Writers for Relief
Vol. 3

*Writers for Relief
Volume III*

Davey Beauchamp
Stuart Jaffe

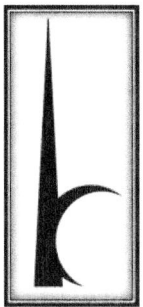

Writers For Relief Volume 3

Copyright © 2013 by Davey Beauchamp

All rights reserved. No part of this book may be reproduced or transmitted in any form or by any means, electronic or mechanical, including photocopying, recording, or by an information storage and retrieval system - except by a reviewer who may quote brief passages in a review to be printed in a magazine or newspaper - without permission in writing from the publisher.

Al l Short Stories are Owned and copyrighted to each of their Authors/Owners

Published by Sapphire City Press

Works Originally Appeared in -
TERRA INCOGNITA: MYTHICAL CREATURES - WordFire Press (May 30, 2011)
GREENHOUSE CHILL - Analog Science Fiction and Fact (January 2000)
PEACEMAKER, PEACEMAKER, LITTLE BO PEEP - Interzone 231 (Nov./Dec. 2010)
THE ONE TREE OF LUNA - The One Tree of Luna (And Other Stories) Foxxe Frey Books (December 8, 2012)
THE SCENT OF APPLES - Glyph: The Journal of Fantasy and Legend No. 8 (Spring 2002)
MEAN-SPIRITED - Jan. 2010 in IGMS (audio)
DOWN MEMORY LANE - Asimov's Science Fiction, 2005
LORDS OF HEAVEN AND EARTH - M-Brane SF, Issue 18, July, 2010
THE SNOW WOMAN'S DAUGHTER - Cricket in 2007

Cover Art by Bob Eggleton

ISBN-13: 978-1492391340
ISBN-10: 1492391344

This series of stories is dedicated to:

All those who have known tragedy through natural disasters or have had loved ones go through it

To the survivors of the Oklahoma Tornados

◊◊◊

For My Mom
-Davey-

*Writers for Relief
Volume III*

Table of Contents

INTRODUCTION — 11

TERRA INCOGNITA: MYTHICAL CREATURES — 13
Kevin J. Anderson

GREENHOUSE CHILL — 33
Ben Bova

THE LAND ABOVE THE AIR — 57
Stephen Euin Cobb

PEACEMAKER, PEACEMAKER, LITTLE BO PEEP — 75
Jason Sanford

MAGNUS: THE APPRENTICE "BIRTHRIGHT" — 107
Bobby Nash

THE ONE TREE OF LUNA — 129
Todd McCaffrey

THE SCENT OF APPLES — 167
A.H. Sturgis

SHE'S GOT LEGS — 177
John Hartness

MEAN-SPIRITED — 207
Edmund R. Schubert

DOWN MEMORY LANE 217
Mike Resnick *too depressing*

COWBOYS 'N' DRUIDS 235
Danny Birt *zzz*

LORDS OF HEAVEN AND EARTH 261
Jaym Gates *zzz*

THE ENTROPY BOX 295
Gray Rinehart *Good but the end is a bearer!*

SONG OF THE SEASONS, SONG 4: FIRE AND RAIN 313
Janine K. Spendlove *Promising start then just end up a mundane 'Forbidden love' story zzz*

LETTER OF REPRISAL 349
Steven S. Long

THE SNOW WOMAN'S DAUGHTER 375
Eugie Foster

AFTERWORD 385

INTRODUCTION

Welcome to *Writers for Relief Volume 3* this time to help relief efforts to those affected by the tornadoes in Oklahoma. I am joined this time by Stuart Jaffe in this endeavor and I couldn't have asked for a better co-editor on this project. It was nice to have someone to talk to about the anthology through all of its steps of creation instead of doing it alone, like I had in the past. It is also thanks to Stuart we have an incredible cover this time around from legendary painter Bob Eggleton.

We have some incredible talent packed within these pages to help bring this anthology to life. If it wasn't for them there would be no anthology. You will recognize some returning authors like Eugie Foster who has always been incredibly supportive with all the anthologies in this series. I feel fortunate to have Todd McCaffery on board again. I have enjoyed everything he has donated to these anthologies.

And I can't thank Stephen Euin Cobb enough. Yet again he has helped get some of the incredible authors you are going to be reading in these pages; Kevin J. Anderson, Ben Bova and Mike Resnick,

Lastly I want to thank everyone who purchases a copy of this anthology to help out the survivors of the Oklahoma

Tornados. Because all of us in this anthology are donating our work, time, and talent for this; all the money raised by this anthology will be donated to the Red Cross for the tornado relief effort going on in Oklahoma.

    Davey Beauchamp

TERRA INCOGNITA: MYTHICAL CREATURES

Kevin J. Anderson

The prow of the *Compass* cut the rough gray waters like a knife carving a Landing Day roast. Prester Ormun closed his eyes and drove away all his pleasant memories of the traditional holiday . . . or any other family memories, for that matter. Those were behind him now; only bleak settlements on the scattered Soeland Islands lay ahead. The prester had a difficult path to follow, even if he did not understand God's reasoning behind it.

The ship's damp sails creaked and sighed, and he felt the cold spray on his face, blown by the coming storm. Dobri, the bright-eyed cabin boy, came up beside him, leaning over the bow to peer down into the choppy waves. "Are you looking for *sylkas*, Prester? They say sometimes you can see them in the whitecaps just before a squall."

"I do not believe in *sylkas*. And neither should you." Prester Ormun knew that for a young man like this, the world was filled with mysteries and wonders, but also ignorance. It was his appointed task to enlighten the people of the islands.

The cabin boy squinted at the sea, which looked leaden under the thick sky. "They're real, Prester—beautiful women with golden hair or seaweed all over their bodies. Other sailors have seen them."

"I don't care what other sailors say. *Sylkas* do not exist. It is written in the Book of Aiden that God created the peoples of the land, but only fish, seals, whales, and sea serpents inhabit the sea—no intelligent creatures. I can show you the Scriptures, if you like." Since Ormun knew the cabin boy couldn't read, the proof would be lost on him.

Dobri was both disappointed and skeptical to hear the prester's pronouncement. He had grown up in a small fishing village, and this was his first voyage away from home; he wanted to believe all the wondrous, imaginative stories, whether or not they were true. Now the boy gazed ahead, intent on spotting one of the imaginary *sylkas* so he could point out the creature to Ormun.

With a pang, the prester realized that his own son Aleo would have been about Dobri's age now. . . .

A large wave gushed over the *Compass*'s bow, and the cabin boy scuttled away, but the prester did not try to avoid the splash; instead, he let it wash away his past again. His family was gone, and nothing remained for him in the city of Calay. That was why he'd been sent across the rough waters to the bleak Soeland Islands. A new chance . . . a last chance.

The church's prester-marshall had sent Ormun to preach among the roughshod and hardy islanders; he would bring them the Book of Aiden to comfort the people in their storms and cold northerly winds. Ormun accepted his first mission with neither enthusiasm nor complaint. He was humble enough not to expect redemption, but he did hope to achieve something positive with whatever remained of his life. That he was all he asked God for. . .

Back in Calay, before he became a prester, Ormun was a shoemaker with a wife and two children, a home, friends—a lifetime ago, or a year ago, depending on whether he measured time by a calendar or the gulf in his heart.

The gray plague had swept through the Craftsmen's District, as it did every few years. Shops closed their doors and latched the window shutters. But Ormun had his family to feed: his son, his daughter, and his wife, a dark-haired, tan-skinned beauty named Risula. And so he kept working, while others hid.

He never knew which customer exposed him to the plague. Ormun lay shivering in bed for days while his family tended him: Aleo, only twelve years old, acting as the man of the house, Risula giving him salty broth to drink; even little Essa brought him flowers that she'd picked outside.

Ormun gained strength day by day, then suffered a relapse, falling back into a deep fever, sleeping like the dead, drenched in cold sweat. His last murky memory was of Risula leading shushing daughter and leading her away, telling her to let her father sleep. And then his wife had started coughing. .

◊◊◊

When his fever broke, Ormun emerged from his coma, very weak, and he could barely open his crusted eyes. His throat was parched, and he called out for water, but heard nothing. The house seemed quiet, much too quiet. After he gained enough strength to crawl out of bed, he found his family huddled together, dead, victims of the fever that he had somehow survived.

Ormun had walked away from his home, wandering the streets in a daze, until he finally came upon the kirk. He stumbled inside, and the local prester cared for him, read to him from the Book of Aiden. It was then Ormun decided what his mission in life must be. The gray plague had left him with an empty heart, no laughter and no love. He clutched onto his service to the church like an anchor of hope, read the Book several times through, and debated with great fervor. When the kindly local prester could no longer answer his questions, he sent the gaunt and intense Ormun to the main kirk in Calay, where he met with the prester-marshall himself.

Cast adrift in life, Ormun begged the church leader for a new course to set. The prester-marshall did not try to explain God's personal message for Ormun, didn't pretend to reveal the purpose behind all the pain he had suffered. "I know a place where you can be of service. The Soelanders need you, and I think you belong there." He anointed Ormun a prester and presented him with the Book and the fishhook pendant that was a symbol of their faith.

No one called Soeland a pleasant place to live, but that mattered not a whit to Ormun. He took his Book and his letters of passage, and begged a bunk on the *Compass*, which was ready to sail back for the islands. . . .

Now the sea grew rough, and waves rocked the vessel. Captain Endre Stillen came to join the prester, looking troubled. He was a red-bearded man with a muscular chest and potbelly as hard as a wine cask. "Your cabin would be more comfortable, Prester. No sense staying out here in the storm—the weather is going to get worse."

"Discomfort doesn't bother me, Captain," Ormun said.

Stillen shot an uncertain glance to the anxious cabin boy who hovered nearby. "Dobri says that you don't believe in the mysteries of the sea." He raised his bushy eyebrows.

"I do not."

"The ocean is vast and uncharted, and we've all seen things we can't explain. I'm as inclined to believe in *sylkas* as in anything else. If nothing else, it gives me hope to know that those dark waters might contain benevolent creatures, should anything happen to my ship."

"I don't need mythical creatures to give me hope, Captain. The Book of Aiden says that *sylkas* don't exist, so therefore they don't exist. It doesn't matter what tales you've heard or what you think you've seen."

The conversation reminded Ormun of a recent outspoken stargazer who had adapted a seaman's spyglass so he could stare at the stars and planets in the night sky. The astronomer convinced himself that he saw tiny satellites circling one of the planets—an impossible idea. To prove his assertion, the stargazer had asked the prester-marshall to observe for himself; but the church leader refused to raise the spyglass to his eye. "The Book of Aiden tells us that God made the world as the center of all things, so therefore other satellites *cannot* circle one of the tiny planets in the sky. I have no need to look, when I already know." He handed the telescope back to the baffled astronomer. Ormun thought it was an amazingly profound demonstration of the prester-marshall's unshakable faith. He only hoped he could be as worthy someday.

Seeing that the prester's mind was set, Captain Stillen

chose not to pursue the argument. "Those legends are a vital part of Soelander life and folklore, Prester. You'll be in for some lively discussions when you get to the fishing towns, that's for certain."

"I'm not afraid of debate."

The captain ordered the sails trimmed against the squall. As the winds picked up, waves hammered the side of the ship. Most of the crew hurried below decks before the rain started to sheet down.

Dobri yelped, pointing off to starboard. "I saw one! Look, Prester—it's a *sylka*!"

Ormun froze, wanting not to look, *almost* strong enough to refuse, but he couldn't help himself. He turned to where the boy pointed—and that was his weakness, his failure.

While he looked in the other direction, a rogue wave swamped the bow and gushed over the rails with enough force to knock him overboard. He reached out, grabbed for anything, and his fingers caught the slick wood, but couldn't get hold. Then the rush of curling foam bore him overboard into the wide gulf of the sea.

Prester Ormun sucked in a breath to shout for help, but he swallowed a mouthful of salt water instead. Flailing, sinking, he coughed and retched as the wave crest bore him upward, then plunged him under again. He clawed at the water with his hands, seeing grayish light above. His face burst from the waves again, and he drew in a deep breath. He rose and sank, completely lost, adrift. His heavy woolen shift pulled him down.

In the pouring rain he spotted Dobri and Captain Stillen struggling to their feet on the deck. He caught a glimpse of the cabin boy, his mouth open in dismay as he saw the prester in the water. Dobri waved and shouted.

Ormun raised his hands to signal, but the seas were too rough. Currents whisked him farther from the ship. The *Compass* could never send out a boat to rescue him.

He tried to stay afloat, but his arms and legs felt leaden. His shoes—good leather boots that he had made in his own cobbler shop long ago in that other life—filled with water. He was going to drown out here.

Oddly, he didn't view the thought with any particular terror, but he did feel a heavy confusion. God's course for him had been so clear—to spread the word out in the Soeland Islands. What was the purpose of saving Ormun from the gray plague only to let him be swept away by a capricious wave, drowning before he even had a chance to preach to his new charges?

He went under again, struggled to the surface, caught another breath. Letting go, he let himself be flung about by the waves. Barely able to think, he experienced a paradoxical sense of calm and peace.

Then clammy hands grasped him from below. A firm grip took his woolen shift, cradled his head, buoyed him up to where he could breathe. But Ormun didn't want to breathe. He struggled and fought against the strange figure below, but he was too weak.

In the end, he simply surrendered to the water and the mythical savior that his imagination had created in his last moments of life. Prester Ormun sank into the darkness, trying to remember a prayer.

◊◊◊

When Prester Ormun awoke, he smelled fish in the dank and cold air around him. Dried saltwater plastered his hair to his head, and he had to pry open his crusted eyes. Before his vision adjusted, he rolled over onto his knees and retched, puking up foul-tasting saltwater.

He saw that he was in an empty cave at the waterline, which looked out upon the open sea. Outside, the waves sounded like drumbeats against the algae-encrusted rocks that he could see beyond the cave opening. With a start, the prester realized he was naked, his woolen shift spread on a rock nearby. The cloth was stiff and salt-encrusted, but reasonably. He shivered and pulled his clothes back on, hiding his nakedness.

He noticed four gutted fish on a flat rock next to him, along with a pile of oysters and clams, all of which had been pried open, ready for him to eat. Weak and starving, Ormun devoured the food without thinking, without tasting, and he felt reborn, as when he'd emerged from his fever after the gray plague. Now, however, questions clamored in his mind, and he looked around, trying to understand what had happened to him.

A figure swam in the sea outside the cave. It seemed human at first—until the creature hauled itself onto the rocks and climbed dripping into the cave. Covered with luxurious locks of golden fur, it was obviously female, with rounded breasts covered by matted weeds. The face was narrow and ethereal, with large brown eyes—soulful eyes, like those of a sea lion. She smelled of salt from the sea. Her lips curved in what was an unmistakable smile as she saw him awake and looking at her.

Ormun squeezed his eyes shut and felt for his fishhook pendant in a protective instinct, but the religious symbol was gone. Perhaps it had washed away when he'd been swept overboard, or perhaps this *thing*—this *sylka*?—had stolen it, fearing the sign of Aiden.

Ormun opened his eyes again, but the creature was still there; he had expected her to vanish like a mirage-shadow. She came forward to squat near him, briny water trickling from her fur, and he struggled away. The *sylka* picked up the empty oyster and clam shells and cast them out of the cave, then she turned back to scrutinize him, like a raven fascinated by a shiny object ... or a predator deciding how best to devour its prey. A thrumming sound echoed from her throat, a call that was at once mysterious, mournful, and hypnotic.

When the creature edged closer, Prester Ormun backed away until his shoulders struck the cave wall. "You're not real!"

The *sylka* trilled at him. Her eyes showed a yearning to communicate. She repeated the sound and chirruped with a higher note at the end, like a question.

"You're not real." Though he could see the *sylka*'s form as if she had been sketched from the logbook of a delusional sea captain, could smell her musky iodine odor, and hear the sound she made, Ormun clung to what the Book of Aiden taught: That God had blessed *mankind* with intelligence, giving only His *chosen children* the minds to understand and worship Him. All other creatures of the land and sea were lowly animals. In another verse, the Book specifically denounced mermaids and *sylkas* as distractions for a devout man, superstitions unworthy of a true follower of God.

But now Ormun found himself faced with the contradiction. The Book of Aiden stated plainly that this *sylka* could not be here. Ormun had read those words of scripture with his own eyes . . . yet those same eyes showed him this impossible creature. Right here.

Back in Calay, the prester-marshall had instructed him in the use of rational thought. If this *sylka* truly existed, then the statement in the Book was in error. A small error, perhaps— and how could anyone know all the mysteries and all the creatures in the vast sea?

Yet one error in one verse was as bad as a thousand errors, for either way it proved that the Book of Aiden was flawed.

And because it was the word of God, the Book of Aiden could *not* be flawed. Therefore, that one verse, and all verses, had to be correct. By definition.

Hence, the *sylka* could not exist, and she was not there. He stared hard at her, willing the illusion to go away.

The *sylka* hunkered down and continued to gaze at him with mournful eyes. She let out a series of complex musical trills, but Prester Ormun closed his eyes and covered his ears.

◊◊◊

The *sylka* left the cave several times throughout the day, diving into the sea and swimming away. She always returned with fresh fish, oysters, or abalones for him, all of which he ate suspiciously. Ormun used the empty abalone shells to capture dripping water that trickled from the moist rocks of the cave. It tasted gritty and dirty, but soothed his parched throat.

Each time the mythical creature went away, Ormun tried to convince himself that she was only an illusion brought about by delirium, perhaps a relapse of the gray fever. Then the *sylka* returned, and they would stare at each other again...

He feared she might bring back others of her kind to show them the strange captive she had hauled from the stormy seas—but, again, the prester knew that couldn't happen, because *sylkas* did not exist. There were no others. Each time she came to him, she was alone . . . and so was he.

When he felt strong enough, and desperate enough, Ormun made his plans and waited for the *sylka* to swim away again. The creature slipped out of the cave one afternoon, and Ormun decided it was time to escape—if he could. He ventured out of the opening and climbed up on the rocks, hoping to find some landmark that would tell him where he was.

If this was one of the Soeland Islands, Ormun could make his way inland, where he might find people—a fishing village, a shack or a boat dock. But when he scrambled up the algae-covered boulders above the tide line, he saw that this island was merely a tiny patch of land, an elbow of reef that barely rose above the waterline—a few acres of forlorn boulders and tufts of misplaced grass. He could see the full swatch of land from end to end, side to side. The island was empty. He was alone.

Staring at the watery horizon with tears burning in his eyes, he discerned the gray hummocks of other islands in the distance, larger shores that might be inhabited . . . but they were much too far away. He could never swim that far, and if he tried to escape, he was sure the *sylka* would come after him, grab his legs, and drag him beneath the water. He still didn't understand why she had saved him in the first place.

As he stood there in empty dismay, the *sylka* rose out of the surf and climbed onto dry land on the other side of the islet. Silhouetted in daylight, she looked like a seductress, her form voluptuous, the golden kelplike fur haloed by the sun. Ormun had looked at women once, had found Risula so lovely that she made him dizzy with desire...but he had been a different man before the gray fever—someone without the same convictions, without the same priorities. He averted his eyes.

The *sylka* came toward him, clearly alarmed to see him out of the cave. On land, her movements were ungainly, like a seal's, although he had seen how sleek and lissome she was in the water. When the creature urged him back to the cave that was his prison, he recoiled at her touch, but could not resist. He saw no point to it; he had nowhere else to go.

Back in her lair, the *sylka* was intent on showing him something. She trilled, inducing him to come to a dank alcove in the rear of the small cave. Under a weed-covered overhang, she had piled rocks to create a protective barrier, a sort of nest. The *sylka* looked at him with great wonder in her eyes as she grasped the rocks with her webbed hands and lifted them away one by one.

Beneath the protective barrier rested a group of pulsating, grayish spheres, pearlescent objects, each one larger than a ripe melon. Ormun counted five of them grouped together with loving care, moist with a filmy membrane—a clutch of eggs! The creature's young. She was reproducing, about to unleash five more of her kind into the world!

Obviously the *sylka* wasn't entirely alone out there in the waters. Ormun imagined her out in the gray cold sea, at night, letting out her trilling song, calling a mate from across the waves. Did she lay her eggs here in the cave and wait for a male to spray his milt on the clutch like a frog? The very idea made him shudder with disgust.

The *sylka* inhaled and exhaled wet burbling breaths, and she crouched closer, cooing. The creature extended a pale finger and stroked the nearest egg. Her touch activated something within, a sparkle in the air accompanied by the smell of ozone, and Prester Ormun felt an overwhelming sense of importance and hope—a magical, unnatural connection.

On the egg's shifting metallic surface, he saw distorted images, like memories seen through the fever fog. The *sylka* touched a second egg, and a third, and more images formed on their reflective shells... the prester's hopes and possibilities from the lost part of his life, things she could not possibly know about him.

Ormun saw the blurry, uncertain features of his son Aleo, laughing, full of tales of fish he had caught or beetles he had collected. The second eggshell displayed sweet, doe-eyed Essa, who loved to pick the flowers that grew in meadows just outside the city. And exotic, beautiful Risula.

But the last time Ormun had seen his family, they were dead, plague-ridden, their bodies huddled on the floor of their home, while he shivered in a coma on the narrow bed. Now, he gasped a quick, perfunctory prayer, but he continued to look. He knew he should turn away, even though those faces made his heart ache.

Sensing his reaction, the *sylka* trilled with happiness.

Then Ormun realized these visions were not just memories, for he saw Aleo as a young man, standing with a thin and pretty red-haired woman. They held each other, kissed—Aleo's wife-to-be? Ormun saw another maiden with fresh-picked flowers in her hair, unmistakably Essa, just at the edge of growing-up. He saw Risula cradling another baby—her own, or a grandchild?

The eggs held possibilities, a wellspring of the future.

"No," Ormun whispered, drawing away. "No, this never happened! This can't be." He covered his eyes. The *sylka* was distraught, not understanding his reaction, but Ormun clung to strength within.

The images that pooled on the shells of her eggs did not represent the path that God had chosen for him. He had endured the pain. He had read the Book. He had fought for understanding and acceptance, like a pathfinder hacking through persistent underbrush, rather than taking a simple and easy trail that did not lead where he wanted to go. These illusive memories were not *his* memories, and that future did not belong to him.

"No," he said again.

With obvious disappointment, the *sylka* piled the rocks again over her eggs.

◊◊◊

Even though the prester understood his mission now, he feared he wouldn't have the necessary strength. As he shivered through the cold, damp night while wrestling with his thoughts, Ormun once again told himself that none of this was *real*. Maybe he had actually drowned when the wave swept him overboard, and this was his test before God let him enter Heaven. The only thing that had kept him alive after the plague, the purpose that allowed him to get through one day, then the next, was the anchor of his faith, his dogged belief in what the prester-marshall had taught him. If he abandoned that, then he would be abandoning everything he had left.

The eerie, tempting images he'd seen in the *sylka*'s eggs—his family, his happiness, a bright future—none of that was true. How he longed for what he saw in those illusions, wanted that reality more than anything else he could ever imagine. But that, in itself, was what warned him. *His* wishes did not matter: It was about what God wanted. Ormun had to be strong, and his only strength was his faith.

On the fourth morning after being washed overboard, Ormun watched the *sylka* return to the cave, climbing out of the water. As the creature sloshed toward him, she looked excited, gesturing with a webbed hand. When the prester didn't follow, she hurried back to the cave opening and stared out to sea, then trilled a sharper sound, more urgent than her soothing music. Ormun felt compelled to look out upon the sun washed waters.

In the channel between the islands, close enough that he could see the sails and rigging, a two-masted vessel cruised in from the north. He even recognized the lines, the look of the hull, the cut of the sails. It was the *Compass*! Maybe Captain Stillen had come back to look for him, or maybe this was just the ship's regular return route through the archipelago.

Thrumming, the *sylka* looked at him with her limpid eyes. Ormun's heart lurched, and he knew the time had come. This was the crux, and he clung to the truth like a man grasping a lifeline. He had not dared to pray for a chance at redemption, to demonstrate his devotion and his acceptance—and now the sailing ship had returned! The *Compass* would rescue him.

He lurched to his feet, uttering a prayer of thanksgiving. The *sylka* gestured for him to hurry, and by her demeanor and bright expression he guessed that she intended to swim out to the *Compass*, draw the attention of the sailors, and get Captain Stillen to change course to the islet. This creature had already rescued him from drowning, and now she would save him from being marooned on the small island. She turned away, looking out to sea.

Ormun picked up one of the melon-sized reef rocks, held it in both hands, and brought it down with all of his strength on the back of the *sylka's* head. He bashed as hard as he could, and her skull was much softer than the rock. The *sylka* collapsed, letting out a mournful hooting sound, and Ormun struck again.

He stood tall and dropped the rock on the floor of the cave. "You don't exist." If the captain, the cabin boy, and the rest of the crew saw her, they would not have the strength to cling to their faith. Ormun had no other choice but to save them from their own gullibility.

He went to the back alcove, pulled away the rocks piled

over the clutch of eggs, and gazed down at the quicksilver pooling—the reflections that were mocking echoes of a past that was already gone and a future he would never have. Useless and dangerous, a mocking temptation. Prester Ormun was strong enough to avoid fantasies, no matter how attractive they might be. He knew his life's course.

Ormun picked up another rock and smashed the first *sylka* egg, obliterating the illusions of things that might have been. Then he destroyed the rest of the clutch, one by one, until he felt safe again.

When he was finished, he was surprised to discover that the *sylka*'s body still lay on the cave floor; the dripping slimy fragments of broken eggs remained strewn about their nest. Now that he had passed his test of faith, Ormun expected them to vanish instantly, but he didn't search for, or want, explanations. It was time for him to be rescued, to return to his role as a prester preaching the Book of Aiden. The Soelanders needed him.

Ormun carried one of the abalone shells as he scrambled out of the cave and onto the high point of the small islet. There, he jumped and waved, seesawing his hands in the air, trying to get the attention of the *Compass*. He caught the bright sunlight with the shiny interior of the shell, flashing a signal. He yelled until his throat was raw.

And finally—finally—he saw pennants raised on the mainmast, and the ship turned toward the rocky island. Someone had seen him.

When the *Compass* anchored at a safe distance from the islet, Prester Ormun watched the ship's boat lowered, saw men rowing toward him. Though he was not a good swimmer, he dove into the water and struck out to meet the boat partway. He recognized the boy Dobri at the front of the boat, and two sturdy Soeland sailors pulling at the oars. The prester flailed in the waves, swimming as far from the islet as he could.

He needed to be away from the persistent imaginary remnants of the *sylka* and her eggs. He didn't want any of these men from the *Compass* to see the evidence, otherwise they would be deceived by what they wanted to believe.

Gasping and exhausted, Ormun reached the boat, and his heart swelled with joy. Dobri leaned over to catch his hand. "Prester, we thought you were dead!"

"I thought I was, too," he said as they helped to haul him aboard. "But I survived, and now I know that God still has more work for me to do."

The cabin boy laughed, and the sailors rowed back toward the *Compass*. Ormun was too tired and shaken to tell his story, and he still had much to think about before he revealed anything.

When they tied up to the sailing ship, he climbed aboard to congratulations from Captain Stillen. "We couldn't believe it, Prester! No man ever survives out here. How did you make it to that small island? We were just continuing our passage among the islands, but Dobri spotted the flashing light."

"An abalone shell," the prester said.

The captain admired his cleverness, and Dobri added, "I was at the bow looking for *sylkas* when I saw it."

"*Sylkas* don't exist, boy," Prester Ormun said, more convinced now than he had ever been.

But while the crewmen took him to change into dry clothes, the prester watched Dobri hurry back to the bow with a spyglass in hand. Seeing the boy's eager willingness to believe, he felt only sadness and disappointment. He had to teach these people the truth, no matter how difficult it was.

Nevertheless, Dobri continued to scan the waves, always looking, always hopeful.

GREENHOUSE CHILL

Ben Bova

"Let's face it, Hawk, we're lost."

Hawk frowned in disappointment at his friend. "You're lost, maybe. I know right where I am."

Squinting in the bright sunshine, Tim turned his head this way and that, searching the horizon. Nothing. Not another sail, not another boat anywhere in sight. Not even a bird. The only sounds he could hear were the soft gusting of the hot breeze and the splash of the gentle waves lapping against their stolen sailboat. The brilliant sky was cloudless, the sea stretched out all around them and they were alone. Two teenaged runaways out in the middle of the empty sea.

"Yeah?" Tim challenged. "Then where are we?"

"Comin' up to the Ozarks, just about," said Hawk.

"How d'you know that?"

Hawk's frown evolved into a serious, superior, *knowing* expression. He was almost a year older than Tim, lean and hard-muscled from backbreaking farm labor. But his round face was animated, with sparkling blue eyes that could convince his younger friend to join him on this wild adventure to escape from their parents, their village, their lives of endless drudgery.

Tim was almost as tall as Hawk, but pudgier, softer. His father was the village rememberer, and Tim was being groomed to take his place in the due course of time. The work he did was mostly mental, instead of physical, but it was pure drudgery just the same, remembering all the family lines and the history of the village all the way back to the Flood.

"So," Tim repeated, "how d'you know where we are? I don't see any signposts stickin' up outta the water."

"How long we been out?" Hawk asked sternly.

With a glance at the dwindling supply of salt beef and apples in the crate by the mast, Tim replied, "This is the fifth mornin'."

"Uh-huh. And where's the sun?"

Tim didn't bother to answer, it was so obvious.

"So the sun's behind your left shoulder, same's it's been every mornin'. Wind's still comin' up from the south, hot and strong. We're near the Ozarks."

"I still don't see how you figure that."

"My dad and my uncle been fishin' in these waters all their lives," Hawk said, matter-of-factly. "I learned from them."

Tim thought that over for a moment, then asked, "So how long before we get to Colorado?"

"Oh, that's *weeks* away," Hawk answered.

"Weeks? We ain't got enough food for weeks!"

"I know that. We'll put in at the Ozark Islands and get us some more grub there."

"How?"

"Huntin'," said Hawk. "Or trappin'. Or stealin', if we

hafta."

Tim's dark eyes lit up. The thought of becoming robbers excited him.

The long lazy day wore on. Tim listened to the creak of the ropes and the flap of the heavy gray sail as he lay back in the boat's prow. He dozed, and when he woke again the sun had crawled halfway down toward the western edge of the sea. Off to the north, though, ominous clouds were building up, gray and threatening.

"Think it'll storm?" he asked Hawk.

"For sure," Hawk replied.

They had gone through a thunderstorm their first afternoon out. The booming thunder had scared Tim halfway out of his wits. That and the waves that rose up like mountains, making his stomach turn itself inside out as the boat tossed up and down and sideways and all. And the lightning! Tim had no desire to go through that again.

"Don't look so scared," Hawk said, with a tight smile on his face.

"I ain't scared!"

"Are too."

Tim admitted it with a nod. "Ain't you?"

"Not anymore."

"How come?"

Hawk pointed off to the left. Turning, Tim saw a smudge on the horizon, something low and dark, with more clouds over it. But these clouds were white and soft-looking.

"Island," Hawk said, pulling on the tiller and looping the rope around it to hold it in place. The boat swung around and the sail began flapping noisily.

Tim got up and helped Hawk swing the boom. The sail bellied out again, neat and taut. They skimmed toward the island while the storm clouds built up higher and darker every second, heading their way.

They won the race, barely, and pulled the boat up on a stony beach just as the first drops of rain began to spatter down on them, fat and heavy.

"Get the mast down, quick!" Hawk commanded. It was pouring rain by the time they got that done. Tim wanted to run for the shelter of the big trees, but Hawk said no, they'd use the boat's hull for protection.

"Trees attract lightnin', just like the mast would if we left it up," said Hawk.

Even on dry land the storm was scarifying. And the land didn't stay dry for long. Tim lay on the ground beneath the curve of the boat's hull as lightning sizzled all around them and the thunder blasted so loud it hurt his ears. Hawk sprawled beside Tim and both boys pressed themselves flat against the puddled stony ground.

The world seemed to explode into a white-hot flash and Tim heard a crunching, crashing sound. Peeping over Hawk's shoulder he saw one of the big trees slowly toppling over, split in half and smoking from a lightning bolt. For a moment he thought the tree would smash down on them, but it hit the ground a fair distance away with an enormous shattering smash.

At last the storm ended. The boys were soaking wet and Tim's legs felt too weak to hold him up, but he got to his feet anyway, trembling with cold and the memory of fear.

Slowly they explored the rocky, pebbly beach and poked

in among the trees. Squirrels and birds chattered and scolded at them. Tim saw a snake, a beautiful blue racer, slither through the brush. Without a word between them, the boys went back to the boat. Hawk pulled his bow and a handful of arrows from the box where he had stored them while Tim collected a couple of pocketfuls of throwing stones.

By the time the sun was setting they were roasting a young rabbit over their campfire.

Burping contentedly, Hawk leaned back on one elbow as he wiped his greasy chin. "Now this is the way to live, ain't it?"

"You bet," Tim agreed. He had seen some blackberry bushes back among the trees and decided that in the morning he'd pick as many as he could carry before they started out again. No sense leaving them to the birds.

"Hello there!"

The deep voice froze both boys for an instant. Then Hawk dived for his bow while Tim scrambled to his feet.

"Don't be frightened," called the voice. It came from the shadowy bushes in among the trees, sounding ragged and scratchy, like it was going to cough any minute.

On one knee, Hawk fitted an arrow into his hunter's bow. Tim suddenly felt very exposed, standing there beside the fire, both hands empty.

Out of the shadows of the trees stepped a figure. A man. An old, shaggy, squat barrel of a man in a patchwork vest the hung open across his white-fuzzed chest and heavy belly, his head bare and balding but his brows and beard and what was left of his hair bushy and white. His arms were short, but thick with muscle. And he carried a strange-looking bow, black and powerful-looking, with all kinds of weird attachments on it.

"No need for weapons," he said, in his gravelly voice.

"Yeah?" Hawk challenged, his voice shaking only a little. "Then what's that in your hand?"

"Oh, this?" The stranger bent down and laid his bow gently on the ground. "I've been carrying it around with me for so many years it's like an extension of my arm."

He straightened up slowly, Tim saw, as if the effort caused him pain. There was a big, thick-bladed knife tucked in his belt. His feet were shod in what looked like strips of leather.

"Who are you?" Hawk demanded, his bow still in his hands. "What do you want?"

The stranger smiled from inside his bushy white beard. "Since you've just arrived on my island, I think it's more proper for you to identify yourselves first."

Tim saw that Hawk was a little puzzled by that.

"Whaddaya mean, your island?" Hawk asked.

The old man spread his arms wide. "This is my island. I live here. I've lived her for damned near two hundred years."

"That's bull-dingy," Hawk snapped. Back home he never would have spoken so disrespectfully to an adult, but things were different out here.

The shaggy old man laughed. "Yes, I suppose it does sound fantastic. But it's true. I'm two hundred and fifty-six years old, assuming I've been keeping my calendar correctly."

"Who are you?" Hawk demanded. "Whatcha want?"

Placing a stubby-fingered hand on his chest, the man replied, "My name is Julius Schwarzkopf, once a professor of meteorology at the University of Washington, in St. Louis, Missouri, U. S. of A."

"I heard of St. Louie," Tim blurted.

"Fairy tales," Hawk snapped.

"No, it was real," said Professor Julius Schwarzkopf. "It was a fine city, back when I was a teacher."

Little by little, the white-bearded stranger eased their suspicions. He came up to the fire and sat down with them, leaving his bow where he'd laid it. He kept the knife in his belt, though. Tim sat a little bit aways from him, where there were plenty of fist-sized rocks within easy reach.

The Prof, as he insisted they call him, opened a little sack on his belt and offered the boys a taste of dried figs.

As the last embers of daylight faded and the stars began to come out, he suggested, "Why don't you come to my place for the night? It's better than sleeping out in the open."

Hawk didn't reply, thinking it over.

"There's wild boars in the woods, you know," said the Prof. "Mean beasts. And the cats hunt at night, too. Coyotes, of course. No wolves, though; for some reason they haven't made it to this island."

"Where's your cabin?" Hawk asked. "Who else lives there?"

"Ten minutes' walk," the Prof answered, pointing with an outstretched arm. "And I live alone. There's nobody but me on this island -- except you, of course."

The old man led the way through the trees, guiding the boys with a small greenish lamp that he claimed was made from fireflies' innards. It was fully dark by the time they reached the Prof's cabin. To Tim, what little he could make out of it looked more like a bare little hump of dirt than a regular cabin.

The Prof stepped down into a sort of hollow and pushed

open a creaking door. In the ghostly green light from his little lamp, the boys stepped inside. The door groaned and closed again.

And suddenly the room was brightly lit, so bright it made Tim squeeze his eyes shut for a moment. He heard Hawk gasp with surprise.

"Ah, I forgot," the Prof said. "You're not accustomed to electricity."

The place was a wonder. It was mostly underground, but there were lights that made everything like it was daytime. And there were lots of rooms; the place just seemed to go on and on.

"Nothing much else to do for the past two centuries," the Prof said. "Home improvement was always a hobby of mine, even back before the Flood."

"You remember before the Flood?" Tim asked, awed.

The Prof sank his chunky body onto a sagging, tatty sofa and gestured to chairs for the boys to sit on.

"I was going to be one of the Immortals," he said, his rasping voice somewhere between sad and sore. "Got my telomerase shots. I'd never age -- so long as I took the booster shots every fifty years."

Tim glanced at Hawk, who looked just as puzzled as he himself felt.

"But then the Flood wiped all that out. I'm aging again...- slowly, I grant you, but just take a look at me! Hardly immortal, right?"

Hawk pointed to the thickly-stacked shelves lining the room's walls. "Are all those things books?"

The Prof nodded. "My other hobby was looting libraries --

while they were still on dry land."

He babbled on about solar panels and superconducting batteries and refrigerators and all kinds of other weird stuff that started to make Tim's head spin. It was like the Prof was so glad to have somebody to talk to he didn't know when to stop.

Tim had always been taught to be respectful of his elders; sometimes the lessons had included a sound thrashing. But no matter how respectfully he tried to pay attention the Prof's rambling, barely-understandable monologue, he kept drifting toward sleep. Back home everybody was abed shortly after nightfall, but now this Prof was yakking on and on. It must be pretty near midnight, Tim thought. He could hardly keep his eyes open. He nodded off, woke himself with a start, tried as hard as he could to stay awake.

"But look at me," the Prof said at last. "I'm keeping you two from a good night's sleep, talking away like this."

He led the boys to another room that had real beds in it. "Be careful how you get on them," he warned. "Nobody's slept in those antiques in fifty years or more, not since a family of pilgrims got blown off their course for New Nashville. Stayed for damned near a month. Ate me out of house and home, just about, but I was still sad to see them go. I..."

Hawk yawned noisily and the Prof's monologue petered out. "I'll see you in the morning. Have a good sleep."

Tim didn't care about the Prof's warning. He was so sleepy he threw himself on the bare mattress of the nearer bed. He raised a cloud of dust, but after one cough he fell sound asleep.

Because the Prof's home was mostly underground it stayed dark long after sunrise. Tim and Hawk slept longer than they ever had at home. Only the sound of the Prof knocking hard on their bedroom door woke them.

The boys washed and relieved themselves in a privy that was built right into the house, in a separate little room of its own, with running water at the turn of a handle.

"Gravity feed," the Prof told them over a hearty breakfast of eggs and ham and waffles and muffins and fruit preserves. "Got a cistern for rainwater up in the hills and pipes carry the water here. I boil all the drinking and cooking water, of course."

"Of course," Hawk mumbled, his mouth full of blueberry muffin.

"We've got to haul your boat farther up out of the water," the Prof said, "and tie it down good and tight. Big blow likely soon."

Tim glanced out the narrow slit of the kitchen's only window and saw that it was dull gray outside, cloudy.

Once they finished breakfast, the Prof took them to still another room. This one had desks and strange-looking boxes sitting on them, with windows in them.

The Prof slipped into a little chair that creaked under his weight and started pecking with his fingers on a board full of buttons. The window on the box atop the desk lit up and suddenly showed a picture.

Tim jerked back a step, surprised. Even Hawk looked wide-eyed, his mouth hanging open.

"Not many weather satellites still functioning," the Prof

muttered, as much to himself as the boys. "Only the old military birds left; rugged little buggers. Hardened, you know. But even with solar power and gyro stabilization, after two hundred years they're crapping out, one by one."

"What is that?" Hawk asked, his voice strangely small and hollow. Tim knew what was going through his friend's mind: *This is witchcraft!*

The Prof launched into an explanation that meant practically nothing to the boys. Near as Tim could figure it, the old man was saying there was a machine hanging in the air like a circling hawk or buzzard, but miles and miles and higher, so high they couldn't see it. And the machine had some sort of eyes on it and this box on the Prof's desk was showing what those eyes saw.

It didn't sound like witchcraft, the way the Prof explained it. He made it sound just as natural as chopping wood.

"That's the United States," the Prof said, tapping the glass that covered the picture. "Or what's left of it."

Tim saw mostly wide stretches of blue stuff that sort of looked like water, with plenty of smears of white and gray. Clouds?

"Florida's gone, of course," the Prof muttered. "Most of the midwest has been inundated. New England...Maryland and the whole Chesapeake region...all flooded."

His voice had gone low and soft, as if he was about to cry. Tim even thought he saw a tear glint in one of the old man's eyes, though it was hard to tell, under those shaggy white brows of his.

"Here's where we are," the Prof said, pointing to one of the gray smudges. "Can't see the island, of course; we're beneath the cloud cover."

Tim looked at Hawk, who shrugged. Couldn't figure out if the Prof was crazy or a witch or what.

The Prof tapped at the buttons on the oblong board in front of him and the picture on the box changed. Now it showed something that was mostly white. Lots of clouds, still, but they were almost all white and if that was supposed to be ground underneath them the ground was all white, too.

"Canada," said the Prof, grimly. "The icecap is advancing fast."

"What's that mean?" Hawk asked.

The Prof sucked in a big sigh and looked up at the boys. "It's going to get colder. A lot colder."

"Winter's comin' already?" Tim asked. It was still springtime, he knew. Summer was coming, not winter.

But the Prof answered, "A long winter, son. A winter that lasts thousands of years. An ice age."

Hawk asked, "What's an ice age?"

"It's what follows a greenhouse warming. This greenhouse was an anomaly, caused by anthropogenic factors. Now the cee-oh-two's being leached out of the atmosphere and the global climate will bounce back to a Pleistocene condition."

He might as well have been talking Cherokee or some other redskin language, Tim thought. Hawk looked just as baffled.

Seeing the confusion on the boys' faces, the Prof went to great pains to try to explain. Tim got the idea that he was saying the weather was going to turn colder, a lot colder, and stay that way for a *really* long time.

"Glaciers a mile thick!" the Prof said, nearly raving in his earnestness. "Minnesota, Michigan, the whole Great Lakes region was covered with ice a mile thick!"

"It was?"

"When?"

Shaking his head impatiently, the Prof said, "It doesn't matter when. The important thing is that it's going to happen all over again!"

"Here?" Tim asked. "Where our folks live?"

"Yes!"

"How soon?" asked Hawk.

The Prof hesitated. He drummed his fingers on the desktop for a minute, looking lost in thought.

"By the time you're a grandfather," he said at last. "Maybe sooner, maybe later. But it's going to happen."

Hawk let a giggle out of him. "That's a long time from now."

"But you've got to get ready for it," the Prof said, frowning. "It will take a long time to prepare, to learn how to make warm clothing, to grow different crops or migrate south."

Hawk shook his head.

"You ought to at least warn your people, let them know it's going to happen," the Prof insisted.

"But we're headin' for Colorado," Tim confessed. "We're not goin' back home."

The Prof's bushy brows knit together. "This climate shift could be just as abrupt as the greenhouse cliff was. People who aren't prepared for it will die -- starve to death or freeze."

"How do you know it's gonna happen like that?" Hawk

demanded.

"You saw the satellite imagery of Canada, didn't you?"

"We saw some picture of something, I don't know what it really was," Hawk said. "How do you know what it is? How do you know it's gonna get so cold?"

The Prof thought a moment, then admitted, "I don't *know*. But all the evidence points that way. I'm sure of it, but I don't have conclusive proof."

"You don't really know," Hawk said.

For a long moment the old man glared at Hawk angrily. Then he took another deep breath and his anger seemed to fade away.

"Listen, son. Many years ago people like me tried to warn the rest of the world that the greenhouse warming was going to drastically change the global climate. All the available evidence pointed to it, but the evidence was not conclusive. We couldn't convince the political leaders of the world that they were facing a disaster."

"What happened?" Tim asked.

Spreading his arms out wide, the Prof shouted, "This happened! The world's breadbaskets flooded! Electrical power distribution systems totally wiped out. The global nets, the information and knowledge of centuries -- all drowned. Food distribution gone. Cities abandoned. Billions died! Billions! Civilization sank back to subsistence agriculture."

Tim looked at Hawk and Hawk looked back at Tim. Maybe the old man isn't a witch, Tim thought. Maybe he's just crazy.

The Prof sighed. "It doesn't mean a thing to you, does it? You just don't have the understanding, the education or..."

Muttering to himself, the old man turned back to his

magic box and pecked at the buttons again. The picture went back to the first one the boys had seen.

Abruptly the Prof jabbed a button and the picture winked off. Pushing himself up from his chair, he said, "Come on, we've got to get your boat farther up out of the water and tied down good and strong."

"What for?" Hawk demanded, suddenly suspicious.

With a frown, the Prof said, "This area used to be called Tornado Alley. Just because it's covered by water doesn't change that. In fact, it makes the twisters even worse."

The boys had heard of twisters. One had levelled a village not more than a day's travel from their own, only a couple of springtimes ago.

When it came, the twister was a monster.

The boys spent most of the day hauling their boat up close to the trees and then tying it down as firmly as they could. The Prof provided ropes and plenty of advice and even some muscle power. All the time they worked the clouds got thicker and darker and lower. Tim expected a thunderstorm any minute as they headed back for the Prof's house, bone tired.

They were halfway back when the trees began tossing back and forth and rain started spattering down. Leaves went flying through the air, torn off the trees. A whole bough whipped by, nearly smacking Hawk on the head. Tim heard a weird sound, a low dull roaring, like the distant howl of some giant beast.

"Run!" the Prof shouted over the howling wind. "You don't want to get caught here amidst the trees!"

Despite their aching muscles they ran. Tim glanced over

his shoulder and through the bending, swaying trees he saw a mammoth pillar of pure terror marching across the open water, heading right for him, sucking up water and twigs and anything in its path, weaving slowly back and forth, high as the sky, bearing down on them, coming to get him.

It roared and shouted and moved up onto the land. Whole trees were ripped up by their roots. Tim tripped and sprawled face-first into the dirt. Somebody grabbed him by the scruff of his neck and yanked him to his feet. The rain was so thick and hard he couldn't see an arm's length in front of him but suddenly the low earthen hump of the Prof's house was in sight and the old man, despite his years, was half a dozen strides ahead of them, already fumbling with the front door.

They staggered inside, the wind-driven rain pouring in with them. It took all three of them to get the door closed again and firmly latched. The Prof pushed a heavy cabinet against the door, then slumped to the floor, soaking wet, chest heaving.

"Check...the windows," he gasped. "Shutters..."

Hawk nodded and scrambled to his feet. Tim hesitated only a moment, then did the same. He saw there were thick wooden shutters folded back along the edges of each window. He pulled them across the glass and locked them tight.

The twister roared and raged outside but the Prof's house, largely underground, held firm. Tim thought the ground was shaking, but maybe it was just him shaking, he was so scared. The storm yowled and battered at the house. Things pounded on the roof. The rain drummed so hard it sounded like all the redskins in the world doing a war dance.

The Prof lay sprawled in the puddle by the door until Hawk gestured for Tim to help him get the old man to his feet.

"Bedroom..." the Prof said, "Let me...lay down...for a while." His chest was heaving, his face looked gray.

They put him down gently on his bed. His wet clothes made a squishy sound on the covers. He closed his eyes and seemed to go to sleep. Tim stared at the old man's bare, white-fuzzed chest. It was pumping up and down, fast.

Something crashed against the roof so hard that books tumbled out of their shelves and dust sifted down from the ceiling. The lights blinked, then went out altogether. A dim lamp came on and cast scary shadows on the wall.

Tim and Hawk sat on the floor, next to each other, knees drawn up tight. Every muscle in Tim's body ached, every nerve was pulled tight as a bowstring. And the twister kept howling outside, as if demanding to be allowed in.

At last the roaring diminished, the drumming rain on the roof slackened off. Neither Tim nor Hawk budged an inch, though. Not until it became completely quiet out there.

"Do you think it's over?" Tim whispered.

Hawk shook his head. "Maybe."

They heard a bird chirping outside. Hawk scrambled to his feet and went to the window on the other side of the Prof's bed. He eased the shutter open a crack, then flung it all the way back. Bright sunshine streamed into the room. Tim noticed a trickle of water that had leaked through the window and its shutter, dripping down the wall to make a puddle on the bare wooden floor.

The Prof seemed to be sleeping soundly, but as they

tiptoed out of the bedroom, he opened one eye and said, "Check outside. See what damage it's done."

A big pine had fallen across the house's low roof; that had been the crash they'd heard. The water pipe from the cistern was broken, but the cistern itself -- dug into the ground -- was unharmed except for a lot of leaves and debris that had been blown into it.

The next morning the Prof felt strong enough to get up, and he led the boys on a more detailed inspection tour. The solar panels were caked with dirt and leaves, but otherwise unhurt. The boys set to cleaning them while the Prof mended the broken water pipe.

By nightfall the damage had been repaired and the house was back to normal. But not the Prof. He moved slowly, painfully, his breathing was labored. He was sick, even Tim could see that.

"Back in the old days," he said in a rasping whisper over the dinner table, "I'd go to the local clinic and get some pills to lower my blood pressure. Or an EGF injection to grow new arteries." He shook his head sadly. "Now I can only sit around like an old man waiting to die."

The boys couldn't leave him, not in his weakened condition. Besides, the Prof said they'd be better off waiting until the spring tornado season was over.

"No guarantee you won't run into a twister during the summer, of course," he told them. "But it's safer if you wait a bit."

He taught them as much as he could about his computers and the electrical systems he'd rigged to power the house. Tim knew how to read some, so the Prof gave him books while he began to teach Hawk about reading and writing.

"The memory of the human race is in these books," he said, almost every day. "What's left of it, that is."

The boys worked his little vegetable patch and picked berries and hunted down game while the Prof stayed at home, too weak to exert himself. He showed the boys how to use his high-powered bow and Tim bagged a young boar all by himself.

One morning well into the summertime, the Prof couldn't get out of his bed. Tim saw that his face was gray and soaked in sweat, his breathing rapid and shallow. He seemed to be in great pain.

He looked up at the boys and tried to smile. "I guess I'm...going to become immortal...the old-fashioned way."

Hawk swallowed hard and Tim could see he was fighting to hold back tears.

"Nothing you can do...for me," the Prof said, his voice so weak that Tim had to bend over him to hear it.

"Just rest," Tim said. "You rest up and you'll get better."

"Not likely."

Neither boy knew what else to say, what else to do.

"I bequeath my island to you two," the Prof whispered. "It's all yours, boys."

Hawk nodded.

"But you...you really ought to warn...your people," he gasped, "about the ice..."

He closed his eyes. His labored breathing stopped.

That evening, after they had buried the Prof, Tim asked Hawk, "Do you think we oughtta go back and tell our folks?"

Hawk snapped, "No."

"But the Prof said -- "

"He was a crazy old man. We go back home and all we'll get is a whippin' for runnin' away."

"But we oughtta tell them," Tim insisted. "Warn them."

"About something that ain't gonna happen until we're grandfathers? Something that probably won't happen at all?"

"But -- "

"We got a good place here. The crazy old coot left it to us and we'd be fools to leave it."

"What about Colorado?"

"We'll get there next year. Or maybe the year after. And if we don't like it there we can always come back here."

For the first time in his life, Tim not only felt that Hawk was wrong, but he decided to do something about it.

"Okay," he said. "You stay. I'm goin' back."

"You're as crazy as he was!"

"I'll come back here. I'm just goin' to warn them and then I'll come back."

Hawk made a snorting noise. "If they leave any skin on your hide."

For a week Tim patched up their boat and its ragged sail and filled it with provisions. The morning he was set to cast off, Hawk came to the pebbly beach with him.

"I guess this is goodbye for a while," Tim said.

"Don't be a dumbbell," Hawk groused. "I'm goin' with you."

Tim felt a rush of joy. "You are?"

"You'd get yourself lost out there. Some sea monster would have you for lunch."

"We can always come back here again," Tim said,

grunting, as they pushed the boat into the water.

"Yeah, sure."

"We hafta warn them, Hawk. We just hafta."

"Shut up and haul out the sail."

For several days they sailed north and east, back along the way they had come. The weather was sultry, the sun blazing like molten iron out of a cloudless sky.

"Ice age," Hawk grumbled. "Craziest thing I ever heard."

"I saw pictures of it in the books the Prof had," said Tim. "Big sheets of ice covering everything."

Hawk just shook his head and spit over the side.

"It really happened, Hawk."

"The weather don't change," Hawk snapped. "It's the same every year. Hot in the summer, cool in the winter. You ever known anything else?"

"No," Tim admitted.

"You ever seen ice, except in the Prof's pictures?"

"No."

"Or that stuff he called snow?"

"Never."

"We oughtta turn this boat around and head back to the island."

Tim almost agreed. But he saw that Hawk made no motion to change their course. He was talking one way but acting the other.

They fell silent. Tim understood Hawk's resentment. Probably nobody would listen to them when they got home. The elders would be pretty mad about the two of them running off and they wouldn't listen to a word the boys had to say.

For hours they skimmed along, the only sound the gusting of the hot southerly wind and the hiss of the boat cutting through the placid water.

"It's all fairy tales," Hawk grumbled, as much to himself as to Tim. "Stories they make up to scare the kids. What do they call 'em?"

"Myths," said Tim.

"Myths, that's right. Myths." But suddenly he jerked to attention. "Hey, what's that?"

Tim saw he was looking down into the water. He came over to Hawk's side of the boat.

Something was glittering down below the surface. Something big.

Tim heart started racing. "A sea monster?"

Hawk shook his head impatiently. "I don't think it's moving. Leastways it's not following after us. Look, it's falling behind."

They lapsed into silence again. Tim felt uncomfortable. He didn't like it when Hawk was sore at him.

Apologetically, he said, "Maybe you're right. The old man was most likely a little crazy."

"A *lot* crazy," Hawk said. "And we're just as crazy as he was. The weather don't change like that. It's just not possible. There never was a Flood. The world's always been like this. Always."

Tim was shocked. "No Flood?"

"It's one of them myths," Hawk insisted. "Like sea monsters. Ain't no such thing."

"Then what did we see back there?"

"I dunno. But it wasn't no sea monster. And the weather

don't change the way the Prof said it's goin' to. There wasn't any Flood and there sure ain't goin' to be any ice age."

Tim wondered if Hawk was right, as their boat sailed on and the glittering stainless steel apex of St. Louis' Gateway Arch fell farther and farther behind them.

THE LAND ABOVE THE AIR

Stephen Euin Cobb

Openhand-Spiraling-Upward was afraid to die; for herself, but even more so for others. *If I die who will care for my babies?*

By human understanding she was a single parent, though for her species the situation was universal. This, combined with the traditions of her people, provided the answer to her question: "No one." Without her, her infant twins would die of neglect.

She lifted a hand to feel one of the two bulges which flanked her stomach on the right and left sides—each was oval and half the volume of her head. Another set of twins would soon join her first. She rubbed both bulges, checking for damage. None was detectable.

Can't die here, she thought. *Must protect my children.*

Half a minute earlier, Openhand-Spiraling-Upward had awakened face down in black dirt. She'd raised her dark gray head from the ground and wiped the fine powdery soil from her eyes by licking each with her cloth-like tongue. Pain pulsed in her head and chest which helped part the veil of grogginess and speed her back to consciousness.

A dozen pieces of fruit lay scattered on the ground before her. Their shape and color were familiar: red with yellow speckles, almost spherical, about the size of a fist. Other than the fruit she saw only dirt—a dirt floor under her and a uniformly curving dirt wall surrounding her on all sides.

I fell into a hole. Pain is from impact.

The hole was as deep as it was wide. The walls were vertical; far too steep to climb without some kind of footing. *Top is too high to reach the lip, even jumping.*

Rolling over, she sat upright, moving much as a human might. Her body's proportions and arrangement of limbs approximated that of a human being, though her people had never seen one and had no knowledge of any life form alien to their world.

The pain in her chest faded but that in her head remained strong.

As she shifted her weight, her back brushed against something larger than fruit and softer than a dirt wall. She turned and discovered the basket she had been using to gather fruit. It was empty and one side was crushed. It was a Naming Basket.

Though not a professional basket-maker, she had woven it herself without assistance. Every set of twins was placed into this type of basket during the birthing ceremony, and every mother would design and make one with her own hands for her event. Lovingly she had decorated it all the way around with writing worked into the weave. The writing proclaimed her love for her new babies, as well as the names they would bare for the rest of their lives. This one was well constructed and artfully designed—naturally. She had woven many dozens over many years. Just as little human females nurture countless toy babies before they grow up and nurture their real babies, the little females of Openhand-Spiraling-Upward's culture wove countless toy Naming Baskets before they finally wove the ones that would matter. Before it could be used in the birthing ceremony, tradition required it be used eight times for fruit gathering. Today's incomplete gathering was this basket's first.

Turning from the basket, she looked for a climbing pole. None lay on the floor, nor leaned against the wall. She checked the rim. One end of a climbing pole extended out over the hole's lip enough that she could see two of its foot-notches. *Diggers must have pulled it up when they stopped work. Too high to grab and pull down.*

She could not have picked a worse time to fall into a hole, and she could not have picked a worse hole to fall into. *I will die here!*

To complete her ritual gathering, she'd stayed outside longer than she should have. She'd been running for the shelter caves when she'd run headlong into this new pit the Circle-Twist brothers had been digging in the hope of capturing a giant stalk eater—good eating if you can get one; good eating for many, and for a long time. She'd seen them start the digging but forgot about it in her haste to return to safety.

She rubbed her head. Her skin was smooth, hairless, and as supple as fine leather, though many times stronger. A bulletproof vest might be as strong—maybe.

Old Fist-Jerked-Backward died this way. He didn't fall into a pit, he just fell and broke a leg, but the result was the same. He didn't get to the caves in time and Father got him.

Again she shifted her weight, but this time she realized why: her bulges were becoming uncomfortable. They were swelling, accumulating water. This was a familiar safety mechanism; one of the ways a mother's body protected her unborn twins from excessive heat or repeated jostling. Swelling was also the first step in the birthing process; but she was not due for thirty-three days, and within her species birthing was predictable to within a day or two.

On the other hand, sometimes when a mother was dying of injuries or sickness the babies would suddenly birth themselves prematurely—sometimes as much as fifty days early, even though they were only half normal size. There were even rumors that this had happened when the mother only *thought* she was going to die—so that fear alone was enough to trigger spontaneous birth.

If Openhand-Spiraling-Upward had been human she might have yelled for help and hoped someone nearby would hear her calls. But that was not possible here.

Her people were perfectly capable of making and hearing noises, and like some of the less evolved creatures of her world, they sometimes used these noises to convey deeply felt emotions, but they did not use sound to share their thoughts. For that they used several thousand hand gestures strung together in uncountable combinations. This was because the last eighty million years of their evolution had taken place within this planet's third and highest ecosphere: a fact they were intensely proud of though their understanding of evolution was still crude.

The lowest eco was the water-covered land. The greed of the Great Moon pulled all waters toward itself, such that their planet—which Openhand-Spiraling-Upward's people called *Underfoot*—had only one ocean. This single ocean covered almost one third of the planet; and the Great Moon, unlike the lesser moons, never moved from above its center. In the water-covered land dwelt the oldest, most primitive and least evolved of Underfoot's living things.

The second eco was the air-covered land. The Great Moon's grip was weaker on air than on water, and so struggle as it might in its terrible greed it could not pull the air nearly as close to itself. The air-covered land skirted the ocean and formed a ring all the way around the planet; a ring which crossed through the north and south poles. Creatures dwelling in this ring were more evolved that those of the water-covered land, some even resembled Openhand-Spiraling-Upward's people, though they could not be taught to share their thoughts or ideas—that is, assuming they ever had any.

In punishment for the evilness of its greed, the Great Moon possessed no name. Openhand-Spiraling-Upward had never actually seen it with her own eyes, but she'd heard tales handed down through generations of its pale visage dominating the bright blue false-sky over the ocean. It was this same Great Moon that also produced the third and highest eco: the home of Openhand-Spiraling-Upward's people.

On the side of Underfoot directly opposite the Great Moon, the youngest and most evolved of Underfoot's living things dwelt. So powerful was the greed of the Great Moon that here the black sky—the *true* sky—was able to reach all the way down and touch the soil. This was the land-above-the-air. A land fully exposed to the hard vacuum of space.

Evolution had expanded its cleverness to new limits in order to colonize and then conquer this land. But like all the difficult places before, given time, victory always fell to the blindly fumbling and infinitely patient tinkerer. If the first billion innovations didn't succeed, you can figure that one of the next billion, billion, billion probably would.

Sealing a living thing's skin and orifices against vapor loss had been the easy part. Extreme temperature variations so common in vacuum had required far more innovation. But it was oxygen-eating that proved to be the final key.

Openhand-Spiraling-Upward's people—indeed all the species within her eco—were oxygen eaters. They satisfied their body's need for oxygen not by breathing, but by eating the fruits and nuts of plants that long ago learned the same lesson learned on Earth by flowering trees during the eons following the decline of the dinosaurs: give the local animals a reason to pluck your seeds and carry them away and they will spread your progeny, and your species will thrive. Fail in this and you will be wiped out, supplanted by those who did not fail.

On Earth, nuts and fruits developed which rewarded the local animals by containing easily digestible nutrition and often an intoxicating dose of raw sugar. In Underfoot's land-above-the-air nuts and fruits tempted their beasts with valuable nutrients too, but also with an indispensable dose of oxygen. This oxygen—loosely bound into chemical compounds giving it a granular sugar-like form—was easily chewed, swallowed, and metabolized by the body for exactly the same function as oxygen within any of Earth's air-breathing creatures.

Openhand-Spiraling-Upward lifted the Naming Basket, turned it upside down and shook from it a fistful of dirt: loose, dry and dusty. She handled its crushed side gently at first, then tugged and stretched to see if the intended future heirloom might still be strong enough to serve its purpose. Surprisingly, it was fine. It just needed a little pushing back into shape. She poked and twisted until it was close to a proper form and set it beside her.

The pain in her head was softer now; enough that it could be ignored. She looked at the illumination inside the pit, especially at the angle on the walls of the brighter of the two overlapping areas of sunlight.

Mother—the lesser of Underfoot's two suns—was visible from where she sat. Mother's orange colored light felt warm and good on her skin. Mother's disk was so small and so faint that it was possible to look straight into it without discomfort; something no one would attempt with Father. All ran from Father. It was Father that got Old Fist-jerked-backward; and it would be Father that would soon burn the fluids out of Openhand-Spiraling-Upward. Burn her until there were no fluids left; until her body was as light as a newborn, as rigid as a carved statue, and as brittle as mother-dried lolalo chips.

I must do something. Otherwise they will return from the caves and find my body has become a husk!

Father was not yet visible from the portion of gritty floor upon which Openhand-Spiraling-Upward sat. The pit's dirt wall shaded her from its pain, but already Father's intense yellow light slanted into the pit at an angle indicating it was well above the horizon and over half way to the zenith.

She was still in fathershadow but would not be for long. Underfoot's day was short, no more than a quarter of Earth's day. In the time needed to eat a large meal Father would reach the sky's highest point and all the fathershadow inside the pit would shrink to nothing.

Her confidence faltered. *Before then, I will die!*

A human might find it surprising to learn that Father was no brighter than Earth's sun. The lack of atmosphere was what made it dangerous. Not because an atmosphere shields those under it from the full intensity of sunlight (though it does this to a small extent) but because an atmosphere is so good at distributing heat.

On Earth when sunlight warms an object the air around it quickly absorbs that heat and rises to carry it away. But in vacuum an object is on its own in getting rid of excess heat. It can either radiate the heat away in the form of invisible light which humans call infrared, or it can share the heat with whatever objects it is touching—which is fine if it is touching an object, and if the object will absorb the heat; some substances are notoriously stubborn about refusing to absorb heat. Such substances make excellent insulation.

The inadequacy of the infrared radiation method of getting rid of excess heat can be observed by looking at the temperature of the Earth's moon which is covered in vacuum and uses this method only. Though the same distance from the sun as the balmy blue Earth, its daytime temperature is 250 degrees Fahrenheit in the light of the noonday sun.

Openhand-Spiraling-Upward rubbed the heat exchangers

which resembled gnarled and twisted tree roots poking out of her flesh along the back of her arms and the sides of her legs. They felt warm to the touch. They always did. Though they radiated heat much better than her skin, they replenished it faster by continually bringing fresh heat out from her body's deep interior.

Just because no one has ever survived Father doesn't mean it can't be done. There must be something I can do.

She tried jumping to grab the climbing pole. This brought her hands into fatherlight, but the exposures were brief enough to produce only mild and momentary pain. Her skin's response was to change color from dark gray to milk white; not over her entire body, only over the portion exposed: specifically, her hands; and even there only on their fatherlit side.

She was not able to reach the pole.

Using her hands and feet, she attempted to dig foot-notches into the wall which would transform the wall itself into a climbing pole. This plan also failed. The dirt of the walls was too hard, like densely packed clay on Earth. With no tools she could barely scratch it.

She walked along the wall poking at it with her fingers looking for weakness. As she worked at this, her hands returned to their earlier shade of dark gray—her kind's usual color when in motherlight. She found an area just soft enough that she could scrape out foot-notches. She dug a set of six; a perfect imitation of those on a climbing pole. But when she tried using them they crumbled into long vertical gouges under her weight. By being soft enough to dig, the dirt was too soft to support her.

Got to stay alive!

She noticed thin vapors rising from the portion of the floor that lay in fatherlight. *Volatiles sublimating out of the dirt.* Then she thought, *Yes, but only from the topmost layer. At a depth of a few fingers the dirt remains cool.*

She kicked at the floor. The dirt moved easily. It flew from the impact of her foot.

Floor dirt is loose!

Her fathershade was steadily shrinking; she could see it shrink by staring at its edge through a dozen heartbeats. Father was now three quarters of the way to high-point. So that three quarters of the floor now lay in fatherlight. What's more, the average temperature of the pit's walls and floor was rising, and in response to this elevated radiant heat all of Openhand-Spiraling-Upward's skin was becoming a much lighter shade of gray.

A piece of fruit came into fatherlight. Its surface boiled and popped for a few seconds and then burst into flame. There was no air to feed the fire, but it did not need air. The fruit contained an abundance of oxygen as part of its nutrition for the oxygen-eaters.

The bright purple flame expanded to become a half-spheroid resting on the dirt. The flame did not dance, did not jump, and did not rise. All of those actions would have required an atmosphere of some sort. Dancing is a result of turbulence; while rising and jumping are the result of hot gasses being more buoyant than the surrounding cooler gasses, since their density is so much lower. The flame was a half-ball as large as the Naming Basket. Its smoke did not rise in a narrow winding column, but simply expanded in every direction equally. Only the walls diverted it from its otherwise uniform movement.

Fatherlight engulfed another fruit, and it too burst into purple flame.

Kneeling near the edge of her fathershade, she started scraping out a shallow hole two hands deep and as long and wide as herself.

Two more fruit burst into bright flame; while the first one to burn's flame shrank and dimmed to reveal a withered black ember with thick cracks glowing red.

She sat down in the hole she had created, stretched her legs out straight in front of her, and started covering her feet and legs with the loose dirt. Then she laid down flat and covered her stomach and chest and one arm and then her face. *But how can I cover my remaining arm?*

As she puzzled over this problem warmth expanded over her feet. This startled and frightened her, though it was not painful; at least not yet.

Got to hide my arm from Father!

She tried slipping the arm under the loose dirt beside her the same way a small animal squirms its entire body into the soil without actually digging, but this only covered the hand and forearm. Her shoulder and upper arm remained exposed.

Then she had another idea. She piled extra dirt on the arm's shoulder, then eased the arm under her back while trying to spill as little dirt from her chest as possible. The position was awkward and made her shoulder joint uncomfortable, but it worked.

The frightening warmth at her feet crawled slowly up her legs. She kept waiting for pain; waiting to scream; waiting to fight the instinct to jump up in response to a terrible agony. A reaction which, since there would not be time enough to rebury herself, would begin a death of many long screams that no one would hear because the vacuum would not carry them beyond her throat. Indeed, even if it could, without air inside her throat her sound-producing organ could not generate as little as a whisper.

The skin over her bulges was stretched tight. Painfully they throbbed in time with her pulse. If the birthing process were to begin there would be no stopping it. She tried not to imagine how terrible that would be right now.

The impromptu insulator still seemed to be working, though her confidence in it did not grow stronger. It would take only one small break, one small breach in its protection, to set her screaming in pain. She waited for it.

She sensed her body's average temperature rising and felt anxiously for its next preprogrammed physiological response. It started on her chest and spread outward over her torso, like a human breaking into a sweat. She could not see it but she knew the sensation well. Her skin had begun secreting a liquid as thick and sticky as molasses, and as silver as polished chrome. The secreting of the silvery liquid spread to all her skin: her arms and legs and even out over the tips of her fingers. The loose dirt piled on her chest and stomach shifted just a little and some of it spilled off as millions of microscopic bubbles formed throughout the liquid, transforming it into a lightweight foam layer three fingers thick—more flexible than foamed rubber and more insulating than a down blanket. Still, she knew even this could not stand up to Father's anger.

Then she remembered something important: It is the

miniscule quantity of volatiles in dirt that causes it to stick together. Volatiles accumulate in dirt over a long period of time by repeated vacuum deposition. But direct fatherlight makes dirt soft and powdery by driving out the volatiles.

At least this seemed important when she thought of it, but she had no idea how to put this fact to use. She continued to lie still; her body temperature rising at about half the rate as before. Now her fear focused less on a small localized burn and more on a gradual rise in overall body temperature. Heat coma, followed by death.

But there was one more physiological response her body had up its sleeve, and she was unsure how that was going to play. She'd experienced it before, maybe half a dozen times; maybe as many times as a human experiences vomiting. It was every bit as pleasant.

The unknown was that she had never experienced it while laying down, or while covered with dirt, or while laying on top of the organ that was about to perform this, its only, function. But perform it, it would. She could feel it building deep inside her.

The organ in question was a matched pair of flat tunnels located just beneath the skin, one on each side of, and parallel to, her spine.

And then it came.

The organ convulsed, squirting pure water into the deepest recesses of the two tunnels. In the vacuum's zero ambient pressure this water boiled explosively long before it could get outside of her body. Two jets of white vapor blew out from just behind Openhand-Spiraling-Upward's shoulders. If she'd been standing they would have blown straight up.

And if he'd been standing this would not have been a problem.

The vapor jets hit the end of the shallow hole in which she lay, which deflected them over her shoulders where they blew all the dirt off of her face. The silver foam saved her from immediate skin burns as well as from near immediate heat coma from a rapidly overheated brain, but its protection would only last a few seconds. Father was now directly overhead—at its highest and most dangerous.

Openhand-Spiraling-Upward jumped up, scooped the silvery foam from her eyes, and with no other conceivable option, tried that important thing she'd remembered. With her jets blowing up into Father's face, she ran to the part of the wall that had been in direct fatherlight the longest and started clawing at it madly with both hands.

She longed uselessly for the flightless vestigial wings she'd had until two motheryears ago. She imagined holding them over her head, screaming as they burned off; screaming as they protected her brain.

Thanks to the jets, she felt her body's core temperature dropping. It felt wonderful, exhilarating, even luxurious, but she knew it would not last. Her body could not sustain such water loss.

I'll soon go into dehydration shock!

In the surface of the wall, she scooped out a tall shallow hole, crudely sculpted to fit her body, then spun herself around and squeezed into it. Its top deflected her jets out into the pit. Their fathershadows danced madly on the floor before her; danced across the dozen fruit which were all shriveled embers now, completely burned black; though half still glowed red in their cracks.

New problem: one of her feet was out too far, getting too much fatherlight. She couldn't bend down and dig its portion of the hole deeper. That would expose too much of her body; absorb too much heat from Father.

Stay vertical! Must stay vertical!

She lifted the problem foot and used its heel to scrape away more of the wall. The knee and thigh absorbed excessive heat for a few seconds, but when she was done the foot fit almost entirely into the wall's fathershadow.

Her vapor jet tunnels vented and vented.

Must stop venting! Stop or die!

But venting was not under conscious control. As the body's last ditch method of dumping heat that would otherwise be lethal, there were only two things that could make it stop: her body temperature returning to a safe operating level, or her body running out of water to feed into the tunnels. It would either save her or kill her. There was no middle ground.

She felt the baby inside her right bulge begin to flail its arms and kick its legs. Every baby did this as its contribution to the birthing process. It was how it got out. To fail in this yielded a stillbirth. For millions of years all the members of her species were descended from infants who succeeded at their first fight—the fight to get out of the bulge.

No! Not now; not here!

The skin across her right bulge split vertically. Water splashed across her hip and down her leg as it boiled explosively in vacuum. She grabbed the kicking infant from the opening and held it in her hand. She could see that it was crying loudly, but she heard only silence through the vacuum.

It thrashed so violently, and was so slippery with birth fluids, that she nearly dropped it; and then nearly dropped it again; and then nearly dropped it a third time. Holding it was impossible. In desperation, she spun around, stepped backward into fatherlight, scraped out a shelf-like hole in the dirt wall about belly high, set the baby in the hole and resumed her former position; thus trapping it in the hole by pressing against it with her lower back. She could feel its arms and legs kicking and poking against her still venting tunnels.

She spotted the Naming Basket near the far wall. The long thin strips of soft bark she had woven it from contained no oxygen to allow it to burn in vacuum. Instead, all its volatiles had been vaporized and, unable to hold together under its own weight, it collapsed into a thin layer of charred black dust.

The baby inside her other bulge started kicking. The second bulge split open on the first kick—too quickly for her to get her hand in position to catch the newborn. The infant—carried along by the birthing fluids splashing down her leg—fell to the ground, then bounced and rolled out into fatherlight a distance equal to its mother's height.

Horrified it would burst into flame, she leapt forward to shield it from the light with her body. As she did this the muscles of her throat and mouth convulsed to produce a soundless scream. Throwing herself onto her hands and knees, her torso formed a roof over the infant and her back began to receive Father's full fury. It felt as if she were on fire.

Grabbing up the baby—along with a sizable amount of dirt—she squeezed it into the hole with the first; then spun around and pressed herself against them. Their tiny limbs bounced off the skin of her lower back as they fought with each other. She wanted desperately to sooth their pain and comfort their fear, but for the moment the best she could do was squeeze them into the dark and let them fight and scream.

Within a hundred more heart beats her tunnels stopped venting.

She waited in fear for dehydration symptoms; waited to drop like a speared animal into unconsciousness which would drop her out of the shallow sculpted hole in the wall and into the killing light. But she didn't drop.

I still have water! Didn't use it all!

At her feet she could see a thin line of fathershadow. Father was past high point. The sculpted hole in the wall would now begin to grow more safe—not less.

Her fear eased somewhat. *Stay vertical. Stay conscious. Stay motionless. Not over yet. Almost over, but not yet. Got to stay still.*

But of course the worst was over. And soon, the thin line of fathershadow grew wide enough that she could safely sit on the floor and rest her back against the wall. She held her babies to her chest, and licked the dirt from their happily squirming bodies with the only cleaning device available at the moment—her tongue. She examined them carefully. Both, she discovered, were female; and both seemed robustly healthy. They'd survived their ordeal without injury.

Her motherly worry was natural. Many of a newborn's organs were not fully developed, so they lacked many of the protections against extreme heat found in adults. They had vapor jet tunnels, for example, but they could not yet vent.

After fathershadow had grown to completely fill the hole—indicating that Father had once again left the sky—she saw several mothershadows moving about on the floor of the pit. Then someone lowered the base of the climbing pole down to her. Rising to her feet, Openhand-Spiraling-Upward slapped dust from her skin in several places and began pondering how best to tell the story of how, by her own efforts and without tools, and even while giving birth, she had survived Father's rage. She also wondered how much of her terror she should leave out of the telling.

Most of it, probably, when telling my children.

The End.

Peacemaker, Peacemaker, Little Bo Peep

Jason Sanford

The sheep led the sheepdogs and wolves to pasture and prepared to gun us down.

They lined us up for execution in an old soybean field as the night clouds above built to rains which never fell, and the wind gusted to burnings we smelled but couldn't see. I stood handcuffed to Victor Braun, a trucker I'd arrested three days before for the murder of a young hitchhiker. I'd caught Victor near the crime scene as he worked with bloody hands on his truck's broken-down engine. When I'd ordered Victor to the ground at gunpoint, he smirked before complying. Muttered about bad luck and cheap-ass foreign trucks and his amusement at being arrested by a woman half his size.

"Care to tell me your name, honey?" he drawled once I'd cuffed him.

"Sergeant Ellen Davies," I announced, and slammed his head against the scratch-rock ground for what he'd done to that poor girl.

But now we stood side by side as the people I'd served for the last decade paced up and down debating the best way to kill us.

Before me, Pastor Albert Jones of the Holy Redeemer Church sadly shook his red-shag head. Jones had baptized me as a teenager, not long after he moved to our little town. One of the proudest moments in my life had been when he once praised me in a sermon as a true protector of the weak and voiceless.

Now, though, he'd be my death. As Pastor Jones looked at me through sad-down eyes I cursed him, causing the woman beside him to angrily spit at my badge. Pastor Jones rested his hand on her shoulder and said to stop – this was a solemn occasion, not an occasion for petty vengeance. He then moved down the row, looking into the face of each person awaiting execution.

On the other side of Victor stood Buck, a lanky rookie who, unlike every other deputy, begged for his life. I refused to beg, and with my free hand wiped the spit from my shield.

"Good on you," Victor muttered.

Ours was a small department of only thirty deputies and half those stood in this old soybean field along with the handful of prisoners from our jail. The others were either dead – killed when we made our final stand at the sheriff's department – or had escaped with their families. And we'd only survived because Sheriff Granville had walked into the thousands of angry townsfolk with a white flag and convinced Pastor Jones to let us surrender.

I'd never seen such bravery – the mob shooting and screaming and throwing Molotov cocktails as Sheriff Granville, already shot twice, waved his flag and shouted over and over, "We're better than this!"

Sheriff Granville now leaned against Sgt. Glosser for

support as blood dripped from the rifle shots to the sheriff's massive gut. He glared at Pastor Jones. They'd been friends ever since Jones arrived in town. Jones, embarrassed, said there was nothing he could do.

"Always something you can do," Sheriff Granville muttered weakly. "We've been there. Helped each and every one of you."

The sheriff's words rippled through the townsfolk. Several people shuffled the dust of old soybean plants, maybe remembering times we'd located a lost child or caught a thief. For a moment I thought the sheriff's words might make a difference, but suddenly Pastor Jones shrieked – an inhuman whine his voice shouldn't be able to make. The high-pitched scream of joy climbed into the word "Peace!" as the people around him joined in. Their voices were unable to match Jones' high-toned shout but they still trilled that cursed word until the mob lost all intelligence and peace no longer sounded like anything I've ever known.

While the crowd trilled, Pastor Jones walked down the line. He pulled out Buck – still begging for his life – and removed the handcuffs before ripping off the kid's badge. He also freed two of our prisoners who'd been in jail for petty crimes. Pastor Jones ordered them to leave and never harm another. Buck didn't glance back as he ran through the dark into the nearby trees.

Pastor Jones shrieked again, causing the crowd to raise their guns even as they kept trilling "Peace!" I recognized the pistol in front of me as my own service weapon, now held by my old Sunday School teacher Mrs. McKenzie.

I could only pray my husband had received my warning

and escaped with our daughter. As if hearing my unspoken prayer, Victor Braun grabbed my handcuffed hand with his own. My palm hot and sweat-slicked. His still coated in the hitchhiker's blood – stains he'd proudly refused to wash away.

I hated his touch. I gripped it tightly.

"Be ready to fall," he whispered. And then Pastor Jones shrieked fire. And then we truly fell.

◊◊◊

Sometimes you fall well before you know. You fall and feel the impact later.

Is it fair to blame a dream for all this, knowing it only released what was inside us to begin with? Or is the dream an excuse? A word to tickle our mind. A mental escape to overlook the horrible things people have always done.

At first the reports of mobs killing soldiers and police and criminals and thugs didn't disturb us. We thought these were simply revolutions and protests from people trying to change their lives – events which happened somewhere in the world on a regular basis.

But then we saw the videos. Heard the eerie trilling. Saw the mobs attack while trilling "peace" as if the word was a sick, perverted joke. Witnessed how the crowds were controlled by a few individuals who shrieked at impossibly high tones, their voices controlling the mobs' actions like a virtuoso caressing bloody piano keys.

And the dreams, don't forget the dreams. Trillers mentioned their dreams with star-gone gazes, as if unable to forget the experience yet unwilling to trust words to describe them. Those few who did speak in detail mentioned the calling they found in dreams, while those the trillers aimed to kill spoke of being rejected by their dreams.

Before the trilling reached our town, Pastor Jones called our congregation to an evening prayer session. I sat on the stiff wood pew with my husband and daughter and wondered if it was really possible for my neighbors, my friends, to kill me because of the work I did. Barry held my hand in his massive grip — his calluses sticky with sap from working all day as a logger — while Lucy leaned against my side, sleepy and wanting to go home.

But Pastor Jones pushed my worries aside as he thundered at our congregation to have faith. "We are all God's children," he proclaimed. "Remember who you are. Don't allow this evil dream to steal your soul."

We all amened, but none of us said the word like we meant it.

Afterward, as the congregation filed out, Pastor Jones walked up. "Makes you wonder," he whispered to me and Barry, "about the truth of what we preach." My husband laughed nervously to the melodrama in Pastor Jones' voice and told our daughter to go play with her friends.

"Are you truly worried?" I asked once Lucy was out of earshot, having long since learned that when people make random observations they're often voicing deeper thoughts. Pastor Jones looked into me — the look people give when they want to say something but are afraid to utter the words. "I worry for you and your family, Ellen," he said. "You should flee before whatever this is reaches town."

I gripped Pastor Jones' hand and told him I appreciated

the concern. "I have a duty to perform, the same as you," I said. "As you said, we merely need faith."

Pastor Jones looked uncertain, the thunder and grace from his pulpit faded. Gone. But before I could press him, my old Sunday School teacher Mrs. McKenzie called to him, demanding Jones decide a theological point about dreams being debated by she and her friends. Pastor Jones chuckled nervously and walked away.

Now, only a few weeks later, I'd love to ask Pastor Jones what he'd truly wanted to say. To ask what had truly worried him. To ask if trillers like him give any thought on the evil their dreams push into the world.

◊◊◊

Into the ditch – mud and screams and cries – the water only a foot deep, hidden by cattails and grass as gunshots and flashlights played over the injured and the dead. The mob shot over and over at the shapes in the mud. They hadn't removed our body armor so many of the deputies survived the initial shots, only to be killed with follow-up shots to the head or rifle rounds which shredded Kevlar and flesh.

But Victor Braun had muttered fall, so when the gunshots rang we fell and rolled into the deeper water of the ditch. We hid in a tall clump of cattails, my leg burning from a bullet while my chest numb-tingled from a round stopped by my vest.

Neither of us talked or moved, knowing sound and motion would reveal our hiding place. However, Sheriff Granville's deep voice boomed out from the ditch, mocking our executioners. He'd survived the initial volley and now laughed at the mob, cursing them as weak and stupid until Pastor Jones himself waded into the ditch and shot Sheriff Granville upside the head. I reached for my service weapon before remembering it was gone.

And there we lay until the mob's eerie trilling died down and they wandered off one by one, leaving only the wind scudding the empty soybean field above us. I began to crawl toward my fallen colleagues, but I was still handcuffed to Victor and he wouldn't move.

"Wait," he whispered. "There may be a few left, watching for survivors."

I glanced at Victor. He was wet and muddy and cold and scared, the same as me. But far bigger than me, over a foot taller with at least a hundred pounds of muscle above my own. If we fought, handcuffed together, he might win. But I wasn't going to wait without checking on my friends.

"If anyone's watching, we'll run," I whispered. "Or kill them."

Victor looked into my eyes as a nasty grin cut his murderous face. No doubt the bastard approved of such bloody talk. We crawled through the ditch back to the other deputies, their moonlit badges glowing against the darker stains of mud and blood on their brown uniforms. We checked each body, but they were all dead.

I'd seen the dead many times in my career, but never so many friends. I searched for a weapon or a handcuff key, or a cell phone to call my husband and daughter, but Pastor Jones had been thorough in his search after we surrendered. While the mob had acted as if in a daze – something tied in with that damn trilling they made — Pastor Jones had shown a deadly intensity I'd never before seen in him.

I told Victor we'd head out with the handcuffs on, but he waved me silent. I glanced around the dark field, looking for the danger, but it wasn't danger. It was sound. A gasp. A low cough.

"Over here," Victor whispered, leading us to Sheriff Granville's body. The sheriff had always been a massive man, as tall as Victor but having long since let his muscle flow to fat. Seeing the sheriff's frozen eyes and face — still set in a look of determination from taunting his executioners — almost broke me to tears.

We heard a low curse. Victor and I grabbed the sheriff's large body and rolled it. Underneath lay Sgt. Glosser, who'd been supporting our wounded boss. Victor and I grabbed Glosser and tried to drag him away but he was still handcuffed to the sheriff, so we pulled both of them out of the ditch and across the field to the nearby woods.

"You okay, Gloss?" I asked. He was covered in blood, but it all seemed to be from the sheriff.

"Bastard like to broke my jaw," he said.

"What?"

"When they started shooting, the sheriff sucker punched me. Knocked me clean out."

I explained how the sheriff taunted the mob after the first round of shooting. "He knocked you out to hide you," I said. "Hid you in the mud under him. Taunted them so they wouldn't notice you."

Glosser nodded, not saying anything, none of us could, only staring at Sheriff Granville's body. Even though he knew he would die, he'd still fought like hell to save one of his people.

Suddenly a car's headlights flickered over the soybean field. Car doors thumped and several men and women with flashlights stepped out.

"We've got to go," I whispered to Glosser. "Do you have a handcuff key?"

He patted his uniform pockets and shook his head. While Victor and I could flee handcuffed together, Glosser couldn't run until we freed him from the sheriff's body.

The people from the car walked toward the ditch. I saw shotguns and rifles. One of them trilled "peace" and they shot at the dead bodies over and over.

"Leave me," Glosser whispered. "Get out of here."

I turned to Victor, ready to argue with the murderer that we weren't leaving Glosser, but Victor merely raised his hand for me to wait. He sat deep in concentration, quietly gagging.

The trillers had now noticed the bloody drag marks in the field from the sheriff's body. They shone their flashlights along the woodline and began walking toward us. Glosser waved for us to go, but Victor again motioned to wait. He gagged a final time as the tip of a handcuff key parted his lips.

He quickly unlocked the three of us and we fled deeper into the dark woods.

◊◊◊

We called them trillers because of the sound they made while killing. It was easier to call them that than friend and neighbor and lover and family, and to know that people once so close could so easily do this deed.

We stumbled through the night, avoiding other people. We saw several fires in the distance and heard screams and gunshots. Anyone who had embraced violence and aggression before the dream hit – whether as a means to harm others, or seeing violence as occasionally necessary to protect yourself and others – was at risk of being killed. Somehow the trillers sensed immediately who these people were and hunted them down.

Never mind that the trillers were doing far worse than those they killed could have ever done.

When morning came we found a partially burned trailer off a backroad and hid there. A man and woman lay dead in front of the trailer, both shot down by trillers as they'd fled the flames. We left the bodies alone and scrounged food and water inside. The water still flowed from the faucets and I washed out the flesh wound on my leg and bandaged it. The wound hurt, but if I kept it clean it shouldn't give me much trouble. Glosser and I also changed out of our uniforms into some civilian clothes we found. But just in case, we kept our damaged body armor on underneath.

Victor seemed amused when he saw me in bluejeans and a flannel shirt.

"What?" I asked.

"Changes the power dynamic, is all," he said. "Amazing what a uniform – or the lack of one – does to the mind."

Glosser eyed Victor warily from the trailer's smoky kitchen. We hadn't found any guns, but Glosser held a machete and handed me a hatchet. Victor glanced around as if to ask where his weapon was before shrugging.

"Interesting trick with that handcuff key," I said to Victor. "How long did you have it hidden down your throat?"

"I always keep one in my mouth while hunting. Partially swallow it if caught. Bring it back up if needed. Trick I learned a while back."

I shifted the hatchet in my hand, remembering the body of that young hitchhiker and knowing instantly what Victor meant by hunting. Her torso split from gut to chest in one knife slice. Her breasts sliced off. Her throat gaping so wide I could have slid my hand up to grab her tongue.

It was the worst crime scene I'd ever encountered, even worse than the murder-suicide I'd investigated a few years ago in the abandoned hotel downtown. That had been the work of a drug-crazed man who hadn't fully known what he was doing to his best friend until he came down, at which point – horrified – he killed himself.

But Victor had known exactly what he was doing to that girl.

After I'd arrested him, I'd found a pair of homemade leather gloves in Victor's back pocket, a human tattoo of a heart visible on the sewn palms. The sheriff and I suspected Victor of being a serial killer and bagged the gloves for DNA testing, figured they were a trophy from another grisly murder. But before we could dig deeper, our world dropped into crazy.

Seeing me gazing at him, Victor spit a grin which would have fried fear through most people. "She wasn't my first kill," he said. "If that's what you're wondering."

"You're proud, aren't you?" Glosser asked in a shaky voice. He'd always had trouble keeping emotions out of his work. Naturally, Victor picked up on this.

"Let me guess," he said. "You take my existence as a personal affront, which of course makes me wonder what you're hiding. Maybe you dip into the criminal now and then...or maybe before becoming a cop you did things you aren't proud of."

I wanted to curse. Not only was Victor dangerous, he was smart – he'd pegged Glosser far too quickly. Before becoming a deputy, Glosser had been involved in a number of breaking and enterings as a teenager, and even one assault. He'd been destined for far worse crimes before Sheriff Granville took him under his wing and refocused Glosser on high school. After Glosser graduated and stayed clean for a few years, the sheriff overlooked Glosser's juvenile crimes and hired him.

Behind me, I heard Glosser step across the burned linoleum, and saw the flash of a machete as he prepared to separate Victor's head from body. I motioned for him to stop.

"Smart," Victor said. "Right now, you need me."

"Why?" I asked.

"Because whatever is causing this is coming after all of us. The sheepdogs and the wolves. Anyone who ever used violence."

Glosser snorted in disgust, but I knew Victor was right. By sheepdogs and wolves, he meant the police and criminals. And it sure did seem that something was gunning for us.

"Victor's right," I said. "There's safety in numbers."

"That's why I'm still with you two," Victor said. Unspoken was that once he felt safe enough, Victor would leave. I lowered my hatchet and sat down across from Victor at the charred table.

"Why didn't you use the handcuff key earlier?" I asked.

"You never gave me an opportunity to escape." I smiled grimly at the compliment and handed Victor the hatchet.

◊◊◊

When dark came we left the smoke-gagging trailer and hiked toward town. We kept to the fence-line trees along the back roads, occasionally seeing bodies beside wrecked cars or burned houses. But most houses stood as they always had, giving an odd normalcy to the night. Groups of people also drove by in trucks and cars, looking as if they were going to a cookout or a party.

But they were actually hunting. We saw three cars full of people pull in front of a wood-panel home. The trillers surrounded the house and yelled at the man inside to come out. Instead the homeowner fired a rifle, hitting two of them. But the trillers fired back and one threw a gas bomb. The man inside kept firing until the whole house was ablaze and all you heard were his screams as he burned to death.

After waiting a bit to make sure the man was dead, the trillers climbed back in their cars and drove off. One of the wounded trillers left with them but the other was dead, her body laying where she fell. As soon as their headlights disappeared, we ran from the woods to the dead woman. Her shotgun had been taken, but she had a pistol and a cell phone in her pocket. Glosser handed me the pistol – an almost worthless .32 ACP Mouse Gun. Still, it might be better than nothing and I pocketed it as we ran back to the woods.

Glosser immediately called his wife. She answered on the

first ring and they both cried. She and the twins were hiding in their attic along with Sheriff Granville's wife, daughter-in-law, and grandkids. When Glosser's wife asked about the sheriff, Glosser didn't say anything. How could he? Glosser's wife knew him well enough to understand.

Glosser promised to reach them soon. "It's almost morning, and we have to hide," he said. "Hang on until tonight, okay?" I heard his wife whisper her love and his two boys say the same.

Wiping his face, Glosser handed me the phone. I called Barry, praying with each ring for the big lug to pick up, refusing to believe the worst even when the phone clicked into voicemail. I left a message and called back, and again. Nothing. If Barry didn't answer, my daughter should have picked up.

"They might not be able to answer," Victor said with more sympathy than I'd expect from a serial killer. "Probably holed up somewhere."

I refused to answer as I slid the phone into my pocket.

◊◊◊

The dream had visited me during a few scant moments of sleep, my head on my desk as I worked on the paperwork from Victor's arrest. Victor sat glumly in the holding cell near me. I shouldn't have drowsed off with him there. But the room felt warm and I felt tired and the next thing I knew I was dreaming.

I sat in a sunny field as a sweet-smelling breeze whistled the grass and daisies around me. Barry sat beside me holding my hand in his giant palm as we watched Lucy practice for her third-grade play. She wore the Little Bo Peep outfit I'd spent far too many hours sewing. But where the outfit I'd actually made for her was barely recognizable as a frock, this dream outfit appeared ripped directly from a high-end nursery rhyme. As if I'd actually had time to make a costume worthy of some damn idealized world's best mom.

Barry looked at me and smiled as Lucy twirled in happiness. The breeze wrapped me tight in its warm embrace. I felt perfectly, absolutely at peace.

But even as I realized this peace the breeze built up and up into a slicing wind, a wind which swirled like a dust devil as it tasted my memories. The wind saw the times I'd had to practice violence. Saw that I'd be perfectly willing to do violence in the future.

"I do wish this could be different," the wind sighed in a voice sounding exactly like Pastor Jones. "That a hero could, for once, be acceptable to us. Unfortunately, I'm not allowed such choices."

I tried to defend myself, explaining that sometimes you had to raise your fist to stop people from harming others. But the wind shivered away my words. The field around me vanished. My daughter screamed in panic before she disappeared along with Barry. As the most peaceful moment I'd ever experienced was wrenched away, I felt the dream condemn me – and condemn my husband and daughter for being so close to me.

I screamed and slammed my fist into my desk, only to realize I was still in the sheriff's department. From the holding cell beside me Victor frantically shook the metal bars, his face a mix of pain and loss from losing whatever dream of peace he'd also experienced. As he rattled the bars we heard a trilling rise from outside the department – a slow moaning of "peace" which mocked the dreams we'd both briefly glimpsed.

"This would be a good time to run," Victor said.

He was right. But I didn't realize how right until we were handcuffed together and falling into that mud and bullet jumping ditch.

◊◊◊

Victor, Glosser, and I wasted an hour trying to find a car to steal, but had no luck. As a result, the sun rose before we made it a dozen blocks into town. The electricity was still on in most houses and we saw a few people holding guns and talking with neighbors. Obviously they were continuing to hunt for us violent people. We needed to hide.

"Buck," Glosser said.

"What's that?" Victor asked.

"Not what," I said. "He's the deputy Pastor Jones released before they shot us. His house is a block away."

Victor shook his head. "We can't trust him. That preacher let him go for a reason."

My gut told me Victor was right, but Glosser shoved the murderer back, pointing the machete at his throat. "Screw you," Glosser whispered. "Buck's a cop. We trust him."

While I'd always been uneasy around Buck – he'd never struck me as top-quality police material – we'd still served together for the last year. So I was with Glosser. We had to trust him.

We reached Buck's back door as the sun lit the neighborhood into a warmer light than it deserved. Several nearby houses were burned and gone, only char and cinder marking their cement foundations. A number of police and firefighters had lived in this neighborhood. I refused to think about what had happened to them and their families.

Glosser tried Buck's door but it was locked. He knocked several times before Buck walked to the window and saw us. But he didn't open the door.

"Son of a bitch," Glosser grumbled. He banged again – far too loudly for my taste – and I looked around to see if any neighbors were watching. After a few bangs, Buck opened the door.

"You shouldn't be here…" he began, but we'd already pushed past him into his den. Victor closed the door and locked it. All of the shades were drawn and the lights out.

"This is not how you greet friends," I said.

Buck looked nervously at the carpet. "Sorry," he said. "I thought you were here to kill me."

Victor walked around the house, checking rooms and closets to see if we were alone. Glosser and I stared at Buck, trying to see the rookie we'd spent so long training in the shivering, fearful kid before us.

"I heard the shots," Buck said. "Anyone else make it?"

We didn't need to answer. "What happened to you?" I asked.

Buck said he hid in the woods until daybreak. As he'd walked back to town, a group of trillers saw him but they merely waved and kept on going. "After that, I figured they wouldn't hurt me."

Victor was drinking a glass of milk in the kitchen and shaking his head at Buck's words. Not that the kid was lying. But something was...wrong with his story.

I wondered how the trillers knew which people were the fighters of the world and which were those they could safely leave alone. No ordinary dream gave people such ability. I remembered Pastor Jones' voice in my dream. Whatever caused this wasn't natural because it involved accessing a person's memories of what they'd done in life – and determining what they might do in the future.

Still, nothing to be done about it now, and we had nowhere to go until sundown. I asked Buck if he had any weapons but he said no, so we made do with my Mouse Gun and the machete and hatchet. "We'll sleep in shifts," I told the men. "Victor, you and me and Buck sleep first. Gloss keeps watch."

Glosser nodded. I trusted him and he trusted me.

I slept exhausted. I again dreamed of Lucy in her Little Bo Peep outfit, only this time we weren't in that peaceful field. Instead, we sat in the school auditorium as she chased costumed sheep around the stage. Pastor Jones sat near me and howled with laughter at Lucy's charming performance, clapping and nodding his red-top head to her every memorized line. But instead of the play ending how it had in real life – with me hugging my daughter – Lucy suddenly ran in panic through our neighborhood, chased by Jones and the trillers as "peace, peace" echoed in my mind.

Remembering how in my first dream Pastor Jones' voice had condemned Lucy solely because of my actions, I begged him not to hurt her. He looked at me with a pained expression and said he'd try to help.

◊◊◊

When Glosser woke me for my turn at watch I again tried calling Barry. No answer. My house was only two miles past Glosser's. After we reached his family, we'd get mine.

I sat in the den's easy chair, trying to clean the flesh wound on my leg. The wound hurt more than before, no doubt from all the running I'd done.

Midway through my watch Buck walked in. "I can't sleep anymore," he said, glancing at my bloody pants leg. "I'll stand watch if you want to shower and dress that wound."

I hesitated, but what could I say? Buck was a deputy. If I said no, it'd mean I didn't trust him.

"Only a few minutes," I said.

In the bathroom was an old radio. I tuned through the dial looking for news, but a recorded message from Pastor Jones was on all the local stations. I showered as I listened.

"Peace is upon us," Jones said as he trilled that word for long seconds. "It is painful, I know, to do these things. We love these people. But for too long the criminal has stolen from us, the murderer has killed us, the soldier has attacked us, and the police officer has merely pretended to protect us. In truth, they are all the same. All the same violent person.

"Once they are gone, peace will be ours. We will beat our swords into plowshares and live in the paradise of a true, eternal peace."

I threw the soap at the radio, knocking both to the floor

with a loud crash.

After drying off, I wrapped my wound with gauze from Buck's first aid kit and dressed. I walked out of the bathroom to find Victor holding Buck at gunpoint, Buck's nose broken and streaming blood.

I pulled the mousegun and aimed at Victor. "Drop the gun," I yelled, loud enough to wake Glosser, who stirred in the back bedroom.

"He ratted us," Victor said in a low, angry voice, keeping his pistol on Buck. "I caught him calling the trillers."

Glosser now stood beside me, machete in hand. I glanced from Buck to Victor. I'd helped instruct Buck, while Glosser had served as his field training officer. Buck couldn't have done this. I refused to believe it.

But the pistol Victor held snapped into my mind – I'd seen Buck shooting it before at our firing range. Victor grin his evil slit. "He had it under his mattress," Victor said. "Guess he lied when he said there were no weapons here."

Buck's bloody face paled and he fell to the carpet, begging like he did in the trillers' firing line. "I promised Pastor Jones," he said. "I promised I'd stay with peace. I even dreamed it. I dreamed the true peace."

Glosser cursed and smashed Buck across the head with the machete's handle, knocking him out. Buck collapsed to the carpet as headlights lit the window shades. Victor glanced out front.

"Two cars," he said. "Seven people."

I looked out and saw Pastor Jones step from one of the cars.

"Sergeant Davies," Pastor Jones yelled. "You have

nowhere to run. Think of your daughter. She doesn't have to follow your violent path. Do the right thing and I promise to gift her a true dream of peace."

I tensed at the mention of my daughter, but Glosser pointed up the street at more headlights approaching. We didn't have long before an entire mob of trillers would be here.

"Out the back door?" Glosser asked.

I looked at Victor and he nodded toward the front door. "No," I said. "We charge them. Rattle them. We're in no condition to outrun them unless they're afraid to follow."

So we charged.

Victor shot two trillers, an old husband and wife I remembered from the church's Christmas choirs, where they always sang a haunting version of 'Silent Night'. Glosser sliced a teenage girl across the face with his machete while I shot the postman who delivered mail to my house. The first shot from the mousegun didn't stop him, but the second shattered the lit Molotov cocktail in his hand, exploding him to a crazy dance of flames. Despite this, he kept trilling peace with the others.

I tried to shoot Pastor Jones but all I saw of him was his red hair illuminated for a moment as a third car pulled up. He ducked behind the car for safety. By then we were past the trillers and running down the street.

"They're not following," Glosser shouted.

"They'll follow," I said. "They'll wait a bit before chasing us. Get up their bravery and numbers."

So we ran for Glosser's house, praying Pastor Jones wouldn't figure out too soon where we were going.

We reached Glosser's neighborhood to find the power out. A fire station down the block had been attacked and the substation next door had exploded when the station burned.

While Victor and I stood guard, Glosser raced up the stairs calling for his family. They opened the attic door and fell into his arms, his twin boys hugging him as his wife cried. Sheriff Granville's wife, along with her daughter-in-law and grandkids, surrounded me. I hugged the sheriff's wife as she wiped her eyes. I didn't need to tell her about the sheriff's bravery. She knew he'd have gone down fighting.

Quickly, Glosser grabbed a duffle bag and began throwing food and supplies into it. Victor and I opened Glosser's gun safe and pulled out a shotgun and an automatic rifle from Glosser's days on our department's SRT team. Victor handed me the rifle and ammo clips and I handed him one of Glosser's old sets of body armor. Victor loaded the shotgun and placed Buck's pistol in a holster which he belted around his waist.

"There's a truck and an old SUV in the garage," Glosser told me. "We drive them both, grab your family, and get the hell out of here."

I was curious where this left Victor. I'd assumed all along he'd leave us at some point. While I didn't like turning him loose, there was no other alternative.

I turned to ask Victor where he was going only to find him staring at Glosser's wife.

Victor looked embarrassed, as if caught in a compromising moment. Even though I'd visited Glosser's wife a hundred times, it took me long seconds to realize what Victor was seeing. Glosser's wife looked like an older version of the hitchhiker Victor had killed.

"What's wrong," Glosser asked in an edgy voice. I was suddenly grateful he'd never seen the girl's bloody body or the nightmarish autopsy photos.

"A destination," Victor said, fumbling away his shocked stare. "You'll need somewhere to hole up for a while. I've got a place."

Glosser pulled out a map and Victor showed him how to drive to his land. About sixty miles outside town, up and down several hills and a number of dirt roads. "Got a supply of food built up, a deep well, a solid rock and cement house that could hold off an army. Best of all, few people know it's there."

Glosser stared at Victor, no doubt knowing like I did what that house had been built to hold off – and likely what Victor had used the isolation for. "I don't know…" Glosser said.

"I won't go there," Victor promised. "I'll head the other way. Wouldn't feel right, you and me together."

Seeing no other place to go, we agreed with Victor's plan. We loaded the truck and SUV and drove to my house.

◊◊◊

Barry lay in our kitchen, his body bled out. There were three dead trillers outside the house and two inside. The shotgun beside my husband was empty and it looked like he'd struggled hand to hand with someone before being shot.

In Barry's frozen right hand, a tangle of red hair gleamed to my flashlight's glow. Torn from the triller he'd fought.

Victor shook his head at my husband's body and kicked a

cabinet so hard the wood splintered. "It ain't right," he said. "All these people – they're sheep. They hate violence. They get people like you to protect them and fear people like me, but end of the day that's all they do, fear and talk and live."

I knew what Victor was saying, and if I'd been thinking clearer I would have told him he was only partially right. That it wasn't wrong to want to live your life in peace. To let others protect you, as it'd been my honor to do. But right then I was as angry as him and wanted to kill Pastor Jones and everyone like him. And I needed to find my daughter.

I thought back to Jones' comment about Lucy being shown the true way to peace. He had her. I knew it.

When Glosser drove up in front of my house he had a young man and woman huddled in the back of his truck and another car following them. "Two soldiers I know, and their families," he said. "I couldn't leave them."

I was proud of Glosser. Proud of how he'd pulled his life together from his wreck of a childhood, and proud I'd served beside such a good, decent man. When he asked about Barry, I shook my head and told him to lead everyone to Victor's safe house. I was going to find my daughter. If I was lucky, I'd join them later.

"What about him?" Glosser asked, pointing his pistol at Victor.

Victor muttered that he was also leaving. Would hike his way out of town. But I quickly told him no. He was coming with me.

Victor looked intrigued and asked what was in it for him. But I didn't answer. Merely tapped my fingers across the oily sheen of my rifle.

◊◊◊

The Holy Redeemer Church sat at the end of our tiny downtown, where it'd stood for the last hundred years. If Pastor Jones and the trillers had their way it might stand for another century as a beacon of humanity's ultimate embrace of peace. Not that I'd be welcome in their dream of peace.

As I expected, the church was also a beacon for trillers across the area. Whatever had infected people caused them to naturally gravitate to people like Jones. I remembered the reports I'd read – how this was happening in communities across the world – before reminding myself to focus on the matter at hand.

As dawn slapped its nasty light down, Victor and I sneaked into the old hotel down the street from the church. The hotel had been built during Prohibition and abandoned for the last few decades. Most people avoided its decaying bulk, which was riddled with small corridors and dusty rooms. But I'd spent long days investigating that nasty murder-suicide here and knew the place inside and out.

"A good defensive spot," Victor said. "But I still don't see why I should stick with you."

I thought again of the murder-suicide and wondered if I could really go through with my plan. Ignoring Victor's question, I climbed the stairs to a fifth floor room, where a small hole in the outside wall let us see the church without being seen.

We watched all morning. Trillers milled around on foot and in cars. Each time the bells in the church's large wooden tower rang – meaning a new victim had been sighted – Pastor

Jones would start his high-tone shriek, which always grabbed the minds of the other trillers and excited them into driving off to kill their prey.

There were also a few prisoners in the church, all children. Through the church windows, I saw Lucy and seven other young kids, each the child of a local deputy, firefighter, or soldier. All looked scared. I remembered my dream and how it had condemned Lucy merely because she was the child of a violent woman.

"Obviously a trap," Victor said. "They're trying to draw out the holdouts."

"Maybe. Or maybe Pastor Jones really believes those kids aren't tainted with the violent tendencies the trillers are stamping out. Maybe he's trying to save them."

That's when Pastor Jones entered the church. Through the large windows I saw him talk to the kids. I don't know what he said but the kids disagreed with him, with Lucy being so bold as to push him away. Pastor Jones shook his red hair in irritation and walked back outside.

I fingered my assault rifle. My daughter was too much like me for the trillers to let her live for long. I had to act soon. But first, I needed to know about Victor.

"If I asked you to help me rescue my daughter, would you?"

"No. Earlier, there was strength in numbers. Now, I'm better going alone. No offense, but that's how I work."

I nodded. That was the answer I'd expected. "Not sure I believe you," I said. "If you're such a loner, why'd you tell Glosser about your safe house? You could have worked your way there. Laid low for a while."

"Again, not my way. I've killed twenty-eight people. Mostly women, but also a few men. People see what I've done, they wonder if the killer's one of the sheep around them. Their neighbor. Their friend."

I shifted the assault rifle nervously in my hands. But Victor could have killed me anytime in the last two days. He grin his evil split at my wariness.

"You and me, we're so similar," he said. "We understand evil, even if we have different reactions to it. The sheep out there, they haven't a clue. They hate you sheepdogs unless we wolves are around, then they tolerate you until we disappear in the night. That's the natural way. That's the life I want."

He glanced at the trillers surrounding the church and shook his head. "I can't say this isn't my fight. And I am curious. I want to see how far you'll go to save your daughter. But I won't risk my life to help you."

And that was that. He'd watch, but not help. His rambling explanation didn't totally make sense. But if I'd asked one of the trillers about their words — for peace, for a new world, because of a damn dream — would they also match their deeds? Too many levels and depths to the craziness around us.

Still, I needed Victor. So I fell back on the murder-suicide I'd investigated here a decade ago, knowing a secret he'd take in trade for his help. Something Victor could only do if I let him.

I handed him my assault rifle and made my offer.

◊◊◊

Victor gave me a hell of a distraction.

From the Prohibition hotel's fifth floor hiding place, he picked off trillers with the assault rifle, sniping them one by one. He killed four before they realized where the shots came from, the sounds echoing in confusing bangs around the downtown streets and buildings. But once they knew where he was the trillers surged toward the hotel.

If Victor did like I said he had a decent chance. It would take the trillers a long time to search every room of that old hotel and by then, well, I refused to think about that part.

I sneaked to the rear of the church, Victor's rifle shots and the returning fire providing more than enough sound to cover my approach. Pastor Jones and an armed man stood guard over the kids in the church, but they casually watched the fight through the windows. I shot the armed man – I recognized him as Mr. Hillsbury, the principal of my old high school – and aimed my shotgun at Pastor Jones.

"You okay, Lucy?" I asked.

My daughter smiled. "I told Pastor Jones you'd save us. He didn't believe me, but I told him."

I wanted to cheer my daughter's faith, but instead told her to lead the other kids to the back room of the church and wait for me. Victor's rifle fire still sounded outside, but I saw the trillers entering the hotel. Victor would soon be forced to go into hiding and I didn't want them to return and find us.

Pastor Jones watched the kids go with sadness. "It's my fault," he said. "While their parents' dreams tainted the kids, I couldn't kill them like I was supposed to. I suppose I've also been tainted. By people like you. I couldn't simply do what I was ordered to do."

I laughed nervously at the meaning behind Jones' words. "How long have you been setting this up? I mean, the people like you?"

Pastor Jones smiled. "Since before I arrived in this town. And be careful about using the word 'people' on us – it's an imprecise term."

I shivered, wondering what exactly I faced. But I understood that there must be Pastor Joneses all over the world directing these dreams and the trillers. Pushing them to do things they might otherwise be reluctant to do.

"It's the human mind," he said. "So malleable. Most of you don't realize how controlled you are by cultural constraints and the desires of other people. You made it easy for us."

"Do you remember baptizing me?" I asked. "You praised me for my work. I'm the same person I was then."

He nodded. "Indeed you are. And I've always been impressed with how strong a person you are. I think that's why I couldn't kill those kids. I thought, maybe I'm the one to stand up to the insanity my kind has brought to your world. Maybe I'm the one to make a difference, much like you have done."

In that moment it almost seemed as if the old Pastor Jones was before me, again caring deeply for his congregation and community. But then I remembered the evil he and his kind had brought to my world.

"When people discover that they've been manipulated, they won't go easy on you," I said.

"Perhaps. But the path to peace no longer runs through you."

Even though Pastor Jones was unarmed, my soul screamed to shoot him. To leave him crying on a church pew as he slowly bled out, just like he'd done to Barry. But I'm not Victor. I made Pastor Jones kneel and I smashed his head with the butt of my shotgun, knocking him out. I then ran to the back of the church and led the children to safety.

◊◊◊

For seven months we've lived in peace. In addition to the people Glosser and I saved, we found other refugees. Soldiers and police and firefighters and others – those who understand the need to occasionally take a violent stand for what is right. We don't worship violence. But we don't fear it either.

We hid at Victor's safe house and several nearby places. But we no longer had much trouble with the trillers. Unless the trillers came face to face with us, they seemed to forget that a few of us had survived. But not many. Over the radio, we heard the trillers' celebratory message of peace echo from all corners of the world. Even though the dream that caused this behavior had begun to burn off – fewer and fewer people were trilling, and fewer and fewer people were being killed – that didn't matter.

The trillers had won. Their peace was at hand.

One cold-shiver winter day, I stood guard duty near the safe house when a solitary man walked up the dirt road. As he neared, I saw his nasty grin and recognized Victor.

I moved from my hiding spot, aiming my shotgun at him.

"I'm not staying," he said. "Heard the bungalow down the

road is more fun."

I chuckled softly. A few miles from here a number of murderers and criminals had banded together, much as we had. While we mostly kept apart from those wolves, they'd agreed to work with us if the trillers ever mounted a full-scale attack.

"Why are you here?" I asked.

"Curious. You tell anyone our deal?"

I hadn't. Truth was, I'd been ashamed to. What I'd offered Victor was the hidden speakeasy in that old Prohibition-era hotel. No one but the few deputies who'd investigated the murder-suicide knew the hidden rooms were even there. When I'd explained the speakeasy's location to Victor, and how that crazed druggie had been able to slowly kill his victim with no one else hearing or seeing, he'd instantly seen the potential. I told him if he sniped the trillers while I saved my daughter, he'd have the perfect lair to fall back on. The perfect place to remind his sheep of the true meaning of fear.

"I stayed three months," he told me. "Came out at night. Caught trillers, took them back to that room. Had a mighty fun time. Way better than that hitchhiker."

I gripped my shotgun tight, fighting the urge to kill this evil man. "Why are you here?" I asked.

"Wanted to see if you'd told the others what you allowed me to do. Wanted to see. That's all."

I didn't lower my shotgun as I told him to go up the road four miles and turn at the hidden driveway under the double oak trees. "They'll take you in," I said. "Tell them I sent you."

"I'll do that. And you're right, you know. Not to kill me. You'll need me in the days ahead."

"Why?" I asked, looking down the road, praying Pastor Jones and a mob of trillers wasn't right behind him. "The trillers are calming down. The dream is easing."

"Think about it. That dream and the way your pastor controlled people wasn't natural. Now that the sheepdogs and wolves are gone, the trillers are going back to being docile. That worries me."

Victor pulled a new pair of handmade leather gloves from his back pocket and slid them on. The bright red hairs on the gloves glistened – laughed – full of Pastor Jones' words from the night we'd prayed together at church.

"Doesn't take another predator to know you attack the sheep when they're peaceful," he said. "The creatures who tricked us with this dream of peace will be coming. I suggest keeping your eyes on the up and up."

Victor waved goodbye with his gloved right hand – the shock red hairs peeking and wafting to the breeze – and walked on.

I gripped my shotgun and watched the road and waited for more to come.

END

MAGNUS: THE APPRENTICE
"BIRTHRIGHT"

Bobby Nash

Is there anything worse than being the new kid in school? Yes, being the new kid who starts two weeks after everyone else.

That summed up Andrew Kenny's current situation. His family had moved from the only home he had ever known in Chicago, Illinois to the much smaller city of Lawrenceville, Georgia. He barely had time to say goodbye to his friends before he was whisked away from Chicago's skyscrapers and transplanted into his new rural setting. In his mind it was analogous to moving to another planet. Everything around his new home was spread out and there were very few things within walking distance except his school and a small strip mall. The only saving grace was that there was a comic book shop in the shopping center.

Andrew's mom and dad had told him that the move was necessary because of his father's transfer, which was a great opportunity for him that they couldn't turn down. While that might have been partially true, Andrew wasn't buying it. His parents loved Chicago more than he did. It would take more than a simple career opportunity to make them pack up and leave.

He knew it was because of him.

The past year had been very rough on Andrew, and as much as he hated to admit it, he took it out on his mother and father. The fact that they hadn't shipped him off to boarding school or some other place to deal with problem kids like him was something of a minor miracle. Lord knows he would have deserved it had they chose to go that route. He had been something of a holy terror the past year and caused his family no small amount of grief.

Looking back he could pinpoint the exact moment his life changed.

◊◊◊

It had started with his grandfather's funeral.

He and Andrew had been very close and spent many long hours together hiking, fishing, or just talking and enjoying one another's company. His name was Jack Magnus, but Andrew called him *Grandpa Jack* because he despised being called *grandfather* because he said he wasn't old enough for that title yet. Grandpa Jack was a brilliant storyteller who often spent hours regaling young Andrew with tales of fire breathing dragons, sword-wielding knights on horseback, vicious monsters, plotting villains, and wizards with powers and abilities far beyond those of mortal men. The stories were magical and Andrew could sit and listen to his grandfather tell those amazing tall tales all day long.

He had even once asked him why he never wrote them down in a book, but Grandpa Jack would always tell him that the stories were for him and him alone. They were not for the world at large. He made Andrew promise that the stories were a secret and not to share them with anyone, not even his parents. At the time it had not made sense why his grandfather had made such a request, but he did as he was asked. It would not be long before he realized how dangerous it was to know this secret.

During a lengthy battle with cancer, Grandpa Jack withered away to nothing. He was frail of body, but his mind remained as sharp as ever. Andrew had been sitting with him when he died. At the funeral he and some of his cousins served as pallbearers, hefting the coffin and carrying it from the funeral home's chapel to the hearse and then repeating the process from the hearse to the gravesite that would be his final resting place.

Andrew could not remember the last time he had cried as much as he had that day. Despite his dad's foolish suggestion that he *"man up"* and not cry, he could not keep the tears from falling. He knew that his grandfather would not have minded the tears. As he stood and listened to the preacher intone about Grandpa Jack's soul and how he had gone on to a better place and was no longer in any pain he realized that none of it mattered. They were only words. He would miss his grandfather and his mother would miss her father.

As they lowered the casket into the earth, Andrew held his mother's hand.

After the funeral the family descended on Jack's house and picked it clean. The furniture, jewelry, clothing, and assorted knickknacks he had collected on his many travels were gone. Andrew stood in the empty den where he hand his grandfather had spent many an afternoon playing chess or Monopoly while Jack told him a story he had never heard before. There seemed to be no end to the new adventures he came up with. His imagination was endless.

That's when his mother walked in dragging a small trunk.

"I think your grandfather wanted you to have this," she told Andrew.

"What makes you think that?"

She pointed at the trunk. "It's got your name on it."

Sure enough, a small envelope was tied to the handle with his name emblazoned on it. He opened the envelope and retrieved the letter that was hidden within. The letter told him how much he was loved and that the contents of the trunk were for him to use when the time was right. The letter also asked that he not share what he found within the trunk with anyone. Like the stories, this trunk was their final secret. He signed it, *Love, Grandpa.*

Andrew read the letter twice before he touched the trunk. It was locked and there was no key, but the letter had explained that as well. Andrew knew where the key was, but had been sworn to secrecy. Grandpa Jack had given it to him years earlier inside a small lunchbox with the comic strip character *Mandrake the Magician* stamped into its metal frame. It had sat hidden on a shelf in his bedroom ever since.

Later that night, alone in his room, he opened the trunk.

He did not expect what he saw inside.

The trunk was filled with papers. Some were in notebooks while others were free floating. There were several items similar to the knickknacks that Jack had kept on shelves in his den. He had referred to them as *totems* several times. These totems oftentimes played a role in the wild stories Jack told. Also inside was a small stick, a box of matches, a yo-yo, an ornately carved ring, a small coin that was slightly larger than a silver dollar coin, and a book with a well-worn moleskin cover. Although the cover was faded from multiple readings, the etching remained.

On it was inscribed the words *Spell Book*.

And Andrew's life would never be the same.

Andrew quickly discovered that the stories Grandpa Jack had told all those years were true after three people approached him a few days after Jack's funeral. There were two men, named Jasper Monk and Harrison Black, plus a woman named Charisma Jones. They all claimed to be Jack's apprentices.

"Why would my grandpa need apprentices?" Andrew asked.

From these apprentices, Andrew learned that Jack had been something of a master wizard in his youth, tasked with protecting the world at large from the forces of evil that threatened to destroy it. All of the business trips he had taken over the years had been a cover to hide his true profession. It was hard to listen to the three of them talk about his Grandpa Jack in such a familiar manner, but the more they told him the more Andrew believed them. Many of the adventures they recounted were familiar to Andrew from the stories he had heard all his life.

As fantastic as it sounded, Grandpa Jack was a wizard.

That's when they Charisma dropped the bomb on him.

She told him that he was a wizard too.

It was at that moment that Andrew's life changed. Gone was the innocent little boy who had listened to his grandfather's stories and dreamed of undertaking some adventures of his own. Jasper, Harrison, and Charisma informed Andrew that their mentor's final assignment was for them to keep him safe while they trained him how to harness his powers. They were his advisors, his trainers, and his protectors.

"There are a lot of people out there that will be looking for you," Jasper told him.

"What kind of people?"

"Bad people," Charisma said softly.

As it turned out *"bad people"* was something of an understatement. During his career, Grandpa Jack had made a few enemies and now that he was gone they were coming out of the woodwork. And each of them seemed to have only one thought on their minds. Revenge. One week after learning the truth from his new advisors, Andrew's school bus was forced off the road when a water main ruptured and pushed a huge metal pipe through the concrete in its path. Luckily, no one had been hurt. His new protectors swooped in to take care of the man who was after Andrew, but he knew that there would be others.

He wasn't wrong.

The next six months consisted of one danger after another. Andrew's powers grew and his knowledge of ancient magic improved daily under his advisor's coaching. Soon he was able to protect himself, but by then the damage was done. The school had labeled him a troublemaker and threatened to suspend Andrew if things did not settle down. The news made his parents, especially his father, angry. They demanded an explanation, but Andrew was bound by his promise and his silence only widened the gulf that had grown between them since Grandpa Jack's death.

The final straw came just a month earlier when he had been attacked while in the auditorium. The man called himself Kurza and he commanded fire elementals, which he hurled at Andrew. In the course of defending himself, the auditorium was burnt to the ground. If not for quick thinking on Andrew's part the entire school would have been lost.

Unfortunately, no one else saw it that way.

Not the school.

Not the fire marshal.

And definitely not his parents.

The news of his dad's transfer came three days later.

◊◊◊

Andrew hated starting over.

The first class at his new school was math, which was not his favorite subject. The principal walked him to the room where class had already started and introduced him to the teacher and the class. The teacher pointed him to an empty seat near the back of the room and continued her lesson. He was now officially a high school freshman. The thought scared him more than the idea of facing down a horde of angry fire demons.

Andrew's sister, Kim, was also starting classes at the same school, but she was a junior. The move had been hardest on her because she was two years from graduating and did not want to move away from all of her friends. Their mom's promise that they would each make new friends here rang hollow for both of them.

Surprisingly, Andrew's relationship with his sister remained solid. Despite everything that had happened, she did not blame him and remained cordial to him. Well, at least as cordial as a sister could be to her baby brother.

He went through the day trying to stay as invisible as possible. The events of the past six months had taught him to be careful of strangers. The irony of it all was that he now lived in a state full of strangers. He was leery of everyone and did not go out of his way to meet his new classmates. That did not stop some of the more friendly students from introducing themselves to him. He met several nice people and even found himself relaxing a bit. Perhaps his mother had been right. Perhaps he might make friends after all.

The rest of his day went pretty much the same. He started each class as an outsider who was behind the class. In most instances he was able to catch up, but there were some homework assignments he would have to play catch up on. However, it was in his last class of the day that Andrew got his biggest surprise.

As he stepped into his American History and Civics class and almost choked on his tongue. Standing next to the chalkboard was Harrison Black, his new teacher. Harrison turned out to be an excellent teacher. He overheard some of the students talking. Mr. Black was a new arrival at the school after the surprise resignation of the teacher who used to teach the class. The rumors behind the teacher's departure varied from the simple "*I heard she was sick*" to the absurd "*I heard she won the lottery and ran off to the Carribean.*" Andrew was fairly certain that his advisors had something to do with it, but of course he couldn't tell his classmates that.

After class dismissed, Andrew stayed behind to ask Mr. Black a question about the homework assignment. Once they were alone, he dropped all pretenses. "What are you doing here, Harrison?" he asked.

"What do you think, kid?" Harrison answered. "My job is to keep you safe and I take my job seriously." He saw the look on Andrew's face. "What? Did you think moving to a new city meant it was over?"

"I was kind of hoping."

"Come on, kid. You aren't that naïve. Oh, and in class, please call me Mr. Black, okay?"

"Okay. So what happens next?"

"Next," Harrison said with a smile. "We resume your training."

The next few days were a blur. Andrew's day consisted of a morning workout with his physical fitness nut dad followed by a full day of school. In addition to Mr. Black teaching class, Charisma had secured a job working in the school's office. Keeping his powers and training secret was still of the utmost importance so Andrew's evenings included his new part time job working at the comic book shop that was owned and operated by Jasper Monk. His parents were overjoyed when they heard the news that he'd found a job. It was the first time he had seen them happy in a long time so Andrew was determined to shield them both from his other life as much as possible. The last thing he wanted was a repeat of the incident in Chicago.

He had to tread more carefully.

The back room of Monk's Comics and Games became the training center where Andrew and his instructors continued to hone his control of the magical powers that were part of his birthright as well as training his body in more traditional ways. The days were long, but Andrew was determined to make it work. At night he would come home, eat dinner, do his homework, and collapse from exhaustion, but it was worth it. It was his job to keep his family safe.

At the moment, his only real problem was staying awake during first period.

Unfortunately, bigger problems were heading his way.

◊◊◊

Lord Lucius Manris slammed his hand down on his antique desk.

The impact released an explosion of color as energy tendrils lanced from his fist in all directions. The desk shattered under the strain of so many mystical energies buffeting it simultaneously. Lord Manris was not prone to outbursts of anger. He held it in, letting the pressure build and build until he was ready to burst. When he did let loose his frustrations his servants knew it was time to buy new furniture.

Lord Lucius Manris was not really royalty. In fact, his birth name was not Lucius Manris. He had fabricated his entire identity from the time his gifts first manifest themselves when he was twelve years old. The child he had been was discarded and Lucius Manris took his place. He eventually came under the tutelage of a master magician who called himself Master Paragon, also not his given name. After a short time spent in Paragon's care, Manris added the illustrious title of Lord to his moniker.

Lord Manris eventually succeeded his teacher and took control of the *family business* after Master Paragon's death. There were many that believed that Manris had hastened his ascension by killing his former master, but there was no proof of that, only conjecture and rumor.

Despite a less than stable world economy, business was booming.

Like so many others, Manris's greatest defeat came at the hands of Jack Magnus. Magnus was a powerful wizard and he had placed barriers in place that hampered Manris and other like him from achieving many of their goals. When he had heard that the *old man* had died, Lord Manris cackled with joy like some comic book super villain. "With Magnus out of the way we can finally move forward with the transfer," he had shouted to the rooftops. After years of waiting, he would finally complete a journey he had started years before.

Unfortunately, breaking down Magnus' mystic barriers proved more difficult than he had anticipated. Lord Manris's abilities were great, but even his power paled in comparison to Jack Magnus.

What he needed was the amulet that his enemy had used to lock the spell that created the barriers that kept him and his followers from leaving this dimensional plane. If he ever hoped to escape he would need that amulet.

Luckily, he had an idea of where to find it. Magnus was a sentimentalist. That was his greatest weakness and Manris planned to exploit it. He had summoned his lackeys, they preferred to call themselves followers, but he didn't feel the need to quibble over such details. After relaying the information to his lackeys he sent them out into the world in search of the amulet.

"Find it," he ordered. "Find my amulet!"

◊◊◊

Andrew Kenny slipped the necklace around his neck.

He had taken the silver dollar sized amulet from the trunk and drilled a small hole in it near the edge, just large enough to slide a small hook into. He then attached the hook to a rope necklace he had in his room. This way he could keep the powerful artifact close at hand in case of emergency. It was also a way to keep Grandpa Jack close to him.

He slipped the amulet beneath his shirt and headed out the door. A school bus passed his house, but it was such a short walk that he and his sister, Kim, decided to walk it every morning. The walk was an easy one, plus it gave them time to talk.

"So, how was your first week of school?" he asked.

"Exhausting. I'm so far behind."

"I know what you mean."

"And I'm trying out for cheerleader," she said, beaming. Kim had been a cheerleader at their last school and she always seemed to enjoy it.

"That sounds cool," he said, trying to be supportive

although he had little interest in sports. Like most fifteen year-old boys he did, however, have a growing fondness for cheerleaders. If his sister joined the team it meant he might get to meet some of them.

The school day went much as Andrew expected. Nothing surprising leapt out at him from a locker or shadow. Perhaps his advisors had been wrong and no one was coming after him anymore.

At least that's what he wanted to believe.

It was his after school activities that Andrew enjoyed the most. His advisors were excellent instructors.

Jasper Monk was a master of several Earth born martial arts. He was teaching him some self-defense moves to start, but promised that offensive training would begin soon. Jasper demonstrated that a melding of wizardry and martial arts could be used very effectively together. His favorite defense was a spell he called the force blast. It was non-lethal, but decidedly effective. After seeing Monk in action, Andrew was more excited than ever for training.

Harrison Black was first and foremost a scholar. As Andrew had witnessed firsthand in class every afternoon, he was quite knowledgeable on a multitude of subjects. Most importantly, he was patient with his students. Andrew began to understand where the magic came from, not just how to use it. Harrison explained that knowing how something works was as important as knowing how to use it.

If Jasper honed the body and Harrison trained the mind, then Charisma was the protector of the soul. She kept Andrew grounded to reality even when his other studies strayed as far away from the realm of normality as humanly possible. She reminded Andrew what it was to be a human being. His powers had the potential for destruction and the more his skills developed the greater the possibility became. They had already witnessed it with the destruction of the school auditorium in Chicago. Without a balance of skill, training, and heart, there was a possibility it could happen again. None of them wanted that.

On Saturdays he worked at the comic book shop during the day so he could have his evenings free. His advisors understood that he was a teenager and still needed time to be a kid. After his Saturday morning workouts, the weekends were his to enjoy.

He walked out of the comic shop and squinted at the bright sun shining overhead. He had heard that it was warmer in Georgia in the fall than what he was used to in Illinois, but it was taking some getting used to. With temperatures in the mid-seventies, it was nice to get out and enjoy it. There would probably be snowing in Chicago soon. He understood they didn't get much snow in the south.

He walked down the sidewalk toward the fast food restaurant at the end of the shopping center. Charisma made them eat healthy most of the time, but the boys had started ganging up on her on Saturdays and vetoed her lunch suggestions in favor of a greasy hamburger with all the trimmings, salty French fries, and a sugary soda. After the first two weeks she gave up protesting and enjoyed a day of gluttony.

The restaurant was crowded and he recognized some of the locals that worked in the strip mall and some that he went to school with. Sitting in a corner booth was his sister and some of her new cheerleading friends. Kim had been accepted onto the squad the week before and was enjoying hanging out with her new friends. Andrew thought about going over to say hello, but decided against it. The last think Kim needed was her dorky little brother embarrassing her in front of her friends.

As he stood in line a strange feeling made the hair on his neck stand up. It was an uneasy feeling that told him something was wrong. He just didn't know what. That's when he saw them enter. There were three of them. They were large men with tattoos running the length of their muscled arms. They took their place in the line next to Andrew's, but only two of them remained together. The third got into line behind Andrew.

He didn't recognize them, but Andrew could feel a mystic energy emanating from them. He had felt such waves before, but never as primal. It felt like waves of raw power buffeting him from each of them and then aftershocks as the waves bounced off one another like ripples in a pond. He had felt something similar before when he faced Kurza back in Chicago. Whoever these men were, they were powerful wizards, but unfocused.

If they were here for him, and he couldn't imagine it was just a coincidence that they had walked into this restaurant at the same time he had, then things could get ugly rather quickly. He had to get away from all of these people. If they made a move here then they could get hurt. His sister could be hurt.

Casually, Andrew stepped out of line and walked toward the exit.

The man in line behind him followed and grabbed him by the shoulder just as Andrew reached the exit. "And just where do you think you're going?" he snarled.

Andrew swallowed hard. The last thing he wanted to do was fight this guy and his friends. People might get hurt. Plus, with three to one odds he wasn't so sure he could take them. His training was good, but he was not ready to deal with these odds yet.

He stared up at the man who towered over him.

"Who sent you?" Andrew asked, trying to keep the fear from his voice.

The big man laughed, but before he could say anything else his friends walked over to them. "Why don't we take this outside?" one of them said softly.

"My thoughts exactly," Andrew said as he pushed open the door.

As soon as he felt the warm sun on his face, Andrew ran.

The big guys gave chase, but the teenager had speed and stamina on them. He quickly widened the gap between them as he leapt over the retaining wall that separated the restaurant from the shopping center.

When he hit the asphalt, Andrew was already moving. He ran around the back of the shopping center. The last thing he wanted was for anyone to get hurt so he made for the closest place he could think of that was empty. Plus, he hoped to get help through the rear entrance of the comic shop. He just hoped Charisma and Harrison were still in the back.

The back of the shopping center was a maze of stacked pallets, dumpsters, empty boxes, and assorted junk that just happened to end up there. Jasper had set up some training exercises back there. At the time Andrew had hated it. Not only was it filthy out there, but it smelled. But now, he was happy for it.

Andrew ducked behind a stack of broken pallets from the sporting goods store. The broken pieces of wood gave him adequate cover, but still allowed him to keep an eye on his pursuers. The three men slowed as they rounded the corner. They had lost sight of him and didn't know where he was. All they knew was that he was close.

They split up. One of the bruisers went around, hoping to come in from the retaining wall that ran the length of the mall. The wall was twenty feet tall and not easily accessible from the other side, but Andrew knew better than to underestimate his foes.

"With my luck these guys can fly," he mumbled.

The other two began moving deeper onto the cracked concrete, but they were careful, walking slowly and checking each potential hiding place for him. It would slow them down, but eventually they would find him. He contemplated making a break for the rear entrance of Monk's shop, but the door was probably locked. Something told him he'd never make it before these guys caught him.

He needed to think of something fast.

One of the first spells he had learned was called *distraction*. It had come in handy in Chicago when Kurza and his goons had come for him. He hoped it would work against these guys as well. He concentrated, his eyes focusing on an area behind them as he mouthed the words to the spell.

A crashing noise made both men turn simultaneously. It had worked. The young wizard had sent a distracting noise directly into both of their minds. For all of their raw power, neither of them appeared to be the brains of the operation. They obviously worked for someone, but he had no idea whom it could be. He had inherited quite a few enemies from Grandpa Jack and they just kept coming out of the woodwork. And there were some he had not yet met.

The men doubled back and looked for the source of the noise they heard. There was nothing there, obviously, but with their backs turned, Andrew made a break for the door to the comic shop. He was about halfway there when he heard a shout from behind him.

"He's over there!"

Andrew had forgotten about the third man who was standing on the twenty-foot wall at the back of the property. Somehow he had managed to reach the top. From his perch he had a perfect view of the entire lot.

His shout had alerted the other two and they bore down on Andrew, who no longer had anyplace to hide. Andrew made fists and pointed them at the two men.

They slowed; wondering what he was up to.

Andrew smiled as a soft blue glow formed around his white-knuckled fists. He mouthed the words, "force blast" around a wide cocky grin--

--Then spun and aimed the blue force blasts at the man on the wall. The blasts hit him square in the chest and head and knocked him off the wall. He dropped twenty feet and landed out of sight with a loud crash on the other side of the concrete wall.

Andrew spun on his heel as he had been taught and aimed his glowing fists at the two men advancing on him.

Having witnessed their friend being dispatched so quickly, they slowed.

"Just hand over the amulet, kid," one of them said. His voice was like a growl.

"What are you talking about?"

"Don't play stupid kid. Just hand it over and this ends."

"Yeah. Right."

The men had been putting space between them as they talked. It was a classic move that Andrew remembered from Harris's history lessons. By splitting his focus, if the young magician attacked one then the other could swoop in and catch him off guard. It was a sound plan and would probably have worked if he hadn't been trained against such a ploy.

The one on the right lunged and Andrew threw the force blast at the one on the left even as he twisted his body against the approaching attacker. The stranger came in wide and his swing missed its target.

Andrew grabbed his arm and used the man's momentum against him, throwing him easily in the direction of the comic shop. Once his opponent was off balance and no longer touching ground Andrew hit him with a double force blast that propelled him toward the rear of the shop.

He hit the wall with enough force to shatter the door inward.

Andrew spun back toward the remaining man. The plan had been to get a bead on him and drop him with another force blast before he knew what hit him. Unfortunately, the man was faster than Andrew expected.

The large bruiser tackled the teen and knocked him to the concrete. The impact expelled the air from his lungs and

Andrew gasped for breath as the big man grabbed at his shirt. The amulet fell from its hiding place and dangled from the string.

The man smiled as he tore the string from the young magician's neck. "I believe this is what I'm looking for," he sneered into the boy's ear.

"Give that back," Andrew said angrily.

The man laughed.

"You heard the man," a new voice said from nearby.

Andrew immediately recognized the owner of the voice, but it was the last person he ever expected.

Andrew's sister stood at the entrance, her hands on her hips and a scowl on her face. He had seen this look before. She was not happy. "I believe you should let him go now," Kim said, her voice never changing tempo.

"And just who do you think you are, little girl?"

"His sister."

"Aw, ain't that sweet?" the bruiser barked. "I've got business with your baby bro here so you should shove off before I decide to have business with you."

"That's not a very smart idea," Kim said as her eyes began to glow. Apparently, Andrew wasn't the only one with a secret. "We won't like that."

"Oh yeah. Who's we? You got an army in your pocket?"

Kim smiled. "Not exactly. They're behind you."

"Do I look stupid enough to fall for that?"

"Don't make me answer that," someone said from behind him.

The bruiser turned and saw Harrison, Jasper, and Charisma. Harrison had the man Andrew tossed through the door held immobile against the wall. The bruiser was outnumbered, but they had to wonder if he was smart enough to realize it.

He was. The man released his grip on Andrew.

Andrew snatched the necklace back and held it firm.

"Why don't we have a little chat," Jasper said as he approached the bruiser. The big man sighed. He had lost the day.

◊◊◊

An hour later they were all sitting around the table in the training room.

After interrogating the men, Jasper had let them go with the knowledge that if they were ever seen around here again it would not end so nicely for them. Jasper explained that the men told him they worked for Lord Lucius Manris, which meant nothing to Andrew or Kim. Neither of them had ever heard of him.

Andrew was more interested in what had happened with his sister. "So what was that out there?" he asked. "With the eyes?"

"Oh, what," Kim said playfully. "Did you think you were the only one Grandpa Jack told his stories to?"

"You mean you're…"

Kim shrugged.

"And all this time you knew about me and never said anything?"

"It was a secret. Grandpa Jack asked me to keep an eye on you. He said you were special. He taught me a few things to help me out."

"I'll say," Charisma added. "That bit with the glowing eyes was effective."

"Just a parlor trick. Nothing more than for show, I'm afraid. Now, that force blast thing you did, that was way cool."

"Yeah. It was, wasn't it?" Andrew said proudly.

"Maybe you can teach me?"

Jasper smiled. "I think we can fit you in."

"Yes!" Kim shouted.

"Well, she is a Magnus," Charisma joked.

"No doubt about it," Harrison added.

"So when do we start?"

◊◊◊

Lord Lucius Manris was not happy.

Not only had his lackeys failed him, but had also told the boy's protectors about him. No doubt they would be on guard now. The one good thing to come from this debacle was that he now had definitive proof as to the amulet's whereabouts. All he had to do was come up with a plan to take it.

"Well, Magnus," he said. "Looks like our game's not done after all."

End

THE ONE TREE OF LUNA

Todd McCaffrey

Every day, just after I get up, I climb on up to the observation dome and watch the Earth rise. Sometimes it's already up, full in its beautiful blue glory, whisked with white clouds and smudged with the darker shades of earth.

"Jenny, you'll be late!" my mother cries most mornings. Sometimes she has to call me twice before I climb back down, close the dome's hatch and get ready for school.

Yes, we do school on Luna. Sorry, if you need to ask the question, you're clearly a grubber -- I mean -- an earthsider. 'An ancestor' as my dad sometimes calls you. 'A tourist' as most of the polite adults will say. But, hey, I'm just twelve and *no* one my age says anything but 'grubber' and sometimes 'grub.' I'm sure you're all very nice but I can't imagine wanting to stay stuck in that overheating, overweighing, deep gravity well you think we should all call home.

I was born on the Moon. I'm a Moony, a Loony, or a Selene if you want to be nice. My parents tell me that if I really wanted to, I could go to the weight rooms and the centrifuges and learn to live on Earth -- but I grew up here. My bones are thinner than yours and it'd take *lots* of work to make them strong enough to live at six times my normal weight.

And I've have to give up flying and I am *not* going to do that, thank you very much!

You probably think flying is the sort of thing you all do down on that dirt ball, don't you? Get a big, powerful engine and have it pull you fast enough so that you can climb through that thick, muddy atmosphere of yours, right? Or maybe you're a bit sophisticated and you've learned to hang glide. Well, if you have, you're closer to *proper* flying at least.

But up here on the Moon, we *really* fly!

And that's why I rushed to get dressed, didn't complain at all when I had to race down the corridors to catch the walkways and arrived breathless at my first class of the day at the unbelievably early time of 9 a.m.

Because if I don't get to school on time, have all my homework done and turned in, then I won't get to fly after school. And I am *not* missing that, not even for a chance at simulator time, no, not me!

And, yeah, when my PE teacher asks me to do another forty sit-ups and another twenty push-ups, I don't complain and I hardly even grumble because he knows what I do after school and he knows my parents, too! (I think that last bit's not fair, really, and I'm not sure that Mr. LePisto would ever tell on me but... you can never tell with adults.)

We do go to school on the Moon, as I told you, but I suppose I should also mention that our schools are a *lot* different from grub schools. We can't afford to spend all our time with our butts in chairs listening to someone drone on. And who'd want to? Our teachers are working as well, you know.

So we're out in the gardens helping our biology teacher, Dr. Philedra with her latest cross-pollinations while we're also talking about mitochondria; we're spinning glass while we're listening to Dr. Lecter tell us about how to stop light in its tracks; we're running photo discriminators on our comps while Dr. Kilstan is telling us about star formation. And we're working on our own, figuring up new ideas in FreeForm (which is probably the hardest class we have), managing younger kids as they work in the bakery or serve on the cafeteria line, knitting, darning, throwing pots, double-checking QA test results, you name it.

How do you think I managed to pay for my wings? Credits don't grow on trees, you know!

Well, okay, they do but there are very few people who are qualified to work on trees here on Luna.

My Dad's one of them. In fact, not to brag, but he's *the* one to work on trees on Luna.

I love my dad like mad and crazy and I think he's the sweetest guy there is but... well, please don't ever tell him, but I think trees are kinda boring.

I mean, who wants to wait twenty years to see if something's gonna work? (I said that once to my mother and she practically burst her sides laughing, "Why not? We're going to wait longer with you!")

Anyway, dad knows more about trees and plants than anyone which is kinda cool and kinda lame. Take Dr. Philedra, she's always giving me that sad look when we're talking botany because she doesn't understand that someone like me is far better suited to quantum space field theory. How are we going to get faster-than-light travel if someone doesn't *research* it, for stars' sake?

But Dr. Philedra keeps giving me those odd looks out of the corner of her eye like she's expecting me to sprout leaves or something or suddenly bounce up and spore all over the place. I'm not; I'm a girl and very well-adjusted, thank you very much. (Even my mother agrees and she should know. Although, on second thought, she *did* marry my dad so she may not be the best judge of things botanical.)

At my house, we have a couple of models that my parents brought up from Earth, models of the clunky old spaceships that were first used to get to the Moon. Of course, as soon as I found them, they became *mine* because, as I said, I'm into all things space and flying and stars and stuff. Mom's a nutritionist which only says about a quarter of what she does as she's not only Luna One's leading nutritionist, she's the leading lunar expert on micro-fauna, intestinal fauna and flora, digestion, and nutritional mutations. She's a great cook, too, which makes sense when you think about it for a while but doesn't seem to mean anything at all when you are eating her cooking. Then, the only thing you can do is either go 'yum!' or 'yuk!' (when she tried to find if I'd inherited the family's distaste for liver).

Ever since I could remember she'd do most of the cooking. Dad was not bad when he took his turn -- he cooked on special days or when Mom was late helping someone on something or other.

Anyway, I never did figure out which of them brought

up the old models or why -- maybe they belonged to one of my grandparents or something. But I had an old Lunar Module model which separated into the Ascent and Descent modules. The Descent Modules legs would open up. As models go, it's nothing like our latest nano-models but it was fun in its own way. And... there was a magic about it, you know? I suppose that something loved acquires its own magic. Yeah, I know, *very* scientific, Jenny! But, still... I kept those models on the shelves beside my bed.

Luna's at the forefront in most things. We kinda have to be because outside the domes -- there's nothing. No air, no safety, nothing but vacuum and even a grubber knows you can't breathe unless you've got air. Some of them are so dumb that they don't understand that you don't need air so much as you need oxygen but... hey, I suppose living with all that weight makes brains work funny.

The one thing that we're famous for is our nanotech. We kinda have to be because without nanotech we couldn't live. You see, there are moonquakes and other natural disasters on the Moon. Yeah, it doesn't rain -- 'cept in our domes -- so we don't have to worry about hurricanes or floods, except when some moron messes with the atmospheric controls and then all that happens is we all get drenched with an unplanned downpour. But we use nanotech to seal our domes. Every airlock and hatch, every corridor, everywhere you go, there's a thin layer of nannies just waiting for a problem. If there's a breach, they'll seal it until we can get a bigger patch in. And they'll sound the alert so we know there's a problem.

But even better, and safer, are our suits. Grubbers

don't believe us when we say that we've always got a spacesuit with us. I remember one old lady looking at me and clucking at my outfit until I activated the suit and then she near-on fainted dead away! Even when we're sleeping, we have our nano-suits like a second skin. Some of the earthers complain that we must smell because we wear the same thing all the time but that's just silly. The suits are self-cleaning.

Of course, we wash and take showers. When we take showers, the suits become the curtains which is another thing the grubs grumble about -- so most of our hostels have additional shower curtains to keep them from moaning on and on.

And even our nanotech wears out after a while and has to be replenished. There's a law that says that every Loony has to have at least a five per cent surplus of nannies on them at all times. Not only does that make sense but, if ever someone is caught out without a suit or if someone's suit gets destroyed (I can't think how), then we can pool resources to help out.

Most of us prefer a twenty per cent margin.

Then there's people like me. I can never get enough nano. I have a special container back in my room for any nano I can't carry around me. It's never very full but whenever I can, I bring it with me.

For wings.

On the Moon, just as on Earth, I mass about forty kilos. Grubbers talk about weight -- which is silly! -- but for them, I'd weigh about 88 pounds in the stupid ol' English system that the North Americans all insist upon using. Really, we're talking somewhere in the field of a measly four hundred

Newtons on Earth -- and only sixty-five Newtons on the Moon. Why talk in Newtons? Well -- duh! -- because Newtons are the force that the Moon exerts on my body. So that's the force I need to counteract to achieve weightlessness. Or lift.

After school, most of my friends gather together in the common area to pod up. If you're a grubber you don't know about pods. Why would anyone want to be a grubber?

Pods. Well, at school we all sort of get together. We're all ages, from toddlers right up to graduates. The oldest of us, Mary Lemieux, has just turned nineteen and, honestly, I think she's getting ready to pod out but -- well, I guess we're too much fun to be around. There's really no age limit on podding. A pod is a group of schoolers who decide to be together. Often it's the same pod as the school pod. Like I said, our schools don't do that silly age thing, we group into pods with the littlest being cared for the by the bigger and the bigger being watched over by the biggest. Pods are cool, they're constantly changing, growing, learning and -- well, I'm not even sure my parents understand us. No, heck! I'm *sure* my parents don't understand 'cuz they keep saying things like, "Oh, it's like a gang!"

I've read about gangs and our pods are almost exactly the *opposite* of those gangs. The gangs on Earth, dirtside, they break things. Our pods are to *make* things.

Sometimes pods hive off from each other, sometimes they grow. There's a core of my pod, a central theme. Pretty much from youngest to oldest we're all space-mad. And not your typical Loony space-mad, either. We're serious. Which is why Mary is working toward a doctorate in astrophysics,

Jordan has specialized in n-space math, little Carey is mad about hydroponics and environments, Matt is all into radiation shielding and I'm -- well, I'm into everything. Starship captain, if you *must* know.

We figure ten years, twenty tops, we'll be ready to head out. So we're figuring more than just a pod's worth -- maybe even two hundred people in all.

I've tried to tell my parents but they don't seem to get it. They say things like, "Wait until you're older" and "Yes, dear, I understand."

You see, Mom and Dad weren't born on Luna. I don't think they understand us. Me and my friends -- my pod -- we're star-children. We know it. It's not just in our minds. It's in our blood.

Okay, okay, so if you're a grubber you won't understand. Heck, half of you can't even *see* the stars; your cities are so polluting. And the rest of you seem to think that Luna couldn't live without Earth. And if Luna can't, then there's no way Loonies can build their own starship without your say-so. Ha!

But here, on Luna, we know better. And my pod, the Third of Luna One, we know what we're gonna do. Where we're gonna go.

Still, that's a ways off but there's no point in not getting ready. So, you might ask, why the flying? Or, if you're a real grubber, you might say: what do you mean, flying?

If you're a tourist or you've been a tourist, they might have brought you to Heinlein Cavern -- as the tour guides call it -- and given you a pair of what they call 'wings' and let you try your hand at lunar soaring. Well, the Cavern is really Air

Holding Station One for Lunar One and yeah, it is also known as Heinlein's Soar in honor of a grub who wrote a silly story about flying on the Moon but that's not flying.

Flying is when you've passed your Free-form Test Five and you've received the full Airborne Authorization. And *that* is so much more than what grubbers could ever hope to do.

So, after school, after saying goodbye to little Carey and big Mary, I moved into a clear space, checked my rear, took a run, leapt -- and flapped my wings.

Wings? Yeah, between that first step and the leap, I closed my eyes, interfaced with my nannies and had them close up around me, fan out -- and spread into wings.

You gotta be strong to fly. You need biceps, triceps, you need to be trim, you use your abs more than you'd imagine and you've got to be light. If it was a choice between starving to lose twenty kilos or flying -- I'd starve. Because there is just nothing like it! Chocolate's great but it's nothing compared to climbing up fifty meters, banking, and seeing the dome floor from a thirty degree angle.

Now tourists come up and spend their time in Heinlein Cave. But those of us born here, who train for it, can go for a full Endurance rating. That's even beyond FFT5. I have a 60 minute full endurance rating. To get that, I had to prove that I could stay aloft for twice that amount *and* that I could fly for 70 minutes at twice my weight.

And *that's* how I can pay for my extra nannies. Okay, not just because I've got the endurance but because of the jobs that that endurance opens for me. You might be wondering what sort of jobs there are for people who can fly on the Moon -- as a grubber you might joke that there's no air up here. Of course, you'd be wrong. There's plenty of air in the colonies. And not just air but high places, too.

My first flying job I got when I was only rated for 30 minutes. That job you could probably guess -- safety hawk for grubbers in Heinlein Cave. It was boring work aside from one or two truly spectacular disasters -- one where I helped and one where I was too far away to do more than give first aid.

But now, with my E60 rating, I have a *real* job. Arborean. Every week, I run the airborne scan of the forest.

It's not as easy as it seems because there are very few stoops on the forest and landing on the trees themselves is frowned upon -- particularly by my Dad.

No, I didn't get the job because of my Dad. I'm sure it helped because he had an extra advantage with me -- he could talk to me any time of the day. I got the job because I'm one of only six who are rated E60 or better. And there's only one better, Stan Morgan, who's got a full E70. So Stan gets the really tough jobs and everyone's scrabbling to hire the rest of us. Heck, they're offering jobs to people as low as E20 nowadays. Because it turns out that once people began to realize how useful it was to have a real live person in the air above, they discovered all sorts of things that needed looking at.

That might surprise you seeing as we on the Moon pride ourselves on our advanced technology. We've got nannies just about everywhere and double- and triple- fail-safe systems where there's the slightest risk of depressurization. But a nanny isn't the same thing as a pair of eyes, ears, nostrils, *and* hands all at the same time. The Council recently priced the replacement cost of a human being -- just regular schooler mind, not one of our top scientists -- at well over a billion credits.

Grubbers don't get credits. Let's just say that on bad days a credit's worth about $200 U.S. and it goes up from there. More specifically, a lunar credit can usually buy a full barrel of oil anywhere on Earth. Somedays an Elsie (Lunar Credit) can even pay the cost of transporting it up to the lunar surface.

Anyway, the cost of replacing a human, even here on Luna is high. So my eyes, ears, nose, hands don't come cheap. Particularly when I can deliver them up to three hundred meters above ground level.

None of the trees in the forest are anywhere near that height -- no one expects them to top more than two hundred meters -- but no one knows for certain what things will be like a century from now. You see, among other things, we've not only got the best soil but we've got the third interstellar seed repository up here on the Moon.

And we've got the first major non-terrestrial conservatory. All our trees are no more than thirteen years old, of course, because none of them were planted until Dad got up here and convinced the Council of their value. It's not just the oxygen generation -- we've got great algae for that -- but also the long-term wood, the environmentalism and... the promise.

The promise that one day the green plains of Luna will be the green forests of Luna. That the tattered redwoods that are losing the battle for survival in California will find a new home up here with those of us who really treasure them.

We're not just growing redwoods, naturally. We're growing pine, we're growing oak, mahogany, ash, cherry, you name it. One of our main thoroughfares is lined with cherry trees and when spring comes the Cherry Blossom festival is so amazing that it's famous throughout the solar system.

We're growing pine and other hardy woods -- including bamboo not just for ecological reasons but also for their value as crops. Not that anything from Luna will come to market anytime soon. And I'd be *really* surprised if any of our wood ever made it back down to Earth.

But Dad says that already some of the trees are outgrowing their terrestrial counterparts. It's not just the lunar soil or the lower gravity but a number of factors, some of which he's still trying to analyze.

Anyway, none of the trees are taller than twenty meters now, so I set my cruise altitude for a safe thirty meters and began to scull my way from one side of the forest to the other, planning my rest stops on the way. The forest is big enough that it takes a good three hours to cover but it's only half an hour wide so I go from side to side, taking a ten-minute recovery break at every side. Not that it's really necessary: climbing takes the most work, once I've got the altitude it's just a question of keeping it.

Anyway, I was waiting (impatiently) for my timer to count down to zero when I saw her. I almost jumped off my perch then and there but I checked myself at the last moment.

"Security, we have an intruder," I said over my comm. The intruder had dark hair, seemed no more than my age and she looked like she wasn't wearing any clothes.

Naked doesn't mean that much on the Moon. Not that anyone ever really *goes* naked -- they have to have their suits somewhere -- but it's possible to roll it up into headgear or even to make it transparent or simply reflect the skin underneath. There's a whole Nudy-Loony contingent up here -- I think they total about sixty and many of them are Naturalists up from Germany or other such countries -- and they do the whole headgear/necklace approach.

It wasn't the lack of apparent clothing that bothered me, naturally. It was that she was climbing *my* tree!

"Say nature and location," a bored security guy replied a moment later.

"Coordinates and video on the chip," I said, glancing at the playback to make sure that I'd got a good shot. There was nothing there but my tree. No sign of the girl that I could plainly see with my eyes. "Uh... wait one."

"Sure." He sounded more skeptical than bored now. The thing is, reporting a security violation is a big thing. Reporting a false security violation was bound to go on my job evaluation -- and not in a good way.

I fiddled with my recorder, changing the speed and depth of field but I couldn't get anything to record.

My timer finally chimed and, with a sigh that was part relief and part irritation, I dropped from my perch and stooped down right above the naked girl.

"What are you doing?" I called as I pulled up from my dive. My muscles warned me that I'd need more than a good hot bath later to recover from what I'd done to them. I didn't care, I was mad. No one was supposed to climb my tree. Heck, no one was supposed to climb any of the trees yet.

"What are you doing?" the girl replied. She frowned at me. "Are you a God?"

"Huh?" I said stupidly. And then I realized -- my suit.

You see, every gram is that much more to lift against the lunar gravity. So early on I made sure that there wasn't a wasted gram on me. I shaved my hair -- and wanted to shave my eyebrows until my mom convinced me that they were necessary to prevent sweat from getting into my eyes -- and wore only my nano-suit. But all that doesn't mean I don't have style. I mean, after all, I own a pretty nice nano-rig and there's no way I wouldn't use it. Particularly with the Animé Parade coming up so soon.

Oh, the Animé Parade! I forgot. So... about the first thing the very first kids on Luna discovered was that they could shape and color their nano-suits any way they wanted to. And in no time they were wearing whatever costume they wanted. And then, to show off, they started a parade. At first the grown-ups just chuckled but somehow news of it made its way to Earth and suddenly it was a *big* thing. Reporters started coming, then fans and then animé and comic people and in a few years it became *THE* thing for rich fans to attend.

And we made it a big deal, too. We'd spent a large part of the year trying out costumes and working on them, each pod trying to out-compete each other. Fans from Earth would come and attend special workshops, pay *zillions* of credits to get special-made nano-suits and the training required to operate them so that they, too, could participate in the Animé Parade.

And that's where my shaved head comes in so handy. Not only does it drop a full kilo or more from my weight, not only does it decrease my aerodynamic drag but I can make the coolest "hair" with my nannies!

And so today, as I stooped on this strange girl, I was

wearing a 'helmet' that was totally cyan-blue with an elongated chin-guard and goggles over my face. My wings, by regulation had the six endurance pennants on them with only two red, two orange and two yellow (we were allowed to pick our own color schemes providing that red was always the 'used' state), the rest of my wings being a coordinated mix of dark blue, white, gray, and steel-black.

Everyone who saw me in the air said I was a shoo-in for Lead Bird in the Animé Parade. Did I mention that one of the perks of being a paid flyer is a chance to practice up for Lead Bird? You know, the Animé character that flies at the front of the whole Animé Parade?

The one who, according to rumor, might be presented to the Emperor himself?

The Emperor of Japan, silly! Luna has no Emperor. Although, there's talk that maybe the Emperor of Japan might settle up here in *Munbesu Nihongo*. Everyone's been talking about it, wondering if that isn't why he and his wife had planned the trip up here in the first place.

"No one's allowed to climb in the trees," I said, forcing my attention back to the girl. She seemed pretty enough although it was hard to say. I tried to imagine her in a costume and was surprised to think that the best outfit for her would be something leafy and green. Like Pan in Shakespeare.

"I am," the girl said.

"I've called security," I told her. It was true, I had, I just didn't bother to add the bit about the cameras not seeing her. I eyed her carefully. "Where's your suit?"

"Suit?"

"Your nano-suit," I said. "Are you running it transparent?" Even as I asked that, I realized that if she was wearing a nano-suit the cameras would have *had* to pick it up. I'd been chewing on that problem -- what can eyes see that cameras can't? -- even as we'd been talking. Cameras recorded a set number of frames per second. I silently sent a command to my suit to up the frames per second and watched the display in the lower corner of my cheekguard until I saw the girl's image come into focus. The frame rate was two hundred and forty frames per second -- ten times normal.

"Who are you?" I blurted, now wandering what I'd wandered into. Was she a ghost or something? Her image was flickering in the playback, even at that high rate. Silently, I ordered it doubled again and the image steadied down. This girl wasn't here most of the time.

"I don't have a suit," the girl said. She looked up at me. "Do I need one?" She pointed at my wings. "Is that what you are wearing?"

"Yeah," I said, stalling for time to think. A girl who can't be seen by regular cameras -- why would she need a nano-suit? She doesn't exist.

We Loonies get laughed at by earthers a lot. They think we're a strange mix between 'eggheads' and 'tree-huggers' that we don't understand 'the real world.' But really, one thing we are is open-minded. We're willing to admit we don't know everything that there might be things outside our understanding. So ghosts -- collections of psychic energy or dark energy or *whatever* -- that wasn't impossible to us (me, at least).

"Could I get one?" she asked.

"Sure, if you've got the credits or ask your parents," I told her.

The girl frowned and looked down at the branches under her feet. "Credits?"

"You know -- money?"

"Money," the girl rolled the word in her mouth as if it were new to her. She looked back up at me, her brows drawing together. "Can you go now? He's coming and he promised to teach me to kiss."

"He?"

"The nice old man who was here the other day," the girl said. She smiled. "He said I was pretty." Her smile faded as she added, "If he sees you, he might change his mind." She made a shooing motion. "You should go."

Before I could find *any* words to respond to that, my emergency warning bleeped. For a moment, horror-stricken, I thought I'd overflown my endurance but then I realized it was the home alert.

"I have to go," I told her.

"Fine," she said, turning away from me and staring intently at the path that lead through the young trees, "just as long as he doesn't see you. He said no one could know."

I wanted to stay, to ask more but the home alert was insistent.

"Coming!" I called over my comm even as I cupped air with my wings and slowly climbed back up to a safe gliding altitude. Once there, I quickly converted height to velocity and skimmed along at max, getting home in less than ten minutes.

◊◊◊

"You just missed him!" Mom said as soon as I entered our house.

"Who?" I asked, still thinking about the girl and her mystery kisser.

"Your father," Mom said. "He's gone down earthside --"

"Earthside!"

"It's an emergency," Mom told me.

"What?" I mean, honestly, what sort of emergency is there that calls a *gardener* back down to Earth? I love my Dad but, really, gardening? Yeah, he's the best and he's cool and I love him so much but I can never, ever understand what makes trees and leaves so important to him.

"His trees," Mom said as if that explained everything.

"His trees are here, Mom," I reminded her. I don't know what it is with adults but it seems like outside of their specialties, they're really pretty dumb.

"Not all of them, miss smarty-pants," my mother -- mother! -- snapped back. Apparently she realized how silly she was because she blushed and turned away from me. "Five there, only one here," she muttered to herself. She turned back to me. "Were you on patrol?"

"Yeah," I said wondering at the sudden change of topic. "Why?"

"Did you see anything unusual?"

I should have told her. I really should have, I realize that now. But then, just after "miss smarty-pants" I wasn't quite thinking at my best. And... ghosts? Can you imagine how my mom would have reacted to that?

"I didn't get to finish the sweep," I told her honestly. "I got this emergency call."

"Your father said to keep an eye on the forest," Mom said. She made a worried face. "I think he's scared..."

Scared? My Dad? Of what?

I should have told her then. I should have but I felt bad that I hadn't told her the first time.

"I can't go into the air again today," I said, consulting my flight log. "But I'll be extra careful tomorrow."

"Okay," Mom said, nodding to herself. "That'll do." She still looked worried as she added, "It's probably nothing."

◊◊◊

"Hey guys, I'm sorry but I gotta jet," I said to the pod as they collected at the end of the last class that day. I pointed to my back. "Angels tread and all."

"Yeah, right," Carey said, rolling her eyes. "You're just going off to try out your latest costume for the parade!"

"Am not, squirt," I told her as I found a clear spot in the crowd. "Stand clear!"

I took two quick steps, leaped up and unfurled my wings. Just to annoy Carey, as I flapped up higher, I strobed the lower edges of my wings in rainbow colors. I could hear Carey's squeal of delight and indignation and the cheers of the others as I made it past fifty meters and then I steered toward the school thermal and slowly glided up to the very top of the safety limit -- can't get too high. It's not that my wings might melt, rather that my wings might tangle with some wiring or other important piece of infrastructure trailing down from above.

A quick check on all my displays and I veered sharply port, towards the agricultural section.

The first thing I noticed was the tree. Actually, the first thing I noticed was all the leaves under the tree. I stooped and dropped down to the top of the tree, swinging in a fast, tight circle, examining and filming every bit of it.

This was bad. It looked like someone had purposely set out to destroy the tree.

The special tree. The one my dad always talked about it hushed tones. The one he planted the day I was born.

I was just about to call him when I realized -- he was on Earth.

Something flickered at the base of the tree. I dropped down to the ground and furled my wings even as I ground to a halt. I squinted at the shape but I couldn't make it out.

"You need to go," a ghostly, faint voice said.

"Are you okay?"

"He's coming back and he won't come if you're here," the voice said. "He'll want to kiss you, not me." And then, the voice went on dreamily, "He kissed me yesterday. I want him to kiss me again."

I cranked my video recorder up to four hundred and eighty frames per second and suddenly the shimmering shape resolved itself into a human form.

"Are you okay?" I said. The ghost of the girl I'd seen yesterday was older, near my mom's age now and she looked listless and weak. Sort of like the tree whose limbs were drooping even as I watched.

"Three kisses," the ghost girl continued, not seeming to

hear me. "Three kisses and I'll be his forever!"

"What's your name?" I asked.

"Name?"

"What do people call you?"

"*He* calls me his life's blood, the heart of his heart, the only thing that matters," the ghost woman replied. Her eyes seemed to smolder as she glared at me. "What does it matter my name?"

"I'm Jennifer," I said, wondering why I was trying to sound so reasonable while dealing with someone who was exhibiting symptoms similar to oxygen starvation. "Can I get you anything?"

"You can leave," she said. "He'll be coming and I don't want him looking at you." She stretched her hands out and held them up to her eyes. "He won't think I'm too old, will he?"

"I thought you said he was an old man," I said.

"He was," she said, a smile fleeting across her lips. She was beautiful in her own way. "But now he's my handsome suitor. Three kisses and he'll be mine forever."

"I should really get my father to look at that tree," I said, pointing to the tree she was leaning against. "And you should treat that tree with more respect. You shouldn't be here."

"My mother doesn't mind," she told me, raising a ghost hand. It seemed to disappear as she wrapped it around the trunk. "She's tired but that's to be expected."

"Your mother?" I said, frowning. I looked around. "Where's your mother?"

"Right here, silly," the girl said with a dry laugh that sounded like wind through leaves.

"We should really get more water for that tree," I said. "And I'm going to have to report you," I added, chiming my comm. Unit. "I think you need help."

"I need *nothing* from you!" She roared and suddenly she loomed up large and charged right through me. A cold, freezing chill took my heart even though none of my sensors recorded it. "Begone!"

A wind rose up and pulled me off the ground before I could react. I was airborne, in gusts I'd never before experienced -- and I was very scared.

I can't say how or how long I battled with the storm that shouldn't have been. For several moments it looked like I was either going to be speared on the trees or dashed against the roof and it was all I could do to survive.

My alarms went off and then my comms went dead and my heart was in my throat as, for a moment, my nano-wings flickered, dissolving into lifeless streams.

Help! I cried to myself, not knowing what to do. The ground was rising and then -- my wings were back. I flexed them, warped to veer away from the storm that had tossed me and finally found myself in still air.

My comms burst back into life loudly with several security guards all calling at once. With a shaky voice I told them that I was all right, that I was about to land and I'd give them a full report when I'd discovered the source of the fault.

"Do you need someone to get you, Jenny?" a voice asked and I nearly died. It was Stan Morgan.

"Did anyone get a read on the freak weather over the forest?" I asked, trying to sound mature and relaxed.

"There are no alerts anywhere in the domes, Jenny," Stan

replied after a moment. "Are you sure you're all right?"

"I don't know," I told him, knowing that honesty was the best policy in a conversation that was monitored and recorded -- and pretty much heard by everybody. "Maybe I hit some micro-climate or maybe... I'll run a systems check when I get home."

"You do that," Stan said. "You never know how those upgrades can interfere with each other sometimes." There was a pause and then he added, "I'd hate for you to run afoul of them."

Did Stan Morgan care about me? My heart skipped a beat.

"Sure thing, clear skies, Stan!"

"You, too, Jenny," he said feelingly -- which might only be because of my recent thunderstorm.

◊◊◊

I was running through diagnostics for the third time when my mom came in. One look at her face made it clear that she had bad news.

"Your father has to stay on Earth," she said without preamble. "He wants to know if you checked up on the forest."

"I did," I told her.

"Stanley Morgan commed me," mother added.

"I had some difficulty with my suit," I told her, waving toward the diagnostics unit. "I've run diagnostics three times but --" I shook my head.

"Maybe you should stay on the ground until your father

gets back," Mom told me.

"Mo-ommmm!" I cried. "You know I've got a job to do and --"

"And there's the parade," Mom finished for me, nodding. She reached a hand toward me. "Honey, I know how important it is to you but your father's worried --"

"Worried?" About me? Why? "I think he'd be more worried about his tree."

"His tree?" my mother said quickly, giving me a sharp look. "What about it?"

I told her. I told her everything and as I did I felt a lump in my heart ease but at the same time, I found another growing in my throat -- because while it was a relief to tell someone, my mom's reaction was terrifying.

"You've got video?" Mom asked.

"I don't know," I said, gesturing toward the suit and the diagnostics. "I didn't download what I got yesterday and if something happened to the suit all of it might be gone."

"You say that yesterday she was a girl and today she's a woman?"

"Yeah," I said. I knew it sounded silly, so I added, "At least she *looked* like the same person and she seemed like she remembered me."

"But -- older?"

"Yeah." I shrugged. "Maybe..."

"Maybe nothing," my mother said. She glanced over to the shelves where I kept the old spaceship models and shook her head. "Oh, I wish your father had stuck with spaceships--"

"Dad?" I cried, completely amazed, turning toward the models. "*He* made those?"

"Well you don't think I did, did you?" Mom snapped with a laugh and then, seeing the look on my face, added sympathetically, "Oh, baby, you mean you didn't know?"

"No," I said, finding my entire world turning upside down. Dad, into spaceships? That was nuts! He was a tree guy, into plants and growing stuff.

"Did you ever ask about your grandfather Ki?" Mom said and then shook her head, "No, of course not." She seemed to be talking to herself as she added, "We thought that there was still time." She shrugged and pulled herself together, letting out a little sigh -- the sort of sigh she gave when she was forced to admit that I was growing up faster than she wanted. She gestured to my bed. "Sit, we're going to be here for a bit."

"But my homework!" I cried. "My projects!"

"They'll wait," mom said, grabbing a chair and pulling it to sit opposite me. She let out a long sigh. "Your father should be the one to tell you but I think it's time you knew."

"Know what?" I asked. Was my dad some sort of Japanese elf or a wood spirit? And then I knew. "She's a wood spirit, isn't she? That tree, dad's tree, she lives in it."

Mom looked amazed and then smiled, reaching forward to ruffle my hair. "Very good! Very, very good! You're as smart as your dad, little one!" She shook her head ruefully. "I suppose I'll have to stop calling you little one, won't I?"

I shook my head. Mothers say silly things -- it's okay.

"But you're only part right," she said when she brought herself back from her reverie. "Your father's tree died long before he came to the Moon."

"It died? How?"

And my mother told me. Now my mom has always been the smartest, most logical, scientific person that I've known -- and I've got lots of other people who agree with me on that. So the story she told me was so far from what I'd expected that my eyebrows rose to the top of my forehead and stayed there pretty much the whole time.

"Mom," I said slowly when she'd finished, "are you sure that dad wasn't just pulling your leg?"

"It's how he won my heart, honey," Cheri Ki told me with a shake of her head and bright spots in her eyes. "I'm a botanist first and I know my craft." She shook her head. "I not only examined the wood but I went to the other plantings --"

"Plantings?"

"There were six seeds," mom told me. "Your father planted five on them on Earth and the sixth one here." She nodded toward the forest. She smiled at me. "You know, we're always learning and we're always discovering that we don't know everything. It was your father showing me those saplings that showed me how much more there was to know and learn." She paused for a moment. "So when he asked if I'd like to live with him on the Moon and make a new garden, I could only say yes."

"But you're a nutritionist!"

"I grow things," mom reminded me. "I grow things that help us breathe, that let us eat, that let *us* grow and survive." She gestured with one arm in a wide arc, taking in all of the Moon. "We've made life where there was none, built a promise for the future." She smiled as she met my eyes. "Built a home for your children."

THE ONE TREE OF LUNA

"You said that dad's tree died," I said, remembering her story.

My mother is a very smart, very empathic person: she caught my unasked question with a twist of her lips. "The tree he planted here in the forest, that's *your* tree sweetie."

"What happened to the other trees?" I asked in a very small voice.

My mother heaved a deep sigh. "Your father is trying to find out."

"But what happened?"

"We don't know," mom said. "All we know is that they're all dead."

"So mine is the last tree."

Wordlessly, Mom nodded.

"Well then, that makes things simple," I said, rising from the bed and moving toward my diagnostic unit.

"What are you going to do?"

"I'm going to save my tree," I told her firmly. My eyes went to the model rocket ships on my shelves and suddenly I realized that I'd begun to understand my father.

This is the point at which, according to all the Earth books I've read, my mom would have taken charge. But you as you've gotta know by now, we're Loonies and we don't do thing the way you do on Earth.

"What are you thinking?" my mom asked instead.

And that's when I knew I wasn't a kid anymore.

To be honest, she took me by surprise. It was a moment before I had a reply.

"Is there a way we can identify this man?" I asked. "I mean, surely if he were a Loony we would have --" I broke off

155

when I caught the way mom was looking at me.

"Hmm," I said as I conceded her unspoken point. It could just as easily be that something in my tree had changed to attract this person. "No, I still think we should check for any recent arrivals."

She gave me a half-nod. Hmm, so I still hadn't figured it all out. "Oh! We should correlate for anyone who's been on Earth near Dad's trees!"

"What else?" Mom asked, making it clear that I was still not done.

"Well," I said, "naturally we need to set up a guard on the tree."

"And?"

I looked at her, stumped. She smiled and patted my knee while moving her hand up by her ear, activating her comms.

"Security, this is Cherie Ki, I am declaring a stage one biological emergency," my mom said. My eyes went wide with surprise. "Do NOT use the alarms -- we have an intruder who may be carrying a biological hazard."

"Dr. Ki, do you have any ID on the intruder?" the security chief came back calmly. I smiled at my mom -- she'd turned on her external audio so I could listen in.

"Not yet," mom said. "We're still working on that. But this is in connection with the earthside emergency that my husband was called away on."

"Yes, Doctor," the security chief said with a tone of increased alertness.

"And Don, I want a twenty-four/seven watch on the tree," my mom added. I knew Don Ostermann, he was the best we had.

"I see," Don said. "Jenny reported an incident the other day but didn't --"

"This is related," my mother said. "It's her tree, you know."

"Oh, yeah, I know!" Don Ostermann said. My eyes went wide and I flushed with embarrassment. The Head of Luna Security knew about *my* tree?

"I'll let you know more as soon as we've got it," mom said, breaking the connection and telling the computers, "Central library, data search."

"Subject?"

"Keyboard entry," my mom said, rising from her chair. Over her shoulder she said to me, "You get some sleep!"

"Mom!" I wailed. How could she possibly expect me to sleep with all this going on?

"I'm going to need you to take over in the morning," she told me. "Your father's not here and you're probably the next expert we have on the dryads --"

"Dryads?"

"Well, who did you expect your tree friend was, honey?" Mom said, tossing me a smile before exiting through the automatic door.

Dryads? Do you know how long it took to look up dryads? 0.32 seconds, that's how long. The network must have been working overtime.

I pulled up a complete download and was checked by a security screen. It prompted me for a passcode. I was astonished, I'd never found anything requiring a passcode on the network before -- we Loonies pride ourselves on our freedom of information. With my tongue poking through my lips -- I do that when I'm nervous -- I entered my passcode and received a priority data assignment.

The Japanese word was *Kodama*, the Scottish had a similar spirit called the *Ghillie Dhu*. Dryads and Hamadryads -- uh, oh, my friend was a hamadryad -- if her tree died, she'd die. And, from the looks of what I'd seen, if she aged, her tree aged. But what had caused her to age so much?

'Three kisses' she'd said. 'Three kisses and I'll be his forever!'

If she looked so bad after two kisses, what would she be like after the third?

I jumped out of bed and rushed out into our living room.

"Mom! Mom, I've got it!" I cried. "I know what happened to the trees!"

But she wasn't there.

◊◊◊

"Stan, Stan, pick up, pick up!" I cried as I rushed outside, wrapping my nano-suit and willing it on me. My chrono told me it was past midnight.

"Huh?" Stan Morgan's voice came into my ear. "What? Jenny, what's up?"

"I need you to meet me at the forest," I told him.

"The forest? Now?" He sounded more awake. There was a silence. "There's a stage one emergency, you should stay home!"

"I'm going out *because* of the stage one emergency," I told him. I spread my wings but I already knew what they'd show -- I'd four red bands and only two yellow. I was thirty minutes from the forest -- I'd be ten minutes into the red by the time I got there. "You've got to meet me; I'm going into the red on this."

"Into the red? Jenny, you'll get your license pulled --"

"Just meet me there," I told him, talking a quick set of steps and leaping into the air. I must have been more tired than I realized for I fumbled the first beat and nearly crashed. I had to work twice as hard to regain the lost height and I was breathing hard by the time I was fifty meters up.

It took work to get to the nearest thermal -- I usually launch from school which has a thermal close by -- and I was grateful to be able to just glide for a bit in a slow turn as I climbed up to one hundred and fifty meters -- just below the safe altitude limit.

"Jenny," Stan called me. He sounded like he was trying to talk sense to me. I didn't have time for sense so I ordered my comms unit to reject the connection.

I glanced at my altitude gage and with a few beats of my wings climbed another twenty meters. Now I was right at the safe altitude but I didn't plan on staying there for long, diving to exchange height for speed.

I didn't know what was happening or when but I knew if I couldn't stop my Hamadryad friend from getting her third kiss she was going to die.

◊◊◊

"Warning, warning, you are entering a secured area," a voice spoke insistently in my ear. "You are in violation of Lunar regulations and penalties will be assessed."

"I know," I said, even as I spotted my tree in the distance. It was surrounded by lights and people. I landed just in front of my mother.

"Jenny!" she cried. She was angry. Don Ostermann was next to her, his expression grim.

"Mom, I know what's happening and I know how to stop it," I told her quickly. Her eyebrows rose. "You've got to leave or he won't come."

"What?" Mr. Ostermann said. "How do you know?"

"Because no one ever saw him," I said. "He went after all the trees on Earth and no one caught him." I looked back at the tree and said, "I'm not sure we'll be able to see him."

"So how are you going to stop him?" my mom asked.

I told her. Mr. Ostermann looked at me wide-eyed but my mom merely took a deep breath and nodded. "She's right, it's probably the best way," she said. "And you've got Stan on patrol?"

"Actually, I've got the whole air corps on patrol," I told her.

"But you only said Stan --"

"Trust me," I told her, nodding up to the skies above as two, then three, four, and finally a dozen sets of wings came into view. "Mr. Ostermann, if you could coordinate with them?"

"What makes you think he won't see them?"

"I don't think he's ever heard of flying men," I told him.

"Do you know who he is?" My mom asked in surprise.

"No," I told her, "but I've got an idea *what* he is." She gave me a skeptical look and I moved close to her. "Mom, trust me, please?"

"This is the last tree, Jenny," my mother said slowly. "We can't lose it, there are no seeds."

"This is my tree mom," I told her. "Dad didn't know what to look for when he was little but I do."

My mom gave me a long look and then she surprised me by stepping back toward Mr. Ostermann. "Jenny's got it, let's go."

Mr. Ostermann had known me a long time, pretty much my whole life. I guess he saw the same thing in me that my mom did because he nodded toward me and smiled. "Good luck!"

"Thanks." I was going to need it. If I was wrong or if I fell asleep, my tree was going to die.

◊◊◊

"Jenny," a voice came quietly in my ear and I startled, surprised that I had nodded off. It was Stan. My face chrono showed me that it was 4:13 a.m. so I guess I shouldn't have been surprised. "From the northeast."

"Roger," I replied. "Show time." I sounded calm, I knew it. But really, truth to tell, I was shaking like a leaf. Which was probably a good thing.

"Nano-suit overload in ten minutes," a computer voice warned. Yeah, I knew. The nano-suit was overworked, overloaded, generating a shutter that flickered over six hundred times a second -- the fastest I could get it to go.

I was pretty sure that whatever was coming for my Hama -- well, I had to call her *something!* -- was flickering in the same ghostly manner as my tree's Hamadryad. I guessed that was why no one had noticed it -- it was flickering too much for our regular cameras to catch it.

There! "Target acquired, confirm lock."

"Locked," Stan's voice was the first among a dozen to reply.

"Engaging --"

"Jenny, are you sure?" Stan cried out. He sounded worried about me. Stan Morgan, the best flyer on Luna?

"-- now," I finished, standing up and moving from the tree toward the approaching figure. There was no time for worries and there was no second plan.

He was dark-haired, dark-eyed and incredibly handsome. He was Japanese, just as I'd guessed. He looked middle-aged, maybe younger. He smiled at me.

"Did you miss me?" he said, moving toward me.

"Are you going to kiss me again?"

"Is that what you want?" he asked, smiling. I could see the hollowness in his eyes and my skin crawled. Whatever he was, he was not human. Some sort of spirit, a creature of darkness or of void -- I didn't know which.

"Don't listen to her!" Hama cried as she burst into view. "She's an impostor?"

"Am I?" I said and, on cue, all twelve flyers swirled into view, each adding their own voice, keyed to match Hama's. "Am I?"

The dark-haired spirit looked desperately from one to the other of us. Hama tried to move toward him but I stepped in front of her as did Stan and Crissie while Moira and Kevin pulled Hama back behind them, executing a quick shell-game even as the rest of flyers interposed themselves.

I shifted out of my flickering just before my nano-suit's power failed.

"This tree is mine, you may not have her," I told him.

"What are you?" he cried, backing away from me in awe.

"The Greeks called me Artemis," I said advancing toward him. "I guard the Dryads, the *Kodama*, the *Ghillie Dhu* and no *jiang shi* will defeat me."

I must have guessed right for the dark-eyed thing winced at the name I gave it.

"You have killed too many, you must depart," I told him.

"What would you do if I don't?" he demanded. "What can you know of my power?"

I smiled. "I know this, you're no match for me," I said, moving forward once more to trap him exactly where I'd planned. I threw a handful of nano-suit at him, using the last of my power to cause it to flash in brilliant light. On that signal, all the other flyers threw flashes of nano-dust light at him and surrounded him in it.

With a horrible scream, he brought his arm in front of his eyes but it didn't matter, it was far too late -- our power-packs were completely consumed delivering that one burst of intense laser light. Stone would have shattered, steel melted. As for the *jiang shi* -- he simply dissolved.

There was a moment's stunned silence and then my Hamadryad moved forward through the group, shouting, "You killed him!"

"No," I told her, turning toward her even as the afterglow faded in my eyes, "he was never alive."

"But -- he kissed me!"

"He took your life force," I told her. "He took it, he took your mother's, and he would have drained you to the death with his last kiss. He's already killed at least five other of your kind -- you're the last that we know."

"The last?" Hama said in dismay. She turned back to her tree. "Mother, is this true?"

The tree my father planted for me shivered as though shaken by an invisible wind and a terrible sorrow and then Hama turned back to me, "She says this is so."

"Jenny?" Stan came over to me. "Who are you talking to?"

"Can't you see her?"

"He has to get my mother's permission to see me," Hama said. She made a face very much like ones I've had when dealing with my mother. "She says I should have asked about that man, too."

"Stan," I said, "go touch the tree and ask for permission to speak with her daughter."

"Jenny, are you all right?" Moira Adamson asked, coming up beside me. She gave Stan a worried look.

I sighed. "Look, it's a long story that you won't believe until you do what I ask. Go touch the tree and ask for permission to speak to her daughter."

"They can't see me?" Hama asked, looking at me in surprise. "Or hear me?"

"No," I said as the others started, with obvious skepticism, to walk toward the tree.

"Then how can you see me?" Hama asked. She turned back to the tree, even as the others reached it, touched it and murmured the question.

"Oh my goodness!" Moira Adamson shrieked as her eyes lit on Hama. "Guys, look, look! There's a girl and she's wearing no clothes!"

Hama looked at me. "What is all this about 'clothes'?"

I laughed. "I'll explain later."

◊◊◊

Okay, so I'm a Loony. I make no apologies. I guess you grubbers have your place, your home and you love it, too. If you want to stay in that gravity well, I'll be okay with that.

You're probably wondering what happened. Well, only the flyers ever saw Hama. With my father's approval, they became the air guard. Mostly that didn't change anything, we still flew our regular patrols, fought and bickered, egged each other on for endurance records and plotted to win the lead flyer position in the animé parade.

It was Hama who came up with the best idea, though.

And so when the Emperor of Japan came to view the Luna Animé Parade, the parade was covered by thirteen different flyers all changing off so that the whole parade had at least three flyers at any point.

At the end of the parade, on a signal, we all stooped from on high and split in an aerial rainbow over the Emperor of Japan

Of course, only we knew that the thirteenth flyer wasn't even human.

And my pod expanded our spaceship designs to include a proper forest; we're expecting seedlings any day now.

Hama kept the name I made up for her.

My name is Jennifer Lynne Ki, I'm a second generation Loonie whose best friend is a Hamadryad.

And we're going to the stars.

THE SCENT OF APPLES

A.H. Sturgis

The waters cradled me like warm life in the womb. The fog shrouded me so I was blind to my own hand before my face. The almost unbearable thrill I had carried with me from the island fell away in that haze and left only peace behind. This day was as natural as breath, and it seemed that the very elements moved in concert to escort me onward.

I trusted the currents to deliver my little craft to shore, the mist to reveal the hillside at the appointed hour. My sisters had left the isle in earlier days, each according to her purpose, and they had painted this world for me in the bold colors of faith and lust and passion. I offered myself up to it without reservation. The cycle, the story, the very world was ready to revolve again in its knotted circle, unending and unyielding, and I was woven into its delicate inevitability.

The veil of fog split before me all at once.

I knew the battle of Camlann from visions and prophesies and songs yet unsung, glorious promises of the defeat of death and the new age of Albion. I had relished the fact I would step onto its stage to perform my duty. I had fantasized of this day and the chaos I would midwife into order here.

Yet I had not once imagined the truth of war. The hillside bled out in garish red streams that ran down to the lake. Twisted bodies, or portions of bodies, lay frozen in death, tangled in final combat. The air stank of blood and torn earth and flesh burning in ceremonial fires.

I did not feel the boat shudder as it ran aground. I simply was there, a part of the shore and the scene, astounded by the ruin I had encountered.

Above me, to my left, a lone knight appeared on a soft swell of ground. He stood under his own power, but I gathered from the rigid awkwardness with which he held himself that some of the blood he wore was his own. He gripped a sword in both hands. The blade was the work of my island, and I knew it at a glance. My instincts told me I was needed in this solemn act, that the Lady of the Lake should accept Excalibur here, in these waters, to complete the movement and fulfill the prophecy.

Instead I sat frozen, captive to the terrible grief this picture presented, able only to watch as he launched the sword over the lake. The blade soared end over end, flashing like shards of shattered glass, and then sank heavily into the deep.

The knight cried out like a wounded animal, and I shivered at the sound.

I had anticipated change, like the budding of leaves after winter frost, a new life born of death, sober yet inherently beautiful. I had not foreseen the raw agony of the hour.

The knight buckled at the knees, grieving. I looked away, but I could offer him no privacy. All around us the blank and rheumy eyes of the dead stared, unblinking, unashamed at

THE SCENT OF APPLES

their intrusion on the living. Their gazes devoured me from every direction. I reached for my thin veil and freed it from its circlet, letting it drape across my face to ease the stench.

And to save me from those eyes.

When the first call penetrated my shock I started, sure that one of the corpses was awake and asking for me. Then I realized that there were live men among the dead, though they looked little better than their lost compatriots. A bedraggled party of three stood before me. They stooped in deference to injuries and exhaustion, yet they all attempted a low bow for my sake. I nodded without speaking, and they rose gracelessly.

I always had planned to walk among the mortals just this once and savor my solitary journey from the island. But faced with the pitiful dregs of an army, men who had funeral pyres to build and hopes to bury, I could not force myself to rise from my boat. I wrenched an unfamiliar voice from my throat to say, "Bring him, good sir knights." The mention of the King sent them up the knoll with more speed than I would have thought possible.

Loyalty, it seemed, was the last to die at Camlann.

Soon they appeared over the rise, a grim and mute procession. I gripped the wooden sides of my craft in the effort to anchor myself against my sea of emotion. In the careful arms of his liegemen came my love, the one I had never known but always adored. I was born to cherish him, to save him, and though I'd not seen him even once, I believed I knew him like no other ever could. Prophecy had promised and fate had sealed this moment between us both. If I was meant for him in this hour, then in a way he, too, was now for me. My sisters be damned; Morgaine might have slept with him, and Morgause plotted with him, and Viviane provided his sword to him, but none of them could heal him as I could.

The knights slipped and stumbled on the upturned and bloodied ground but the King remained secure, high atop their shoulders on a litter fashioned from their battle shields. I wanted nothing more than to remove him from this place. The knights looked to me as they progressed toward my canoe, and I straightened in silent salute.

They continued on into the water until they could lower him into my little craft. I closed my eyes and opened my arms. Even now I remember the first thrill of warmth as they settled him before me, his shoulders upon my lap and his head against my chest. Only the mild splashing of wounded men in shallow water disturbed the silence of the moment. I kept my eyes shut until I could feel them grow still and expectant around me. Looking to each of them in turn, I nodded thanks for their final act of obedience to our shared destiny. At my sign, they pushed us off into the lake.

Then the mist returned and there was no more Camlann with its grotesque landscape of carnage, no broken warriors with dying dreams of the Round Table. There was only the King.

Finally, I looked at him.

He appeared older than I had imagined he would. The thought was ludicrous, of course, but it struck me all the same. Silver had invaded his curls, his beard, and vanquished much of its vivid dark mahogany. The dull brown of dried blood tracked from the corner of his lips to his neck. I followed the trail until it met the wicked scar of his wound, a jagged tear from shoulder to breast. His men had stripped him of armor and left him in simple cloth garments to expose his injury. I gathered the folds of my cloak and pressed them against the spot where bright red blood still trickled.

At my touch, he trembled.

I began a tuneless, instinctual hum as I brushed the fingers of my free hand against his hair. The cool air I once had found comforting now chilled me as the mud and gore from the fallen King seeped through my skirts and down my bare legs. I dared not shiver and add to his pain.

His eyes, when they opened, were not the cornflower blue I had heard described so many times. Instead they were the fathomless grey of the sky before a storm, pregnant with power but quiet for now. He looked straight ahead into the fog.

I wondered what he saw there. Or whom.

He had, after all, no lover to conjure. His woman was another man's, or perhaps God's by now — I had paid little heed to the stories of Guinevere's fate. His only child lay slain by his father's hand, but not before dealing the King this terrible blow. His friends were piled high on funeral pyres, their bodies' oily smoke climbing to the heavens. His advisor was gone, disappeared into the woods, the victim of the very sorcery he once had wielded so well.

As I listed the King's losses to myself, I began to marvel at how truly alone this man was. Apart from the ragged handful of survivors I had encountered lakeside, I was all he had. And though I knew the story of his deeds, the detail of his every campaign, I was to him a total stranger.

A legendary life spent in service to others, to ideas, and to justice, and now, helpless, he depended for his very survival on the care of those he did not know. It was foretold, of course, and he knew it. The thought made me unutterably sad. Suddenly my compassion overwhelmed my passion, and I saw him as a man rather than a king.

I could find no words to say to him, and so I simply held him as we floated on the patient waters. After a time he shuddered, and I felt his breath catch as he fought to brace himself against new torment. Jaw clenched, air hissing between teeth, he tried valiantly to endure in silence. As I watched his knuckles go white against the floor of the boat, I wondered how long he could survive. Without me and my healing mysteries, his suffering soon would end forever.

It was a strange notion. Quite unexpected. Before, sheltered on my island with only the foolish dreams of a naïve girl for company, I had not imagined Arthur's life as one of suffering. He was a ruler and a beloved one at that, a legend in his own lifetime. When I had envisioned that King, however, he had not been filthy and agonized, bereft of all he had known and loved. Only now did I see that Arthur had spent himself for his subjects and land. He had given away everything he treasured and denied himself any comfort. The healing I promised was not the restoration of a man: it was the renewal of a monarch. I was to save Arthur so he could offer himself up to the next cycle, the next story, as fate demanded. It would happen all over again, and I was to be the agent of his self-sacrifice.

He saved me from my bleak thoughts then as he eased back against me with a sigh. The spasm was over, or perhaps he had drifted beyond all pain now. He turned his head, sending curls to tickle my nose, and encountered my heavy sleeve. Like a child or small pup, he nuzzled against my arm, burying his face in the fabric there. Then he sank back against me limply.

"Apples," he whispered with a brittle voice like dry leaves in autumn.

Avalon had taken its name from the fruit that grows there, and I suppose I carried its scent on every fiber of my dress. I had been told that the Britons believe the apples are enchanted. Of course there was magic all about us; the women used it to enter men's hearts, the men used it to enter women's skirts, and the chosen used it to usher prophecy to life. The apples, however, were natural. Reports that they remained red and ripe year-round were folktales, hyperbole expanded over generations. We sisters had little to do between our meetings with destiny, and thus had time and talent to develop our farming arts. It was as simple as that.

The fruit was delicious, I admit. The thought of it made my mouth water.

I nodded my response to him, although his eyes were closed again and he could not see me. He had confirmed what I had surmised, that he knew of me and our destination. Perhaps, I mused, he thought of the reputed magic in the apples, and then considered the magic I would soon perform on him to repair his mortal wound and restore him to his kingdom. Or perhaps — it was a far more chilling thought — he knew the fruit possessed no magic, that every season we performed the same gritty tasks to coax apples from the trees. Life works in circles, I thought. Could I truly return this man to his, knowing how it would end?

He was consenting, of course. He curled in my canoe like a lamb en route to slaughter. No, he was not like a lamb, innocent and unaware. He knew the rise and fall of kingdoms, the tragic descent that was his fate. He knew, and yet he was willing. Or resigned. Somehow that made it more horrible.

I wondered at the path brave men like Arthur and foolish children like me follow. After this bloody morning, I understood that it led to Camlann and to death. And why did we follow it? We trusted in prophecy, in the elegance of the cycle and the justice of the preordained. Blaise and Taliesin and Merlin and others foretold, and we marched into their visions without a backward glance. We did not select the path. In fact, we had never once made any choice. Arthur and I, we were both offered up on the altar, given to destinies we had never questioned. Puppets had pushed the kingdom down into the muddy field Camlann.

Camelot fell, I realized, because we let it fall.

All at once I grew angry. How pathetic it was that I had discovered my will here, on the lake, with the dying King in my arms. I might have made a difference at Camlann. I might have turned the tide for Arthur. I might have spared fair Albion the horror of such bloodshed and destruction. But instead I had remained on my island, obedient and unimaginative, able only to play the part others had written for me.

Arthur shifted slightly and sagged into my embrace. I reached for my veil and lifted it back to the crown of my head so I could look at him with naked eyes. I adored this man so, but I had never really known him. And he, I supposed, had never really known himself. I wondered what he would change if he knew he could.

We had been on the lake for some time, cocooned in the fog without sound or sight. The island had to be drawing near. As I realized our hours alone were short, a thought attacked me with sudden urgency. I was meant to mend him and send him back to begin the cycle anew. I was meant to allow him to think only of others, not himself. I was meant to return him to heartbreak and treachery and grievous pain.

I was meant to, but I did not have to. The choice was mine to make.

Mercy can take many forms. I trusted my fledgling sense of discernment and made my decision.

I eased Arthur back against my left shoulder. He gasped but allowed the move. As his weight shifted I drew my right leg to my chest and found the small dagger strapped at my ankle. My hand was familiar with the blade, and I unsheathed it with one swift move. A moment later, its edge caressed Arthur's throat.

His curls brushed my cheek, and I turned and kissed them. His gaze found mine. Those eyes were a bright blue now, clear and lucid. I read surprise in them, then understanding. I saw no fear. I pressed the blade more harshly against his skin, indicating that he, too, had a choice.

His eyes fell shut. Trembling with weakness, he raised a hand and wrapped it around mine on the hilt of the weapon.

I held my breath and waited for him to push me aside.

Instead, he drew the steel closer to his neck and broke skin.

Cracked lips turned up in the promise of a smile.

I drew the dagger ear to ear with all my strength. Arthur's

body jerked once in my arms and stilled.

His blood drenched and warmed me even as his limbs grew cool. For a time I rocked him as a mother would a child, cradling him in his first moments of freedom. I did not weep. If I had healed him, then I would have wept.

When my reason returned, I realized that my sisters could perform the rites I knew and give life when there was none. If they ever found him or me, they would return us to the cycle we had escaped. I had to move quickly.

The craft halted at my command. I stood in the little boat and drew Arthur up with me, summoning magic to supply strength when my arms failed. I embraced him with all my power, my palms against his shoulders, my head at his chest. We would have fit together perfectly, my love and I, had we met under different skies.

The words came to my lips, incantations that would allow us to sink to the bottom of the lake as Excalibur had, alone and undisturbed, invisible to those who would hunt us. My voice echoed back to me, angling off the heavy wall of mist that protected us. When the words ran dry, I drew the blade against my own wrist and mingled our blood together.

◊◊◊

The circle is broken.

I grow weary now. I crave sleep in the arms of my King.

The boat sways, and I lean us both back into the inviting waters.

THE END

SHE'S GOT LEGS
A Bubba the Monster Hunter Short Story

John G. Hartness

"I hate I-40." I said to the air as my tires sang out at about 85 miles per hour. I was making good time since I got out of Memphis, but the bad taste of that long-ass highway tends to linger with a body.

"I know, Bubba, but there ain't a whole lot of ways to get from North Georgia to Forrest City, Arkansas that don't involve I-40." Skeeter, my technology expert and the world's worst wingman, said into my Bluetooth earpiece.

"That don't help." I grumbled, reaching for the radio. Mojo Nixon was screeching on my satellite radio and I needed a little relief. I turn the radio down and focused on Skeeter again. "What's the job this time?"

"Don't you read your email? I explained all that when I gave you the destination."

"I only read the ones that promise to make my pecker bigger or give me a million dollars. Crap from you I know I don't have to read - I can just ask you about it later."

"You're a huge pain in my ass, Bubba."

"Yeah, what are best friends for, anyway? So what's the

gig?"

"Men are disappearing out of the greater Memphis area, mostly around the St. Francis National Forest."

"You sure they aren't just going on the lam after a bad run in Tunica?"

"We have seven men, all vanished from within fifteen miles of the edge of the forest in the last month. Only three of them had been to Tunica within a month of their disappearance, and two of those three had actually *won* money. So no, they aren't dodging a casino debt."

"All right, then ditching a girlfriend or wife?" Money and women were the reasons I'd beat a hasty retreat from more than one small Southern town. Usually both of them together.

"Only four were married, one was gay, and none seemed to be particularly unhappy in their relationships. And other bright ideas?" I hate it when Skeeter gets snide. Snide is my shtick, and he needs to leave it alone.

"Nope, I'm not the idea guy, Skeeter. I'm the shoot things until they don't move guy. What about you, any brilliant ideas?"

There was a pause at the other end of the line. "Actually, no. There haven't been any signs of struggle, or any signs of anything, really. These guys just wander off into the woods and are never heard of again. Or at least they haven't been heard of for a couple of weeks, at this point."

"I guess I'll check it out. Got any real leads for me?"

"Yeah, turn off at the next exit and head into the park. The last guy just disappeared a couple days ago and Amy was able to get the locals to keep the campsite secured for you." Amy Hall is an agent for DEMON, the federal Department of

ExtraDimensional, Mystical and Occult Nuisances. She's part of a super-secret government agency that does pretty much the same thing I do, just with a bigger budget. And black helicopters. No matter how often I ask Uncle Father Joe, our liaison to Rome, the Vatican keeps refusing to buy me a black helicopter.

"So I gotta be official?"

"Kinda. They're park rangers, so you don't need a real shirt or anything like that. Just flash your badge and you oughta be okay."

By this point I was pulling into the St. Francis National Forest. I parked my F-250 in the gravel lot at the front of the ranger station and got out. My beat-up old Wolverine boots clumped on the wooden porch, and I banged on screen door.

"Anybody home?" I yelled.

No answer. I walked around to the back of the ranger station, peeking through windows and banging on doors. The only thing I found was a very confused squirrel scampering over a woodpile. I pressed the Bluetooth earpiece, calling Skeeter.

"There's nobody here, Skeeter. Was the ranger a guy? Maybe we need to add him to the list of missing dudes."

"Maybe we do, 'cause Jerome Davis is the ranger you're looking for. He's supposed to take you to the last known whereabouts of one Aaron Kennedy, a climber last seen in the park Friday morning."

"Well ain't nobody here, so I'm going on in." I opened the screen door and stepped into the abandoned ranger station. The place was small but neat and clean, with all the maps and logs in their place. I picked up a clipboard from the lone desk in the room. Titled "Climbers," it had a list of names in small, tight handwriting. There was a check mark by each name except for the last one, Aaron Kennedy.

"Looks like our ranger went off looking for Mr. Kennedy on his own, Skeeter. I don't see any signs of a struggle, and there's an empty spot in the gun rack."

"How can you tell it's not just an empty spot?"

"The dust in the floor of the case has an oval spot in it, like the butt of a gun usually rests there. And nobody leaves an empty spot one from the left in a gun rack, Skeeter. Even you're redneck enough to know that."

"I'm redneck enough to never have seen a gun rack that wasn't full." He had a point, Skeeter's daddy owned more guns than even my family, and we were better armed than some third-world countries.

"Well lemme look around and see if I can find out where Ranger Jerry might have gone off to, then we'll try to figure out what's been stealing men in the Arkansas woods." I sat at the desk and looked through the stacks of papers arranged neatly on the blotter. Nothing. I flipped through the stack of pink message slips by the phone. More nothing. I looked over the blotter for notes. Even more nothing. I was just about to give up and start randomly wandering through the woods, always a good way for me to find trouble, when I remembered the list. I grabbed the clipboard and looked at it, then smacked myself in the forehead with it.

"What?" Skeeter said in my ear.

"The clipboard."

"What about it?"

"It lists their planned climbs. It tells me right where to

look for this Kennedy fella. . . "

"And by extension, Ranger Jerry."

"Yup. Sometimes I think I'm a real dumbass."

" . . . "

"Shut up."

"I didn't say nothing!" Skeeter protested.

"I heard you thinking." I said, and pushed the button to sever the connection. I grabbed the top page of the clipboard; a topographical map that Ranger Jerry had lying around, and then went back to the truck to gear up. I grabbed Bertha, my Desert Eagle in her shoulder rig, slid my Taurus Judge revolver into a paddle holster at the small of my back, and threaded a Ka-Bar through my belt loops. My backpack had a couple bottles of water, a handheld GPS and some camping supplies, just in case. I didn't bother with a tent or anything that heavy, since I wasn't planning on being gone more than a couple hours. I used the map to figure out GPS coordinates for Ranger Jerry's most likely destination, plugged them into the handheld unit, and headed off into the woods, machete in one hand and MP3 player in the other. Nothing like a little Alabama Shakes to help guide a brother through the deep dark woods, I always say.

It took an hour or so of hard hiking to get to the right GPS coordinates. The trail, if a deserted deer path could be called that, opened up to a clearing at the base of a three-story rock incline. It looked like a pretty simple climb, as long as you weren't a thirty-something 350-pound redneck weighted down with thirty pounds of guns and gear. In other words, it looked damned impossible to me. But the bright purple rope running down the face of the rock told me that somebody thought it looked like a good idea, and recently.

But it wasn't the cliff that stood out most of all. That honor went to the small cottage nestled up against the base of the cliff, complete with chimney and delicate white smoke wafting up into the afternoon sun. I pressed the Bluetooth button, but got nothing. I pulled out my cell phone and saw the blinking "No Service" icon.

"Shit. Well, I guess I can find a bunch of lost hikers without Skeeter's help." I hoped I could, anyway. I'd never tell him this, but Skeeter's pretty important to my hunting. Not only does he look up how to kill whatever I find, but just having his voice in my ear keeps me kinda calm. Like having somebody to bicker with keeps me centered. If I believed in therapy, I'd probably talk to somebody about that. But since I don't, I just drink.

The only sign of a climber was the rope dangling from the rock face, and there was nothing to indicate that Ranger Jerry had been by here at all, so I did exactly what everybody in their right mind screams at the TV for people not to do in horror movies - I walked up to the front door of the mysterious cottage that appeared where it had no business being, and knocked.

The door swung open silently at my touch, not even an eerie creak to warn me of what was about to happen. But that was probably because the little old lady that opened the door seemed to keep a neat house.

She looked up at me from just inside the door and said "I wondered if you were ever going to have the guts to come knock. What took you so long?"

She was a little old lady in all ways. Skinny, stooped over, maybe five and a half feet tall if she stood up straight, with white hair pulled into a bun on top of her head. She smiled up at me from underneath bright blue eyes and I got the distinct impression that this lady didn't mess anything that happened in her woods. No matter how weird it was that she was in the woods to begin with.

"Sorry, ma'am. I was a little confused. I didn't think anybody lived out here, it being a national park and all."

"Oh, dearie me, we don't pay much attention to nations out here. My sisters and I have lived in these woods for years and years. Now what brings a strapping young lad like yourself to my doorstep, and here in my old age no less." She sounded disappointed, like she wanted me to go away and come back later.

"May I come in? I'm looking for a few friends of mine and was hoping that you might have seen them."

"Of course, of course, please come in. She stepped back and I followed her into the cottage. It was a small, open room with a tiny kitchen, a table set for three, and a living room with three chairs. A doorway opened up off the back of the room, leading to bedrooms I supposed.

"Do your sisters live here with you?" I asked, waving at the place settings.

"Oh no, but we do like to gather for dinner from time to time. I usually do the cooking. Grissy does most of the hunting, because she's the youngest. The animals just seem to flock to her for some reason." She glanced away when she said that last bit, like it offended her somehow. I decided I didn't want to get into family politics, especially not a fight over which sister was prettier. There was no way that ended well for me.

I followed her into the living room and sat down on one of the chairs. Fortunately for me, antique furniture like her house was filled with was built to last, and to support big men. The chair creaked a little and maybe even whimpered as I sat down, but it held me, and was pretty comfortable to boot.

"Ma'am . . ." I started, but she held up a hand.

"Call me Esme, darling. It's been so long since a man called me that."

"Well . . . Esme, I'm looking for some people, and since a couple of them were last headed in this direction, I was hoping you could help me."

"Well, of course, dear. I suppose you're looking for that boy with all the climbing equipment and the nice park ranger, aren't you?"

"Yeah, I mean, yes, ma'am. That's two of the folks I'm looking for. Do you know where they went?" If I could wrap this up before dinner I could get out of these woods and get something real to eat, not just the granola bars I had in my pack.

"Well, they were both here. The climbing fellow a couple of days ago, and the ranger just this morning. The climbing man played around on the rocks behind the house for a while, but then he fell and hurt his arm. My middle sister Minerva is a wonderful healer, so I took him to her house so she could help him out. I suppose he decided to visit with her for a while until his arm was all better. That's what I told the ranger when he came by this morning. He took off for Minerva's house without even finishing his tea." She motioned to a cup sitting next to the chair I was in. Sure enough, it was three-quarters full of what looked like tea.

"Can you show me on this map where your sister's house is? I really need to find these people." I unfolded my topo map and dug a Sharpie out of my backpack. Esme looked at the map for just a second before taking the marker and putting a small circle down. I plugged the GPS coordinates into my handheld and figured it was a little more than another hour to get there. My watch told me it was about two o'clock, so if I wanted steak for dinner I was gonna have to get a move on.

"Thank you so much for your help, Esme. I really appreciate it." I stood up to leave, but she grabbed my wrist. Her grip was strong for somebody so apparently frail.

"Please come back by and visit me sometime. It gets very lonely here in the woods, all alone." She pressed herself into my side in a distinctly *non*-old lady fashion, and I felt myself blush a little. I danced backwards a little and got out of the cottage before Granny Esme decided to really throw herself at me. I mean, I love the ladies, and I'd dipped my toe in some older rivers from time to time, if you know what I mean, but I draw the line at fooling around with women who remember V-J Day.

Once I was back outside, I followed the GPS southwest past the house and was soon back into the deep woods. I kept trying the Bluetooth, but even though it felt like I was traveling higher and higher, there was no signal. I guess there are still a few places that cell phone companies haven't invaded yet. And of course I end up in all of them sooner or later.

I trekked deep into the woods, so deep that I could barely see the sky. My sense of time went all wonky, and I couldn't tell if I'd been walking for one hour, or three. All I was sure of was that my feet were sore, my water bottle was empty, and if I didn't find this woman's house pretty soon, I was going to need to find a stream or some other source of fresh water. Just when I was starting to think thirst was a serious problem, I stepped out into a clearing, almost identical to the last one.

Just like her sister's place, this cottage sat in a cleared patch of woods, with a nice little picket fence and a neat little chimney blowing a thin plume of white smoke up into the late afternoon sky. There was no cliff behind this cottage, just more woods, but otherwise it was almost indistinguishable from the first one. I stepped through the gate and up to the front door, raising my hand to knock.

The door opened before I touched it, swing in to reveal a beautiful fifty-ish woman dressed to kill in slinky black pants and a clingy black shirt that wrapped around her midsection and fastened in the center of some truly impressive tracts of land with a sparkling pendant. The brooch, not that my eye was drawn to that area at all, was a Celtic knotwork that looked familiar somehow. Then I remembered that her sister wore a necklace of the same design. I supposed it was a family thing.

"Hello," she said with a raised eyebrow and a smile. "I'm Minerva, and you must be Robert. Esme told me you were coming." Her dark eyes shone with anticipation, and her red lips turned up to mine invitingly. I stepped forward, into the cabin . . .

And shook myself back to my senses. "Sorry to barge in

like that, ma'am. Could I trouble you for some water? My bottles ran out a while back and I think thirst has made me forget my manners. I'm really sorry about that."

Something flashed across her face faster than I could track, but it was gone before I could even swear it existed, and was replaced by a sweet smile.

"Of course, dear. Let me hold your . . . sack and I'll refill your supplies." I handed over my backpack and watched as she walked over to the sink. I took in a deep breath as I checked out her ass. For an older chick, she was smokin'! Her butt cheeks looked like s pair of kittens playing in a pillowcase.

I snapped out of my contemplation of her rear to see her looking at me, a little smirk on her face. *Busted.* I realized she was waiting on me to answer, and had no idea what the question was.

"I'm sorry, what did you say? I guess I was out there a little longer than I thought. Do you mind if I sit down?" I stepped over to her couch and took a seat. The cottage was almost identical to Esme's on the inside too - a little sitting area, a kitchen, a dining area, and a hallway leading off into the back. I noticed one thing conspicuous by its absence, though.

"Ya'll don't have TVs?" I asked.

Minerva paused halfway across the living room and looked at me like a startled rabbit. "Um . . . No, we . . . Um . . . never have enjoyed television the way some people do."

"Huh." I shrugged, reaching out for the water glass and knocking back half of the tumbler in one gulp. "Well, can't say as I blame you. There's never anything on except smut and bad news. You're probably better off reading a book." I looked around, but there were no bookshelves, either. Or board games, or computers, or anything a person might amuse themselves with. These women kept some strange households.

"Yes, well, the library is in the back of the house. That's where I spend much of my time. There, and the bedroom." Her voice was like smooth velvet, and before I noticed, she was on the couch with me, pressed tight against me. "Is there anything else I could get for you? *Anything?*"

I looked down into those dark pools and felt myself slipping away, just comfortable to sit there on the couch with her and leave the lost men to their own devices. But then I remembered Skeeter, and Agent Amy, and that steak I wanted for dinner, and my focus went sharp again.

"Yes ma'am, there is. I'm looking for some hikers that vanished near here, and a park ranger that went missing this morning. I visited your sister because her cottage is near the last known destination of one of the hikers, but she didn't seem to know anything. She told me I should talk to you, because you might have some idea where these men have vanished to."

That shadow flickered across her face again, almost too fast to see but not quite, then she answered me. "Well, there was a man by here this morning, looking for another man he said was missing. I told him I hadn't had the company of a gentleman caller in some time, and that he should talk to Grissy."

"Who's Grissy?" I asked.

"Grissy is our youngest sister. She lives a little further into the wood." Just what I needed, another hour of hacking through honeysuckle and dodging deer poop. My steak was fading into dream territory with every minute.

"I thought Esme said she brought the climber here. She said he was hurt and you were nursing him back to health."

"Well I was, but he got better and went to visit Grissy for a few days."

"I thought he just went missing two days ago?"

"Well, I don't know anything about that, young man. I just know that he was hurt, and the moment I got him all healed up right as rain, he ran off with my little sister." Her dark eyes flashed, and I got the feeling this wasn't the first time a guy she was interested in made a play for the younger sis.

"So you told this to Ranger Jerry?"

"I did indeed, and just like all the others, he ran off to little Grissy's house." *Bitter, party of one. Your table is now available.* I decided it was time for me to get out of there before this chick started boiling bunnies and swinging cutlery around. I stood up from the couch and reached for my bag.

"Thanks for the water, but now it looks like I need to go see your sister and get this mess all cleared up."

She just sat there on the couch, looking up at me like an abandoned puppy. An abandoned puppy with huge knockers spilling out of her shirt, but a puppy just the same.

"Do you *have* to leave? Aren't you sure you wouldn't rather stay here? With me?" At that last bit she stretched out one long leg and ran her bare toes up the inside of my leg. As her foot approached the Promised Land, I stepped back out of reach. Her foot dropped to the floor, and she gave me a pout before standing and going to open the door.

"Well, you have fun with little Grissy, but remember how to get to my house when you want to talk to a *real* woman."

"Yeah . . . That reminds me. I don't have any idea where your sister lives. Could you mark it on this map for me?" I held out the map and a Sharpie, and she took them both in a huff. She stomped over to the little table, marked an "X" on the map, and stomped back.

"Here. Now get out."

I just that, and kept one hand on my knife as I backed away from the cabin. No way was I letting that one out of my sight. I thought to myself as I left the clearing that maybe it was a good thing these chicks lived deep in the woods. I heard the sound of something big and probably hungry rustling around in the woods nearby, but that didn't worry me nearly as much as the thought that Minerva might be following me.

The map took me over a couple of rivers and through a helluva lotta woods, but Grandmother's house was nowhere to be found. Okay, it was more like a couple of little streams that I managed to hop over without even getting my boots wet, but there were plenty of woods. Another hour or so of clumping through the woods brought me to one more clearing, marked just where Minerva said it was on the map. And once again, there was a tidy little cabin in the center of it.

The cabin looked a lot like the other two, your basic log cabin, but with a nice picket fence around is and a little flower garden out front. There was a big overturned pot by the front door of this one, though, and I couldn't for the life of me figure out what it was for. It looked like a giant stewpot, a good five feet deep and six feet around, but it was made out of porcelain instead of cast iron. On the ground next to it was a porcelain stirrer, but it was thicker than anything I'd ever seen before. In me stew experience, you just needed a cast iron pot about four feet around and three feet deep, and growing up we always stirred ours with a busted oar from somebody's jon boat, but this rig was a lot fancier.

The rest of the cabin could have come out of a fairy tale, it looked so stereotypical. There were even window boxes full of flowers. A thin tendril of smoke wafted up into the air from the brick chimney, and the scent of cooking spices filled the air. I stepped into the clearing and walked up to the front door, a little entranced by the delicious smells. I raised my hand to knock, but the door opened before I had the chance to bring my meaty fist down on it.

A blast of good food smells wafted out and floated around my head, taking me back to some of the best meals I've ever had. Mama's fried chicken and gravy danced on my tongue, while memories of my college girlfriend Brittany's spaghetti sauce tingled feelings a little lower. I even thought I smelled Waffle House chili in there for a second. Don't judge me, you ain't lived until you've been knee-walking drunk at three-thirty in the morning in Birmingham, Alabama eating Waffle House chili at the bar with one hand while you hold your buddy's head out of his grits with the other hand.

I blinked a couple of times to cut through the food smells and the memories and looked down at the woman who stood in the doorway. I had to catch my breath all over again when I saw *her*.

"Y-you must be Grissy." I managed to stammer while I drank in every inch of her. And they were some good-looking inches, too. She had long, dark hair cascading down over her shoulders, exotic part Asian-part Latina-part American-all hottie features that made Angelina Jolie look boring, with big brown eyes, dimples in her cheeks and a smile that melted my heart and stiffened a couple of other things.

She had a slender neck, smooth skin and long, long legs in a short, short skirt. She was barefoot, and her toes were painted a crimson to match her fingernails. She had on a men's tank top tied up to show a flat belly with a silver ring in her bellybutton and exposing enough cleavage to make me want to dive in there and explore for a day or so. In short, she was *hot.*

"Yes, I'm Grissy. What brings a big, strong man like you all the way out here?" She reached up and stroked my shoulder as she asked the question, and when the words came across her lips, I had no idea what the answer could be.

"I - I - I'm just taking a hike, I guess," I said after a minute of staring into those pools of blue. I might have diverted my gaze a little further south once or twice, too, but it was in a purely respectful way. And I didn't drool. Or if I did, my beard caught most of it.

"Wow, you must be thirsty. Why don't you come in, have a drink of water, and sit down for a minute. After all, it's soooo hot out there." She turned and walked into the cabin with me in tow. I followed her like a bulldog chasing a convertible, not having any idea what I was going to do with it when I caught it. She motioned to the couch and I sat. She didn't so much sit next to me as she *oozed* in beside me, pressing all her curves up to every inch of the side of my body. All thoughts of water went right out of my head. Come to think of it, pretty much every thought went right out of my head. I just sat there, enjoying the feel of all that soft womanliness pressed up against me.

"Now," she continued, trailing a fingertip down the line of buttons on my shirt, "what brings a big, strong man like you out to my cabin deep in these woods?"

Somehow I focused my thoughts enough to answer her question. "I'm looking for some people. Several men have gone missing in these woods lately, and when I spoke to your sisters, they thought maybe you might have seen them." I pulled a couple of pictures out of my back pocket and showed them to her.

She glanced down at the pictures for about an eighth of a second, then turned her dazzling smile back to me. "Never seen them before. Now, why don't we get better acquainted before dinner?"

I was all set to call her out on not even looking at the pictures, but then she had to go and mention dinner. Now let's review - I arrived on her doorstep after traipsing through the woods all damn day, chatting with her oldest sister, practically being molested by her middle sister, and now this most delectable thing had to go and mention food with me sitting in the middle of an olfactory orgasm zone. Well, my stomach did what it does when somebody mentions food - it grumbled out a little "hello" to the room just to remind us all that it was there. She heard my stomach growl, hell, people three states away probably heard my stomach growl, and giggled. Like she thought my barbaric manners were *cute*.

I've been called a lot of things by a lot of women, and a lot more by their fathers, husbands, brothers, boyfriends and priests. But I'm seldom what anybody thinks is *cute*. And it's even more rare that I get *giggled* at. So I didn't really know what to do with the situation. So I sat there like a jackass with a giggling sex kitten laughing on his chest, with all the appropriate jiggly bits of her doing what jiggly bits of women do when they laugh. So yeah, I didn't mind being giggled at so much.

After a few seconds of confusing frivolity, she looked up at me and said "Sounds like somebody's hungry. Would you like to join me for dinner?" And she batted her eyelashes. She batted. Her. Damn. Eyelashes. It was about as cute as a bucketful of kittens. And I was hungry.

"Of course. I'd hate to leave you out here all alone to eat by yourself. Besides, it smells delicious. What are you having?"

"Oh don't worry about that. I won't be alone. As a matter of fact, my sisters should be along in just a few minutes. We always take our meals together." I wondered about this, since old lady Esme didn't look like she could walk across her living room without breaking a hip, much less meander through the woods for two hours to get here. But then I caught another whiff of whatever was in the oven, and I didn't care so much about Esme. I did make sure that Bertha was still in her holster, though. Minerva scared me a little.

"Do you have anywhere I can wash up?" I asked. "I've been tromping through these woods for hours and I'd hate to sit down at your table all grimy."

"Of course. Right through there." She pointed down the hallway that led, I assumed, into the rest of the house. I heaved my bulk up off her couch and walked down the hall. The door to the right was open a little bit, so I peeked inside.

Nope, that ain't it. I pulled the door to her bedroom shut, but not before I took in the huge canopy bed in the center of the room and thought about all sorts of gymnastics that a guy my size could put a woman her size into in a bed that size. I turned to the opposite door and tried the knob, but it was locked.

The door at the end of the short hall opened into a small bathroom with an old-fashioned claw tub and a cute little pedestal sink. I closed the door, took a long-needed leak, and set about making myself some level of presentable. My hair looked like a bigger rat's nest than normal, so I took my ponytail down and ran my fingers through the mop, trying to tame it a little bit. I had no luck, so I opened the medicine cabinet in hopes of finding an old boyfriend's comb or something that I could use. I wasn't snooping, really. Much.

No comb, just a bunch of old glass bottles with paper labels on them. I grabbed one down, but couldn't read it. The script was spidery and faded, but also written in some kind of Latin or Greek or hell, if I was being honest it coulda been Korean for all I knew what it was saying. I put the bottle back and went back to washing my hands and face. I reached over to the side of the sink for a towel, and with all my usual bull-in-china-shop grace, knocked it to the floor. I knelt down to pick up the towel and saw something gold and shiny behind the toilet. Never one to leave something shiny behind, I reached down and pulled out a cheap gold star with the name "Davis" on it below the symbol of the National Parks Service. My brow knit, I slid the badge into a pocket and clambered to my feet.

Or at least I started to clamber to my feet, because just

about the time I got to kneeling position, the door opened behind me. I turned to see Grissy standing there, looking *pissed* and holding a black iron skillet. In my experience, that's always been a bad combination.

"You just *had* to get all snoopy, didn't you? Couldn't just leave well enough alone, could you?" I didn't bother trying to answer, because she swung the skillet at my head like Babe Ruth in Yankees Stadium. I dove under the swing and scrabbled forward, trying to get out of the bathroom and somewhere that I could defend myself without having to shoot the really hot girl with the really big pistol. I ran into Grissy's legs, and instead of bowling her over like I would expect a 350-pound dude to do to a hundred-or-so pound woman, it was like I'd run into iron bars. I looked up in surprise, and saw nothing but skillet rushing down at my face. The world exploded into stars, and that was the last thing I remember.

I woke up butt-naked and hanging by my wrists from a pair of handcuffs. The handcuffs were suspended from the ceiling by a chain that went up to a thick wooden beam, but I couldn't see how it fastened up there. The cuffs had just enough slack in them to let me stand on tiptoes, but I couldn't get much relief from the pressure on my shoulders. As my vision cleared, I realized that unlike every other time I'd woken up naked swinging by handcuffs in my life, this time wasn't a dream. And there were no Playmates anywhere. I was a little disappointed, then downright disconsolate when I looked around enough to see that I was hanging naked in a room with two other guys.

"Ranger Jerry, I suppose?" I asked the one hanging closest

to me.

"Yeah, how'd you know?" He observed the talking at urinals section of The Guy Code and looked only at my face.

"I'm Bubba. I been looking for you. And I reckon the rest of these guys, too."

"Yeah, they're all here. I don't know what she's going to do to us . . ."

"But it probably won't be near as much fun as what I had planned, Jerry old pal." I grinned, and he chuckled. I heard a weak laugh from behind me, and spun around to look at the other guy. He was hanging the same way I was, and looked a lot worse off than me. I him as Aaron Kennedy from the pictures Skeeter'd sent me, and figured that I'd found some of the folks I was supposed to rescue, now I just had to get on with the rescuing.

Suddenly the floor lurched and I lost my footing, putting all my weight on my wrists and shoulder sockets. I tried to reach up to the chain to take some of the strain off my wrists, but couldn't get twisted right, so I just hung there in agony as the floor rocked back and forth, like we were suddenly on a boat in the middle of a storm.

"What the hell is that?" I asked Jerry.

"I don't know. I just got here this morning." He said.

Aaron didn't have anything useful to add, and after a few minutes, the ride stopped and I managed to get my feet under me. My shoulders gave a sigh of relief, and I took another look around the room. In one corner was a big sturdy table, with enough knives and saws hanging over it to make a dozen Ginsu knife commercials. Dark brown stains covered the surface of the wood, and my stomach did a little flip-flop.

"Hey, Jerry. Did she say anything to you about coming to dinner?"

"Yeah, she did. She mentioned dinner just before she drugged my tea."

"What about you, Aaron?" I raised my voice. He answered in the affirmative. That sinking feeling in my gut came back, stronger than ever. We'd been invited to dinner, but not as guests. We were the entrees.

I looked up at the cuffs and the chain again, mentally measuring the strength of the average set of police-issue handcuffs against my own sense of self-preservation. I figured most days it was about fifty-fifty. I jumped as much as I could off my tiptoes and grabbed the chain, then started to pull myself up hand over hand.

"This might be uncomfortable, Jerry." I told the ranger as I started to swing my feet back and forth. The more I swung, the closer I came to Jerry. He started to pull back from the giant naked redneck swinging at him from handcuffs, but I wrapped my legs around his torso, using his body to take some of the strain off my arms for a second.

"Don't get any ideas, pal. I'm really not interested. But I gotta get us out of here before she decides who she wants to be the appetizer. I managed to wriggle around until my ankles were on Jerry's shoulders, and pulled myself up until I could at least see the end of the chain. I heard a choir of angels singing in my head when I saw the tiny shackle holding the chain wrapped around the beam. Obviously Grissy hadn't expected anybody to be crazy enough to get to the beam, so she just used a normal screw-pin shackle to hold the chain together. If I could get my hands up there, I could unscrew the pin and be free.

But that meant that I had to get my big ass up there, and even pulling myself up the chain and getting my feet onto Jerry's shoulders, I was still a good four feet under the beam.

"Crap. This is gonna suck." I muttered under my breath.

"Well it ain't exactly peaches and cream from here." Jerry muttered right back, keeping his eyes squeezed shut against the sight of my dangly bits hanging right in front of his nose.

I pulled myself up a little more on the chain, then reached up with one foot as far as I could without losing my grip or my footing. Imagine a Sasquatch doing one of those aerialist acts with the bands of silk, only bare-ass naked, and you get a little idea of how bizarre that whole thing must have looked. I got my foot high enough to loop one big toe over the edge of the beam, then I pulled the other foot up. I managed to get my whole right foot hooked over the beam, then pulled my left over and locked my ankles together.

I let out a huge sigh and relaxed my grip, swinging upside-down from my crossed ankles and almost bumping into Jerry's face. He jerked back, a look of horror on his face.

"Don't worry," I said, grinning at him. "I don't kiss on the first date." I took a deep breath and swung up to the beam using my abs and the chain to pull myself up. I got my left hand on the beam and set to unscrewing the shackle pin with my right. A few seconds later, I dropped down from the beam to land on both feet in front of Jerry. I was still cuffed, and still had six feet of chain hanging from the cuffs, but I wasn't dangling in midair anymore.

And of course that's when the door opens and Grissy walks in holding a cleaver and a carving knife that could have doubled as a short sword.

"You are a very naughty entree," she said, with a grin spreading over her face that said "I am batshit, paste-eating, carve my initials in your butt cheeks *crazy*." She walked towards me, he pace slow and deliberate, her path cutting off any chance of escape, weapons flicking out side to side like she knew exactly how to use those toys to carve up a whole side of redneck *du jour*. I backed away, always keeping one hanging dude between me and Grissy, until my butt hit the table.

"Nowhere to go, Bubba. What are you going to do now? There's nowhere to run, no place to hide, no way out. What do you do?"

"Like Rowdy Roddy said, I chew bubble gum and kick ass. Only I ain't got no bubble gum." I butchered the quote, but I spun around and grabbed a couple knives of my own and charged Grissy with a lot more bravado than most folks expect from a naked dude.

The key to a knife fight isn't in not getting cut. It's in understanding that you're *gonna* get cut. You just try not to get anything cut off that you care too much about, and you try to cut more bits off the other guy than they cut off you. I had a serious reach advantage over Grissy, but she was a lot faster than me, and she didn't have her hands cuffed together.

She dodged my first charge without any real effort, but she got a little too close to one of the dangling men, who put a knee in the small of her back for her troubles. She winced and turned to him, then remembered that she was fighting me and spun back around. I was almost on her then, and she ducked aside again. Again she danced too close to one of her captives and got a kick in the side as a reminder. We kept dancing that way for a long minute or two, me charging, her dodging, the other guys kicking. It was starting to wear on Grissy when suddenly her eyes gleamed with an evil idea and she ducked behind the nearest hanging dude and threw the cleaver at me.

I knocked it to the ground with my chain, not willing to let it fly past and maybe kill somebody, then I froze as I saw her plan. She was using the hanging guy as a shield, hiding behind him so I couldn't get at her, and he had her hand wrapped around his pride and joy with the edge of her knife pressed against it.

"One more step and I geld this stallion." She giggled at her cleverness, and the guy whimpered. Aaron Kennedy, missing climber, was about to be missing a piton unless I thought fast. Too bad for him thinking fast ain't what they hire me for.

"Go ahead." I said, and took one step closer.

"I mean it!" Grissy screeched.

"Dude, stop!" Aaron Kennedy was looking very concerned, and I didn't really blame him.

"I don't care, lady. Cut it off. You want to chop us all up and serve us in a stew, so go ahead and start with the shrimp cocktail." Sometimes I amaze myself with my wit.

"What? What kind of hero are you?" She looked baffled. I get that look from women a lot. Especially when they're looking at me naked.

"I'm no hero, lady. I'm a hunter. I'm here to find out what happened to these dudes and kill whatever was making it happen. I found out there's a psycho hosebeast out in the woods that wants to chop dudes up into Hamburger Helper, so now it's time for Part 2 - the killing part. Now you do what you gotta do to Aaron there, but I'm gonna rip your head off regardless."

She looked at me for a long time, like she was trying to see if I was serious. I was, by the way. I'm sure Aaron Kennedy is a nice dude, but I didn't really care if he got to keep his pecker or not. I was hired to kill the bad guy, or girl in this case, and I was gonna do that no matter what happened to him. After a minute that probably felt like a year to the guy with a butcher knife on his junk she burst into tears and fell to her knees. The knife clattered to the floor and Aaron let out a huge breath.

"But I don't WANT to get old!" She wailed, pounding on the floor with her fists. I looked around, but none of the dudes hanging like sides of beef had anything to contribute. I stepped forward, picked up the knife and snatched Grissy up by the hair and dragged her over to the table. I threw her face-up on the table and pressed my knife to her throat.

"What the hell are you squalling about?"

"I have to eat the stew to stay young. It's the flesh of men that keeps the change from happening."

"I repeat - what the hell are you talking about?" She curled up in a little ball on the table, sobbing uncontrollably. I wasn't getting anything useful out of her until she got her crap together, so I frisked her. For the keys, not just for fun. The keys were in her pocket, so I unlocked my cuffs and used them to chain her to the table. Then I let the other guys loose and sent Ranger Jerry off to look for our clothes.

He made it almost to the door when he froze. "Uh,

Bubba? We've got company."

I turned to the door and there stood Esme and Minerva. Grissy's older and way, *way* older sister, and they looked pretty irritated.

"Hey y'all. How's it going? I hope you weren't expecting dude stew for dinner, 'cause there's been a little change in the menu." I motioned to Grissy, tied to the table, and the roomful of naked men.

"That's how she was doing it." Esme said, as if I'd unlocked some great secret.

"Of course, how could we be so stupid!" Minerva replied.

I was confused, but that's pretty much my normal state around women, so I waved Ranger Jerry on to go find clothes. "I'm not gonna have to fight y'all too, am I? 'Cause I really feel like I've hit my quota on beating up crazy women for the day."

"No, Bubba, you won't have to fight us. Why don't you come into the den and we'll explain everything." Minerva turned and walked away, Esme following. I shrugged and started after her. Then I paused and handed the knife to Aaron.

"If she tries anything, stab her. A lot." He grinned a little and stood over Grissy with the knife. I decided that she really didn't want to move right then.

Minerva and Esme were on the couch when I made it back into the den. Ranger Jerry came out of the bedroom dressed in his uniform and carrying a pile of clothes. I held up a finger to the ladies in a "just a sec" gesture and retrieved my pants from Jerry. I pulled on my jeans and t-shirt, then strapped on Bertha and sat down in a chair facing the sisters.

"Would you mind telling me exactly what the hell is going

on here?" I asked.

"Where to begin?" Minerva asked.

"Try the beginning, dear." Esme chimed in.

Minerva glared at her, then went on. "Have you ever heard of the Baba Yaga, Bubba?"

"Yeah, I think so. Flies around in a mortar and pestle, house with chicken legs, that Baba Yaga?"

"That's the one." Minerva replied. "Except there isn't just one of us. We are all the Baba Yaga."

"Wait, like you're all three the Baba Yaga? Like, *all* of you?" Then it hit me. *Shit.* The Crone, the Mother and the Maiden. The Furies. *Double shit.* I just chained one of the Furies to a butcher's table and left her with a bunch of pissed-off naked dudes. This might be bad.

"Are you sure I'm not going to have to fight you two now? I did just beat up your sister, after all."

"Not only are you not going to have to fight us, you have done us a great service. Griselda has held the form of the Maiden for longer than is natural, using her manflesh stew to prevent the rotation from taking place." Minerva explained calmly.

"It's my turn to be young and beautiful, and that bitch has held on too long!" Esme spat.

"So what, y'all take turns being . . ." I wasn't even sure what I was trying to say, so I shut up and waved at Minerva.

"Yes, exactly. We alternate which aspect we represent. We change with the solstice, the holy days."

"But the summer solstice was like a month ago." Then it all fell into place. "And she's been making dinner for y'all ever since, making some excuse as to why you weren't changing.

And I bet it was stew every time."

"Once it was meatloaf." Esme said. I felt like puking, but I kept it together.

"So you've been eating the men that went missing in the forest, and that's what has kept you from changing into your other forms." I stood up and loosened Bertha in her holster.

"Where are you going?" Minerva asked.

"I'm going to shoot your sister in the face."

"You can't do that."

"Would you like to watch? Because I'm pretty sure I not only can, but I'm going to. You see, that's how the whole monster hunter thing works. I find monsters, I shoot monsters. Crazy witch-hotties that eat dudes definitely qualify as monsters. So I'm going to go shoot the crazy witch-hottie."

"It won't matter. It won't kill her. We're immortal."

"Let's test that theory. I've got white phosphorous rounds for the fire-haters, blessed rounds dipped in holy water for the demonic, cold iron rounds for the Fae, silver rounds for the lycanthropic, and hollow-points for every damn thing else. I bet I can find something that she doesn't like."

"I never said she'd like it, I just said it wouldn't kill her. She'd just heal, and then she'd hunt you down forever. And with the flying mortar and the house, there's nowhere she can't go."

That created a problem. I thought for a minute, then offered Minerva a deal. She and Esme talked about it for a long time, then finally agreed. They packed up their crazy-ass sister and toted her off into the woods, her shrieking the whole time about revenge.

Ranger Jerry and I went outside, turn the mortar over and

set it up to be the enormous stewpot I'd originally mistaken it for, and used the furniture from the cabin to build a roaring fire. Then we did the only thing you *can* do to disable a magical walking house on giant chicken legs. We cooked the legs into chicken stew. Let me tell you, magical-house chicken legs really do taste like chicken.

MEAN-SPIRITED

Edmund R. Schubert

As I picked up my pistol one last time, I found my attention wandering away from the weapon itself and to the withered hand that held it. It looked like a mummy's hand, collapsing from the inside after too many millennia of desiccation. What a grotesque hand. My entire body was so close to death, why not finish the job?

Yes, at seventy-eight years old, I could easily come up with plenty of reasons to kill myself, some of them even logical, valid reasons. Blowing my brains all over Trish's favorite Monet for pure spite probably wasn't one of the better ones, but it was good enough.

I had considered blowing my brains out on the Jackson Pollock in the main hall, but given the nature of Pollock's work, I wasn't sure Trish would even notice. She neither knew nor cared anything about art; she collected it simply because that's what obscenely rich people do. However, a spray of blood-red blood over the renowned Frenchman's white water lilies -- that would not only get her attention, it would really piss her off. Oh, how it would piss her off.

Dear God, how that made me smile . . .

And it wasn't the loss of the money that would make Trish mad. Even if the painting hadn't been insured, the ancient hag had enough cash to buy fifty more. She'd probably let some museum clean the painting, then donate it to them and use the insurance money to spend a month sunbathing, topless, on the French Riviera. The wrinkled, sagging, melanoma-ridden bitch.

No, what would piss her off to no end was the knowledge that I had ruined a century-old masterpiece *just to piss her off*. Trish and I had raised the art of spite and malice to that high a level. We were grand masters; we had been at each other's throats for thirty-seven years now.

Turning my attention back at the black-barreled .45 caliber pistol in my hand, I imagined Trisha coming into the library. Her hazel eyes would go wide as she beheld the horror of the scene. I prayed that the power of the moment, the memory of it, would haunt her for years. Hell, for all eternity.

I could envision the scene with transcendent clarity. Standing in the doorway, one of her hands would unconsciously drift to her open mouth, the tip of her forefinger coming to rest on the tip of her nose. Her hand would then drift slowly away from her face as her dumb-struck expression transformed into one of unexpurgated rage. She'd rush forward, hurdling my still-bleeding corpse in her haste to get to the painting. "Nooooo!!" she'd howl as her fingers hovered inches away from Monet's bloodstained masterpiece, afraid to touch it for fear the blood might still be damp, that it would smudge the delicate petals of the water lilies beneath.

Then she'd turn back to my body, looming over me like I was an old dog who had just relieved himself on the carpet for the thousandth time.

"You . . ." She'd kick me in the head. "Arrogant . . ." She'd kick me again, even harder. "Pompous . . ." Another kick. "Prick . . ." Kick.

Her tempo would increase, and she'd punctuate each word with a blow, as if her legs were gigantic, living exclamation points. "You think you've won, don't you," she'd rant, legs pistoning merrily into my corpse. "You think you've stuck the last needle under my fingernails and gotten away with it, don't you? Well you haven't. This isn't over; do you hear me?" Aiming a final kick at my ass, her rage would crescendo. She'd be shouting at the top of her lungs, her eyes bulging, her hair disheveled from the fury of her efforts. "This isn't over *until I say it's over!!!*"

Of course, she'd be wrong.

That was the beauty of it; it would be over. And I would have won. After nearly four decades of tormenting each other, I would have finally, ultimately, unequivocally won. There was no way for her to retaliate because I'd be gone, gone, gone, and there was nothing she could do about it.

I felt like doing a little song and dance.

Nothing you can do about it; nothing you can do about it; nothing you can . . .

Not a good reason to kill myself? I was giddy with excitement. I couldn't imagine a better reason.

I brought my .45 to my head, made sure I was properly aligned with the Monet so I would splatter it without putting a bullet through it, and stuck the bitter tasting barrel into my mouth. I embraced the trigger.

◊◊◊

I had expected a loud noise when the gun went off, followed by nothing. Darkness. Sweet oblivion.

What I got was pain.

Dear God, what pain. Agonizing, excruciating, unimaginable pain. Vicious, angry icicles of pain clawing their way out from the center of my brain, tearing through flesh and bone in an effort to be free. But every time they broke through to the surface, they'd vanish -- poof, just like that -- only to start over again from the center, digging and clawing their way through my brain over and over, again and again.

Had I screwed up? Had I managed to put a pistol in my mouth, pull the trigger, and not kill myself?

I dearly hoped not. That would give Trisha too much satisfaction.

But those cruel icicle claws wouldn't stop. They went on and on and on, ripping and tearing, and all I could do was clench my eyes and endure the unendurable. I heard nothing; saw nothing; and felt nothing. Nothing but pain.

I *was* pain.

Finally, after what seemed like days, I managed to open one eye. It wasn't that the pain had lessened. It had not. I'd simply become more accustomed to its presence. Not much; just enough that I could tolerate the movement of one eyelid by about half an inch.

What I saw jolted both of my eyes open.

Lying beneath me . . . was my body. *My body!*

It didn't move. If it had, I would have been stunned, because the hollow-point bullet had blown away a massive chunk of skull and brains. There was no chance I had survived that.

Which meant I was dead -- and still experiencing the gunshot. I was frozen in that split second where the hollow-point tore through the roof of my mouth, mushroomed out, and then shredded my brain before blowing open the back of my skull.

And suddenly I knew I would feel this way forever. I had no idea how or why, but I knew. Whether it was punishment from God or simply a unknown fact of the afterlife made no difference. I was trapped in this moment of Promethean pain for all time.

◊◊◊

They say people can get used to anything. Apparently this applies in the afterlife, too, because a week later I was in no less pain than before, but I had grown accustomed enough to it that I was able to think and move with a little more ease.

All those schmucks who had heart attacks while getting laid. They had no idea how lucky they were. I pondered that fact angrily. Of course, I did everything angrily. The pain kept me in an eternally sour mood.

And as if the pain weren't enough to maintain my foul demeanor, when I first began to move around, I quickly learned that I was not only trapped in the moment of my death, I was also trapped in the room where I had shot myself. I could open and close the library door, pull books off the shelves, even stumble over my own rank-smelling corpse. But leave the room? Never.

I grew angrier with each passing moment.

And speaking of rank smelling, where the hell was Trish? An entire week and she hadn't come home yet.

For that matter, where was the staff? The maid? Butler? Cook? They were all gone. I was glad enough they were out of the house the day I shot myself; I really didn't want to be interrupted. But someone should have come home by now. Especially that wretched wife of mine. The thought of her seeing what I had done to her Monet -- and I had made a royal mess of it, more than I ever could have hoped for -- that was all that kept me going. So where was that witch of a . . .

"Honey?"

Trish! I hadn't heard her come in, but that was her voice. No doubt about it.

I made sure the door to the library was open and sat down in an over-stuffed chair to watch the show.

Briefly I wondered if she would be able to see me sitting there. That would certainly present some interesting possibilities. I hadn't considered it before, but being trapped here like this . . . well, as long as *she* stuck around, I could haunt her to my heart's content. I was a poltergeist. An angry, noisy ghost with a foul disposition -- one that I would be more than happy to inflict on her for as long as possible. That had the potential for some real fun.

"Honey?" I heard her call again. "Margot and I jetted down to the Bahamas for the week. Since you'd be all by yourself I didn't think you'd need any help, so I took the staff with me. That didn't cause you any problems, did it? I *surely* hope not."

After all these years, that was the best she could come up with? Take the staff away to inconvenience me? She was losing her touch.

"By the way," she began . . .

Ah. Here comes the big one. I should have known better; taking the staff had just been foreplay.

"I got tested about three months ago and I have AIDS. You should have contracted it by now, too."

Wow. So smooth; so matter-of-fact. So calculated. Based on her delivery, I couldn't help but think that she had intentionally sought out a way to get AIDS just to infect me.

It also explained a lot: why she had suddenly grown amorous again, as well as those new medications she had recently started taking. She had hidden them well enough that I couldn't find them, but I knew she had been taking a new drug cocktail.

If I hadn't been dead, that would have really gotten to me. That would have infuriated me.

But I was dead. Beyond her. If my head hadn't hurt so much, I would have laughed. To tell you the truth, though, I hurt too much to ever laugh again.

I heard Trish call out again; obviously she was expecting some sort of reaction. "Sweetie pie," she called, "did you hear what I said?"

I grabbed a paperweight off my desk and threw it against the wall, hoping to attract her attention. It *whumped* twice, once against the wall and once more when it hit the floor.

"Sweetheart?"

Her voice was getting closer. Finally, an advantage to

being a poltergeist. I threw a book.

"Are you in here, pudding?"

She came through the door . . .

And froze.

Oh, it was beautiful. She spotted my body with her eyes at the exact same moment that the smell hit her nose. She wears so much perfume that there was no way she could have picked up the stench until she was right on top of me, and it was perfect. I couldn't have planned it any better.

Stunned, she brought her hand to her mouth, just like I had anticipated. But she just stared at my body. She couldn't take her eyes off of it.

I wanted to shout, but I knew she wouldn't hear me even if I tried. But wanted to. Oh how I wanted to. *The painting, damn you! Look at the painting!*

I contemplated throwing a pen or something in the direction of her precious Monet; she took two steps toward the spot where my body rested.

"Nooooo!!" she wailed.

I was stunned. After all these years, was she actually distraught over losing me?

Snatching up my pistol, she fired three quick shots into my fetid corpse.

Okay - now things were getting interesting.

"How did you find out?" she screamed. "*How did you find out I gave you AIDS?*"

This time she kicked my body in the small of the back.

"How did you find out?" She screamed again, bending closer to my body as if I could hear her better that way.

Straightening up, she looked around the room - but she

never saw the stupid painting. The look in her eyes was one of someone gazing off into infinity. Then she started shaking her head.

"Oh no," she said. Very softly. "You're not leaving me here to deal with this infernal disease all by myself. You don't get to do that to me. I decide when this is over; not you."

She brought the gun to her head, lowered it for just a second, then brought it back to her head again. I saw her fingers stiffen with resolve as she said again, "I decide, not you."

And just like that, the ramifications of what she was about to do hit me like a Learjet.

Nooooo, I wanted to scream. Noooo!

Damn it, no! *No!* Kill yourself if you want, I don't care. But not in here. Please, God, *not in here!* I'm not spending eternity trapped in this room with --

Ka-blam.

This time I heard the gun shot.

It was much louder than I expected . . .

DOWN MEMORY LANE

Mike Resnick

Gwendolyn sticks a finger into her cake, pulls it out, and licks it with a happy smile on her face.

"I *like* birthdays!" she says, giggling with delight.

I lean over and wipe some frosting off her chin. "Try to be a little neater," I say. "You wouldn't want to have to take a bath before you open your present."

"Present?" she repeats excitedly, her gaze falling on the box with the colorful wrapping paper and the big satin bow. "Is it time for my present now? Is it?"

"Yes, it is," I answer. I pick up the box and hand it to her. "Happy birthday, Gwendolyn."

She tears off the paper, shoves the card aside, and opens the box. An instant later she emits a happy squeal and pulls out the rag doll. "This is my very favorite day of my whole life!" she announces.

I sigh and try to hold back my tears.

Gwendolyn is 82 years old. She has been my wife for the last 60 of them.

◊◊◊

I don't know where I was when Kennedy was shot. I don't know what I was doing when the World Trade Center collapsed under the onslaught of two jetliners. But I remember every single detail, every minute, every second, of the day we got the bad news.

"It may not be Alzheimer's," said Dr. Castleman. "Alzheimer's is becoming a catchword for a variety of senile dementias. Eventually we'll find out exactly which dementia it is, but there's no question that Gwendolyn is suffering from one of them."

It wasn't a surprise—after all, we knew something was wrong; that's why she was being examined—but it was still a shock.

"Is there any chance of curing it?" I asked, trying to keep my composure.

He shook his head sadly. "Right now we're barely able to slow it down."

"How long have I got?" said Gwendolyn, her face grim, her jaw set.

"Physically you're in fine shape," said Castleman. "You could live another ten to twenty years."

"How long before I don't know who anyone is?" she persisted.

He shrugged helplessly. "It proceeds at different rates with different people. At first you won't notice any diminution, but before long it will become noticeable, perhaps not to you, but to those around you. And it doesn't progress in a straight line. One day you'll find you've lost the ability to read, and then, perhaps two months later, you'll see a newspaper headline, or perhaps a menu in a restaurant, and you'll read it as easily as you do today. Paul here will be elated and think you're regaining your capacity, and he'll call me and tell me about it, but it won't last. In another day, another hour, another week, the ability will be gone again."

"Will I know what's happening to me?"

"That's almost the only good part of it," replied Castleman. "You know now what lies ahead of you, but as it progresses you will be less and less aware of any loss of your cognitive abilities. You'll be understandably bitter at the start, and we'll put you on anti-depressants, but the day will come when you no longer need them because you no longer remember that you ever had a greater mental capacity than you possess at that moment."

She turned to me. "I'm sorry, Paul."

"It's not your fault," I said.

"I'm sorry that you'll have to watch this happen to me."

"There must be something we can do, some way we can fight it..." I muttered.

"I'm afraid there isn't," said Castleman. "They say there are stages you go through when you know you're going to die: disbelief, then anger, then self-pity, and finally acceptance. No one's ever come up with a similar list for the dementias, but in the end what you're going to have to do is accept it and learn to live with it."

"How long before I have to go to . . . to wherever I have to go when Paul can't care for me alone?"

Castleman took a deep breath, let it out, and pursed his lips. "It varies. It could be five or six months, it could be two years, it could be longer. A lot depends on you."

"On me?" said Gwendolyn.

"As you become more childlike, you will become more curious about things that you no longer know or recognize. Paul tells me you've always had a probing mind. Will you be content to sit in front of the television while he's sleeping or otherwise occupied, or will you feel a need to walk outside and then forget how to get back home? Will you be curious about all the buttons and switches on the kitchen appliances? Two-year-olds can't open doors or reach kitchen counters, but *you* will be able to. So, as I say, it depends on you, and that is something no one can predict." He paused. "And there may be rages."

"Rages?" I repeated.

"In more than half the cases," he replied. "She won't know why she's so enraged. You will, of course—but you won't be able to do anything about it. If it happens, we have medications that will help."

I was so depressed I was thinking of suicide pacts, but Gwendolyn turned to me and said, "Well, Paul, it looks like we have a lot of living to cram into the next few months. I've always wanted to take a Caribbean cruise. We'll stop at the travel agency on the way home."

That was her reaction to the most horrific news a human being can receive.

I thanked God that I'd had 60 years with her, and I cursed Him for taking away everything that made her the woman I loved before we'd said and done all the things we had wanted to say and do.

◊◊◊

She'd been beautiful once. She still was. Physical beauty fades, but inner beauty never does. For 60 years we had lived together, loved together, worked together, played together. We got to where we could finish each other's sentences, where we knew each other's tastes better than we knew our own. We had fights—who doesn't?—but we never once went to bed mad at each other.

We raised three children, two sons and a daughter. One son was killed in Vietnam; the other son and the daughter kept in touch as best they could, but they had their own lives to lead, and they lived many states away.

Gradually our outside social contacts became fewer and fewer; we were all each other needed. And now I was going to watch the only thing I'd ever truly loved become a little less each day, until there was nothing left but an empty shell.

◊◊◊

The cruise went well. We even took the train all the way to the rum factory at the center of Jamaica, and we spent a few days in Miami before flying home. She seemed so normal, so absolutely herself, that I began thinking that maybe Dr. Castleman's diagnosis had been mistaken.

But then it began. There was no single incident that couldn't have occurred 50 years ago, nothing that you couldn't find a reasonable excuse for—but things kept happening. One afternoon she put a roast in the oven, and at dinnertime we found that she'd forgotten to turn the oven on. Two days later we were watching *The Maltese Falcon* for the umpteenth time, and suddenly she couldn't remember who killed Humphrey Bogart's partner. She "discovered" Raymond Chandler, an author she'd loved for years. There were no rages, but there was everything else Dr. Castleman had predicted.

I began counting her pills. She was on five different medications, three of them twice a day. She never skipped them all, but somehow the numbers never came out quite right.

I'd mention a person, a place, an incident, something we'd shared together, and one time out of three she couldn't recall it—and she'd get annoyed when I'd explain that she had forgotten it. In a month it became two out of three times. Then she lost interest in reading. She blamed it on her glasses, but when I took her to get a new prescription, the optometrist tested her and told us that her vision hadn't changed since her last visit two years earlier.

She kept fighting it, trying to stimulate her brain with crossword puzzles, math problems, anything that would cause her to think. But each month the puzzles and problems got a little simpler, and each month she solved a few less than she had the month before. She still loved music, and she still loved leaving seeds out for the birds and watching them come by to feed—but she could no longer hum along with the melodies or identify the birds.

She had never allowed me to keep a gun in the house. It was better, she said, to let thieves steal everything then to get killed in a shootout—they were just possessions; we were all that counted—and I honored her wishes for 60 years. But now I went out and bought a small handgun and a box of bullets, and kept them locked in my desk against the day that she was so far gone she no longer knew who I was. I told myself that when that day occurred, I would put a bullet into her head and another into my own . . . but I knew that I couldn't. Myself, yes; the woman who'd been my life, never.

◊◊◊

I met her in college. She was an honor student. I was a not-very-successful jock—3rd-string defensive end in football, back-up power forward in basketball, big, strong, and dumb—but she saw something in me. I'd noticed her around the campus—she was too good-looking not to notice—but she hung out with the brains, and our paths almost never crossed. The only reason I asked her out the first time was because one of my frat brothers bet me ten dollars she wouldn't give me the time of day. But for some reason I'll never know she said yes, and for the next 60 years I was never willingly out of her presence. When we had money we spent it, and when we didn't have money we were every bit as happy; we just didn't live as well or travel as much. We raised our kids, sent them out into the world, watched one die and two move away to begin their own lives, and wound up the way we'd started—just the two of us.

And now one of us was vanishing, day by day, minute by minute.

◊◊◊

One morning she locked the bathroom door and couldn't remember how to unlock it. She was so panicky that she couldn't hear me giving her instructions from the other side. I was on the phone, calling the fire department, when she appeared at my side to ask why I was talking to them and what was burning.

"She had no memory of locking herself in," I explained to Dr. Castleman the next day. "One moment she couldn't cope with a lock any three-year-old could manipulate, and the next moment she opened the door and didn't remember having any problem with it."

"That's the way these things progress," he said.

"How long before she doesn't know me anymore?"

Castleman sighed. "I really don't know, Paul. You've been the most important thing in her life, the most constant thing, so it stands to reason that you'll be the last thing she forgets." He sighed again. "It could be a few months, or a few years—or it could be tomorrow."

"It's not fair," I muttered.

"Nobody ever said it was," he replied. "I had her checked over while she was here, and for what it's worth she's in excellent physical health for a woman of her age. Heart and lungs are fine, blood pressure's normal."

Of course her blood pressure was normal, I thought bitterly. She didn't spend most of her waking hours wondering what it would be like when the person she had spent her life with no longer recognized her.

Then I realized that she didn't spend most of her waking hours thinking of *anything*, and I felt guilty for pitying myself when she was the one whose mind and memories were racing away at an ever-faster rate.

◊◊◊

Two weeks later we went shopping for groceries. She wandered off to get something—ice cream, I think—and when I'd picked up what I needed and went over to the frozen food section she wasn't there. I looked around, checked out the next few aisles. No luck.

I asked one of the stock girls to check the women's rest room. It was empty.

I started getting a panicky feeling in the pit of my stomach. I was just about to go out into the parking lot to look for her when a cop brought her into the store, leading her very gently by the arm.

"She was wandering around looking for her car," he explained. "A 1961 Nash Rambler."

"We haven't owned that car in 40 years or more," I said. I turned to Gwendolyn. "Are you all right?"

Her face was streaked by tears. "I'm sorry," she said. "I couldn't remember where we parked the car."

"It's all right," I said.

She kept crying and telling me how sorry she was. Pretty soon everyone was staring, and the store manager asked if I'd like to take her to his office and let her sit down. I thanked him, and the cop, but decided she'd be better off at home, so I led her out to the Ford we'd owned for the past five years and drove her home.

As we pulled into the garage and got out of the car, she stood back and looked at it.

"What a pretty car," she said. "Whose is it?"

◊◊◊

"They're not sure of anything," said Dr. Castleman. "But they think it's got something to do with the amyloid beta protein. An abundance of it can usually be found in people suffering from Alzheimer's or Down Syndrome."

"Can't you take it out, or do something to neutralize it?" I asked.

Gwendolyn sat in a chair, staring at the wall. We could have been ten thousand miles away as far as she was concerned.

"If it was that simple, they'd have done it."

"So it's a protein," I said. "Does it come in some kind of food? Is there something she shouldn't be eating?"

He shook his head. "There are all kinds of proteins. This is one you're born with."

"Is it in the brain?"

"Initially it's in the spinal fluid."

"Well, can't you drain it out?" I persisted.

He sighed. "By the time we know it's a problem in a particular individual, it's too late. It forms plaques on the brain, and once that happens, the disease is irreversible." He paused wearily. "At least it's irreversible today. Someday they'll cure it. They should be able to slow it down before too long. I wouldn't be surprised to see it eradicated within a quarter of a century. There may even come a day when they can test embryos for an amyloid beta imbalance and correct it *in utero*. They're making progress."

"But not in time to help Gwendolyn."

"No, not in time to help Gwendolyn."

◊◊◊

Gradually, over the next few months, she became totally unaware that she even had Alzheimer's. She no longer read, but she watched the television incessantly. She especially liked children's shows and cartoons. I would come into the room and hear the 82-year-old woman I loved singing along with the Mickey Mouse Club. I had a feeling that if they still ran test patterns she could watch one for hours on end.

And then came the morning I had known would come: I was fixing her breakfast—some cereal she'd seen advertised on television—and she looked up at me, and I could tell that she no longer knew who I was. Oh, she wasn't afraid of me, or even curious, but there was absolutely no spark of recognition.

The next day I moved her into a home that specialized in the senile dementias.

◊◊◊

"I'm sorry, Paul," said Dr. Castleman. "But it really is for the best. She needs professional care. You've lost weight, you're not getting any sleep, and to be blunt, it no longer makes any difference to her who feeds and cleans and medicates her."

"Well, it makes a difference to *me*," I said angrily. "They treat her like an infant!"

"That's what she's become."

"She's been there two weeks, and I haven't seen them try—really *try*—to communicate with her."

"She has nothing to say, Paul."

"It's there," I said. "It's somewhere inside her brain."

"Her brain isn't what it once was," said Castleman. "You have to face up to that."

"I took her there too soon," I said. "There *must* be a way to connect with her."

"You're an adult, and despite her appearance, she's a four-year-old child," said Castleman gently. "You no longer have anything in common."

"We have a lifetime in common!" I snapped.

I couldn't listen to anymore, so I got up and stalked out of his office.

◊◊◊

I decided that depending on Dr. Castleman was a dead end, and I began visiting other specialists. They all told me pretty much the same thing. One of them even showed me his lab, where they were doing all kinds of chemical experiments on the amyloid beta protein and a number of other things. It was encouraging, but nothing was going to happen fast enough to cure Gwendolyn.

Two or three times each day I picked up that pistol I'd bought and toyed with ending it, but I kept thinking: what if there's a miracle—medical, religious, whatever kind? What if she becomes Gwendolyn again? She'll be all alone with a bunch of senile old men and women, and I'll have deserted her.

So I couldn't kill myself, and I couldn't help her, and I couldn't just stand by and watch her. Somehow, somewhere, there had to be a way to connect with her, to communicate on the same level again. We'd faced some pretty terrible problems together—losing a son, suffering a miscarriage, watching each of our parents die in turn—and as long as we were together we were able to overcome them. This was just one more problem—and every problem is capable of solution.

I found the solution, too. It wasn't where I expected, and it certainly wasn't *what* I expected, but she was 82 years old and sinking fast, and I didn't hesitate.

That's where things stand this evening. Earlier today I bought this notebook, and this marks the end of my first entry.

◊◊◊

Friday, June 22. I'd heard about the clinic while I was learning everything I could about the disease. The government outlawed it and shut it down, so they moved it lock, stock and barrel to Guatemala. It wasn't much to look at, but then, I wasn't expecting much. Just a miracle of a different sort.

They make no bones about what they anticipate if the experiment goes as planned. That's why they only accept terminal patients—and because they have so few and are so desperate for volunteers, that's also why they didn't challenge me when I told them I had a slow-acting cancer. I signed a release that probably wouldn't hold up in any court of law outside Guatemala; they now have my permission to do just about anything they want to me.

◊◊◊

Saturday, June 23. So it begins. I thought they'd inject it into my spine, but instead they went through the carotid artery in my neck. Makes sense; it's the conduit between the spine and the brain. If anything's going to get the protein where it can do its work, that's the ticket. I thought it would hurt like hell, but it's just a little sore. Except for that, I don't feel any different.

◊◊◊

Wednesday, June 27. Fourth day in a row of tedious lectures explaining how some of us will die but a few may be saved and all humanity will benefit, or something like that. Now I have an inkling of how lab rats and guinea pigs feel. They're not aware that they're dying; and I guess before too long, we won't be either.

◊◊◊

Wednesday, July 3. After a week of having me play with the most idiotic puzzles, they tell me that I've lost six percent of my cognitive functions and that the condition is accelerating. It seems to please them no end. I'm not convinced; I think if they'd give me a little more time I'd do better on these damned tests. I mean, it's been a long time since I was in school. I'm out of practice.

◊◊◊

Sunday, July 7. You know, I think it's working. I was reading down in the lounge, and for the longest time I couldn't remember where my room was. Good. The faster it works, the better. I've got a lot of catching up to do.

◊◊◊

Tuesday, July 16. Today we got another talking-to. They say the shots are stronger and the symptons are appearing even faster than they'd hoped, and it's almost time to try the anecdote. Anecdote. Is that the right word?

◊◊◊

Friday, July 26. Boy am I lucky. At the last minute I remembered why I went there in the furst place. I wated until it was dark and snuck out. When I got to the airport I didnt have any money, but they asked to see my wallet and took out this plastic card and did something with it and said it was OK and gave me a ticket.

◊◊◊

Saturday, july 27. I wrote down my address so I wouldnt forget, and boy am i lucky I did, because when I got a cab at the airporte I coudlnt' remember what to tell him. We drove and we drove and finally I remembered I had wrote it down, but when we got home i didnt' have a key. i started pounding on the door, but no one was there to let me in, and finally they came with a loud siren and took me somewere else. i cant stay long. I have to find gwendolyn before it is too late, but i cant remember what it wood be too late for.

◊◊◊

Mundy, august. He says his name is Doctr Kasleman and that i know him, and he kept saying o paul why did you do this to yourself, and i told him i didn't remember but i know I had a reason and it had something to do with gwendolyn. do you remember her he said. of course i do i said, she is my love and my life. I askt when can i see her & he said soon.

◊◊◊

wensday. they gave me my own room, but i dont want my own room i want to be with gwendolyn. finaly they let me see her and she was as beutiful as ever and i wanted to hug her and kiss her but wen i walked up to her she started krying and the nurse took her away

◊◊◊

it has been 8 daz since i rote here. or maybe 9. i keep forgeting to. today i saw a prety littl girl in the hall, with prety white hair. she reminds me of someone but i dont know who. tomorrow if i remember i will bring her a prezent

◊◊◊

i saw the pretti gurl again today. i took a flower from a

pot and gave it to her and she smiled and said thank you and we talkt alot and she said i am so glad we met & i am finaly happy. i said so am i. i think we are going to be great friends becauz we like each other and have so mucch in commmon. i askt her name and she couldnt remember, so i will call her gwendolyn. i think i nu someone called gwendolyn once a long time ago and it is a very pretti name for a very pretti new frend.

-end-

COWBOYS 'N' DRUIDS

Danny Birt

As he swung down from the saddle, Drew's frown deepened. He had been driven out of his cabin this morning by the feeling that something was not right on his lands, and the further east he had ridden the feeling had only increased until he reached this spot and, frustratingly, found nothing amiss.

Drew took off his beaten cowboy hat and wiped his forehead with his sleeve while he continued to scan the area. The day was hot and likely to get hotter, given that the summer solstice had happened only the day before. The drought was obvious in the way the detritus of withered trees and shrubs crackled under his feet, throwing up little puffs of dust as he walked away from his dun stallion. Drew didn't bother to tie the horse to anything; he knew Frey would not wander far.

The oak and hazel trees were thick around him, providing shade and peace for his walk. The wildlife noted his presence, but continued to play, eat, chatter, work, and generally continue on with life: they knew him and recognized his belonging on this land.

He knew he had to be close to whatever was bothering him, but still finding nothing unusual in sight Drew chose to continue his search by alternate means. He bent over to pick up a fallen tree branch, looked around to orient himself to the time and place, then closed his eyes and let his subconscious soak into the wood. When he opened his eyes once more, he found that his arm was pointing off to the right. He walked on with renewed purpose, yet he only took twelve steps before he stopped cold.

A brown rabbit lay dead at his feet, caught in a spring steel-jawed trap. That the animal was dead did not upset Drew, but the manner by which it had died most certainly did.

Drew tossed his tree branch aside and squatted to examine the rabbit and bloody trap more carefully. The rabbit had died messily: all around the base of the trap, the ground had been mixed into a blood-and-dirt gruel by the rabbit's death throes. Further away from the trap, Drew's experienced eyes took in the trail the rabbit had worn into the ground in its comings and goings, and he saw the hole under the root of the tree that surely led to the rabbit's burrow. Those same eyes narrowed in burgeoning anger as his fingers felt at the rabbit's carcass and found that the doe had given birth recently. This steel monstrosity had committed the doe's helpless kittens to starvation.

Grasping the rabbit and trap in his left hand, Drew stood up. The trap was anchored to the ground, but Drew was too angry to take the time to dig it up. Instead, in a fit of serious overkill he pulled his old Colt revolver from its holster and shot the chain, breaking its link to the ground. The trapper would be angry that his property had been damaged, of course, but Drew was well within his rights: the trapper in question had knowingly trespassed on his lands after being warned to stay off three times already.

Besides, Drew planned on seeing to it that Bruce Jacobowitz had more to worry for than mere materialism.

◊◊◊

"Old man!" Drew bellowed as he gave Frey a light swat on the rump, urging him toward the stable behind the cabin. He did not bother staying outside to make sure the horse would do as he was directed. Instead, he clomped up the porch steps and through the front door. "Get yourself up; I need help!"

"The only times you ever admit you need me nowadays is when you're trying to do something tricky or morally questionable," a petulant voice from the loft said.

"This one's both."

A white-haired head poked itself over the rail of the loft. "What's this?"

Drew held up the trap by the severed chain, rabbit and all.

"Jacobowitz." The elder shook his head. "That man will never learn to leave well enough alone, just like his pappy. What's this now, the third trap?"

"Fourth, including the one I gave back," Drew answered. Three months ago he had almost stepped foot in a trap along the border of the McConnell and Jacobowitz ranches. He had confronted Bruce at his cabin, and left the trap along with a word of warning against further trespassing. Since Jacobowitz had obviously chosen to ignore him, the only positive thing that had come of that encounter had been Drew's first chance since last winter to visit with his old high school crush, Laura. She was still the same pretty, happy girl she had always been, despite night-and-day exposure to her father's venomous personality.

The old man continued to speak in a different tone of voice. "That was a fine job, sensing the rabbit's death from that far away, Drew. Combined with the way you handled the solstice ceremonies last night, I think you're prepared to officially take over as primary protector of the lands come next equinox." As if he could sense Drew's sudden bout of pride, the father added, "After that, all you'll need is a woman to be a proper man."

Drew dropped the rabbit to his side and rolled his eyes. His father had been on his case to go take a roll in the hay with a girl since his first ejaculation (as if having his father know exactly when that had occurred hadn't been embarrassing enough!). His classmates Laura and Jenny had been his father's first suggestion — both at the same time, no less, mortifying young Drew to no end — but he hadn't stopped there when Drew demurred. Drew acknowledged his duty to continue the ancient McConnell family line, but he wanted to marry someone he could live with, not just someone to incubate offspring and leave like his own mother had.

"It's not like you let me take weekends off to go look for likely prospects, Dad," Drew said peevishly. For three years now Andrew McConnell had done little more than supervise his son's stewardship over the lands, and more and more often Drew was moving proactively to care for their property rather than waiting for his father to tell him what needed doing.

Andrew let out a hmph. "A druid doesn't 'take weekends off' any more than his lands do. Besides, if you work so hard, why aren't you more in touch with the wyrd yet? Why, if you ever set your mind to actually developing yourself, you'd be a shoe-in for the Supreme Druid in about thirty years, no doubt in my mind."

"And why would I want to do that?" Drew asked.

"Why would you-" his father choked. His mouth formed words, but nothing came out until he took a deeper breath and hollered, "You and I need to have a serious talk about your priorities, young man! Why, if our ancestors of some *two thousand years* heard you talking that way about their most sacred, most revered..."

Drew let the tirade wash over him as he always did. His ancestors had forsaken Europe some time before the birth of the Christ and sailed to America based on a wyrd prophecy of doom from the most gifted druid of the times. The prophecy had been proven correct, many centuries later, when Europeans followed them to the North American continent and brought their histories with them – histories that included druids as no more than an ancient footnote of the second-century Roman Empire. So Drew McConnell and a few other landowning 'ranchers' in the West and Midwest were all that was left of the druidic way of life, and their lands were all that remained of the pure, untainted, natural magic of the druids.

"...why, I'm of half a mind to find a woman to impregnate and start all over without you!" Andrew continued to rant.

"Right," Drew said sarcastically. "Like your wedding

tackle still works at your age."

The old man glowered at Drew in the way that only older people can, brought his hand and arm over the rail, and before Drew could defend himself he found that his nipple had been crushed and twisted by no visible means.

Drew roared in pain and threw the trapped rabbit away from himself to clutch at his twisted nipple. He held his shirt away from his chest. "It's bleeding!" he gasped. He looked angrily up at his father. "You almost twisted it straight off!"

"That's what you get for doubting your father's abilities," the old man said smugly. "Speaking of which, what was it you needed me to do? A spell to preoccupy ol' Jack-Off off the lands? Or maybe to bespell his traps to keep critters away?"

"I'm tired of chasing him off our lands, and I don't want him setting even more traps to make up for poor luck on the originals," Drew said, now in a doubly foul mood. His chest was going to be sore for days if he didn't fix himself a soothing poultice soon.

"So what do you want?" his father repeated.

Drew answered succinctly: "I want to kill him."

"No."

"He deserves it!"

"No, he doesn't."

"How can you say that? He's invaded our lands and spilt blood four times now! Hunting is one thing – it returns the vivacity of the chase to the land – but trapping wastes a creature's vital energy!"

"And who taught you that?" The old man started stumping his way down the stairs, pausing only to tie his fraying brown bathrobe when his son pointedly looked at the ceiling.

"So why-" Drew started to cross his arms, then uncrossed them with a hiss when he brushed up against his injured nipple. He spoke through gritted teeth: "Why doesn't Jack-Off deserve to die?"

"I didn't say that."

"You did so, Dad!"

"No, I didn't. What I said was he didn't deserve for *you* to kill him. Death by a druid's hand is an honor."

Drew grudgingly conceded the point. Besides, he had the sheriff to worry about. Sheriff Porter was the sort of fellow who had been born with the ability to tell if a man was guilty or innocent just by looking at him, and being Jacobowitz's neighbor would surely bring the sheriff around to the McConnell Ranch asking questions. It may have been an honor for a druid to kill someone, but in this century it was an illegal honor.

"So what do you have in mind?" Drew asked.

"A plan that only an older and far more devious mind could devise," his father answered with a wily smile. He kicked aside a rug and opened the exposed trapdoor. "Bring the rabbit."

Drew did as he was told; closing the trapdoor behind him and exerting the mental strength it took to move the wool rug over the trapdoor, just in case someone came visiting at an inopportune moment. He then clambered down the last few stairs to enter the holiest place on all of the McConnell's lands.

The cellar was nearly as old as was the entire McConnell's claim. The natives had resisted the druids when they had first arrived, but their shamans' magic had been no match for the focused powers of the druids. The later Spanish conquistadors had thought to take these lands, and their muskets had failed them, too. The newly-minted Americans had tried to assert their dominance next, and the McConnells had still triumphed save for the loss of one parcel of land because of a lawyer's sleight of hand. That the Jacobowitz patriarch had stolen the McConnells' land still rankled three generations later, but there was little they could do about it: nature magic held no sway over such ephemeral ideas as laws and lies.

The fact that his father had come down to the cellar told Drew he meant business. The cellar was no more than rough clay walls and sand floor, but its contents made it the holiest and most powerful spot on the claim. The ancient McConnell who had claimed these lands had planted concentric groves of oak and hazel around this very spot, and as the trees had grown the druids had encouraged them to grow taproots to this cellar.

Not only were there roots from all the sacred trees above them, but in jars on clay shelves all around the room there were seeds from every single type of plant that grew on the McConnell Ranch. There were bones and exoskeletons from all the animals and insects, too. There was water jarred from streams and ponds and rain, as well as soil and stone from every corner of the ranch. Even lightning and wind had been caught in carefully prepared jars, though those needed to be refreshed every solstice. Everything of which the land was embodied resided in this room within easy reach of its druidic caretakers, each ready to lend its vital energies at need.

Drew's father had gathered several jars from the shelves, and was arranging them in a pattern on the floor, drawing in the sand between the jars with an oak wand as he went.

"Take the rabbit out of the trap, place her in the middle of the room, then get off the sand," Andrew commanded.

"Yes, Father." Drew had felt the difference in the old man's presence from before he spoke. Far from the irascible old geezer he had been talking with upstairs, Drew was now in the presence of a druid acting in his most awesome capacity as his land's protector.

Drew watched from the step as the spell's intricacy grew jar by jar, line by line, connection by connection. His grasp of druidic magic was no match for his father's lifetime of experience, but he was catching up quickly enough that he had a general grasp of what his father was going to do by the time he actually did it.

When he had finished his setup, Andrew McConnell held the wand in both hands like a knight with a sword, took a deep breath to center himself, then began his spell. First swirling the oak wand around one mason jar then another, Andrew drew out the essences of various elements of his lands, morphing them into a powerful tool. In between each jar he sewed ever more complicated patterns in the air, and his steps took on the look of an intricate dance. When he was at last done with the complicated sequence, he very carefully brought the wand tip with all its pent up energies down to touch the rabbit carcass precisely on the tip of its ear.

Despite himself, Drew recoiled from the sharp sting of warped nature that his father brought about. Nature did not relish being toyed with in such ways. Growing a calf bigger was simple because calves already grew; drawing rain out of clouds that otherwise would pass overhead was not hard because clouds rained eventually. But what this spell was designed to do was unnatural. Indeed, Drew's father would likely have been unable to make it if Jacobowitz had not left himself karmatically vulnerable to its effects.

Then it was done.

Disregarding the lines he had drawn in the sand, Andrew McConnell walked over to a shelf to get a set of tweezers and an empty mason jar. He returned to the middle of the room to pluck a single hair from the rabbit's ear. He dropped it in the glass jar and screwed on the lid, then strode over to Drew and handed it to him.

Drew looked at his father's face in amazement. Despite having seen the effect before, Drew was still in awe of just how much youthful vigor a druid was engorged with when he practiced high magic. Unlike other forms of magic from the old land – sorcerers and wizards; their kind was hopefully dead and gone for good, not in hiding like the McConnells – when druids nurtured their lands, their lands nurtured them in turn.

"Take this hair and place it on Bruce's skin," Andrew instructed. "It *should* only work on him, but don't touch it yourself, just in case."

"Will this have the effect that I think it will?" Drew asked with an anticipatory smile.

"If you studied your theory properly, yes," his father grumped good-naturedly. He looked back at the dead rabbit and jars, then stomped up the steps. "Toss the carrion outside for the scavengers. And you can clean up the rest of this mess before you come upstairs, too."

◊◊◊

Drew crouched behind a log, peering into the Jacobowitz cabin. The lights had gone out more than an hour ago, but he waited still to make sure that Bruce was asleep.

Of course, Bruce was not the only person in the house. His wife had passed away many years ago, but Laura still lived with him. She rarely ever left the Jacobowitz lands at all, in fact, as her domineering father had forbidden her going into town without him. Since she lived with Bruce, Drew virtually never saw her despite their being neighbors and despite his more than casual interest in her. Drew regretted the necessity of putting Laura through the terror that she was about to experience, but he was intent on his purpose.

Silently, Drew rose and made his way toward the cabin. He felt even more off-balance than he usually did when he was not on his lands and did not have access to most of his powers because the Jacobowitz land recognized a McConnell, and it was crying out to him in a sickly, dwindling sort of way for help, all the while offering a meager trickle of power to him. It was hard to ignore, but he had to concentrate for now.

A locked front door proved little obstacle to Drew. He could not use his sort of power to unlock a lock – there was nothing of nature in such mechanisms – but he had learned how to pick locks back in high school.

The door squealed as it opened. Drew froze in place, listening for any reaction to the alarming noise. He could not hear anything after several seconds, but that did not mean that a hand was not reaching under a pillow for a revolver right now.

Though the door was not even halfway open, Drew decided to not risk a second noisemaking. He could have muffled the hinges if he had been on his own lands with full access to his powers, but that was impossible here. Instead, he had to rely on his abilities as a man. With a remarkably acrobatic feat, Drew slithered between the doorjamb and door without making a sound.

He stood up and took in the room as best he could in the meager light. Everything was silent, though any loose floorboard might give away his steps with further squeaks if he wasn't careful. The house smelled of freshly baked bread and a slight hint of the perfumed soap Laura always used. The main room where he stood was dark, with the open kitchen a little beyond it. To his left were two doors; near the kitchen was a third door – a smaller one; probably the bathroom – and one more door led out from the kitchen, likely to the back porch.

"Which door leads to whom?" Drew whispered to himself. He moved silently toward the two doors, avoiding the shadowy outlines of a couch and table here, a lamppost there, and was halfway to the doors before he received the clue for which he had been hoping: a resounding snore came from the door on the right.

"It takes a bigger nose than Laura's to make that much ruckus," Drew whispered with a smile. Unless she had a live bear in her bedroom, he had found Bruce.

Once he had reached the bedroom door, he hesitated. If

these hinges squealed on him like the front door had, he was going to have to move fast and hope that Laura did not wake up in the ensuing scuffle. In preparation, Drew took the glass jar out of the fur-lined satchel at his side, unscrewed it, and put the lid back in the satchel. Holding the open jar in his right hand, Drew grasped the doorknob, turned it, and opened the door in one swift motion.

The door made not a sound.

Despite his relief, Drew did not pause his forward motion. Without a bit of ceremony, he arrived at the bedside of Bruce Jacobowitz and dumped the rabbit hair out of the glass jar and onto Bruce's already hairy chest.

The spell took effect instantaneously, and did exactly as Andrew McConnell had directed.

◊◊◊

"Hello the cabin!"

Drew had felt the sheriff come onto his lands from the west – from town, likely – so he had had enough time to work through the worry that had gripped his heart by the time the sheriff arrived. There was more than one reason the McConnells had never suffered a road to be cut through their lands.

"Sheriff Porter!" Drew called with a friendly wave.

"Drew." The sheriff tied up his horse on the hitching post and entered the cabin at Drew's welcoming gesture. "How's things?"

"Slow," Drew replied as he shut the door. "Weather's too hot this summer for my usual clientele to be out here trompin' around the woods. I reckon business will pick back up come autumn."

"As long as we don't get a fire through here," the sheriff said.

"As long as," Drew agreed amiably. Though he could not make his lands a verdant paradise in the middle of a dozen otherwise dry ranches without drawing his neighbors' suspicions, he would never allow the drought to affect his lands that badly. "How's town?"

"In a bit of an uproar, actually. Bruce Jacobowitz's gone missing." The sheriff took off his uniform hat and hung it on the hat rack by the door. Though he had ostensibly been concentrating on his hat, he had been watching from behind his tinted spectacles for any overt reaction from Drew McConnell.

But Drew gave him nothing to work with when he nodded fully. "Rachel down at the diner filled me in on the whole thing this morning when I went to town for supplies. I tell you, Sheriff, you've got to get Rachel to be your secretary; she knows every bit of information this county has to offer."

"Well, if she knows what happened to Bruce, she ain't telling me." He removed his tinted spectacles from his nose, hung them on his breast pocket, and peered curiously at a caged rabbit sitting on the coffee table. "You keepin' pets nowadays?"

"Nah," Drew answered. "That little guy's just not quite himself. If he doesn't recover by tonight, I'm thinkin' about puttin' 'im out of his misery."

The rabbit squealed and kicked the cage, making the sheriff jump back. He chuckled at himself. "Almost like he knew what you said."

"Mayhap he did." Drew smiled, looking at the rabbit. "So what can I do for you, Sheriff?"

"I came by hoping you might have some information on Bruce, what with your bein' neighbors and all."

"Information like what?"

"Oh, any strange happenings, unusual comings and goings from his place. Anything."

"Wouldn't Laura know better?"

"I've already talked with her. I'm talking to you now. Answer the question, Drew." The sheriff's gaze had sharpened at the lack of straightforward answers.

Drew shrugged. "I don't keep Jack-o's day planner for him, and I don't go anywhere nearer his lands than I have to. I have plenty to do on my own lands without stickin' my nose in neighbors' business."

"Uh huh." Sheriff Porter was nonplussed. He pulled out a pad of paper and a pen. "When was the last time you saw Bruce Jacobowitz alive, Drew?"

Drew's countenance clouded a bit. "That sounds like an awfully formal question, Sheriff."

"I suppose it does."

"Is this a formal inquiry?" Drew pressed.

"Should I make it one?" the sheriff shot back.

Drew put his hands on his hips and exhaled noisily, yet when he spoke his voice was calm and reasonable. "Let's cut to the chase, Sheriff. You've always told me that you can smell a liar a mile away."

"That's the truth."

"Then take a good whiff o' me when I say this: I ain't killed

Bruce Jacobowitz."

The sheriff scrutinized Drew intensely, looking for any sign that he was telling an untruth. But, ever so slowly, his head nodded and he put his paper and pen away. "Alright, Drew. I believe you. I think there's something you're not telling me about Bruce, but-"

"I'll tell you, Sheriff, if you want me to," Drew said. "I'd rather not, but I don't want you thinking that I'm hiding something. That sort of doubt in the eye of the law can come back and bite a fellow in the uncomfortables."

The sheriff pulled the paper and pen back out. "Drew, we're probably dealin' with a man's life here. Now if you know something that could help, you'd best tell me right quick."

"It won't help with your search."

Sheriff Porter cocked his head. "Why don't you let me be the judge of that."

Drew shrugged his acquiescence. "Jack-Off was trapping on my lands. I've told him to keep off three times, but... well, you know how that son-of-a-monkey acts."

"Do you have proof of this?" Porter asked.

"I still have all but the first trap I found over there in that chest." Drew pointed over near the door. "The first trap I gave back, thinkin' that maybe he'd crossed over to my property by mistake."

"How can you be sure it wasn't a mistake?"

"Word around town is he's been defaulting on some debts, but since he doesn't take care of his property, he's runnin' out of things to trap on his own lands."

The sheriff frowned, and made a note. "How can you

gauge how much of what he has on his lands?"

"I don't. Bobby over at the Grocer and Furrier keeps track of what a man brings into the shop for sale. He said Jack-o's account's been on the decline for years but for a big jump in numbers over the past three months – which just so happens to be when I found that first trap."

"That still doesn't prove that he was intentionally trespassing. It's not like there's a line painted down your lands' border."

"True. And I wouldn't get too upset about a trap on our border – that's just bein' neighborly. But the last trap I found was near to smack dab in the middle of my lands. And I can't have that, Sheriff! You know that most of my yearly revenue comes from city hunters staying the weekend at my lodge. If one of them lawyer types steps his dainty little foot in a steel-jaw trap on my property..." Drew gave the sheriff a pointed look.

"Why didn't you come to me with this, Drew? I could've had a word with him."

"Not to put you down, Sheriff, but you know that a word's about as strong as water to Bruce Jacobowitz. The only thing he would respect from you or me would be a bullet. And that," Drew pointed his finger, "Sheriff, is why I didn't want to tell you about this. I didn't want that law-enforcing head o' yours ponderin' over how I had 'motive' to kill him. But you have me trapped because, again, I didn't want you thinkin' that I was hiding stuff from you, neither."

Sheriff Porter stared Drew in the eyes, and saw nothing but truth. The entire town knew Drew McConnell to be an odd bird, but he tended to be honest, and the fact that he had been willing to halfway implicate himself straight to the law's face made Sheriff Porter all the more certain that Drew was innocent. In the sheriff's experience, a man would not do something that blatant if he was not absolutely sure there was no evidence of his wrongdoing.

"Well, Drew, I still wish you would've called me in on this -- that's what you pay your taxes for, after all," the sheriff said, putting his pen and paper away once more. "We could've saved you a lot of heartache, mayhap. And if Bruce does show up, you and he and I are *going* to have a sit-down, you hear me?"

"I do." Drew nodded.

The sheriff made his way toward the door. "In the meantime, I'll take those traps off your hands."

"You're welcome to 'em. I'd been trying to figure out what to do with those for a while now; I didn't want 'em in my home, but I'd sooner eat my hat than give 'em back to Jack-o." Drew opened the chest and handed the sack to the sheriff.

"I'll be headed off, then. Say, Drew, would you do me a favor?" the sheriff asked as he put his hat back on and opened the front door.

"What's that?"

"Have a look around your lands for Bruce's body. And don't be thinkin' that I'm picking on you, now, alright? I'm gonna ask the same of George and Rory, since their lands border Bruce's. Chances are, if he was trapping that deep into your lands he was trapping on theirs, too. He may be layin' out there somewhere that nobody would think to look."

"I'll do that, Sheriff."

"Bye, now."

"See you 'round town."

Drew listened to the sound of Sheriff Porter walking down the porch steps and reclaiming his horse. He stayed by the door until he felt the Sheriff pass off his lands.

He turned to the caged rabbit and smiled.

"Well, Jack-Off, you heard. There's a search going on for you, just like I'm sure you were hoping, but that search won't turn up a thing. You saw: the Sheriff himself was right here, laid his very eyes on you, and didn't recognize you for you."

Drew came closer to the cage and sat on a stool so he could be eye-level with the rabbit. "Now, I don't know exactly what's going on in that head of yours. Maybe you're thinking this is all a nightmare; maybe you're thinking this is impossible. Well, you'd be half right: it isn't impossible, but it's a nightmare alright. It's a month-long nightmare."

The bunny was staring at Drew with an intensity that no naturally-born rabbit could manage. Drew knew he had a captive audience, and that his audience would surely have picked up on what that last sentence implicated.

"Yes, Bruce. That spell I cast on you will only last a month. At the zenith of the next full moon, you'll turn back into a man – a man with a much healthier respect for nature, I would hope.

"Of course, that transformation is predicated on your surviving for a month."

The rabbit squealed and kicked at the cage door again.

"Calm down. I'm not gonna kill you, Jack-o. In fact, I'm gonna set you free." Drew paused for a moment to let Bruce ponder his words, for the hope to well up in him, then for it to come crashing back down when he realized the implications. "Yep. I'm gonna open this cage door right outside my cabin, and I'm gonna let you run around on my lands like you've so enjoyed doing these last few months." Drew smiled spitefully. "Good luck avoiding all your own traps."

His smile went away. "Now, a word of warning, Bruce. If you do happen to survive for an entire month as a rabbit – which I don't expect you will – then you'll be coming back to a community of folks who won't believe a word of your story about a magic spell cast on you to turn you into a rabbit. A wolf, they might just think you've been reading one too many dime novels, but... a rabbit? No. No, what they're gonna think is that you ran out on your daughter for no reason you care to admit. They're gonna take that to mean you found yourself a woman somewhere, and that when she finally got to know the real you, she kicked your sorry behind out. You're gonna be persona non grata around these parts, as the Romans used to say.

"Now. *If* you're alive by the end of the month and you find yourself human again, I'll tell you what I'm gonna expect out of you.

"First, you're gonna tell everyone that you've decided to move, all sudden-like, and you've only come back to sell off your effects so you can settle your debts and buy your new home out of state.

"Second, as you're selling off everything you own, you'll sell your land to me -- *directly* to me, and for a more than generous price. I know that you know your grandfather stole that land from my grandfather in the first place, so don't even think about complaining.

"Third and finally, you're not gonna pressure your daughter to move with you. Laura could have an awful good life in this county if it weren't for your deadweight 'round her neck.

"I'll give you to the time of the moon's next wane to do as I told you." Drew leaned in close to the cage. "Or else."

Drew picked up the cage, opened the front door, and unceremoniously dumped the frightened rabbit off the side of the porch. The rabbit sat there for a moment, looking around at the world, at the ground no more than an inch away from his eyes. He took a hop in one direction, then another.

"You'd best be learning to run on four legs a little faster, Bruce," Drew said conversationally as he leaned against the rail. "There's an eagle up there eyeing you."

The rabbit bolted into the underbrush.

Drew erupted in laughter and walked back inside.

"As enjoyable as that was to listen to," Andrew McConnell called down from where he lay in his bed in the loft, "I'm afraid I have to rate your little homework assignment a B minus."

"What now, Dad?" Drew asked exasperatedly.

"You left a thread loose. According to your instructions, Bruce can't take his daughter with him."

"And?"

"And he's selling us our land back, finally."

"So?"

"So where's his daughter supposed to go?"

Drew smiled slightly. "Who says she has to go anywhere?"

There was a rustle of bed sheets, and a moment later

Andrew's tousled head popped over the loft balcony to peer down at his son. What he saw softened his countenance to a look of great pride. "Well then, son." He nodded his paternal blessing without a further word.

◊◊◊

"Laura? You home?"

Drew took his time tying Frey up to the hitching rail, trying to give Laura any extra time she needed to tidy the house or make herself more presentable. His horse didn't need to be tied up, but whenever Drew went visiting other humans, he played by their rules. Tying Frey up was a small price to pay if it helped him fit in better.

Laura still had not come to the door, so he fiddled with Frey's saddle a bit, loosening the straps. It was late for a social call – the sun was near to setting at his back as he had ridden to the Jacobowitz lands – so she probably wasn't prepared at all. But Drew's delay tactic gave just enough time for Laura to open the front door to him.

"Drew McConnell!" Laura exclaimed, fist against hip. "I haven't seen you in a coon's age!"

The stress of the past few days was obvious in Laura's puffy eyes and her reddened nose, but Drew still found her a beautiful and welcoming sight, as always. He smiled. "Laura. It's good to see you, too."

"Now, I didn't say that it was *good* to see you," Laura said with a twinkle in her eye and a shake of her finger.

Drew laughed.

Laura waved her arm. "Get yourself up inside, Drew. I've

got a jug o' sweet tea brewin' on the back porch with your name on it."

In short order, Drew and Laura were sitting on a couch in the main room with glasses of tea and a plate of freshly baked cookies, chatting away.

"So why *don't* I see you more often, Drew?" Laura asked lightly. "I always thought you and me were more than just neighbors."

Drew winced slightly.

"What's wrong?" Laura asked, this time sounding serious. "Do you... do you know something about Daddy?"

"It's not that. I'm sorry, Laura," Drew said contritely. "I never expected to have to bring this up with you at all, and the timing makes it even worse. ...How much do you know about your Daddy's trapping business?"

"Not much," she admitted.

Drew nodded. "Not to go into detail, but he's been trapping on other people's property to make up for lost revenue. That's sort of got him in hot water with those who've figured it out." He intentionally did not name himself one of the wronged parties to avoid the tension that would add to the situation. "Sheriff Porter dropped by my cabin and asked me to look around my lands to see if your Daddy had got himself hurt somewhere that nobody would think to look for him. He says he's asking Rory and George to do the same. They may have better luck than I did."

Laura bit her lip and nodded. "Thank you, Drew. And thanks for coming to see me despite all that."

"Hey, I'm not the type to leave a damsel in distress," Drew said gallantly.

"I know that. You've always looked after me, even way back in grade school." She smiled. "Is that why you came by? Just checking in on me?"

"Actually, I was gonna ask if you needed anything from town – I know it's hard for you to get down there without your Daddy, and with him gone I thought you might be running low on a few things."

"That's mighty considerate of you, Drew," Laura said.

"But," Drew added, "now I'm not so sure I want to make that offer."

Laura looked like she was expecting to be hit. "Why's that?"

"Because I don't think that would be good enough."

She shook her head. "I don't understand."

Drew hesitated again, then said, "Can I speak plainly with you on a delicate subject, Laura?"

She set her tea glass on the table. "Of course, Drew."

"Now, I don't mean to alarm you, but you know how the grapevine works in these parts. I'm sure everybody already knows that you're living here on your own, without your Daddy to look after you. And some types might try to take advantage of that fact, if you take my meaning."

"I've been sleeping with Daddy's revolver on the nightstand every night," Laura admitted with a nervous little laugh.

"That's good," Drew praised her. "I'm thankful to hear you've prepared yourself. Still, I'd hate for anyone to force you into finding out whether or not you have it in you to pull a trigger. You're a sweet girl, Laura – sweeter than sweet tea," he toasted Laura with his tea glass and took a sip before continuing, "and I'd hate to see you lose a single drop of that gentle nature."

"What are you saying, Drew?"

"What I'd like you to do is come live where I can keep an eye on you. Nothing improper," Drew said hastily at the startled look in Laura's eyes. "I don't mean in my cabin. But my hunting lodge is completely vacant until autumn, and you're more than welcome there. You'd be far enough away from me that folk won't gossip, but close enough so that if someone comes onto my lands and heads your way I'll know it, and I can drop by for 'a friendly visit' shortly thereafter."

"That's awful nice of you, Drew," Laura said slowly. She looked around the house. "But what if Daddy comes home and finds me gone?"

"Leave a note tacked to the door," Drew said. "You and I can ride into town, too, and let everyone know where you'll be for the duration – town's a lot closer to my place than it is to here. In fact, I think I'm gonna stable Frey's sister Freyja at the lodge with you, so you can ride her into town any time you like."

Laura blinked, as if the concept had never occurred to her. "Any time?"

"Well," Drew amended, "if you go on a shopping trip at midnight I doubt it would be too productive, but yeah, any time." Laura laughed, and Drew smiled, then he made his face as sincere as he could make it. "You're your own woman, Laura; you can make your own decisions. And staying at the lodge is one such decision – I'm not gonna force you a smidgen. In fact," Drew set his tea on the table as he stood, "I think I'm gonna head on my way right now and leave you to think. I'll drop by tomorrow after you've had time to consider." He took a step toward the door.

Laura hurriedly jumped up and grabbed his hand to turn him back around, surprising him. "Actually, would you mind stayin' for supper?"

"Would I mind?" Drew looked incredulous. "Would I *mind* having a proper meal that my father hasn't somehow both undercooked and burnt?"

She laughed. "You can take some home with you, too, then. Shoot, you'd be doing me a favor: I already have three nights worth of leftovers still in the ice box, and if you hadn't come over, I'd have a fourth simmerin' away on the stove right now. I..." she paused, blushed, and cast her eyes downward. "I guess I just don't know how to cook for one person."

Drew squeezed her hand. "It sounds like we're each the answer to the other's problem."

Laura met his eyes once more, and Drew could see the slight change in how she looked at him. "Yeah," she said in a revelatory sort of tone. "I suppose we are at that." Slowly, hesitantly, she stepped forward, tucked her arms around his waist, and placed her head gently on his chest. "Thanks for looking after me, Drew. You always have, for whatever reason."

"I always will, Laura." Drew enfolded her with his arms. "And I sincerely hope that you already know the reason."

LORDS OF HEAVEN AND EARTH

Jaym Gates

Super-House engines roaring to life, the Nidhogg shook himself loose from temporary hibernation and stretched his wings. The shockwave flattened the sagebrush and sparse, dry grass. The power stored from a week of hard flight surged through the systems. Lights blinked on, startling red in the colorless sunlight. The non-launch crew grumbled and pulled blankets over their heads.

Outside, the launch crew went through the barely-familiar routine of pre-flight checklists. Well, the practice itself was familiar. It was the Nidhogg who jumbled their routine with all of his new tech and organic modifications.

"We're all clear!" yelled Technomancer Williams. She battened down a final clip and hopped off of the wings. "Wings are cleared for take-off."

She wiped her hands on her breeches and stepped into the cargo bay. "There's some frayed silk on the inner sub-seven. Should last till Atlanta, but we better replace it then."

Captain Scott Janus nodded and drew an orange X on a large diagram taped to the wall. Only one other X, a yellow one on a tail-joint, marred the hand-drawn blueprint of a classic Nidhogg.

"Should get someone to draw a new 'gram," said Williams. "There's so much stuff on him that isn't here, we're going to miss something."

"Got a hand with art?"

"Nope." She shrugged. "Plenty of old techs who do, though."

"You want to let people in on his secrets? 'Sides, it would take months for someone to figure him out even a little. Not even sure who'll be able to do the repairs. We need to get an in-house mechanic."

She shrugged again and took a seat in front of the tech console. "Someone's going to find out, sooner or later."

Janus stepped onto the lowered deck. The early-morning sun blinded him for a moment, until the inner-eye shields slid dark. "Best biosci invention ever," he muttered.

He walked around the Nidhogg. He'd captained Dracul before, the massive half-tech, half-organic warships, but never a Nidhogg. His experience was with the quicksilver Fireflies, the serpent-sleek Sheshas, the half-feral Amalindas. Never a Nidhogg, especially not one like Prometheus.

Gun-metal scales shone with silky softness, even smudged and scratched from the long, grueling flight. The sinuous neck flung upwards, loosening joints and cogs and bones in a flurry of creaks and clicks.

"Good morning, captain," said the Nidhogg, lowering his head.

"Good morning, Prometheus." Janus checked Williams' work. He trusted her implicitly. She'd been flying with him since their first classless mongrel-flyer, back during the Rising.

She knew the Dracul, inside and out. She would check his work, too.

Never too careful. Not with the Dracul. Not with a prize like Prometheus.

The guns had to be triple-checked. The facial armor had to be applied, and strapped down. Lights had to be double-checked, engines and wings checked every time someone turned around. Gears and cogs, intake systems, neural monitors. Claw and landing systems. Thousands of tiny parts, both mechanical and organic.

And the eyes. Eyes, eyes, eyes. The eyes couldn't be checked often enough. Dust or grit sliding beneath the ten-layer silk and crystal shields could blind the Dracul. A blinded Dracul would crash within minutes. That was their one failing. Though their sensors and radars were more advanced than any warship on earth, sea or sky, the Dracul were still too organic, too easily panicked by blindness.

Janus had been in one of those panicked behemoths. Aeternitas, the Grandship, the Flying Fortress, King of the Skies, The Second. Janus had watched Aeternitas, blinded by acid, claw his eyes out.

Remembered wheeling, falling, wailing.

He and the remaining crew had parachuted to safety and watched as their beautiful, mighty Dracul fell helplessly to shatter on the shores of the Salt Lake. They had laid there and watched Vritra, the rogue organic Dracul, melt the metal exoskeleton around Aeternitas's organic core. They'd watched, helpless, as Vritra encased Aeternitas in a useless shell of warped gears and singed silk.

They'd trekked to Salt Lake City, on foot, in the

summertime heat, to look for a mage. All of the mages were in Denver, protecting the walls from the Texans. The crew had stolen a mongrel flyer and flown to Carson City. The mage could only kill Aeternitas. There was no saving him.

Janus remembered that death, more clearly than any other moment of his life. The days, the nights. Quivering, grinding creaks of ruined metal. Flaring arcs of wild energy as Aeternitas' power railed uselessly against Vritra's subtle rape. Aeternitas wailed and wept, voice human and something far older, far more heart-wrenching.

By the end, in the silence left by that last, agonized wail, even the mage had wept. The captain, clinging to the wreckage of the Dracul's head, shot herself before the echo of the scream had faded.

Janus wiped the outer eye-shield with an oiled rag, lost in his memories. He missed Aeternitas. The ancient Dracul, battle-scarred and mighty, had carried them through the Rising. He had turned the course of the battle and saved the West Coast from Imperial Rule.

Even Prometheus did not have the weight of presence, the power of the old serpent.

Janus flicked a grit of sand out of the corner of the eye. It swiveled, focused on him. Janus smiled, weakly.

"Everything feel good?" he asked the Nidhogg.

The great eye blinked, once. The signal for yes. Though Dracul emotion could not be read through their eyes, they projected well. Tentative concern prodded him. Prometheus could not speak while Janus was clinging to his face. Too easy for the human to fall to the ground.

"I'm okay," Janus replied. "I'm okay."

Janus climbed down and Prometheus shook his head carefully, testing the tightness of the straps.

"Tighter on the nose-line," the navigator said over the PA. "It's chafing at one of the visual sensors."

Janus climbed back up the rigging and tightened a strap of leather wider than his thigh.

"He says we're good!"

Prometheus lowered his head to the ground, allowing Janus to clamber down. He patted the Nidhogg on the cheek and jogged back to the hold.

"Batten down the hatches," he said. "Let's get to a real way-station tonight."

◊◊◊

The wastelands of New Mexico stretched away to the mountains, painted black and white by the young sun above them. Prometheus paused for a moment in the harsh white sun, his organic tongue flickering, taking in the subtle, myriad scents of his world.

"Preparing for launch sir," the navigator reported, and Janus strapped himself in as the thrusters under the engines began to roar.

"You've got that shit-eating grin again sir," the technician said.

"Always gonna," he said, and flipped a switch to seal the cabin doors. "No way this can get old."

Intercontinental flights had been obsolete by the time Janus was born. Their national unity becoming a distant wish, and the threat of failing fuel resources, life in America had shifted back to a more local pattern. Gradually, the coasts established their own empires, and the rest were left to fend for themselves.

Besides that, new and frightening things haunted the earth, and there were times when technology went abruptly hay-wire without warning or recourse. Staying close to home became more attractive every day.

The images of those old jets had appealed to Janus as a young boy. His grandfather had flown some of the last fighters, before fuel became more precious than blood. Janus grew up with stories of the thrill, the danger. It was in his blood, and captaining a Dracul was more than he had ever imagined it to be.

The new era had brought challenges that threatened to shut technology down forever, reducing the majority of the world to third-world status. But pockets of resources remained, and these became the locus for war after war. Instead of trying to find a way to expand those resources, to better life, humanity did what it had always done: it expended the last bit of known resources to create bigger, better war-machines.

Prometheus and his fellow Dracul were the pinnacle of those war-machines. Genetic engineering had failed. Brutal, uncontrollable monsters were the eventual result of any tinkering. But the Apocalypse—as everyone referred to it now—had brought them one thing: myth. The myths were too powerful to subdue, too unique to clone, too intricate to tinker with. But many of them were caught in decaying, starving bodies that were too big to be supported by an ecosystem that was struggling to survive.

The dragons taught the humans how to exploit them. It was their only chance to survive. Humanity gained terrifying new weapons, and the dragons lived.

The Dracul had been born from necessity of man and beast. Flying war-machines, blended from the finest meld of beast and machine. Metal beasts equipped with intelligence, with cunning and emotion and loyalty.

Taking off in Prometheus must be like the pre-Apocalypse jets had been, or so Janus imagined. The chassis shook from the power flooding through it; the control panel twinkled and glittered as he and Prometheus ran through diagnostics and system checks.

But Janus didn't think the old jets opened their mouths to roar happily as they took off. He didn't think the old jets would zig-zag through the air like a puppy chasing a ball, just because they could.

Prometheus finished playing and set his course for Bloomington, New Texas Republic, and Janus realized that he was laughing.

In a perverse way, he was glad for the Apocalypse. It had opened his skies.

◊◊◊

The lights of Bloomington flickered uncertainly on the horizon, shrouded by the fog rising off the bay. The continental upheaval that had broken America in half had spared the little town, and brought more oil to the surface. The New Texas Bay provided port for ships laden with supplies that could be trucked overland to Santa Fe or Denver, the only thing that kept those cities in contact with the outside world.

"We've been given permission to land sir," Morgan reported, punching a button on the console. The navigator, recently transferred from a decommissioned Amalinda, still had the tremor of uncertainty in her voice.

Janus nodded. "Prometheus, set a landing pattern for East Field according to coordinates."

An agreeable hiss of static answered him and the wings shifted. The Super-House engines slowed, and the Nidhogg lowered, sweeping along the runway. Wind-generators spun backwards to create drag and steam-thrusters slowed his headlong rush. With a jolt, his feet connected to the ground. His wings tilted. Broad-side to the wind, the huge sheets of metal and engineered steel-silk braked him as he galloped down the runway.

A final shift, the wings folded and tucked gently to the side, and the Nidhogg stood calmly, steaming from the exhaust ports as his engines powered down.

"Well done crew, well done Prometheus," Janus said, and unfastened his seat-belts.

Technicians and orderlies came running with their scanning gear. Landing at any officially-recognized way-station required a full set of diagnostics and scans, and Prometheus submitted to them with bored gentility.

"Super-House class Nidhogg Prometheus III certified clean ma'am," a technician reported to his supervisor.

The woman nodded and raised her radio. "Hangar C, prepare to house Super-House Nidhogg Prometheus III," she ordered.

"There anyone else here tonight?" Janus asked the

woman, climbing down the ladder. Williams would take Prometheus into the hangar to be unharnessed and tended. Janus had paperwork to fill out. He felt so very fortunate, in a certain irked sort of way. At least there were still way-stations that could require paperwork. Most of them, like the one that they had planned to stay at the night before, had been burned out by Apophis and Vritra.

"We've got twenty Fireflies on permanent station," the administrator replied, "and Veles landed two days ago. He'll stay until the damage to his wings is repaired."

"Rogues?"

"Yeah, some new nuisance out of the mountains. Pirates captured an Amalinda breeder a few years ago, seem to be breeding some weird variant, probably with Apophis. Now they want a

Nidhogg I guess. All the cities have pulled theirs back, doubled their escorts."

Janus sighed. There were simply too few of the larger classes of dragon still in the control of the city-states. There were plenty of Fireflies and Amalindas, smaller and weaker creatures that had bred indiscriminately in the hidden places for decades.

But the Dracul—the Nidhoggs, the Tanises, the Sheshas—these were rare, beyond priceless. As new territorial lines were drawn in America, the Dracul were becoming even more desirable.

The highest, most delicate inter-state government contracts weren't made in money or goods, but in the hours of service one government's Dracul could provide to the other. Since the creatures were alive and sentient, yet another level of complexity layered into the equation. Entire branches of government had sprung up around the politics and rights of the Dracul.

And here he was, the captain of a Nidhogg with no alliance or allegiance.

"Your life is about to get a whole lot more dangerous, captain," the supervisor said. "Belynda was struck down a few months ago during an attack on Atlanta, and repairs are rumored to be impossible. Have to create a new frame for her. You are the only free agent on the east coast, and nobody knows where you are, so word will spread like wildfire, especially in that behemoth."

Janus groaned, following her into the office. "Do me a favor, don't report me until you absolutely have to. I'm already worried about making it back there in one piece."

"Got it. I'll lose the paperwork for a few weeks. Firefly kits steal enough of it on their own."

Janus grinned, but paperwork was suddenly the least of his worries. Like a pretty girl at a dance, everyone would be trying to seduce them to their side now...or kill them.

◊◊◊

Veles, a smaller variant of the Nidhogg class, snored. Captain Allie Iglesias sat on the beast's metal nose, her bare feet swinging gaily between his nostrils. Janus met the captain's eyes, and they erupted in a fit of laughter.

"Haven't been able to convince him to leave it off," the captain admitted ruefully. A petite woman in her late forties, Allie was a top pilot and an activist for Dracul rights and privileges. "Drives me bloody fucking nuts, so he'll keep it up."

Laughter sparkled in her brown eyes, a welcome relief from the subdued mood that had followed them east. Allie still wore her pretty floral skirts and white blouses and grease around her nails, looking just like the girl he'd met in the Academy.

Janus laughed, knowing well that Prometheus would do the same if he thought of it. "Still basing in Margate?" he asked, following her to the back of the hangar.

He paused by the burnished copper-tone scales the Nidhogg's head. Veles twitched an eyelid and peered fuzzily at the intruder for a moment before the snoring resumed. The noise shook the entire hangar and vibrated the ground under Janus's feet.

"Nah, got too dangerous there. New boy, name of Kai. Got some big ideals about rivaling Atlanta and Philadelphia, but some weird-ass religious leanings that aren't making him any friends. He's a vicious little prick." Allie was nearly yelling to be heard above the rumble.

"The Kendalls are gone?"

"Jordan's dead, Devin's holed up in a rebel camp with Jordan's daughter and about a hundred refugees. City's primarily underground now, had some really bad disasters."

"Any Dracul in Margate to watch out for?"

Her lips thinned. "Rumor is, Apophis and Vritra stop in there sometimes. But, no room for a Drac in city limits anymore, too dangerous outside."

"I'd been planning to take cargo from Houston to Margate on the way east."

Allie caught his arm with such force that he swung

around, staring at her. "What?"

"I need the money if we're going to survive in Atlanta."

"Keep him as far away from Margate as you can, or you're gonna find yourself and your beastie slaves to Kai."

"But there's nothing between Dallas and the East that's safe."

"Anything's safer than Margate right now darlin'," she said, shaking her head. "Apophis and Vritra've got free rein out there now, with Veles and Belynda grounded."

"Texas is going to get cut off if Margate isn't safe for travel."

"Veles and I are going west," she said, "soon as he's mended, to open a way-station between here and Denver. The West's got all Organics, and the supplies to keep them in the air. Denver's been isolated from the east for so long that they're sending a squad down to help us hold it open. Wouldn't hurt to switch back to Western support. The East is getting hairy."

◊◊◊

They ate dinner together that evening, musing about the Rising and the years since. They had been flying together, he training a young Sheshas, and she providing support and guidance with Veles. They were the ones who had overheard the rumor of a wildly-advanced Nidhogg in Mexican control. A simple campfire tale at a waystation on one of their long flights.

A simple tale that had turned into a three-year mission, the death of a Sheshas and twenty long-term crewmembers, and the loss of everything that Janus had worked so hard to build.

Janus told Allie as much of their adventure as he could remember, from the first sight of Prometheus to the challenge of fighting the reclusive Southwestern vigilantes.

"We're all that's left," Janus said. "An army went with us to get Prometheus, and they all got killed, except for a few Dracul who are still recovering in the West. But it wasn't even the Mexicans that hurt us. Was the damned Revelators."

"Was it worth it?" asked Allie.

"The Mexicans have the deserts, and mountains. I don't even know how long the Organics have been awake, but the Mexicans know how to take care of them, how to grow them. Prometheus... I don't know where they got him. But they treated him well."

"Why'd he come with you? More money in Mexico," Allie asked. "They treated him good." She poured them a little more whiskey.

"He said he was bored, wanted to go home. He wanted to fight, but they were keeping him grounded until they were done shaping him."

As the evening progressed, the topics grew darker, slipped back to the days of the Red Sun—a time now only myth to most of them—and the changing of the world since then.

Cheered by the rare opportunity to talk to a fellow captain, especially one of the few who had run Draculs as long as he had, it was almost dawn before Janus said goodbye.

Allie caught his arm again as he prepared to leave. "Two of the Kendalls are still alive Janus. Bad blood between us now, so they won't have Veles, but they need a Dracul bad."

"Thought Margate wasn't safe?"

"Isn't. Stay *out*! But Jordan left a daughter before he died, a hell of a little war-witch if I'm not mistaken. Devin's not worth a shit, he's broken and done. If Margate's going to be retaken, got to be her. Prometheus is..." She hesitated, turned away. "No, forget it."

He caught her arm. "Forget what? What have you found out about him?"

"Just take him to Angel's Crest. Keep him away from Margate, from the big cities. He's a pawn to them. He'd be a god to the refugees."

"You told me to keep Prometheus out of trouble."

"I told you not to be stupid. You've been gone for a long time, Janus. America's still tearin' apart at the seams. These ain't the times to stay out of trouble. You've got the best thing there is in the skies, use that power, 'cause the gods aren't gonna help save our asses."

"But a girl? How old is she?"

"Twelve, and an older soul I've never met. Try her, Janus. See if they've got the heart left. They need help."

Janus laughed until his stomach hurt. "Allie, are we talking about the same clan? The Kendalls. Black Jack and Ax, the worst gangsters and madmen of our generation? Vicious to the bone, all of 'em, the daughter can't be any better. Why do you want them taking the city again?"

"Because they may be criminals and hell-sons, but they know the place. They're magicians. We need Margate open, Janus. We need the Kendalls there. It's cursed ground, and they know better than anyone how to keep it alive. If Kai's got it, Hydra's got it, and that means that Apophis and Vritra will be able to take over the continent, given enough time."

Janus studied her for a long few minutes. "I trust you, Allie. I owe you. We'll go into the Wilds, get around Margate if we can. Where are we aiming?"

"A place called Hungry Valley. Valley's all weird, but there's landing space on some of the ridges. The Kendalls are on Angel's Crest, above the valley." She rummaged through her gear, pulling out a notebook and jotting down numbers and directions. "Here's your path. Stay out of the cities, fly high, watch out for Organics."

He put the paper in his pocket and kissed her cheek. "Safe flights for you and Snore."

Allie laughed. "You too," she said, and watched as he returned to his Nidhogg.

"And may the gods protect you from him," she whispered.

◊◊◊

Prometheus was alone when Janus came back.

"Change of plans," said Janus, waving the paper.

The Nidhogg lowered his massive head, settling it near his captain with a metallic clatter. "We will not be flying to the east?" he asked, the auditory translator echoing a touch in the warehouse.

Janus shook his head. "Allie said there's something up north. Wants us to go offer help."

"You trust her?"

"Always have. Margate's been taken by some cult, Kendalls are gone. Since that's somewhat important to the trade in the area..."

Prometheus blinked, acknowledging. "We must take back the city."

"You don't mind then? There's danger. Too many Organics out there to be sure we'll make it. And pirates. Vritra."

An alien ripple passed across the metallic face, through the robotic eyes. "And storms, accidents, frightened people, politics, other Dracul, assassins, coups and skies only know what else," teased Prometheus. "It's all rather thrilling, really."

After twenty-plus years of working with the Dracul, Janus had thought himself immune to their surprises, yet Prometheus continually surprised him. On impulse, he pressed his hand to the scaled nose and grinned.

"You're just an old Victorian adventurer in a dragon's body, aren't you? Alright brother, we'll see this one out together."

"Will the rest of the crew come?"

Shrugging, Janus opened the access door and stuck his head inside, looking for his gear-bag. "They will if they want a job."

Prometheus's laugh startled Janus into cracking his head on the doorway. Rubbing his head, Janus backed out and glared at Prometheus. "What?"

"Adventure! Fear, fire, foes! We might even miss tea!" said Prometheus. He laughed again, a deep rumble of shifting metal.

Janus shook his head. "And here I thought that they'd neglected your education."

Together, they laughed, and the walls vibrated.

"What's so funny?" Williams asked, coming into the

hangar with the navigator and two other crew-members.

"Have a seat, and our brave Captain will tell you everything," Prometheus announced in stentorian tones. He rolled his head, slinking it close to Morgan. "But beware, for this is not a tale for the weak of heart."

Morgan and Williams blinked and looked from Prometheus to Janus, who was choking on his laughter.

Janus shrugged. "Don't ask me, he started it."

Prometheus swung his head to Janus. "There captain, they are ready for you to talk."

"I'll bet they are," he muttered.

Looking vastly pleased with himself, Prometheus settled into a resting position, his nose propped on the floor.

And when the rest of the crew arrived, Janus did talk.

◊◊◊

Bloomington faded in the distance as Prometheus set a course according to the coordinates Allie had given them. Settling into a flight-path high in the heavy clouds, Prometheus dampened every heat signature possible and drifted silently through the sky, riding the air currents.

The only chance they had was to disappear off the map. So Bloomington Air worked with them as if they were flying to Dallas, and then slipped them all the help she could on the side. They had registered a false flight-path at Bloomington, and hugged it until they were out of radar reach.

A sweeping turn, a thrust of power sent a shock-wave through the air, and Prometheus was off to the north.

Janus unstrapped from his seat and went into the

weapons-bay. Allie and the Administrator had sold or given him every weapon they could scrounge, leaving themselves with just enough to ward off an attack.

Everything from buckshot for Prometheus to heavy artillery for the rebels was stashed here, giving them another reason to avoid detection. An unregistered Dracul with this much weaponry would be summarily disabled and both Dracul and captain court-marshaled. The patrols did still run the routes, quick fleets of Fireflies slipping from rock to hill, under the eaves of forests and wrapped in clouds.

Janus checked weapons bindings, nodded at the gunners, and went to the bunks. Williams had found an old war-witch, Michelle Henderson, at the base, and hired her for the journey. Janus sought her out now to ask about the danger of the Organics.

"She's sleeping sir," Morgan said, drawing him aside. "She's been through some rough things getting here."

Janus raised his eyebrows and led the way to the common room.

"She was Belynda's war-witch for a few years, came to a disagreement with the captain and left. I'd say she feels responsible for Belynda's failure."

"She tell you this?"

Morgan shook her head. "The Administrator did. Michelle was on her way back from a stint in Denver studying the Organics when she heard about Belynda. Apparently she was sick for weeks."

"As long as she can fight now."

Morgan grinned. "That, and better. She's one of the foremost human experts on the Organics."

"We'll need that," said Janus.

◊◊◊

"Looks to be about ten of them, hatchlings probably sir," Williams reported. The unmanned drone—barely larger than a crow—buzzed through the rocky outcroppings below and gave the crew a visual of the pride of young Organics basking in the white sun.

"Prometheus, can you see this?"

An agreeable static hiss.

"Any ideas?"

A less-agreeable static hiss, and Prometheus's voice came over the line. "The dominant males in the area are mostly sons of Apophis, the females are ferals, equivalent to the Chumana. These won't be able to fly probably, although they run fast."

"Then we're in Organic territory for sure."

"We've been in Organic territory since we set wing out of Bloomington," Prometheus snapped. "The Dracul do not claim territory, but the Organics snap up every bit they can."

The edge in Prometheus's voice sent a chill through Janus. "Will you be able to tell if there's a dangerous Organic within range? Before it hits us I mean?"

The static hiss again, equivalent of a shrug. "Depends on the Organic. Apophis and Vritra can be in the middle of a city, and you'll only know it if they get careless."

Janus looked at the screen again as panic filled him for a brief moment. What had possessed him to come out here? There wasn't any back-up, no one to receive a distress signal.

The Organics loved collecting Dracul parts in their hoards, and humans were delicacies.

"Get hold of yourself, Captain," warned Prometheus. "If there's a chance of making it past Margate, I'm it."

Damn the creature for reading him so well, thought Janus, but he nodded. "Of course. Keep high, power down everything that you can to avoid detection. Silent sonar on."

Gears and engines whined around him, screens shutting off. The drone remained on-screen, an eerie white glow cast around the cabin. As they left the immature Organics behind, Janus saw one young male, larger than the others, raise his head to peer at the sky, his blue throat startling even in the washed-out light of the sun. Vritra's child. His throat burned at the thought of that treacherous, beautiful serpent.

"Stay high Prometheus, and watch out for storms. Vritra has been around."

Another static hiss, and the super-house swung upwards.

◊◊◊

The weather worsened throughout the day. Lightning flickered against Prometheus's sides, the feeds showing blue light webbing his metal skin. Heavy winds on the plains finally forced the navigator to recall the drone, leaving them ground-blind, although the rain had reduced visibility to a few feet, even for the drone.

The gunners readied the weapons, afraid to load them prematurely in the wild weather and everyone sat tensely on the edge of their seats. Only Prometheus seemed undisturbed. His engines never caught, no static filled the lines.

Hours later, Janus sent the drone back below into the lightening rain. The winds had subsided and lightning no longer touched down. A visual of the area showed them flying to the east of the burned-out husk of Oklahoma City, tornadoes riffling through the wreckage like abandoned puppies. The city had been one of Vritra's first conquests, his nest for years before he became a prime target of every city-state and alliance on the east coast. Now the shell of the city was a hellish wasteland, haunted with thousands of ghosts and throttled by the captive storms Vritra always wrapped around his territory.

Prometheus veered a little farther east to avoid the city. Nestlings still squatted there, squabbling over territory in a strange, endless turf-war.

"Captain, we've got a sighting!" Morgan called a few hours later, punching buttons on the console. The drone-feed magnified and Janus leaned over. A red blip in the corner indicated that Prometheus was paying attention too.

Long and serpentine, a white and blue Organic slithered through the air. No wings sprouted from her back—and the delicacy of her horns clearly indicated a female—yet she rode the air and storm with an ease that even Prometheus must have envied.

"A Sheshas 'broodmare' sir," Michelle said, startling Janus. He cleared room for her at the console. "The red along her back, a sign that she has young and is not available to the males."

"Is she dangerous?" asked Janus as the sleek Organic coiled up on herself and surveyed the plains.

Michelle nodded. "She can be. The males have huge territories and will defend those, but a broodmare settles on her territory as soon as she can defend it, and never leaves."

The Organic looked sky-ward and the drone slipped close enough that a blue tongue could be seen flickering as she tasted the air.

"Vritra is rare for his kind sir," the witch said. "Most of them will defend territory, but not attack like he does. Unless she feels we pose a threat..."

"Load weapons!" Janus roared into the intercom, "We've got an Organic coming at us, broodmare class Sheshas!"

"Sir wait!" the witch cried, catching his arm. "Don't fire yet, she may simply be curious. Organics seldom care if another passes through their territory."

"She could inform Vritra."

Michelle shook her head. "Not likely sir, the breeders have little to do with the warriors, and barely speak to the kings. This one is young. No more than a concubine to a warrior at best. Vritra's queens are the only ones you would have to worry about. But if you killed her, it would be known by every Organic in the nation."

"Hold fire till order," Janus said, reluctant, and focused on the screen again. He marveled as the female slipped through the air, climbing without visible aid. She really was a thing of exquisite beauty—all of the Sheshas were—and deceptively delicate.

She broke through the clouds a few hundred feet west of Prometheus and he slowed a bit. His head dipped, a submissive pose. She ruffed a little, a thin white membrane half standing around her head, warning him off, but offered no further challenge. In fact, as they moved through her territory, she began playing with the huge Nidhogg, looping her long body around him and nipping at his metal sides.

Steadfastly ignoring her invitation to play, Prometheus kept steady and she soon grew bored, leaving them alone in the sky again as she plummeted towards the ground in a free-fall, pulling up scant feet from the earth and whipping off in another direction.

Mesmerized by her acrobatics, the crew lost a little of their fear. "She's stunning!" Morgan cried as the female skimmed along the river, raising plumes of water.

"And those love-nips she gave your beast would have crushed a man into pulp," Michelle reminded them. "She probably doesn't know about the Dracul, and be grateful for that."

The flight-path required nearly a day's flight to detour a safe distance around Margate. Without way-stations or friendly outposts—Apophis *had* succeeded in razing this part of the country—Prometheus conserved every bit of fuel he could. Lights were kept low, crew-members layered on whatever clothing they had as the temperatures dropped. The wind-collectors hissed and hummed, feeding raw energy into the converters. Prometheus set his wings and glided through day and night, keeping his pace slow enough to detect any threats.

The hours stretched endlessly, the crew clustered around the instrument panels, the guns, the heat-vents.

"The land is angry," Michelle whispered suddenly, sometime in the night. "Its rulers have been cast out, its soul is corrupted, ravening dragons rule it. It bears man no sweet will."

Williamson shivered, her eyes glued to the screens showing the ground. "What could the land do?" she asked, "It's just...land."

Michelle laughed and laughed, and finally patted Williamson's hand disdainfully. "Oh child, the land is the true Queen here. She always has been. That's why America died. That's why the world died. She got tired of us."

Janus shook his head. "We're not touching down here anyways. Nothing friendly in this quarter on land or air."

And as the white sun rose, stripping away the soft illusions and rest of night, the skies did indeed become unfriendly.

"Sir, there's something big over to the east. Organic I think."

Prometheus hissed assent, altering his course to the west.

"Ready weapons," said Janus, and turned to Michelle. "Well?"

Her eyes were already closed, her right hand slightly raised. As he watched, her lips parted, her tongue flickering at the air. He shivered, seeing the resemblance to the Organics she had studied for so long.

"The wind moves with him, his scent is strong on it. The Lord of the Skies is coming."

Vritra. Only he, of all American dragons, could claim that title. Sure, Aeternitas had tried, and the half-decayed skeleton in the Great Salt Lake bore testimony to how well that had worked. Anzu had almost succeeded, but in the end, he was driven back to the Old World, dripping black blood into the sea.

Apophis, black-hearted, ancient, wise and cunning, had tried to wrestle that title from Vritra in a duel of words, song and claw. Apophis was Vritra's first lieutenant now, cringing

whenever his master came near.

Janus remembered hearing the tale of Vritra's second-known kill in America. A young female Dracul, one of the first hybrids. Vritra had seduced, tortured, raped and dismembered her while the crew watched helplessly from within her. Vritra had left a few humans alive. The others, he had devoured with relish.

Vritra. Lord of the Skies. King of America. Father of Serpents.

The cries of the fallen Aeternitas thundered in his ears again. Janus's throat dried and he tasted vomit. Prometheus was the greatest of the Dracul, the son of the Fire-Bringer—the first dragon to wake in America—a new breed in his own right, and...a shadow of Vritra's power. Hybrid against Organic.

"Sir?" Morgan asked, her clenched hands as white as her face. "What do we do? Can we avoid him?"

"No," Prometheus's voice came over the speakers. "We cannot avoid him. He has scented us, and he will overtake me within moments."

"Don't fight him!" Janus cried, punching buttons. Override, redirect, deploy cargo, deploy lures, distract distract distract!

Prometheus laughed wildly, shutting down the systems that allowed his humans to control his movements. Metal purred against metal as his huge wings unlocked from their glide. They had to grab hold of hand-rails to keep on their feet as Prometheus changed course.

Janus swore. Dracul were not able to override their protocols! They couldn't be hacked, and they couldn't take control away from the captains! That was the safety net, the ritual, everything that kept the relationship between the Dracul and the captains possible.

But Prometheus was flying to meet Vritra head-on, and Dracul and war-witch were laughing madly together.

Janus grabbed Michelle by the shoulders and shook her. "Stop him, you idiot, he's going to kill himself!"

The laughter was gone, a cold glee in her eyes. "Vritra's found you, he ain't stopping. Least one of you has balls. Let him go."

Janus shoved her away and yelled into the intercom. "Stop damn you! You can't win! I"ll lose you and watch you die like Aeternitas died!"

Prometheus's snarl was low and primal. "He is a blood enemy. I am the king of the Dracul, and he is their blood enemy as well. It is my duty to kill him."

"You aren't strong enough!"

The world dropped away around Janus. He was in darkness. Without footing. Without ceiling or wall. Empty. Bitter cold chewed into his bones; wind cut gashes in his cheeks. And something massive and primeval surrounded him, coiled around his mind and body. The power shifted, and a golden-red eye opened, and Janus stared into the eyes not of a Dracul, but of a King-Dragon.

"In the world of serpents, the rattlesnake is most feared in the West. Yet the King Snake hunts and eats them." The massive eye blinked once, slowly. "Vritra is my prey today. You will have your revenge, but do not stand in my way."

Janus cowered from the knowing in those massive eyes. None of the Dracul were supposed to have true power, to be able to meet the Organics in a show of every sort of strength a dragon possessed. The blood and bones of the Organics were their magic, something never replicated in the Dracul. The Organics had souls, the Dracul did not!

But this, this was power! This was a dragon! It should not have been possible! He would have sensed it, something would have been said.

"They did not put me into a body," said Prometheus, "they put the body into me, shaped and changed me to be the pinnacle of all things."

The coils eased around him a bit, and Prometheus raised his head, towering above Janus. "Tell your crew to ready the weapons. Whether Vritra falls or not, he will never forget this day."

Janus was back on the bridge. His teeth chattered helplessly and he fell to his knees now, retching. He was dimly aware of a soft cloth wiping his mouth, of being helped to a chair.

Prometheus wasn't Dracul. He was King. He was going to punish Vritra.

"Ready the weapons!" he cried, jumping to his feet. "Vritra's going to remember today!"

And I hope we live to remember it too, he thought, and took a seat at the console.

Prometheus flew slowly, powering up the piezoelectric Super-House engines to full absorption and switching on the wind-generated turbines.

Only the shock-waves of his wings could be heard in the

hold, thumping against his sides.

Flicking on the video screens, Janus connected to the armory. "Listen to Prometheus, deploy the moment he commands it."

"Yes sir!" the gunners replied, throwing grinning salutes. Ralph, the shorter of the pair, bounced to his bank of Copperhead G30s and checked them for readiness. Close-range armor-piercing rockets, the Copperheads could unearth a bunker or dent a Dracul. Knife-nosed, they would cut through the hide of even the Organics to explode deep inside, and their remote-controlled functions meant they could be recalled if they missed.

Ralph tossed a thumbs-up over his shoulder and Mike shook his head. "Lemme throw Ralph at the son of a bitch sir, he'll do more damage."

Janus laughed, glad for the banter.

"Hold on," Prometheus warned. A little red light blinked on the console: Claws deployed. Five-foot long claws of tungsten steel scythed through the air on dragon-bone legs, weapons twice the size of Vritra's.

Janus switched on the drone feed and brought it in close to record the battle. If they didn't make it, the drone would go to Angel's Crest and replay the scene, give the rebels some idea of Vritra's weaknesses.

Vritra filled the viewscreen, long and white and furious. He coiled in the air and his mouth gaped. Shock-waves buffeted against Prometheus, knocking the drone wildly off course, the war-cry of a jealous King. Magic—magic that no Dracul was ever able to call—rose in shimmering streams from the patches of blue at throat, horns, chest, belly and genitals to surround him in a crackling blue shield. Janus knew with sinking certainty that the Copperheads would malfunction before they ever hit flesh.

And then Prometheus screamed and swerved, and there was no more time to think or know. Only time to hang on and pray that Prometheus had not misplaced his pride.

Slashing at Vritra with his heavy tail, his talons raking through the white dragon's magic and gathering it up in handfuls, Prometheus dropped on Vritra. Vritra shrieked too, in pain and rage, as his shields were ripped, and he struck, snakelike, coming away with a mouthful of alloy scales.

Twice Prometheus battered against Vritra, using his weight to advantage to keep the white dragon off balance. His claws scored the Organic over and over again, Vritra's ineffective legs scrabbling for purchase against Prometheus's slick scales. Battered and harried, Vritra threw his magic at them, buffeting winds, lightning and storm against Prometheus's sides. Greedy teeth of unnatural blue lightning dug at Prometheus, opening gouges along his neck and haunches.

Now Vritra was on Prometheus's flanks. Prometheus screamed as Vritra flung himself in great coils around Prometheus's body and struck like a snake.

Prometheus screamed, furious and hurting as Vritra choked on another mouthful of metal...and blood. Magic seeped into the air around Prometheus, black and venomous. Another terrible scream, and Prometheus set his wings sideways against the wind, turning all thrusters to reverse. Rising for another strike, Vritra slid forward and was flung off. He rolled through the sky in long coils, flailing.

Then Prometheus swept away, his engines and wings straining as he fled Vritra, and the white screamed in victory and chased after.

"What's he doing?" Janus yelled.

Michelle raised her hand, hushing him as her eyes closed. The cabin grew bone-chillingly cold again; the blue mist filtered through the walls to collect in the war-witch's hands.

Prometheus keened, a long, wailing note, and the crew covered their ears as Michelle joined in. Eerie, grating as nails on chalkboard, they wailed together. The black mist filtered through the walls. It mixed with the blue, swallowed it and changed it until a net formed of black-hearted blue strands.

Michelle opened her eyes and smiled as Prometheus plunged around a hill, Vritra on his tail. The Dracul's secondary engines boomed to life, braking him. Vritra dropped underneath, twisting to rake at Prometheus's belly with his lightning.

Michelle flicked her fingers. The net dropped through the floor.

Vritra screamed and twisted, clawing at the the filaments twining around his body. More black mist fell from Prometheus's claws and he spat a mouthful of it at Vritra. Blue and black warred over the white dragon's hide, the black opening rents in the blue. Blood, deep blue and thick, welled from long tears in Vritra's hide. The Sheshas screamed, and his cries echoed through the hull with all the power and fury of an ancient, dying god.

Janus watched, his mouth dry. "Can you kill him now?"

"No," Prometheus said, "He will not die without battle that would kill you too. But I can do other things."

The world blurred as Prometheus dove at Vritra. Claws glittering in the white sun, Prometheus spread his talons and drove them deep into Vritra's body, a roar of pain shaking the Dracul as the magic penetrated into his own body. Prometheus ripped free, taking chunks of meat with him, dripping blood and power as he soared upwards to fall on his enemy again.

With a cold heart, Janus listened to Michelle and Prometheus singing together. He understood Allie's fear. He understood his mistake. He could betray the great dragon, reject his power, or he could accept what Prometheus was: a predatory god, flush with youth and power and fury.

They were trapped, watching helplessly as the King-Dragon mauled and harried Vritra. Streaming blood and blue mist, Vritra gave up his fight for supremacy and locked with Prometheus, fighting for survival.

Disengaging to pounce again, Prometheus shook Vritra loose and spiraled upwards. The white dragon plummeted towards the ground, caught himself, and coiled, hissing at the stooping Prometheus.

Vritra was gone. Leaping out of his coil with a speed only a Sheshas could conjure, he fled towards the river.

"Choose, captain," said Michelle. "Choose if you will be the first council to the first Drac King."

Her eyes were not unsympathetic. "Choose. Call him from the fight. He will listen. He loves and trusts you."

Janus's finger hovered over the com button.

"Choose."

His finger mashed on the button with desperate decision. His voice was dry. Something squeezed his chest and throat shut.

"You can't keep up with him," Janus managed to say, "and we're running low on energy. Turn. Let's go to Margate."

The King raised his head and screamed a war-cry, the sound shimmering in visible waves. Dirt exploded from the ground. Clouds changed shape from the force of his cry. Prometheus hovered, daring any to challenge him.

Vritra was gone.

Faced with a King-Dragon who wanted to stay and claim territory, Janus reached into his old bag of tricks. "Prometheus, Margate is still their nest. You need to go to Angel's Crest, help the rebels destroy Hydra, remember? Vritra IS Hydra. There's nothing you could do that would hurt him more."

He watched the drone-screen breathlessly, waiting for the hulking Nidhogg to listen to him. He breathed a sigh of relief when the arched neck softened, when Prometheus lowered his head to lick a dripping wound on his chest.

"We go to Angel's Crest," the dragon agreed. "And when we are done there, Vritra is my prey."

A breath rushed out of Janus's lungs, an exhalation that loosed fear and grief and hope all together. They were going to war. Together.

Massive, curving wings lifted Prometheus towards Angel's Crest, blood streaming behind him. As Janus watched, that blood slowly dripped to the earth. The land would know Prometheus now. It remained to be seen if it would answer his call.

"The land is changing," Michelle said softly. "He has Territory now, marked in the blood of the defeated and the victorious kings."

"What have we unleashed?" Morgan asked, her face bloodless.

"Change," said Michelle.

THE ENTROPY BOX

Gray Rinehart

Charles Eckhart died a week after he built his perpetual motion machine. He was thirty-four years old, but wrinkled and bleached as a man over ninety.

The machine did not pause at Charles's passing. His sister Katherine put it up in the attic with some of the other sad and useless things she inherited. That's where her son found it. Twice.

◊◊◊

Five days after his mother's funeral, Paul pulled the attic stairs down from the second floor ceiling. The empty, creaking old house was his now, along with the rest of Katherine's estate except what she had set aside for an endowment to the local college.

The hinges squeaked, the spring protested, and a rain of fine dust fell from the hatchway. Paul unfolded the flimsy steps and climbed up into the darkness.

The attic was smaller than he remembered it. It was still spacious--big enough to convert into a bonus room--but not the cavernous place he remembered. He'd been ten when he first climbed the stairs by himself and spent any time in the attic. It was hot and dry and dusty, but it was a place of wonder.

Paul pulled the string hanging from the light fixture, but the string broke. By the light from the open hatch he reached up to the fixture and pulled the chain. He blinked at the sudden brightness.

The attic smelled the way it always had: the peculiar damp-dry smell of age that found its way to the back of his throat and almost choked him. And it looked the way it always had: zinc-coated roofing nails poking down between the rafters, dust-covered plywood spanning the joists, boxes and toys and other debris of modern life too precious to throw away but nonetheless unwanted. Out of sight, out of mind, as his father used to say.

Paul gave a moment's sad, swift thought to his father. Fred Marshal had blazed through life like a forest fire, igniting passion in everyone he met until he finally burned himself up with his own excesses. Paul's arm remembered throwing a football, while his eyes remembered his father's wrecked Oldsmobile and the deeply polished wood of his casket. Suddenly the attic felt much bigger; the house also felt bigger, and emptier.

Paul shook off the memories and grinned to see a particular corrugated box halfway down the length of the attic, on the left. The box sat atop a pile of thin metal sheets, and as Paul opened it one of the top flaps came away in his hand. It felt crumbly as a dry graham cracker, and he silently snapped his fingers across his thumb to get the gritty residue off them.

The clock sat in the box just the way Paul remembered it. It was a square cube of brushed aluminum, with four separate faces scribed directly on the metal sides; each consisted of a circle and a single mark where the twelve would be on a regular clock. One face was marked α, one υ, and two were marked S. Each face had only one hand, the hub of which hugged the surface so tightly that Paul couldn't see where the shaft went through the face. From where he stood he could only see two faces; as he watched, the S hand moved minutely forward and the alpha hand turned a bit backward.

Paul's legs quivered and he sat down on the floor, gracelessly. The plywood sheeting shook and more of the box crumbled away. Paul sneezed into the choking cloud of dust, and as it settled he saw the hands move a bit more, and more still, and he shook his head in disbelief.

It was impossible--no battery could last so long--but the clock was still running.

◊◊◊

Paul originally found the cubical clock on his first foray into the attic. His father wouldn't burn out for three more years, but at the time he was still blazing--and God knew where. So Paul asked his mother what the thing in the attic was. She scrunched up her face as if trying to remember something, and finally told him it was his uncle's clock--Uncle Charlie's crazy clock, she said. At the time, Paul wondered if his uncle was the same Charlie who inherited the chocolate factory. The clock seemed as strange as anything out of that wondrous story. His mother told him nothing more.

Paul noted the movements of the crazy clock, but couldn't decipher the time it told. The faces were next to each other such that after the forward S hand came the backward one, then the α hand moving forward, and finally the u hand moving backward. Usually the clock's hands moved slower than the second hand on the wall clock downstairs--the only other clock with hands in the house--but sometimes they turned faster. He tried to discern rhythms in the speeds of the hands, but any patterns that might be there eluded him. The clock was heavy, as if its metal shell was completely solid, and it was so cold Paul's hands hurt for two days after the first time he picked it up.

Paul checked out a book about clocks and other machines from the library, and read a lot of fascinating facts about how the Chinese and the Muslims built great water clocks and how the sixty-minute hour came to be. But he didn't see anything that looked like his uncle's clock.

Paul sometimes looked at the clock during brief adventures among the boxes, old luggage, and other artifacts in the attic, but he eventually found other things to fascinate him. He burned with temporary enthusiasms just as his father did, and nothing held his attention for long. Over the years, Paul's interests became more esoteric: from baseball, caterpillars, and the stream behind the house; to model cars, radio-controlled airplanes, and miniature rockets; to wind tunnels, Bernoulli's principle, and particle physics. Only infrequently did the clock draw his attention.

Paul's first kiss was in the attic, in shared fascination of the clock.

His eccentric interests and scholastic reputation, along with his teenage awkwardness, combined to thwart his romantic ambitions, but still he found a kindred spirit in Krista Strickland. She was dark, and beautiful, and smart: she was fifteen, a year younger than Paul, but they were both Seniors set to graduate early. Krista looked at the clock with great interest; she knew the Greek alphabet, but besides telling Paul what the alpha and upsilon were she couldn't say what his uncle meant in using them.

They examined the clock together. Paul's stomach twisted, as much from being so near to Krista as sharing the mystery of the clock. And in the way that infatuated boys will give a girl whatever interests her, Paul gave the clock to Krista on her sixteenth birthday.

He wore gardening gloves and carried it down the stairs, and was only slightly embarrassed to put it in a red wagon and pull it around the block to Krista's house. He carried it inside and put it on the desk in her room, and got another nice kiss for his generosity. But when Krista's mother saw it, she said it was too much for a teenage boy to give a girl and made her give it back. So back into the attic it went, and before too long Paul's interests moved on from Krista.

◊◊◊

Paul looked around the attic. He frowned and let out something between a sigh and a chuckle. The crazy clock was still running, almost a decade after he first saw it.

He upended a plastic milk crate--Property of Selig's Dairy Farm, it said--in the middle of the attic floor. Wearing the same old gardening gloves, though he remembered them being bigger and less threadbare, Paul put Uncle Charlie's clock on the overturned crate so he could see it better.

He wondered if it might have a radioactive source in it--maybe that was what the alpha face indicated. That might explain the clock's longevity, and shielding would explain its mass. He decided to borrow a survey meter from the physics department and check for decay signatures; it shouldn't be too much trouble, since he was well-liked among the professors. They'd liked him ever since he'd taken a special physics class during his last semester of high school.

That first class, three years before, had focused his mind temporarily on the clock when he learned that S was the symbol for entropy. The nomenclature made little sense to Paul, other than that E was already taken as the symbol for energy, but it made even less sense as a label for two of the faces on the clock. Eventually he decided that Uncle Charlie must have meant something else: the entropy of the universe was always increasing, so it was absurd for one entropy hand to move forward and the second to move backward.

Now, he wished his mother and father had told him more about it.

He searched through some of the boxes in the attic, each one evoking some memory or another, until the early summer heat drove him from the uninsulated space. He carried a disintegrating file box with a few of his Uncle Charlie's papers downstairs into the cool of the house. Some were quite straightforward, though faded: sketches dated before Paul was born, of different odd clocks--with more or fewer faces than the attic clock, with several faces aligned in a row, and so forth. Other papers were illegible, and a few crumbled in his hands until the pieces fell to the carpet like snow.

Paul spent the rest of the day studying the attic scraps and trying to find relatives who remembered his Uncle Charlie. The family tree written in the big Bible was stunted: his mother and Charles had been the only Eckhart siblings. With no other relatives on his mother's side, he turned to his father's side of the family. No one knew anything about Charles' occupation, whether he had been some kind of nuclear researcher, and at first Paul learned only that Katherine had also inherited a metal lathe, milling machine and other tools Charles had kept in the basement of his apartment building, but had sold them and used the money to set up his college fund. Then Tracy, his cousin on his father's side, remembered something strange about how preternaturally old Charles looked when he died.

Paul hung up the phone and thought of his mother's aged face.

In her casket, Katherine had looked far older than forty-two. The worries of single motherhood had taken their toll, but the funeral director, who was also the town coroner and had gone to Paul's parents' church, said it looked as if she'd aged by decades since Paul had moved into the dorm. After the funeral, her doctor had told Paul he suspected it might be some new kind of late-onset progeria--perhaps a new form of Werner's syndrome--that unfortunately had gone undiagnosed. But Paul shouldn't worry, genetic disorders of that type were exceedingly rare.

This news about Uncle Charlie planted a seed of worry in Paul. He read through the annotations in the big Bible and wondered if there were some test he should undergo. The rest of his ancestors on his mother's side, he saw, had lived into their sixties and longer. But Paul's mother and her brother were both prematurely old.

As he lay in bed that night, Paul wondered about the backward-spinning hands on his uncle's clock. He did not sleep well.

◊◊◊

The next morning Paul went to the college and borrowed a Geiger counter and some measuring instruments. He went back up into the attic around noon; sweat oozed from him as he climbed up into the heat. He swept the survey meter all around the clock, but picked up no unusual emissions. He had hoped the clock would peg the meter, even though it meant he would be in danger, because radiation was a known danger. Now he wasn't sure what to think.

Had Uncle Charlie meant *S* for entropy? Perhaps the clock was some kind of entropy engine, decreasing the entropy inside but adding entropy to the world the way a refrigerator stays cold by adding heat to the world.

Paul sat down on the floor and watched the clock's hands spin. Were they moving a bit faster than before?

He moved his hand and saw that it left a dark, wet imprint on the plywood. It was far too hot to stay in the attic. He glanced around at the other detritus of the attic--an upright vacuum cleaner missing its bag, an old sewing machine encased in a dusty plastic carrying case, various other forgotten relics--before his gaze settled back on the fantastic, impossible clock. He put his hand back out to push himself up off the floor, and brushed against the sharp edge of one of the metal plates the clock used to sit on.

Paul vaguely recalled looking at the plates years ago and thinking little of them. Now he lifted them up, one by one, and examined them. They were thin sheets of stainless steel, and he realized they were templates his uncle had used to mark, cut and drill the sides of his clock. Paul laid them out across the plywood floor, and dripped sweat on them as he looked for clues about the mechanism. They were shiny and silent and disappointing.

Paul retreated from the attic, and the house felt almost cold: more shocking than refreshing. The garage was pleasantly warm, though, as he looked around for tools he could use to open the clock. Uncle Charlie had been dead for seventeen years, but his clock was still running. Paul had to figure out why.

Paul remembered taking apart his grandfather's pocket watch when he was five. He had destroyed that watch, unable to reassemble it. He didn't want that to happen again, but the mystery of the crazy clock pulled him as surely as if the clock were magnetic and he was made of iron.

That night, Paul carried the clock down out of the attic. It was cold, freezing cold, through the gardening gloves and through his shirt as he clutched the heavy metal cube to his body. Twice he almost dropped it, but he clung to it fiercely. Its mystery was too much a part of him.

He put the clock on the kitchen table and examined it closely, desperate to discover its secrets. It revealed nothing. The hands just turned, each at a different rate but a little faster than they had when it was in the attic. Since the survey meter had detected nothing, Paul turned to more mundane methods. He measured the case precisely with a micrometer and calipers he'd found in the garage. The clock was a perfect cube, five and eleven sixteenths inches on a side. The circles scribed for each face were each three and nine sixteenths inches in diameter. The case had no slot or cover behind which a battery might lie, and definitely no cord or plug. The brushed aluminum faces fit together so closely that Paul couldn't slide a piece of paper between them; each was secured by twelve Phillips head screws. Apparently, from the orientations of the screws, they were attached to an internal frame--or else the sides were at least a half inch thick.

Paul gently shook the cube, but it made no noise. It made no noise at all, in fact. He put his ear close to the alpha face and listened for the scrape of the shaft that turned its hand, or the hum of a motor or the click of an escapement. Nothing. Gently, so gently he had to close his eyes to focus on the sense of touch in his fingertip, he touched the hub and felt it turn under the pad of his finger. As he touched it, it sped up, but he felt no vibration at all. It should have been warm, by friction if nothing else, but it was frigid. The chill seeped into his finger until it burned with cold. Paul left off his investigation to run some warm water over his finger, but that just made it throb.

Paul contrived to stop one of the hands to see if the others stopped. He chose one of the S hands, the one moving backward. His right index finger pulsed with freezing pain, so he put his left index finger against the hand's pointer. The metal barb pushed into his fingertip, just a little, before the hand stopped. The other hands appeared to march on as if nothing had changed; they did not stop or even jerk. Within a couple of seconds, Paul became aware of pain in his finger. He let go of the pointer and the hand resumed its backward movement, this time with a drop of his blood that quickly dried on it until it matched the pointer's black color.

Paul put his finger in his mouth and tasted blood and metal. When he looked at it, the wound was just deep enough to break the skin. It didn't hurt like getting stuck with a pin; instead, it throbbed like a deep ache. Unlike his right index finger, which was moving beyond pain into numbness, this pain spread backward into his hand. He walked into the living room and sat down on the couch as pain crept up his wrist and into his elbow. Should've worn the damn gloves, he scolded himself, or jammed it with a wrench or something.

He made his way to the bathroom and took four extra-strength Ibuprofen, then went to his bedroom to lie down. The pain gradually subsided, but left his arm aching as he fell asleep.

◊◊◊

Paul broke his fast next to the inscrutable machine. The last remnants of the neighbors' food gifts were molding in the refrigerator, but he would clean them up another time. He itched a little from neither showering nor changing his clothes. His right hand and left arm still ached.

After he laid his cereal bowl in the sink, he picked up a screwdriver and removed the screws from the top of the clock. His hands hurt to turn the screwdriver, no matter which he used. Finally he just kept pressure on the end of the screwdriver with his left hand, his palm on the end of the handle the way he'd seen his dad put up curtain rods, and turned as best he could with his right hand. Picking the screws up, though, his hand began to shake. The screws were small and his hand shook so badly that more than once he dropped a screw and had to sweep it off the table into his open left hand. It took more than twenty minutes for Paul to get all the screws into an old baby-food jar, itself emptied of the wood screws his father kept in it in the garage.

He couldn't grip the cube well with gloves on, so he endured the cold as he clawed at the top. The lid was tight, as if fused to the four sides. Paul stuck the blade of a penknife in the miniscule crack and pushed, but the blade slipped and his knuckle scraped across the edge of the box. It left behind a ribbon of blood that turned from red to rust to black as he watched.

The spinning hands sped up.

He took a few minutes to bandage his hand, then drove the point of the blade into the crack and wiggled it back and forth. Almost imperceptibly it slipped into the joint. Paul twisted the knife carefully, afraid to break the blade, until the crack spread a bit more. He worked his way down the side of the cube, and progressed from the penknife to a jeweler's screwdriver to a standard screwdriver. Looking at the corner of the faceplate, the edges appeared to be beveled; the piece should lift up easily, but it resisted being taken off. It was almost as if it had been glued, but Paul saw no evidence of that; he wondered for a second if it might be held down by a strong magnet, but that made no sense if the sides were really aluminum.

Then the lid flipped up, backwards onto the table, as suddenly as a cork popping out of a bottle. It rang against the wood and settled to the surface.

Paul looked into the clock, and thought he was looking into glory.

As his eyes adjusted, it looked as if the box was full of liquid gold. Paul knew that couldn't be true: gold would have to be hot to liquefy, and the box was still icy cold. On closer examination the liquid looked like some kind of heavy oil, shining silver and gold under the kitchen light. As he bent his head to the left and then right, the liquid reflected the light in all the colors of the spectrum, except where it met the four sides of the box. There, the liquid faded to the same uniform silver of the aluminum sides. But in the middle, where its meniscus gave it a distinctive convex hump, the gold color was richest.

Paul gazed into the clock until his neck and shoulders ached. His left leg was numb from standing still so long. He shifted position and his right knee popped. He sat down and rubbed it a little, pondering the crazy old clock.

One of the hands had stopped.

He hadn't noticed it at first, so enraptured was he by the liquid in the thing. He watched carefully until he was sure. It was one of the S hands--the one that usually moved backward--and it was definitely still. He stood up and leaned on the table to look at all the faces, but the other three hands were still moving.

He jostled the table as he sat back down.

The liquid sloshed from side to side, and a little spilled out and down the alpha face. It didn't move like water: it rolled down the face in a little misshapen ball, like the mercury Mr. Oakhampton had shown his general science class back in high school. The alpha hand stopped as the tiny golden droplet touched it. The liquid ball lost color as it fell, until it was a uniform dull grey rolling across the polished Malaysian hardwood. It was almost black by the time it reached the edge, and Paul lost sight of it when it sank into a crack between the floor tiles.

He had leaned all the way over to his right to watch the escaping droplet. It reminded him of that *Terminator* movie, and he hoped for a few seconds that the clock would call the liquid metal back up out of the floor. He watched, but nothing happened.

Paul sat up, slowly. He pushed against the arm of the chair to right himself, and his wrist and elbow creaked. He looked again at the faces of the clock. The forward-running S hand and the backward running upsilon hand were still moving. Perhaps they were moving slower than Paul had seen before, but he wasn't sure because they usually moved slowly. He thought about his grandfather's pocket watch and knew he should put the lid back on this clock and be done with it. He thought of Krista, of how fascinated she would be by the inside of the clock.

With an effort, he stood and reached across the clock for the lid. Looking down into the open top, he saw that the gold sheen on the liquid surface had disappeared; the liquid was now almost wholly silver, fading to black at the edges. In the reflection he saw with only mild surprise that he had gone quite grey. Maybe it was a trick of the light, but the glory seemed to be fading--

He pulled back his hand from the lid, then reached down and touched the image of his face in the silvery liquid.

It burned him with cold.

He jerked back his hand, and ripples moved across the surface of the liquid. He held his freezing finger in the palm of his other hand and watched as the liquid level began to drop. He looked around and under the table to see where it was leaking, but there were no holes or drains and no stream of silver-turning-black liquid staining the floor. He wondered if he should worry about breathing it in if it was evaporating.

He leaned back over and watched the abrupt, unexpected phase change run its course.

As the oily liquid dropped, it grew translucent. A little solid block of crystal was suspended in the center of the box, black as his mom's onyx ring, but shinier. Dark shafts projected out from it to the four faces. It wasn't smooth like a cube; it was rough, more pebbled than jagged, and maybe an inch on a side, but definitely crystalline even though it wasn't as sharp and misshapen as the crystals he'd grown on a string in sugar water many years ago.

The liquid level fell until the black crystal was exposed to the air. It appeared to dissolve, and when the surface reached the shafts they dissolved, too. The four hands clattered to the table.

The liquid level dropped until only a thin film of oily residue was on the bottom of the clock. It became thinner and thinner until only the aluminum case remained.

Paul leaned on the table, staring into the empty clock.

◊◊◊

Paul stood over the clock for a long time, until once again numbness and pain made themselves evident. His back cracked as he stood up straight.

He wanted to cry, the way he had wept over the pieces of that old pocket watch, but his eyes were too tired and dry. So he laughed instead: a short, low chuckle that sounded strange in his ears, as if it echoed back to him out of a deep well.

Paul's hands shook as he gathered up the clock's. He sat down and turned the metal hands over and over in his own. One hand was marked with an alpha, one with an upsilon, and two with the enigmatic S. The backs of his own hands were marked with wrinkles--he touched his face and felt deep lines there, too--and his right index finger was starting to turn black. How would he explain getting frostbitten in the summertime? He tapped the S hands together and chuckled again at the absurd explanation: my Uncle Charlie's entropy engine did it, Doctor.

A wave of fatigue lapped its way from Paul's feet upward through his body. That's entropy, he decided: the universe getting tired--tired of holding itself together. But he had to hold himself together; he had no one around anymore who could do it for him. He might live a long life as an old man, and had to live it the best he could. He wouldn't sell his parent's house, at least not yet. He would rent it out, and use the income while he finished school, which, he realized, might take a long time. The entropy box was too tantalizing a puzzle; he'd need a good deal more study in order to duplicate Uncle Charlie's research.

Paul pulled the broken clock to the edge of the table. He looked inside, hoping for a glimpse of the glory it once held, but saw only bare aluminum. He dropped the hands into the case. They clinked against the bottom like nails in the scale at the hardware store; otherwise, the box was empty.

But not for ever.

THE END

SONGS OF THE SEASONS, SONG 4: FIRE AND RAIN

Janine K. Spendlove

She kept tossing her long red hair, arrayed in dozens of braids, over her shoulder, unconsciously exposing the dryad gills positioned directly behind her pointed elf ears.

I sat across from Adair in the Ailesit's sitting room while my master conversed with the Ailesit (she called herself a "human," of all things) outside on the porch overlooking the channel. I was staring at the half-blood before me, while trying not to stare at the same time.

A half-dryad, half-elf was unheard of.

It wasn't that our peoples didn't get along exactly - and Ai knew that dryads would lie with anyone - but it was her elf half that intrigued me.

I returned Adair's smile with a tentative one of my own. After all, I didn't want to be rude.

"Hello, I'm Eisrus." I held out my hand for her to grip in the traditional elf greeting among new acquaintances. She just stared at it for a moment, blinking her silver elf eyes at me, when suddenly a dash of orange sparked across them.

She took my warm hand in her cool one and pulled me down into a crushing hug.

"Hullo, Eisrus, I'm Adair, and it's so very nice to meet ya."

I immediately stiffened then found myself unexpectedly relaxing into her embrace. Her voice, lilting and musical, with an accent so different from my own, immediately put me at ease.

She squeezed tighter and I gasped for breath while my mind swirled around the memory of the flash of color I'd seen in her eyes. She'd known me for all of a minute and was already sharing her emotions with me. I was touched, yet also confused; what did she mean by it? I'd been training under my master for years now, and only recently had Eáchan allowed me to see some of her colors.

The girl released me, grinned, and flopped back down on the stuffed chair behind her.

"Don't worry, hunter. I'm not goin' to kiss ya. Da says I can't go 'round kissin' elves in greeting, or you may all faint or somesuch. Says it would be scandalous."

She looked at me, one red eyebrow raised against her alabaster skin. "You're not goin' to faint, are ya?"

I realized that I was still standing there, mouth hanging open like a squalling gnome babe, and snapped it shut.

"I am not a hunter." I recalled the moment, nearly six years ago when Eáchan took me on as her apprentice. It was the proudest day of my life. She was the greatest hunter my clan had ever seen, and she wasn't just any hunter, she was the Hunter, the clan chief.

"At least, not yet. Not for many years yet." I looked behind me and sat carefully back down in my carved wooden chair.

Adair grinned broadly and continued to stare at me with glittering orange excitement coloring her eyes.

"What do you find so humorous?"

"You." She cocked her head to the side. "Are you always this uptight? Maybe you should take a bath."

"Excuse me?" Confused by her turn of conversation, I surreptitiously tried to smell myself. I'd bathed last night before retiring for the evening and hadn't done anything strenuous yet today. Was I breaking out in a nervous sweat? But what did I have to be nervous about? She was just a girl.

Was she somehow using her alluring dryad magic without me even noticing? I sat up straighter in my chair, determined not to fall prey to her.

"Take a bath, or go for a swim." She slung her shapely legs over the arm of the chair.

I quickly averted my eyes, and looked around the spacious, sunlit room, as her minuscule, green sarong gapped open momentarily near her stomach. I supposed I should have been grateful she wore anything at all. From everything I'd heard, dryads abhorred clothing as a rule. Though, given that we were in the queen's palace, it made sense that she was trying to maintain some semblance of decency.

I realized she was still talking, completely oblivious to my distraction.

"...I always go for a swim when I'm feeling out of sorts. Or a bath. Water in general soothes me."

"But do you never commune with the trees? You are half-elf, are you not?" The words were out of my mouth before I could recall them, and I felt my cheeks heat with embarrassment. That was a very personal question, and we'd only just met.

Her eyes darkened to blue and she looked away, focusing her gaze on a yellow vase holding purple spring flowers on the other side of the airy room, near some gauzy window coverings. "Do you commune with the trees, Eisrus?"

"Yes, of course." I sat back in my chair, once again confused by her question, and at the same time fascinated by the sound of my name on her lips.

"While I'm certain you talk to the wood in your own way, the only way elves can now, it can be nothing to what a dryad feels when in touch with water."

She turned to look at me, and I realized the blue in her eyes was not sadness for herself, but pity for me.

"The only way elves can... now?" I stiffened. Elves, like any creature in Ailionora, were tied to nature. We would die without it. "Just what are you implying?"

She straightened, her casual manner gone. "I don't mean to offend, I just thought, that without your magic..."

"You thought that with our access to magic gone, we couldn't talk to trees?" I narrowed my eyes, struggling to keep my emotions at bay. What was wrong with me?

"Well..."

"We may not be able to wield magic anymore, but I assure you, it is still there in the wild of nature." I closed my eyes and took a calming breath. I hardly knew this girl... why couldn't I control my emotions around her? "I still talk to trees. Just because I can't hear them, doesn't mean they don't listen."

"I'm sorry, I didn't mean-"

"Eisrus!" My master strode into the room, her brows furrowed, and her lips pressed into a thin line. I'd never seen her so close to losing her composure. "We are leaving."

She scooped up her precious iron-tipped bow from the low table before me. Giving Adair a scathing look, my master stormed out of the room, leaving me nothing to do but follow in her wake.

◊◊◊

The six wood sprites emerged from between the trees, their red eyes glowing in the darkening sky. Adair and Eisrus stood back to back, and he felt her reach behind and into his quiver. She pulled an arrow out and held it before her, and Eisrus wished she had heeded him by mounting Ped and running for the sea.

The little tree fey scuttled forward on their short legs, and Eisrus drew his bow and aimed – though what good a stone tipped arrow would do against them while they were at full strength, he didn't know. Iron was precious and difficult to come by.

The sprites raised their spindly arms, each hefting a rock, ready to throw.

Eisrus could feel Adair's breath quickening beside him and he spared her a glance. Her eyes were orange! She wasn't frightened at all – if anything, the mad dryad was excited.

So typical.

His moment of distraction nearly proved fatal as he only just managed to duck as a rock flew past where his head had been before. Eisrus loosed his arrow directly into the maw in the bark that he assumed was the offending sprite's mouth, hoping to slow the fey down, and Ped — their selkie companion — leapt out of the woods, trampling one of the sprites beneath his saucer sized paws. He gave a barking growl at the shrieking faerie and clamped his jaws around its crown and began whacking it against the trunk of a tree, knocking autumn leaves to the cold ground with every blow.

Eisrus felt the flow of the hunt come over him, marveling in the fact that he could now feel the magic coursing through him, thanks to the Ailesit. He drew another arrow and watched as Adair danced gracefully between a pair of sprites, dousing one with a spray of salt. It shrieked as the salt burned through its bark, and Eisrus loosed another arrow, putting the now weakened and injured fey out of its misery.

There were only three sprites left and they backed away, chittering loudly amongst themselves. Adair met his gaze from across the clearing and smiled.

"See, I told ya—"

The temperature dropped, and Eisrus watched as his breath suddenly became visible before him in a condensed cloud.

"No..." Eisrus felt his breath catch in his chest as he moved his trembling fingers back to grasp another arrow.

A swirl of stinging snow exploded between Eisrus and Adair, and when it cleared the largest bear the elf had ever seen stood between them.

Pure white and standing erect on his hind legs, the bear's intelligent, mad gaze swiveled until it trained on Adair.

The Winter King had found them.

◊◊◊

My people tended to stay away from those not of our kind. It's not that we were intolerant – or at least I didn't think so at the time - just that when a race is dwindling, it tends to turn inward in preservation. Right or wrong, elves didn't couple with other races. It just wasn't done.

I had heard stories and I knew that it wasn't always that way. Elves used to be immortal, so the fact that male elves could only sire one child was not a bad thing – in fact, it kept Ailionora from being overrun by undying elves.

But everything changed when we were betrayed by the Lord of the Spring. Cursed with mortality, we were slowly dying out. It was genocide over millennia, but genocide nonetheless. And so, for an elf to waste that one shot at a child on another race, especially one as flighty as the dryads... well, it was the deepest betrayal fathomable.

And yet, an elf had done it, and I watched from a distance as the evidence of that coupling swam in the Ailes channel around the Queen's Island. The water was wide and deep here, and I knew Adair would not be able to resist getting in.

I honestly don't know why I followed her there. Perhaps it was because I felt badly about how I'd snapped at her the previous day. Or because I'd seen the way the other elves avoided her and I felt bad for her. Or perhaps it was because she was a curiosity, something so different from anything else I'd experienced in the limited scope of my life up until that point.

All I'd ever known before Adair were these islands – primarily the Hunters' Isle as both my parents were hunters –

and a year spent with each of the other eleven clans learning about their ways as well. But I never doubted that I'd be a hunter.

When the inverted triangle ailach showed up under my left eye, signifying me a member of the hunter clan, everyone else knew it as well. My life became nothing but the hunt then. Years of arrows and stalking. Targets and trails.

But Adair, she was different. She was new.

She was wild.

A blast of cold water hit me square in the face.

"What in the name of Ai..." My words trailed off as I took in Adair grinning at me over the edge of the wooden dock.

"Thought you could sneak up on me, did ya?"

"No, I just... Eáchan is in a clan chief meeting with the Queen, and after how we rushed out yesterday..." I realized how pathetic my explanation sounded and dragged my fingers through my short, muddy brown hair in frustration. I was a fool.

"Aww, did you come to check on me, hunter?" Her eyes swirled a mischievous orange, and I was beginning to wonder if they were nearly always that color.

"I told you, I'm not a hunter. Yet." I sat down on the edge of the dock, dangling my booted legs over the edge. A chilly wind ghosted by, and I was thankful my mother had insisted I wear a long sleeve tunic and a wool cloak today. The sun did not yet give much warmth, though it was nearly spring.

"That's right." She cocked her head to the side, tossing her long braids back over her shoulder. "When do you suppose you will be a hunter?"

I shrugged. "That all depends."

"On?"

"My master. Though she says I'm doing a good job. So I suppose perhaps five or ten more years? But I could be wrong. Some apprentices train until they are forty." I didn't tell her my secret hope that it was actually closer to two or three for me.

"And then you'll be a hunter?" She lowered herself back down into the water and began a backstroke. It was only then that I realized she was not wearing a stitch of clothing.

Dryad indeed!

I averted my eyes and tried to ignore the blush I felt while I scanned the shoreline across the way. Normally the sight of the woods across the way would have calmed me, but all I could think of was the naked dryad swimming back toward me. My mind raced back to the threads of our conversation, and I focused on coming up with a proper response.

"And then I will not be a hunter. Then I will go on my Grand Tour, and when I come back - if I come back - a formal Ascension ceremony will be held and then I will be proclaimed a hunter."

"Oh..." Treading water before me, she tapped a finger on my left toe, leaving a wet spot on the suede leather there. "That sounds overly complicated. If the ailach shows up on its own, who are the clan leaders to test you? Magic knows where your heart is."

"So you do know something of our ways."

"Aye, my da is an elf after all." She laughed, her musical voice blending naturally with the sound of the water lapping against the dock. "You know, I always assumed he had friends here, but I had no idea Queen Eánna numbered among them."

"What?" My head came back down to meet her curious eyes. The traitor and the queen... friends?

"Aye, she housed us in the palace after we arrived, and I thought that was just to be courteous because we brought the Ailesit with us. But no, she came to visit night before last, and she and da talked all night, and then yesterday morning she asked me to bring the Ailesit to the meeting after she woke up – humans sleep a lot, did you know that?"

Barely giving me a chance to process everything she'd said, much less respond to her question, Adair pressed on.

"They eat a lot, too. But I took the Ailesit to the meeting – her name is Story and she's my friend – and at the meeting I helped come up with the plan to restore *The Ailes*." She beamed with pride at this fact, and all I could do was nod.

This was all new to me. What plan? Restore The Ailes? If the tree that embodied our magic was restored, then that would mean....

"Oi, are you listening to me?"

I blinked my eyes and looked back down at Adair. She was releasing my boot after giving it a hard tug, leaving a wet handprint on it. "I'm sorry, I was distracted."

She just laughed again. "Oh, I'm not upset. I often get distracted. Da says I need to work on my focusing. On paying attention when other people speak, that I shouldn't do all the talkin', but sometimes people don't talk, and then it's quiet, and that's odd, and I don't like that. Friends should talk." She cocked her head to the side and her orange eyes swirled with a bit of yellow.

What could possibly be causing her concern?

"Are we friends?"

I stiffened, feeling my bow and quiver dig into my back at my sudden movement. What kind of questions was that?

I was an elf.

She was... well, an elf, too. In a way.

I looked at her worried eyes, and realized I wanted nothing more than for a smile to come back to her face.

I didn't see why we couldn't be friends. As long as my master didn't know.

"I don't know." My mouth betrayed me as a corner tipped up in a smile of its own accord. "How old are you? I'm not friends with children."

"I'm not a child! I'm nearly fifteen."

"Nearly fifteen is fourteen." I leaned back against my elbows, enjoying the sunshine sparking off the clear water.

"I'm old enough to have pups of my own, therefore, I'm an adult."

I raised an eyebrow, trying to maintain my cool façade when all I could I think of was what Adair had just said. "Is that all it takes in dryad society?"

She nodded her head, quite seriously. "Oh yes. Old enough to have pups means you're old enough to work and contribute to the whole." She rested her arms against the dock, leaving a trail of warm water pooling around her skin. "And what about you? How old are ya?"

"Twenty three."

She snorted.

"What?"

"*You're the child.*"

"Says the fourteen year old." I knew I was being unfair.

She was marked as an adult by her people, and I was still viewed as... well, not quite as a child, but certainly not as an adult by mine. Still, my pride had been wounded.

"Says the fourteen year old who has seen more of this world than you can even imagine." Her eyes had darkened from orange to blue, and I swallowed my retort. I'd hurt her feelings.

"Would you tell me about it?"

"What, the world?"

"Aye, if you wouldn't mind. Ailionora is vast — I can only imagine the things you've seen."

Her grin was back, as were the orange sparks in her eyes. I found I never wanted them to leave. Unless they were replaced by purple. I quickly banished that improper train of thought and focused on what she was asking me.

"What do you want to hear about first? Gnomes, trolls, or da'nan?"

◊◊◊

"Run!" Eisrus screamed at Adair. Their only chance was to get her away from the Winter King, else he would sacrifice her to unleash Chaos and end all the worlds. Ped ran over and tossed the half-blood onto his back while the bear hurled Eisrus against a tree, silencing him.

Eisrus's bow flew out of his hand and he could hear the arrows in his quiver crack from the force of the impact. He blinked, trying to get his vision to clear. Groaning, the elf rolled to get back to his feet and froze with horror as a double vision of Adair leaping from Ped's back assaulted him.

"Go! Get help!" She shoved the selkie away and dove toward Eisrus's bow.

Winter cocked his head to the side and casually blasted a band of ice around Eisrus's arms and legs, immobilizing him. The bear watched as Adair raised the elf's bow, aiming an arrow straight at his chest.

"You don't want to do that, little half-blood."

"Shows what you know." She loosed the arrow and the bear easily batted it away with a grace and speed belied by his bulk.

"Adair, run!" Eisrus knew it was too late, but he couldn't give up hope. He struggled against his frozen bonds as they burned coldly through his clothes.

"Yes, go ahead and run. I do love a good hunt, don't you, elfling?" The Winter King turned toward Eisrus and smiled, revealing a mouthful of sharp teeth. His eyes fixed on the elf's hand and he froze.

"My son is a clever Sidhe, yes he is." Without looking over his shoulder at the creeping Adair, he extended a massive, furry paw toward her. Ice bands encircled her arms, chest, and legs as she fell to the leaf covered ground. A final band circled her mouth, silencing her protests.

Winter dropped to his front paws and lumbered over to Eisrus slowly, while the elf followed the bear's gaze toward his closed right hand, Winter's intent quite clear. A fear almost as great as the one he felt for Adair threatened to consume him, as Eisrus tightened his fist. He would not give it up. He would not. The Spring Prince had been clear about that.

Tears pricked his eyes as the bear used a claw to pry open Eisrus's hand. The bear's tongue slurped out and slid across his palm, and Eisrus forced himself not to gag. He felt violated, assaulted, and the sunshine pulsing in his hand shied away from the darkness that oozed from Winter's presence.

The Winter King sat back on his haunches, a look approximating sanity crossing his features. "Yes, Spring is very clever indeed."

The bear lowered his massive muzzle over Eisrus's head and face, his fetid, dank breath washing over the elf. Eisrus struggled not to tremble, both from the cold of the ice bands, but also from the madness he saw just below the surface of the Winter King's eyes.

"Release it."

"N-no." *If he released the sunshine, the Ailesit and Spring Prince would think he and Adair had made it to Vevila safely. That Adair was no longer in danger of sacrifice. That all the worlds were no longer at risk of total destruction.*

The bear leaned closer, drool and snot dripping onto Eisrus's forehead.

"You are brave, and I admire that, so I will give you one more chance, elfling. Release it."

Eisrus shifted slightly to his right and locked his gaze with Adair's. Laying on her side, fully bound by ice bands, silver tears leaked from her eyes as she shook her head in a clear 'no.'

He looked back at the Winter King, his voice clear and strong.

"No."

Winter recoiled as if struck.

"No? No?" *He shook his massive white head.* "That is a pity. There was no need for you to die yet."

Turning to the wood sprites, the Winter King slung Adair over his shoulder as if she weighed nothing.

"Take it off. Then have whatever sport you wish with him."

Adair and Eisrus locked eyes once again, and Eisrus hoped his colors showed everything he was feeling for her in that moment.

With a scattering of snow, the bear and the half-blood were gone.

The remaining three wood sprites stepped into the forefront, moonlight illuminating the grotesque smiles on their bark surfaces. The center sprite hefted a sharp rock, and their red eyes gleamed.

◊◊◊

I approached the end of the wooden dock warily. I knew Adair was there. The Ailesit, Eirnin, and Adair had returned only yesterday from their mission to restore *The Ailes*, and I was anxious to see her. I'd heard they'd run into some trouble. I just wanted to make certain my friend was unharmed.

I flattened to the ground as a spray of water jetted over my head. The wooden splinters of the dock dug into my chest, but I couldn't help smiling as Adair peeked over the dock's edge with an impish grin on her face. She looked just fine to me.

"Oi, you're no fun!" She cocked her head to the side and the sun glistened off the seashells and other baubles woven into her braids.

"What, just because I don't feel like getting wet?" I pushed myself off the dock and unslung my bow, quiver, and cloak – I needed to make certain my kit was in order after a drop like that.

"What's wrong with getting wet?" Adair's hand snaked out and wrapped firmly around my ankle. Her eyes were glittering orange.

"Adair, no! I'm in all my hunting—"

I just managed to close my mouth in time to prevent ingesting a lungful of water. Kicking my legs upward, I broke through the surface of the channel, sputtering.

"See, isn't this nice?" Adair swam up next to me as I wiped the water out of my eyes with one hand and used the other to tread.

My vision cleared and then I lunged back, startled. She'd been right in my face, grinning.

"I don't know if 'nice' is how I would describe it." My teeth weren't chattering, but it was still definitely early Spring and the water was frigid. Unlike a dryad, I did get cold when wet. I looked around for the ladder to pull myself up and my gaze flicked back over Adair, momentarily lingering on the attractive spray of freckles spread across her nose, before my gaze froze on her right arm, or rather lack of one.

"What in Aisdeann happened to your arm?" I felt my chest compress – no one had mentioned an injury.

She turned so that I could see her right shoulder more fully and I bobbed under the surface of the water, momentarily forgetting to tread in my surprise. Coughing, I surfaced, and got a better look. Her arm was not gone, but had somehow shrunk to the size of an infant's. To say it was perhaps the most bizarre thing I'd ever seen in my life was an understatement.

"Oh, that." She waggled her stubby little fingers. "A kraken decided to snack on me, but not to worry, a fishing pod got it, and I snacked on the kraken instead. *Delicious*."

"Wait, are you saying something bit off your arm?"

"Snapped off with its pincer more like." Adair made a clawing motion with her full sized left hand and pinched my shoulder.

"So that means your arm grew back."

"*Is* growing back, actually." She waved her tiny hand again. "Should be good as new in a month or so." She made a disgusted face. "Honestly it's far more trouble than it's worth. It stings like you wouldn't believe, and it's fairly useless in its current state." She lifted it with her left hand and then let it flop back down to her side.

I clung to the wooden ladder rung next to me, tired from all the treading. "But you would have been maimed your entire life it hadn't grown back. An invalid. Crippled."

Adair's eyes darkened as she narrowed them, and I was under water once again.

I tried to kick back to the surface, but she held me there firmly, until I stopped thrashing about, trying not to panic.

"*Do I look crippled to you?*"

I knew dryads could send their thoughts under water; still, the experience was both thrilling and a bit frightening. Could she hear my thoughts too? Could she read my mind?

I realized she was patiently waiting for an answer from me and my air was rapidly running out. Shaking my head "no" I felt her let go of my leg and push me toward the surface.

Breaking through, I gasped for air, coughing and wheezing all at once.

Adair treaded water next to me, her usual smile once again on her face. "I would have been fine without my arm, really. I can still swim and cast a net or a trident without it." She wrinkled up her nose in distaste. "But this, this is painful, and a hassle."

"Right." I pulled myself up the ladder, determined to not get another dunking at the hand of a mad dryad.

"Leaving already?" She swam a lazy circle in the water on her back, and I forced myself to keep my gaze averted. I didn't think she was purposely trying to be enticing, but dryads were often called sirens for a reason.

"I don't see why I should stay if I'm to be bathed against my will."

"Aw, come on, stay. I won't do it again... today." She swam back to the dock and pulled herself out just far enough to clear her full-sized arm but keep her chest covered by the edge. It seemed she did have some consideration for elf culture, after all. I found I was a bit disappointed by that, and I quickly shifted my thoughts to other less inappropriate things.

"Very well." I sat down and unlaced my boots, hoping they weren't ruined. "I need to dry a bit at any rate."

Adair smiled and lowered her chin onto her bent arm. "Did you know I met the Summer Queen yesterday?"

She had my full attention now. "I had heard she dropped by to see the queen and council. What was she like?"

Scary. Fierce. Like a walking flame and a little girl at the same time. But mostly scary." Her eyes tinged with yellow. "I don't think I ever want to meet another Sidhe again."

I laughed. "Well, I don't see why you'd have too. Mortal affairs are none of their concern." She still seemed worried, and once again, I didn't like that. "How about, once your arm grows back, I teach you how to shoot a bow?"

She raised her head and gave me a half a smile. "Oh, Eirnin already did that."

I made a scoffing sound in the back of my throat. Eirnin was a good hunter, if a bit eccentric, but I was better. "Alright, how about once your arm grows back I teach you how to shoot a bow *properly*?"

She laughed, and it was music to my ears.

"I'm going to tell him you said that."

"Go ahead. I'll bet my arm against his any day." It wasn't pride speaking, truly. Nor jealousy. I'd seen the two of them together, and it was clear that Eirnin was like an older brother or uncle to Adair and, from what I could see, completely in love with the Ailesit. Then I realized I'd just considered if I should be jealous. Where had that come from? What did I have to be jealous of? Adair wasn't mine. I didn't think of her in that way... did I?

"What's it like to have your magic back?" Her lilting voice broke into my thoughts.

I expelled a deep breath and pondered on how best to answer.

"It's... it's wonderful. I talk to the trees, and they—"

"Talk back?"

"Well, not exactly... it's more like humming. But I know they hear me. And I can sense them. I can sense all my surroundings when I'm in the wood now. But it's been only a few days. We are all, as a race, still trying to sort out what our abilities are and what we can do." I looked at her. "And what about you? Has your elf half awakened?"

Adair pursed her lips, as though deep in thought. "A little. I definitely feel more connected to the earth now. It's not quite like what I feel for the water, but I think that'll change in time."

I hesitated in asking my next question. I desperately wanted to know, but wasn't sure if it would be too personal.

"Go ahead and ask it."

"Ask what?" I lowered my eyes, feeling slightly embarrassed.

"Whatever it is you're dying to know."

"Is it true that the queen and your father...?"

"Bonded? Yes, that's true."

"And... and that the queen will bear an heir. And that your father...?" I hardly dared to hope. If Eilath had sired another child that meant our race had a chance for life once again. That we wouldn't be condemned to a slow extermination.

"My da is also the unborn babe's father. Yes, that is true as well." Her eyes sparkled with excitement. "I'm so happy to get another sister. I've always only had brothers among the dryads."

"What's it like?"

"What's what like?" Adair dipped back into the water before pulling herself back against the dock.

"Siblings. Having them. While I understand the concept in theory, aside from the very rare occurrence of twins...." I shrugged, unsure of how to finish.

"I suppose that definitely cuts out cousins, uncles, and aunties as well, doesn't it?"

I nodded.

"Well, the truth is they can be a right hassle, all of them. But...." Adair turned and faced the slowly lowering sun. "But I wouldn't give them up for the world. Take my brother, Corcoran, for example—"

"Eisrus!" Eáchan's voice boomed from the end of the dock, and I shot to my feet.

"I'm sorry – I must go." I bent over to pick up my things as quickly as I could. "But I will see you again, yes?" I found I couldn't bear the thought of not seeing her again.

Adair smiled, her face lighting up. "Of course, that's what friends do."

◊◊◊

Eisrus maintained his composure long enough to feel the first bite of the sharpened rock against his upper arm. The fey only needed his hand, but why settle for a hand when they could hack off an entire arm?

He tried to be strong, to protest, to fight back, but the wood sprites held him tight. Their wicked red eyes gleamed in the starlight, and their wooden bodies were splattered with flecks of the elf's silver blood.

The blood loss was too much, his vision tunneled, and eventually, his screaming stopped.

Later, how much later he didn't know, Eisrus realized he was no longer bleeding. Mud and leaves coated the stump directly below his right shoulder.

Why would they use their magic to heal him?

Eisrus could see his right arm, only a hand span away,

severed and lying in a dried pool of blood. He watched, transfixed, as the bit of sparking sunshine the Spring Prince had embedded in his hand slowly detached itself once his arm died. It hovered for a moment, and then sped off, back to its master.

And his master and the Ailesit would think he and Adair were safe in Vevila.

He swallowed around the lump forming in his throat. The wood sprites were all facing him and smiling with malicious intent.

No one was safe now that Winter had Adair.

A rock slammed into his chest, and he let out a strangled cry, wondering if he'd cracked a rib.

The sprites cackled with evil glee, and it became clear to the Eisrus why they had healed him just enough.

He couldn't scream if he was dead.

◊◊◊

I couldn't find her. She wasn't in her usual places. Not the dock, not the springs in the queen's garden, not her rooms, or the spacious tub for swimming Queen Eánna, her stepmother, had given her.

Three weeks. I had been off with my master for three long weeks trying to come to an accord with the red dwarves. It was all for naught, and I found I was frantic to see Adair again.

Perhaps we could go for another swim, so long as Eáchan didn't find out. Or maybe a picnic. Our last picnic had been nice.

It had been Adair's birthday. She'd caught a fish, and I, a

hare. I promised her all the archery lessons she could ever want as her gift and she kissed my cheek in thanks. After our meals she laid her head in my lap as we watched the sunset, and she told me all about dancing with gnomes in Stoneybrook.

I'd left on the mission to the dwarves shortly after that, and while I was glad to finally be seeing more of our world, I found I didn't want to do it at the expense of not getting to know Adair.

I rounded the corner of one of the long hallways in the queen's palace and nearly lost my footing on the slick, marbled stone floors. Leaning against a marble pillar, I forced myself to take deep, calming breaths. I knew I would have to leave on another mission soon, but behaving like a fool wouldn't do me any good, or help me find Adair any faster.

And suddenly there she was, in the courtyard just to my left.

Her arms were wrapped around the thick trunk of an oak that shaded her from the hot summer sun overhead. Her eyes were closed, and she had a soft smile on her face, as if she was guarding a secret.

My heart calmed at the sight of her and I knew in that moment that I loved her. I'd suspected it before now. I could feel myself slipping. But this was the moment I knew.

I couldn't fully explain even to myself what it was that she did to me, but I knew I didn't want to live without her. Her voice soothed me, her laugh cheered me, and I wanted nothing more than to see her smile. I felt more alive than I ever had when I was with her.

I crept into the courtyard, determined not to disturb her,

but the tree must have told her I was there, or I wasn't as quiet as I thought I was. She waved me over with one hand, never moving her head away from the trunk, or opening her eyes.

Settling in beside her, we listened to the tree's music. It was a perfect moment. The sun shining bright overhead, birds singing in harmony to the tree's thrumming, the girl I loved finally embracing her elvish side—

"You stink."

"What?" My eyes popped open.

Adair's eyes were still closed, but she wrinkled up her nose in distaste. "When was the last time you had a bath?"

"Well, I only just got back. As in just this last hour. And I came straight to find you as soon as I did."

"That's no excuse for smelling like a mountain troll." Her eyes were cracked open, and I could see orange flickers of merriment in them. I was mesmerized. I had to tell her. I couldn't go another moment without her knowing.

"Adair, I have something I need to tell you. I... I—"

"Shall we go for a swim?" She tried to get to her webbed feet, but I took her hand in mine, gently pulling her back down alongside me.

"Later. I need to tell you—"

"Please don't ruin the moment." She didn't pull away, but she wouldn't meet my eyes. "Please don't ruin what we are, what we have."

"Ruin what? Our friendship?"

She nodded her head.

"I'm not trying to ruin it, I'm trying to make it better."

"Eisrus, you know your family would never approve of us

courting."

"That's not true – with *The Ailes* restored we can be with anyone we'd like now, regardless of race." I tried not to sound pleading.

She shook her head slowly, still not looking at me. "While I know that's technically the case, a thousand-year-old culture doesn't change overnight. I've seen how your people treat Story and Eirnin. The Ailesit saved your entire race, and some elves would still spit on her, given half a chance."

"Not all of us feel that way."

"But enough do."

"But, Adair, I—"

She placed a hand over my mouth.

"Don't say it. Please."

I moved her hand away and placed a soft kiss on her fingertips. "Don't say how I feel?"

She shook her head, still refusing to look at me.

"What are you so afraid of? I don't care what my family thinks. And I know how you feel about me. I've seen it in your eyes! Do you deny it?" I gripped her cool hand in mine and watched as a tear slid down her cheek. Why was she crying? This should be a joyous occasion!

Adair took a deep breath and wiped away the tear before facing me with a cool silver gaze, doing her best to hide her emotions.

"You forget, dryads don't have *your* kind of relationships. We love everyone. We don't bond ourselves to any one person. It goes against everything I know and believe in."

I sat back feeling slapped.

"But... you're half elf. You were just listening to the trees.

I thought... I thought...."

"You thought I would just throw over my entire way of life and reject the one society that has always accepted me regardless of my parentage, all because a boy professes to love me?"

"No, I just... I just...."

"Wanted me to put aside the dryad, and fully embrace the elf?" She dislodged her hand from mine roughly, her eyes burning red. "You don't really know me at all, do you?"

She left me sitting there alone against the tree, the rough bark pressed against my cheek, trying to make sense of what had just happened.

◊◊◊

Eisrus drifted back to wakefulness, but forced himself to maintain the façade of unconsciousness.

He'd learned over the past few hours... or was it days? Either way, it didn't matter. They wouldn't torture him if he wasn't awake to scream.

It was dark now, he could tell even through his closed lids. He could hear the three of them around him. Waiting. Patiently waiting. He felt one of them shift closer.

Perhaps not so patiently waiting, after all.

Eisrus could sense through the wood the approaching presence of two beings, likely more sprites.

He had to escape, and soon.

He had to tell the queen that Adair had been taken.

They had to rescue her. They just had to.

Eisrus was no longer bound, the ice bands had long since

melted, and the sprites thought him too weak to move. He hoped he was not.

His bow! If he could make it to his bow, he'd... do nothing.

The horror slowly washed over him as he realized he would never draw a bow again.

A low moan of anguish escaped his mouth before he could clamp down on the sound. The sprites reacted instantly and the one on his right thrust one of his stick-like fingers into Eisrus's amputated stump.

Eisrus screamed as his back arched up and his eyes flew open in pain.

The sprite on his left leaned over his face, the bark splitting into a smile. Quick as lightening, the fey jabbed a finger into the elf's left eye, and slowly began pulling.

◊◊◊

I paced in the main room of my home, my bare feet sweeping across the ancient wooden floor, worn smooth by generations of my family. My parents were both out. My father, who, as the former clan chief, was first advisor to Eáchan, was at a council meeting. My mother was with her apprentice.

I was grateful for the solitude, for I didn't think I could bear to answer their questions. They knew something was wrong. I could never hide my emotions from them, so when I'd returned from my encounter with Adair yesterday I'd shut myself up in my room.

"How dare she say my parents wouldn't approve?" I flung myself into my father's reading chair, shoving it against the wood paneled wall. "She knows nothing! My parents are wonderful. She is wonderful. They would get along so well if she would only try." I crossed my arms over my chest, fuming. "And I'm not asking her to stop being a dryad, I'm just asking her to embrace her elf half a bit more. Is that so awful?"

A tentative knock sounded on our front door, interrupting my solitary tirade. I stomped over, wondering who could possibly have the nerve to come.

It was Adair. And she had been crying.

"Oh, hullo." Her blue eyes took in my angry expression. "If now's not a good time, I can come back." Her voice cracked on the last word, and she dissolved into sobs, throwing herself into my embrace.

Any anger I'd felt toward her melted away as I lifted her into my arms and carried her back into my family's bathing room. Our tub was not so large as the queen's, and our stone walls not as fine as the queen's marble, but we had running water, and in that moment that was all that mattered.

I settled her inside the tub, clothes and all, and despite her small frame, she nearly filled it. I turned on the clay spigot, and cool water poured out, over Adair's legs. I pulled up a stool behind her, swept aside her mass of red braids, and while the tub slowly filled, gently rubbed her back, shoulders, and neck.

I don't know what possessed me to do this, as an elf would never have been so familiar with someone they were not bonded to, or at the very least courting. But I knew dryads were a much more affectionate race, and hoped that my touch would soothe her. Eventually her weeping quieted, and apart from the occasional sniffle, she seemed calmer.

The tub now full, I turned off the water, and resumed my ministrations on her shoulders, as she seemed to like it. I tried to not exult too much in the joy of actually touching her this intimately, given that I knew for her it was simply a source of comfort, nothing else.

"D'ya want to know what's wrong?" Her voice was quiet, timid, and so unlike her, it nearly broke my heart.

"Only if you want to tell me. Otherwise, I find I am quite happily engaged in learning all the curves and lines of your back."

She gave a sniffling laugh and patted my hand. "Thank you."

We continued on like this in a companionable silence for a long while. Long enough that even my eager hands began to weary, and I wondered what I could next do to resolve whatever had upset her.

"The queen and my da are sending me away."

My hands stilled.

"What?" I slid my stool around to the side of the tub and started massaging one of her hands.

Adair nodded and rubbed the back of her free hand along her eyes. She still wept.

"They told me this morning that I have to spend the rest of summer and all of autumn in Vevila with my mother. They said I can come back after the Winter Solstice."

I stared down at her hand, unsure of how to respond.

I was furious.

Furious with myself, with my master, the queen, and yes, even my parents. They had somehow found out about my interest in Adair and had conspired to send her away, under the sea, back to "her kind" where she belonged.

Of all the close-minded—

"And here I thought Queen Eánna loved me like her own daughter. Da, too. Of course, that all changed once their own child was coming. A pure-blooded elf daughter. What do they need me for? Their flippant, unpredictable, scandalous, half-dryad daughter." She pulled her hand away and covered her face, sobbing once again.

I reached out and pulled her toward me in a tight embrace. The water sloshed over the edge of the tub, soaking me, but I didn't care. All that mattered was Adair. I kissed the crown of her head and stroked her hair as her shuddering sobs overtook her body.

"That can't possibly be true. Is that what they told you?"

She shook her head, wiping her nose against my sleeveless green tunic. "No. But why would they specify that I had to be gone until after the Winter Solstice? That is when the baby is due to arrive. They clearly want me out of the way."

I could think of nothing to counter what she had said.

"When do you leave?"

"Tomorrow. Story and Eirnin are taking me. Ma wants to see Story for her birthday, so they'll escort me." She sniffed again. "More like, make sure I don't swim off."

My heart was racing. Tomorrow was so soon. Too soon. She would be gone for the better part of four months!

"But they can't leave tomorrow, whether it's the Ailesit's birthday or not. They'll miss the clan chief elections... perhaps they'll delay a week?"

Adair heaved a ragged breath and buried her head against

my chest even tighter.

"No, they are leaving tomorrow. And me with them."

◊◊◊

Unfamiliar voices, definitely not fey, permeated Eisrus's unconsciousness.

"Dude, what the hell happened to him? Is he alive?"

"I do not know, Joshua, and as a reminder—"

"Yeah, yeah, your name's not 'dude.' Check him for a pulse, will you?"

He felt one of them place a hand over his chest, and another placed two fingers along his neck.

"His heart still beats, though faintly. We must get him to a healer, quickly."

"Yeah, no sh…" The voices faded and Eisrus wondered if these were spirits of Ai come to take him across the Ailes Sea to join the rest of his kin who had passed before him.

But if they were spirits, and he was dead, why did he still feel so much pain?

Eisrus blinked his eyes slowly open. Or rather, eye. His left eye didn't want to obey him. Ignoring the needles of pain coursing through his arm when he moved it, Eisrus reached up to feel his eye.

There was nothing but an empty socket.

He remembered now. The sprites had taken his eye.

Looking around, he saw three piles of ash.

All that remained of the wood sprites.

A fair-skinned, red-headed young man's face filled Eisrus's vision. Like the Ailesit, his ears were strangely rounded.

Another human perhaps?

"Hey buddy, you're gonna be okay. We're here now, and we're gonna get you to a doc real quick." His had been the first voice Eisrus had heard. It was kind and caring, with an unfamiliar twang and several words the elf had never heard before.

"You... you are not spirits...." The words cost him dearly, and Eisrus nearly lost consciousness again. But no, there was something he needed to tell them. Something important. What was it?

"No, hunter, we are not spirits." A dark-skinned, blue haired dryad moved into the elf's field of vision. "I am Corcoran, and this is Joshua."

"Actually, it's just Josh."

Eisrus's mind latched onto that name.

Corcoran.

Why was that name important? It meant something. There was something he needed to do. Someone they needed to save—

"Adair!" Eisrus croaked. "I'm so sorry, I failed." *Tears leaked from his eye.*

The dryad was suddenly close, scrutinizing the elf. "What about Adair? Is she all right?"

"Dude, can't we worry about that later? Shouldn't we be more worried about getting this guy to a hospital or something?"

"Adair is my sister." Corcoran focused his intense blue eyes on Eisrus. "Where is she? I have been journeying for many months. What has happened, hunter?"

"He has her. He has...." Eisrus felt what tenuous control he *had on his consciousness slip away.*

◊◊◊

"We should not be stopping, Adair. The Ailesit and my master were quite insistent that we go straight to Vevila and use the protection the sea will afford you from the fey." I stomped up from the shore after Adair while she paused to shake out her hair. "It won't be safe for you until after the Winter Solstice."

She frowned at me over her shoulder and patted Ped, who'd transformed from seal to dog once he'd reached the dry land, on his flank.

"It's not safe for Story either, but she's still out there." Adair stuck out her jaw like a petulant child. "I want to help save Eírnin too, not be sent away like a child. I'm not a child, yet Story will never see me as anything but!"

I closed the distance between us and placed a hesitant hand on her shoulder. "*I* know you're not a child. Which means you need to make responsible choices, which, in this case, is to seek safety from the Winter King. More is at stake than just your life."

She flinched away from me. "Why didn't you tell Story all this? She's risking her life too."

"You think because the Ailesit is behaving poorly, that gives you an excuse to do so as well?"

Adair sighed and leaned her head against Ped's broad shoulder.

"No." Her voice was muffled by the selkie's fur. "But it's just not fair!"

"No, it is not. I'd rather be searching for Eírnin too." That was a lie. I'd rather be right where I was, drinking in the sight of Adair for the first time in months. My love for her had not waned in the slightest during her absence. If anything it had strengthened.

"Fiiiiiiine." She drew out the word and flopped down against a tree. Holding out her hand toward me, she tugged me down.

"Should we not be getting back to the sea?" I did not fail to notice that she still had my hand in hers and had, in fact, interlaced our fingers. Granted, that may have been due to the bit of sunshine currently residing in my palm. The Spring Prince had said to release it once we arrived in the dryad city, Vevila, in order to inform him, my master, and the Ailesit that we'd safely completed our journey.

I didn't want to ever release it and found both myself and Adair staring at it for long stretches of time. But I supposed everyone craved a bit of sunshine in their lives.

"Not just yet." Adair recalled me to our conversation. "We haven't seen each other in months. We should talk."

And by "we" she meant "her," which was fine by me. I enjoyed listening to her tell tales, and all the while, she held my hand tightly in hers.

But eventually, as I noticed the sun sinking low in the sky, I disengaged my hand and got to my feet. It was past time to go.

"No, not yet." Adair's eyes fixed on my bow, wrapped tightly in waxed paper and leather to keep it dry. "You promised me an archery lesson."

"What, now?"

"Yes, now."

"Adair, I hardly think—"

She pressed her fingers over my lips and left them to linger there a moment. "Then don't think. You promised me archery lessons for my birthday whenever I wanted them, and now I want them."

I stared at her lips, only inches from mine. All I would have to do is bend slightly and….

But I was too late. She was already gone, unwrapping my quiver and motioning me over. I heaved a sigh and began unwrapping my bow.

"Very well, but only a short lesson. I don't like the feel of these woods."

"Thank you!" She hugged me, and pressed a quick kiss on my cheek before she slung my quiver over my back. She averted her gaze from mine, but not before I glimpsed a flash of purple in her orange eyes.

I forced myself to focus on the task at hand. Give Adair her lesson and then bundle her back onto Ped and get her to the safety of the sea. Drawing an arrow from my quiver, I picked out an oak tree near enough to easily aim at in the darkening sky.

"Proper archery techniques begin with a proper stance—"

My hunting sense flared, and I calmly shifted my aim to a dark patch of underbrush to the right of the oak.

"Adair, get on Ped and run."

She froze. "What's wrong?"

"There is no time to explain." There were at least six of them, and it took everything in me not to toss Adair on Ped myself. But I knew the moment my back was turned, they would attack. "Please trust me in this, Adair."

Her eyes, yellow with worry, scanned the surrounding wood, and I thought for a brief moment that she might actually listen to me.

But then her gaze met mine and I knew the moment had passed.

"I'm not leaving you." Her eyes flooded with green and purple. "I love you, too."

LETTER OF REPIRSAL

Steven S. Long

The afternoon was fading as night approached the forest, slow but inexorable. Walking along a game trail came a man carrying an armful of branches. That he was a wolf's-head was obvious to anyone he saw him — the combination of unkempt look, cruel features, weapons showing signs of frequent use, and his unwashed stench said "bandit" to whomever he might meet on the high road... much to their dismay unless they were equally well armed.

He headed up a low hill toward a small plume of smoke rising into the darkening sky. Without warning or challenge a black-fletched arrow took him through the back of the neck, dropping him in his tracks with little more than the sound of the branches tumbling out of his arms and onto the ground.

A man dressed in brown cloak and garb appeared on a tree limb twenty yards back. Dropping lightly to the ground, he hurried forward to confirm that the man was dead and retrieve the arrow. *Now I must move quickly*, he thought. *They won't miss him much longer.*

Running swiftly but almost silently, he continued up the

trail until he could just see over the hill. Crouching behind some forest brambles, he observed the scene. Four more men just like the one he'd killed had made camp in a small clearing next to a stream. It was an ideal campsite, right next to water yet not so far from the high road that they couldn't easily get back to their filthy work of robbing and killing. But they were overconfident fools, with no guard or watchman.

The brown-cloaked man drew a second arrow and waited. *The darker it gets, the better my advantage... and I need all the help I can get against four. But they'll realize he's not back soon.*

As if hearing his thoughts, one of the bandits chose that moment to speak. "Hey, what's taking Corbin so long? Won't be nothin' left for him if he doesn't get back with that wood soon."

One of the others stopped his eating and guzzling. "Maybe we should go find him."

That was the brown-cloaked man's cue. He drew his bow, aimed at the first man who'd spoken, and let fly. Before the arrow struck home he quickly drew and fired again at another bandit.

The first man jerked with the pain of an arrow through his chest, then convulsed and fell over. The second target took the arrow in his belly and let out a hoarse scream of agony as he toppled over.

The brown-cloaked man burst from the underbrush and charged, hurling a throwing knife as he ran but missing the other two outlaws, who'd jumped to their feet and reached for their swords. He drew his own weapons as he ran. In his right hand was an axe short-hafted enough to serve as a tool but heavy enough to make a good weapon; in his left a baselard — a crescent-hilted blade longer than an ordinary dagger but smaller than a short sword. It had a pommel shaped like a hawk's head.

He was on the first man almost before the outlaw had time to get his sword. Blocking the bandit's clumsy swing with the baselard, he brought his axe down on the man's skull, splitting his head with a sickening crunch. He jerked the axe free and turned to face the other man.

The second bandit was quicker and cleverer than the brown-cloaked man had hoped. He slashed at his attacker with the calm, swift aim of a seasoned fighting man, not the panicked flailing about of a man taken by surprise. The brown-cloaked man winced as he felt the blade cut through his leather armor and bite into his side.

In return the brown-cloaked man lashed out with his own blade, forcing the bandit to pull his sword back quickly enough to defend his right side... and then the axe flashed forward, catching him on his unprotected left side where neck met shoulder, driving deep into the man's chest. The bandit wobbled for a moment, trying to bring his sword up for one final, defiant blow, then collapsed.

The brown-cloaked man freed his axe, then stood quietly for a moment, alert and on guard. He'd only seen five of them since he began trailing them earlier that afternoon, but it never hurt to be cautious. Twenty seconds later, convinced no further threat existed, he relaxed. He cleaned the axe on a bandit's grimy cloak and began to search the camp.

It didn't take long. The outlaws had five horses and a pack mule, plus an assortment of sacks and pouches holding the spoils of their banditry: plenty of food; a few dozen silver coins (and, surprisingly, a pouch with a dozen gold royals); some items of clothing and personal possessions. There was nothing of any great value.

Then something caught his eye — a pouch one of the bandits was wearing. It was well-made of fine leather, with sturdier stitching than one was likely to find so far away from the cities. Looking inside he found a few small coins and tiny keepsakes, but nothing more. Something wasn't right, though; this pouch wasn't something any common traveler or bandit would carry.

A-ha! On the back, hidden by what was made to look like some stitching — a concealed pocket! Opening it up he drew forth a small letter on fine paper, carefully folded into a rectangle and closed with red wax bearing a seal.

Carrying the letter over to the fire for better light, he examined the seal... and felt a chill rise up his spine. The twin bears of Krond! This was no ordinary letter, this came from some highly-placed Krondian nobleman. But how did it get this far into Valdaron? These bandits hadn't been anywhere near the border or they'd have been reported — and dealt with — sooner.

He carefully opened the letter with his knife and scanned the contents. Worse and worse: it was some sort of code. He couldn't read it and had no tools with him for puzzling it out. This was definitely something to be brought to his superiors, and as soon as possible.

But now it was first night, no time to start traveling. One by one he dragged the bodies a short way downstream and dumped them in the water, then sat down to enjoy the bandits' fire and what remained of their meal.

◊◊◊

Two weeks later he rode into Accara, the king's seat of Valdaron. The other four horses and most of the bandits' goods he'd given to surprised but grateful farmers and other folk along the way, leaving him with just one stout chestnut horse and a bag of coins.

Amidst a straggling of peasants bringing their wares to the day's market he rode through the Brandenar Gate, named for the king who built it centuries ago. The guards saw him and nodded acknowledgement, letting him go forward in peace despite the many weapons he wore. Only a very new guard wouldn't recognize one of the Drusaidi Shanir, the scout-assassins who served the throne of Valdaron by patrolling the roads and wilds in search of bandits, orcs, enemy soldiers, and any other threat to the King's peace.

He rode toward the palace, cutting his way easily through the crowds with well-timed nudges of his horse. At the outer gate a password gained him admission and he headed for the King's stables. "Here's a new addition for the King's herd," he said to the boy he handed the reins to when he dismounted. "He won't win any races, but he has plenty of endurance and is accustomed to the wilds."

"Yessir," the boy said, leading the horse off to an empty stall.

Bag of coins in hand, he took the staircase leading up to the castle storerooms, then walked out into a corridor near the kitchens. Snatching an apple from a basket being carried by one of the serving girls, he walked on until he found one of the palace guards.

"Is Seneschal Merekal in the castle?"

"Aye, m'lord, 'tis court-day."

"Send word to him that Vilkun has returned and awaits him in the East Tower."

"Aye, m'lord."

Vilkun walked quickly to the East Tower, taking care to be seen by as few people as possible and talking to no one. Once there he went up two flights of stairs, unlocked a door with a key he took from his belt pouch, and entered a small chamber decorated mostly in grey. The furnishings were simple — a table, a few chairs, a cabinet, a small fireplace. No fire burned on the hearth, but with summer coming the room was warm enough that he felt no need of one.

He took off his cloak, threw it over the back of one of the chairs, and sat down to wait. He was there less than half a glass when the door opened again. In walked a middle-aged man, stout but not too heavy, richly dressed with a well-kept black beard: Merekal, Duke of Tanevar, the King's Seneschal of Valdaron... and, as only a handful of men in the kingdom knew, commander of the Drusaidi Shanir.

"You've returned early, Vilkun," in his usual dry tone. He almost sounded bored, but Vilkun knew he was not — behind that courtier's exterior was one of the brightest minds and sharpest pairs of eyes in Valdaron. "I trust there's some reason?"

"I was up in the Gordaut Hills. I heard word from some of the folk about a gang of bandits robbing travelers on the high road and hunted them down. After I left them all for the crows, I discovered an exceptionally fine pouch on one of them. In a concealed pocket in the pouch I found this." He drew out the letter and handed it over.

The seneschal examined it quickly, then frowned. "A coded message from Krond? Was it to the bandits?"

Vilkun shook his head. "Couldn't be — it was sealed when I found it, and still in the concealed pocket, so I doubt they were even aware it was there. I opened it, but as you see it's in code. I have no idea what it says... but these bandits haven't been anywhere near the border. Whoever carried it brought it a long way into Valdaron."

"I know someone who might be able to read these signs — one of the king's spies, a man with the Devil's own cleverness. I'll take it to him right away. Was there anything else?"

Vilkun heaved the sack of coins onto the table. "Just this — a gift to the King from the bandits."

Merekal looked inside. Pulling out the pouch, he poured a dozen gold coins from it into his hand. "Genuine?" he asked.

"As far as I can tell. I'm no forger to distinguish true coin from false, though."

Merekal placed six of the coins on the table in front of Vilkun, then poured the rest back into the pouch. "I'll see that all this makes its way to the King's treasure-chambers. Get a room in the town and let me know where you are; I'll send word when the King decides what next he wants you to do."

One of the King's gold royals bought Vilkun a fine room at the Boar & Panther. He could spend weeks alone in the wilderness with nothing but the cold ground for a bed — but when there was no need for such privation, why suffer?

He'd only had three days to enjoy the city when he received the Lord Seneschal's summons. Gathering up his gear, he told old Horgen the innkeeper to put the rest of the royal toward his longstanding bar tab, then hurried over to attend on Merekal.

He hadn't been seated long when the seneschal walked into the room — and not by himself. Behind him was a tall, middle-aged man, handsome, with a dark beard and hair, sumptuously dressed and wearing a crown: King Janos. "My liege!" Vilkun said, quickly getting out of his chair and kneeling.

The King's usual good humor hadn't deserted him entirely. "Up, Vilkun, up — there's enough dirty business here without your dirtying your knees on the floor as well."

After all three were seated, Merekal spoke. "My man broke the code. The letter seems to be the latest in a long line of communications from the Regent of Krond to Lord Thelborn. Krond plans to invade over the Estula, and Thelborn will rise in support of him and attack us from behind."

"Thelborn," Vilkun said as if he were spitting. "We've often kept watch on him, and never liked what we saw. That family has orc's-blood in it somewhere, I'll warrant."

"I wouldn't doubt it," Merekal replied. The King said nothing.

"Why does King Tenec want to attack Valdaron?"

"King Tenec is a seven year-old child and probably knows nothing of this," Janos replied. "But the Regent, Lord Rudegar, is a treacherous snake who'd love to add Valdaron's lands to Krond's. He'd parcel them out among his own sons and other nobles as a way of securing his grip on power. If he succeeds, no doubt young Tenec will meet with an "unfortunate accident" and he'll simply assume the throne for true."

"If only Bernwald hadn't died so young," Merekal said bitterly.

"I'm not so sure Rudegar didn't have something to do with that as well, but it doesn't matter at this point. What matters is making sure this attack fails. And for that we need your help, Vilkun."

"All my service is yours to command, Your Highness, but I'm not sure I understand how one person, even a drusaidi shanir, can aid you — besides wielding a sword in battle like any other loyal King's man."

"The service I require of you now is far more difficult than fighting at my side, Vilkun," the King said. "I need you to stop Lord Thelborn's attack. I must take my army east to meet the main thrust from Krond — if Thelborn comes upon me from behind there's almost no chance of victory."

"How can one man stop a lord's army, Your Highness?"

"Isn't that what you drusaidi shanir do — the impossible?" the King asked with a half-hearted grin. "I would not ask this if you were it not so necessary, but you are the only man for the job. All the rest of your comrades are out on patrol and cannot be reached."

"If that is what I must do, that is what I shall do," Vilkun answered. "By your leave I will depart immediately, Your Highness. It's a long ride to Thelborn's lands, and I'll need every moment I can get."

"Go at once, and may the gods go with you," Janos said, clasping Vilkun's hand in his own briefly. "Buy me the time I need and we'll dispose of Thelborn for good."

"I will, Your Highness."

Vilkun headed for the stables, where he retrieved not the bandit's mount he'd ridden in on, but his own horse — a tall black charger named Hringli, from the old word for "swift." Trained for battle and with the endurance of an ox, he was the perfect horse for a drusaidi shanir in need of all the speed he could muster.

Three days' hard travel later he entered Thelborn lands... though not by any route Lord Thelborn or his men were likely to be aware of. Even here, the drusaidi shanir knew the land well.

All three days one thought had occupied Vilkun's mind: *How can I stop Lord Thelborn?* Just slowing Thelborn considerably would likely be enough, but even that task seemed beyond his means. A week's rain would do the job nicely, but unfortunately he was no wizard to command the weather.

Dawn of his fourth day of travel found him on a forested ridge overlooking Lord Thelborn's castle. The place was a hive of activity. There were men at arms everywhere — training, packing mules, loading wagons, and performing the countless chores necessary to get an army on the move. From the looks of it Thelborn had mustered nearly a hundred men and would be ready to leave no later than the next day. *Where did he get so many men?* Vilkun wondered. *He wouldn't need more than two or three dozen at most to control his fief. Perhaps those rumors of orcish blood in his house have truth to them. For all the orcs we've killed, many still reside in the mountains to the west.*

The sun was rising; he backed away from the edge of the

ridge so no one below would see him. Could I infiltrate the castle in all the confusion and kill Thelborn? he wondered, but almost as soon as the thought occurred to him he dismissed it. Even amidst the seeming chaos Thelborn's guards would be alert, and just killing him wouldn't necessarily stop the attack — whoever intended to rule Thelborn's lands after him would pick up the banner and continue the charge. No, he had to stop the entire army, not one man; Lord Thelborn's demise would be for the King to accomplish.

Moving through the forest as quietly as a cat, Vilkun returned to where he'd hidden Hringli near the road. Watching Thelborn's soldiers load supplies wouldn't help him; he needed to scout the route Thelborn would likely take and see what possibilities it offered.

The route, at least was obvious: Thelborn's army would journey south to join the great east-west road that ran the length of Valdaron, and even into Krond. He got to the road quickly and began riding it eastward, looking carefully for anything he could use to his advantage. He'd come this way many a time before, but the need of the moment brought a fresh perspective on the passing landscape. *How can I defeat an entire army by myself?*

As noon approached he crested a rise and entered Red Rock Valley — a broad, flat land between two ridges. It narrowed and gently sloped to the south, where it finally gave way to the lowlands at the Cataracts of Carthana, formed as the stream that ran down the center of the valley poured over the rocks to form an impressive waterfall.

Vilkun stopped Hringli and looked over the valley carefully from his high vantage. Even with the slope, the ground becomes boggy here during the rainy season, and in the spring when the snows melt. Could I dam the stream and flood the valley to block Thelborn's march?

Almost as the idea came into his head he dismissed it. Even if there was time for a lake to fill the Red Rock — which he doubted — any dam he could build as one man, Thelborn's hundred men could quickly destroy. At most he could hope to delay Thelborn for a few hours, and that would not buy the King enough time. On he rode.

By late afternoon he was still in the high hills, riding through a region where rocky hills frowned over the road. Another possible solution presented itself: I could cause a landslide and block the road. He began eyeing the hills more closely, to see which might suit this plan well. He found several where the hills closed in on both sides of the road, creating a pass he could easily block if he could cause enough rock to fall.

But again the scheme had more flaws than strengths. If too little rock fell, Thelborn's men could clear the road easily enough, even if they had to leave some of their supply wagons behind. If too much rock fell, or he collapsed an entire hillside, the road could be blocked for months... perhaps even forever, cutting western Valdaron off from east. The King wouldn't thank him for buying the safety of half the kingdom at the price of the other half! It was hard enough to keep the western lordlings under control as it was.

Vilkun slept that night in a small dell between two hills, keeping his fire as small and smokeless as he could to avoid betraying his presence to any scouts Lord Thelborn might send ahead of him. He awoke at first light and was soon on the road once more. Desperation was beginning to eat at him.

◊◊◊

All morning he followed the road west and a little south, looking for some obstacle he could place in the path of Thelborn and his hundred. But from this point, he knew, the road ran over flat and rocky ground until it reached the bridge that spanned Ogreskull Gorge. He could destroy the bridge if he had to, but that too would cut the rest of the kingdom off from the eastern lands until the king could have it repaired — which would take not only time but money.

And ultimately it would be a futile tactic anyway, he realized. Thelborn could simply turn back and take the little-used road that led south around the gorge and past Gnispa Heath. It would take him longer, but...

The Heath! The thought burst into his brain like a flash of lightning. He stopped his horse and considered the plan forming in his head. It was not without its risks, but it was more likely to work than any other idea he'd had... and he was running out of time.

Standing in the stirrups he stared at the sky, using his well-honed drusaidi shanir senses and wilderness lore to judge what the weather would be for the next few days. Satisfied with what he read in the clouds, he put his heels to Hringli's ribs and rode for the village of Larbach as fast as he could go.

◊◊◊

Vilkun crossed the great wooden bridge over Ogreskull Gorge and rode into Larbach, a small village on the eastern side, late that afternoon. The village square, if it could be called that, was where a small inn, a smithy, and a cartwright's shop faced one another across the dusty road. Two people sat on benches in front of the inn, drinking beer in the golden sunshine, and the sound of hammer on anvil ringing from the forge filled the air.

He reined Hringli in and gave a long, loud, sharp whistle. The hammering stopped, and the two drinkers looked at him in puzzlement. Villagers soon came out of the buildings with the same expression on their faces.

"People of Larbach! I am Vilkun, a Druisadi Shanir in the service of King Janos of Valdaron." He held up his cloak-pin, which like those of all druisadi shanir was made in the shape of their emblem, the leaf and thorn. "I am here on the King's business to protect you; Lord Thelborn marches east from his stronghold with a hundred men at his back."

A babble of confused voices broke out, shouting questions or fears. Vilkun raised his hand for silence, and soon got it. "Who among you leads this village?"

A tall, well-muscled man — the smith, obviously — stepped forward. "That would be me, Otmar. Or perhaps Mokus the innkeeper there."

"I'll need your help if we're to keep Thelborn away. Call all the villagers here as soon as you can."

Otmar stood his ground stubbornly. "Why? Anyone could show us that badge. How do we know you're not one of Thelborn's men, trying to trick us?"

Before Vilkun could respond, Mokus the innkeeper spoke.

"I recognize him, Otmar. He's stayed at my inn before. He's who he says he is."

"All right," the burly blacksmith said, no longer looking quite so sullen. "Get you a drink, King's man, and I'll have the villagers here in a glass."

◊◊◊

An hour, a meal, and two mugs of the inn's fine beer later, Vilkun left the inn to find a group of villagers assembled. No more than three dozen, they were farmers and craftsmen and laborers, good subjects of Valdaron who possessed little but still carried themselves with pride. He hoped their loyalty to the King was as strong.

He stepped up on a bench so all could see and hear him. Dusk was upon them, and someone had lit torches; he grapped one and held it up. "I am Vilkun, of the Druisadi Shanir. No doubt word has spread of my reason for coming to your village. I have a plan to stop Lord Thelborn and save your homes, but I must have your help if it's to succeed. I need you to bring every barrel and crock of lantern oil in the village to me by dawn tomorrow, a cart big enough to carry it all, and several men to work beside me for a day."

Grumbling broke out at that. "All our lantern oil?" someone said. "What will we do when we need light in our homes?"

"You must rely on torches for now, until you get more oil."

"We can't afford any more oil! You're taking all we have to last the year!"

"I will replace what I take. Who among you can write?" Mokus, his wife, and his daughter raised their hands, as did two others Vilkun didn't recognize. "Now, who has a good horse and can bear a message to Accara?" Two men raised their hands.

"Very well. I will write a message to the King himself this night, telling him what I have asked of you and requesting that he send oil to replace what I have taken... as well as other things you will need. Mokus will read it to assure you I do not play you false, and these men will carry it to the King in the morning. Go now, bring me the oil!" The crowd broke up, some people muttering among themselves as they went.

At Vilkun's command, Mokus brought him parchment and ink. By candlelight he wrote a message beseeching King Janos for six large barrels of oil, as well as wood and engineers enough to rebuild the bridge.

Mokus read the letter with a grim look on his face. "You mean to burn the bridge, my lord?"

"I do. There's no other way, if Thelborn is to be stopped. From the other side of the gorge his army cannot hurt you or your homes... and the King's men will be a long time rebuilding the bridge. They'll need somewhere to stay and to eat, hey?" That brought a smile to the innkeeper's face.

Vilkun sealed the letter with a large blob of wax, impressed his cloak-pin into it to show who sent it, and wrote MEREKAL on the outside in large letters. Then he tucked it into his jerkin beneath his leather armor.

◊◊◊

Early in the morning Vilkun met the two messengers, Andel and Tevan. He gave them the letter, five silver nobles apiece, and two packs of food prepared by Mokus. "Deliver this letter to Seneschal Merekal at the King's palace in Accara as soon as you can. Don't ride your horses to exhaustion, but travel quickly. If anyone in the city questions you, show them the seal on the letter and tell them Vilkun sent it." They nodded their understanding and set out east along the road.

Next he turned to the oil. There were several small casks of it and a host of small jars and crocks. I pray the gods it's enough, he thought. He told two of the men helping him to pour all the smaller containers into one large barrel provided by Mokus. He instructed the others to gather small boulders, fell pine trees to make stout poles, and bring all of it to the Lorbach side of the bridge.

All that day Vilkun worked with the two men, driving the cart back and forth across the bridge, spreading the oil over the wood. Dry weather for the past few weeks had left the wood parched and cracked, eager to soak up the golden liquid. Vilkun poured it out carefully to ensure that the bridge would instantly go up in flames when he wanted it to, but not putting so much oil in any place that the smell of it would alert Thelborn's men. He kept an eye on the sky and prayed no rain would fall. Fortunately there were few clouds.

Meanwhile Vilkun's other helpers gathered a large pile of stones and crude wooden poles. When the spreading of the oil was done, he directed the men in the building of a barricade to block the bridge. The sharpened poles were lashed to the stones to give the barrier some strength — it didn't have to hold Thelborn's men back for long, but if it were too fragile it would fail in its purpose altogether. Seeing Vilkun's purpose, the villagers brought other things to help: the remnants of a cart that no longer worked; a cracked barrel they filled with earth and pebbles. They left only a small gap for him to use on the morrow.

By the end of the day the work was done. An exhausted Vilkun and his helpers returned to the inn, where he bought them all beer and stew. Before retiring to his bed, the drusaidi shanir ordered two villagers to maintain watch over the gorge, in case Thelborn had traveled quicker than he expected.

The next day Vilkun arose early. After breaking his fast, he put on his armor, gathered his gear, and prepared to set out. Before he left he had some last words of warning for the villagers. "If my plan fails and Thelborn's men make it through the barricade, they'll likely be angry. Flee if you must, or tell him I forced you to do it and perhaps he'll be merciful." Several of the villagers gave him sour looks, but the rest seemed to have faith in his scheme. He rode through the gap in the barrier, then watched carefully as the villagers plugged it with more rocks and wood.

Vilkun rode Hringli quickly across the bridge and then turned south, looking for a way up into the hills that lined the gorge. He finally found one, taking care when he used it to leave no trace of his passing. Within a glass he made his way to a rocky, forested outcropping on a hill overlooking the bridge. He tied Hringli loosely to a tree, knowing he'd need to leave swiftly when the time came. He sat down behind a stone, strung his bow, got out two arrows with oil-soaked cloth wrapped around the head, made sure his flint and steel were to hand... and waited.

Hours passed. At last, not long after noon, he heard the sound of men talking from the road to the west, and then the jingle of harness and mail. Peering up cautiously from behind the stone, he was soon rewarded with the sight of Thelborn's vanguard reaching the bridge. Spying the barricade at the far end, they halted in confusion, waiting for their lord to arrive.

Thelborn and the bulk of his forces arrived soon enough. They bunched up on the western edge of the gorge for a few minutes. Vilkun couldn't hear what they said, but he could see Lord Thelborn, tall and proud aboard his black steed, his arms — three towers on a blue field — adorning a pennon fluttering above. *So easy to end this now with just one arrow,* Vilkun thought. *But I cannot be sure that would stop his army too.* Nevertheless he drew a third arrow from his quiver.

Lord Thelborn gestured and two squads of men rode forward. One was apparently to remove the barricade, for they went down the center of the bridge with no weapons drawn; the other saw to their protection, riding along the sides with shields at the ready.

◊◊◊

Vilkun struck flint against steel and lit the two arrows, carefully keeping them below the edge of the stone so none of Thelborn's men would see the fire. He waited as the warriors moved across the bridge... closer and closer to the barricade.

When they were but a dozen yards from the eastern end of the bridge, Vilkun fired his first arrow in their direction, then turned and fired the other nearer to the western side. They hissed through the air unnoticed and struck the oil-soaked timbers. Within two heartbeats the bridge was engulfed in flames. On the bridge men shouted in fear and agony; horses reared and screamed, throwing their riders. To the west Lord Thelborn and his men drew back from the conflagration. Some of the soldiers on the bridge rushed to the barricade, but in panic and pain could make no headway against it; like their comrades they died among the flames.

Vilkun risked one more shot, this time at Thelborn. That was a mistake. The turmoil and motion among the enemy forces made Thelborn too difficult a target — the arrow struck a warrior near him, who went down howling. Worse, some of Thelborn's men spotted him. He turned and ran uphill into the deeper cover, arrows striking the ground and trees around him.

Soon he was beyond the archers' range and made it back to Hringli. He tore the reins free and leaped into the saddle, spurring his horse to the best possible speed on the uneven ground. He burst out of the hills and onto the more level ground west of them, riding south as fast as he could while bent close over the saddle. He lofted a silent prayer that none of Thelborn's men would give chase.

An hour later he reined to on the southern side of a small forested ridge. While Hringli rested and gulped water from a spring, he crept back up to the edge of the ridge. Carefully concealing himself among the trees, he peered northward with his sharp drusaidi shanir eyes. Minutes passed, but he could detect no signs of pursuit. But he could see the heavy plume of smoke from the burning bridge. Now if only

Thelborn would turn around and bring his surviving men down the southern road....

After allowing Hringli a little more rest, Vilkun headed south again, this time traveling at an easier pace. He thought he could reach the Heath by nightfall, and while the thought of spending the night there disturbed him, it meant he had plenty of time. Even at best speed Lord Thelborn couldn't turn his army around, get to the south road, and arrive at the Heath for nearly two days.

◊◊◊

Gnispa Heath: a desolate, almost barren land covered only by patches of low, sickly bushes. In the distance, over its rolling swales and rises, Vilkun could see line of higher hills that was his ultimate destination. Preferring healthier ground, he rode back north a short distance and made his camp near a small copse.

In the morning he rode onto the Heath, keeping a watchful eye on the hills. Hringli became restless and harder to control; the smell of the heath, apparent even to Vilkun, disturbed him... and Vilkun knew it would only get worse as they approached the hills.

Further onto the heath they rode, and slowly but surely the hills loomed larger. At last Vilkun saw what he was looking for: a thin plume of smoke rising up from one of them. The sight reassured him that his plan could still work even as he felt an unaccustomed stab of fear in the pit of his stomach.

He turned Hringli more to the east, away from the plume of smoke, but still south. He continued on. Before they began to climb into the hills, he stopped and tied Hringli to a shrub. Then, leaving his weapons on his saddle, he lay down and began rolling around on the ground. When he finished he was covered in dirt and dust from head to toe; his black hair was now ochre-colored from it. Hringli snorted and shied away, but he climbed quickly into the saddle and continued his journey.

Slowly he worked his way up into the hills, then turned west back toward the plume of smoke but still well south of it. Soon he stopped and dismounted once more. He dared bring Hringli no closer. He had to hope that the horse's training would hold, that it would not whinny or scream or stamp despite the unpleasant smell of the place and the hunger and thirst it would soon feel. Taking his axe, bow, and arrows, he continued west.

Moving with all the stealth he could muster, Vilkun crept across the hills. By mid-afternoon he reached the spot he wanted: a few dozen yards south of the plume of smoke, which he could see wafting into the sky over the top of one of the hills just to the north. He found a comfortable spot and sat down.

He spent the night there, hardly moving. He ate cold trail food from his pouch, knowing that to light a fire would ruin all his plans. He watched the stars awhile, then drifted off to sleep.

The next day brought more of the same. He stayed in place, making as little noise as possible and keeping his eyes on the road to the north.

It was late afternoon when he finally saw it: the glint of sunlight on steel along the road. He watched for a few minutes as the glint grew: this could only be a force of armed men. And only Lord Thelborn's men would march to war down this road.

Now was the time to act! He ran forward, making as little noise as possible, until he was on the hill next to the plume of smoke. Soon he was overlooking the mouth of a dark cave from which the smoke rose. The smoke and air from the cave smelled foully, like the brimstone in an alchemist's workroom.

Along the hillside above the cave-mouth were many stones, from small ones to boulders. Moving to one of the boulders, Vilkun stood behind it and pushed with all his strength. It barely budged. Pulling forth his axe, he used it as a primitive lever and finally managed to dislodge the large stone. It rolled down the hillside and over the edge to land with a heavy thump in front of the cave. A trickle of smaller stones and dirt followed behind it. Rushing over to another, smaller, boulder, he pushed it over the side.

Suddenly the plume of smoke ceased. Vilkun retreated, quickly finding a small stand of scrub brush to hide in that would still allow him to view the road.

From out of the cave something emerged: red-gold, wedge-shaped, an enormous reptilian head. The rest of the dragon's body followed slowly as it gazed around itself. Then it saw the men on the road and its lethargy vanished. Flicking its wings, it lifted into the air with unearthly grace, a fearsome, deadly arrow burnished golden by the afternoon sunlight and pointed straight at Lord Thelborn's army.

Some of the soldiers saw the wyrm and screamed. Horses' terrified whinnies added to the tumult, drowning Thelborn's shouted orders. Spying his pennon, the dragon flew that way, belching fire, and in that horrific burst of flame Lord Thelborn and his captains died. Then the dragon fell upon the rest of the army, his fangs, talons, and breath wreaking bloody havoc. Arrows bounced off his flanks; sword-blows skittered harmlessly over his scales.

Vilkun was running now, back to the east toward Hringli, caring little how much noise he made. He had to escape immediately, while the dragon was still busy, or else he'd die just like Thelborn's men were dying now. He reached his steed, mounted, and rode eastward as fast as the frightened horse would carry him.

◊◊◊

Two weeks later Vilkun was once again seated in the grey chamber in the East Tower awaiting Seneschal Merekal. He was well-rested, well-fed, bathed, and happy. King Janos's battle with Krond had been a success. Without Thelborn's forces in support, Lord Rudegar's army had been unable to overcome Valdaron's army. Rudegar remained Regent of Krond, but it would be long and long before he once again cast covetous eyes across the Estula.

The door opened; Seneschal Merekal entered. He'd been at the battle and taken a minor wound in the right arm, which was now in a sling. "At least one of us kept himself safe while in the King's service," he said.

"Aye, but it was a near thing at times," Vilkun replied.

"Let's hear your report. How did you do it?"

Vilkun told his tale, holding nothing back. "Did my messengers get through to you?" he asked when he described the fight at the bridge.

"Yes, though they had to wait awhile. They've been rewarded and sent home; I've already given orders for the rebuilding of the bridge and replacing for the oil you used — plus enough food to give the villagers a fine feast. What next?"

"Next I waited for them to come past Gnispa Heath and turned the dragon on them," Vilkun said with a grin.

Merekal's look turned dark and grim. "You awoke the dragon of Gnispa? That's worse than Lord Thelborn! You fool, he'll devastate the kingdom before we can muster the force to put him down... if we can put him down at all!"

"Relax, sir, relax," Vilkun said, raising his hands placatingly. "His Highness should live so long that the Dragon of Gnispa will be such a problem to him. Think about what I did: I sent the dragon after an army of nearly a hundred men and horses. By the time it's done gorging on their remains, it will be so full it will only want to go back to sleep again. There's no need to fear the return of the dragon! It won't awaken for decades... or until I have need of it again."

Merekal considered his words, slowly calming down as the truth of them dispelled his fears. "One thing I don't understand, though, Vilkun. Why didn't the dragon eat you, too?"

"I was covered in the dirt and dust of the heath. I kept out of sight and made no noise, and I smelled just like the land around him. Once he spotted Thelborn and his men, he assumed they were what woke him up."

Merekal laughed. "Well, Vilkun, never let it be said you're not willing to get dirty to get a job done."

THE SNOW WOMAN'S DAUGHTER

Eugie Foster

When I was a little girl, I thought my mother's name was Yuki, which means snow. That was part of her name, but I didn't learn the rest of it until the night my father died.

My mother left us on a slate-gray evening when I was five, with her namesake falling from the sky and piled high around the windows and doors. Awakened by raised voices, I watched through a tear in the curtain that shielded my sleeping mat as my mother wrapped her limbs in a shining, white kimono. As far back as I could remember, she had always worn the dark wool shifts that all mountain people wear, spun from the hair of the half-mad goats that give us milk and cheese. In her kimono she looked like a princess, or a queen. Her skin was paler than mine, and I am thought quite fair. Roku, the boy who lived on the northern crest, used to tease me when we were little, calling me "ghost girl" and "milk face."

That night, my mother was so white, it was as if a candle shone within her breast. It made my eyes crinkle as I squinted through the thick cloth.

I saw her come toward me and I scrambled to return to my mat. She wasn't fooled, but then, she had never been deceived by my tricks.

"Sekka," she said, "I am going away."

I sat up, dropping my pretense. "Where are you going, Mama?"

"I am returning home. Your father broke a promise to me."

Through the swept-back curtain, I saw Father huddled miserably by the fire.

"When are you coming back?"

"Never."

The finality of her reply stunned me.

"But if you need me," she continued, "call my real name three times, and I will come for you."

"Your real name?"

"Your father will tell you what it is."

Her arms were cool as they embraced me. Soothing and restful when I was sick with a fever, now they chilled me through.

She pulled away from me, and I began to cry. I trailed after her, frightened and cold. Through my tears, I watched her open the door of our house, dressed only in the thin, white silk of her kimono. The breath of winter rushed in, sucking away the cozy warmth of our hearth fire. She stepped into the snowstorm raging outside.

I wanted to run after her, but Father caught me up in his arms, and we both watched my mother walk away, melting into the whiteness of the falling snow.

I asked him that night what my mother's real name was,

as I intended to call her back immediately. But he didn't tell me.

I asked him every year on the anniversary of that night until I was sixteen. He would not relent, and eventually the worries and uncertainties of a maiden approaching womanhood overshadowed family mysteries.

Most pressing of these was Roku. Somehow, between rambling trips together to the market and snowball fights among the trees, he had become more than the brat who tugged on my braids and poured ice water on my head. My heart tripped and fluttered when our fingers brushed together, and heat filled my cheeks when he remarked upon the ribbon I had sewn to my skirt.

The intervening years had not been good to my father, though. He had withered from a strong, healthy figure to a feeble shadow, a wraith of a man. He merely blinked when Roku came one day, bearing a sprig of wild honeysuckle, and asked to wed me. It was as though the betrothal of his only daughter was of no more consequence than a discussion of the weather.

I had always assumed I would marry, but it had been a distant eventuality. Now I was as bewildered as if I had woken on a December morning to discover summer skies and the snow all melted away. How could I leave my father, our home, and become a wife and mother?

After Roku left, my father slumped in his chair before the fire. He pointed at Roku's engagement bracelet, heavy on my wrist, and said, "There drops my last excuse. The day I have always dreaded, when I must lose you, too, is nearly arrived. So tonight I will tell you your mother's real name."

Forgetting my trepidation about my impending marriage, I sat at my father's feet, waiting.

"When I was a boy," he began, "I was apprenticed to the woodcutter, Mosaku. One evening, we were out in the forest chopping logs, and a sudden blizzard overtook us. We ran into a tiny cave for shelter and prayed for the storm to end.

"Mosaku fell asleep. Eventually, I drifted off, too, and I dreamed.

"In my dream I saw a beautiful woman. Her kimono was made of ice crystals, and it glistened on her body like a sheet of diamonds. Her face was like the moon, cool and impassive, and her eyes flashed like sunlight on the snow.

"She bent over Mosaku and breathed out white smoke. It covered my old master, sheathing him in a layer of spangled silver. Turning from him, her eyes fell upon me.

"I wanted to shout, cry out, but I was dazed by fear. I watched her walk to me, each footstep as graceful as a dancer's. She leaned close to my face, and I was sure I was going to die.

"'I had intended to kiss you as well,' she said in a voice as smooth and flawless as a pane of ice. 'But you are so handsome with your wide eyes and strong shoulders. I will spare you, but you must promise never to speak of me. If you even whisper of so much as the hem of my kimono, I will know it and I will return to blow my kiss of everlasting sleep over you. Do you promise?'

"I nodded, and she was gone. I startled awake and saw poor Mosaku, quite dead. By then the snowstorm had stopped, and I fled home.

"Everyone asked me what had happened, and I told them

we had been caught in the snow. I did not mention my dream of the white maiden with her breath of frost.

"The next year, I met your mother at the winter festival. She said her parents had died and she was looking for work as a servant girl. But her hands were far too pale and soft for the harsh work of a washerwoman. I invited her to be my wife for I had fallen in love with her quiet voice and laughing eyes. She agreed, and the next week we wed.

"Of course, she was the snow maiden in disguise. At first, I did not recognize her without her white kimono. But the chill of her arms and the pallor of her skin, who else could she be?

"I remembered my promise to her, and for six years, I said nothing. Then one night, as she was sewing a torn shirt for me, I saw her in the firelight, and her skin was whiter than lilies, and her eyes danced brighter than the flames. I was overwhelmed by love for her and could not believe how fortunate I was. How could someone as beautiful, as elegant as she, love a common woodcutter like me? In my stupid insecurity, I asked her:

"'Do you ever regret sparing me, that night in the cave?'

"I had not expected her to react so harshly.

"She flung down her sewing. 'You promised never to speak of so much as the hem of my kimono!' she shouted. 'You broke your promise! I should kill you for that, but for the sake of Sekka, I will spare you.'

"I was frightened by the terrible look in those eyes that had always been so full of laughter.

"'Don't you love me?' I whispered.

"'Didn't I show you how I loved you by sparing your life?

Didn't I prove my love by coming to you in this mortal guise? Have I ever given you reason to doubt my love when I held you in my arms, cared for your house, and bore you a daughter? So why now do you question my devotion?'

"I had nothing to say to that. So she donned her white kimono and left us.

"I have mourned her ever since. I hoped she would forgive me and return to us, but she never has. I was afraid to tell you her real name for fear she would take you away, leaving me alone. Now I am dying, and it doesn't matter anymore. Your mother's name is Yuki-hime-kami, the snow spirit."

The moment his mouth finished shaping those words, he drooped forward and died.

I wrapped his body in a blanket and laid him on his sleeping mat. My father had lived so long with a shattered heart. In all that time had Mother even thought of us? Had she ever loved us?

I spoke her name.

"Mother! Yuki-hime-kami!" I cried. "Yuki-hime-kami! Yuki-hime-kami!"

The fire's light turned from orange-red to a cold, lifeless blue. It crackled and sang, not with the snap of burning wood, but with the sharpness of ice warmed by sunlight. White smoke gushed into the room from the chimney, and it was neither sooty, nor hot, but cold, and smelled of the clean tang of fresh snow. She, my mother, stepped out of the smoke in her white kimono. While my father's face had become creased with age, and strands of gray mingled freely with darker locks, she had not aged. She was as beautiful, as young, as the day she had left.

"My daughter, you have grown up." She held her arms wide for an embrace, but I did not go into them.

"I am eighteen years old," I said. "Next week, I am to be wed to Roku."

She let her arms drop to her side. "You say that as though you spoke of a funeral and not your own wedding. Don't you love him?"

I was angry then. "Who are you to speak of love? Father loved you, and look what happened to him."

She gazed at my father's swaddled body, and a tear glittered in her eye. It fell and shattered on the floor, a droplet of ice. "I loved him, too, my handsome woodcutter. It is why I had to leave."

"What do you mean? You left because of some silly promise."

"I left to save his life. I am a snow spirit, Sekka. I am frigid death. I fell in love with your father, but by the laws of the winter gods, I had to kill him. So I hid and gave up my immortality, content in your father's love. But the moment he spoke of the night we met, the last night I was Yuki-hime-kami, the gods remembered me. I had to leave, or they would demand I kill him."

"Are you here to kill me now?" I asked.

"Of course not. You are half snow spirit, Sekka. You may come with me and live forever. I can show you winter caves where the sun dances from icicle to icicle, fragmenting into a rainbow prism; midnight pools, cold and deep, that shelter the bones of creatures so old, their memories are no more than half-remembered stories; and the perfect silence of a snow-covered cliffside, hovering on the verge of avalanche. These secrets I would share with you."

"And will you also teach me to kill men with my breath?"

"Yes." My mother had the decency to lower her eyes. "It is the price of immortality. We remain young and beautiful forever, free to go where we will, unrestrained by the laws of man. And truly, what else have you to look forward to? Growing withered and old, Roku's children growing in your belly, sucking away your life, in toil and hardship?"

I thought of Roku, with his silly, crooked mouth that quirked on one side when he laughed. And the way his eyes had been so eager and hopeful when he asked my father for my hand, lingering on my face for the smallest sign of encouragement. I thought of sitting at his hearth, listening to his voice telling me of his day as I mended a series of clothing--his, mine, our children's. And I imagined my hands growing gnarled and the light fading from my eyes as my children grew up around me.

"I choose life and love, Mother," I said. "For the price of immortality is more than murder, it is love. You cannot love."

My mother smiled. "You have chosen wisely, my daughter."

Whatever it was I had expected, it had not been her blessing.

She gazed at the stiffening shape of my father's body. "But in one thing you are wrong. I can love. I never stopped loving him."

I felt tears sear my eyes and I was once again five years old. I went into her waiting arms, no longer chilly with cold, but warm and yielding. There was so much I wanted to tell her: awkward kisses in the forest with Roku, how the mere sound of my name from his lips made me smile with joy--all the vital moments of my life she had missed.

She pulled away, and it was just like the last time, thirteen years ago, when she had untangled herself from my arms. Except this time, she went to my father, instead of leaving him.

She lifted his body as though he were made of paper, or snowflakes. The door blew open, sending a spray of needle-sharp ice crystals flurrying inside. A winter storm, a blizzard, had sprung up as we talked. She carried him out into the whirling snow.

As the world grew formless and indistinct in the storm, I watched as she became mist, fading into the soft whiteness that poured out of the sky. My father's body in her arms faded with her.

◊◊◊

Roku and I married and are happy together. We have ten plump children, and though all of them are fair like me, they are vibrant and alive, with the hearty laugh of their father.

I have no regrets, even though sometimes life has been hard. I have always had Roku standing beside me, and his warm arms hold me at night. He tells me every day how beautiful I am, even though my face is seamed with years and my back is bent.

But in winter, sometimes, when the fire blazes high and hot, I peer out through the patina of frost on the window. Occasionally, I think I can see two figures: a man, tall and proud, with a woodcutter's breadth of shoulder, dancing with a beautiful woman in a white kimono. And other times, all I can see is the whirl of snowflakes in the air.

    The End

Afterword

I stumbled into co-editing this anthology by offering to donate story. See, Davey had put together the previous two volumes of *Writers for Relief* on his own. They were successful enough that, when tragedy struck, many of us writers would ask him if he was going to be doing another volume to help. When I offered a story for his latest volume, he told me that he couldn't handle the workload on his own this time around. Either I pitched in, or *Writers for Relief* might not have been able to continue. So I did.

Now, I don't tell you this to shine a halo around my head. Rather, I want you to know how important and rewarding it is to participate in helping people altruistically. Or if you prefer the Dawkins selfish gene idea -- helping people for the warm fuzzies you'll receive. Either way, working on this project has been more fulfilling than I had expected.

Unfortunately, there will be another tragedy at some point. And when it happens, it's good to know that there are opportunities like this one in which to use our skills for more than just telling fun stories.

Thank you to all those who donated stories, art, and time in helping us bring this to fruition.

And a special thanks to you, our reader, for purchasing this book, and in doing so, for helping the good people of Oklahoma get back on their feet.

Stuart Jaffe

Printed in Great Britain
by Amazon